POWERTOWN

POWERTOWN

—

MICHAEL LIND

HarperCollins*Publishers*

HarperCollins books may be purchased for educational, business, or sales promotional use. For information please write: Special Markets Department, HarperCollins Publishers, Inc., 10 East 53rd Street, New York, NY 10022.

FIRST EDITION

Designed by Nancy Singer

Library of Congress Cataloging-in-Publication Data

Lind, Michael, 1962–
   Powertown : a novel / by Michael Lind.—1st ed.
     p. cm.
   ISBN 0-06-017510-9
    1. City and town life—Washington, (D.C.)—Fiction.
2. Politicians—Washington (D.C.)—Fiction.   I. Title.
PS3562.I482P69   1996
813'.54—dc20   96-13266

96 97 98 99 00 ❖/HC 10 9 8 7 6 5 4 3 2 1

ACKNOWLEDGMENTS

I would like to express my gratitude to Rick Horgan and Eric Steel, my editors at HarperCollins, for their enthusiasm and expertise; to Earl Shorris, for his helpful criticism; and to my agent, Kristine Dahl, for everything.

1

The eagle slants. It hungers through space, its talons unknotting, its wingspan ragged as a saw blade.

"Oh, darling, it's been forever!" One matron in diamonds envelops another. From a splintered cask of ribs, a diorama's buzzards look up. A man in festive black with a waxed head assesses a young woman beyond his drink. A red-tailed hawk prepares to dive.

"I think we're lost," Stef repeats.

"No, we're not," Avery tells her. "See, there he is. O ye of little faith."

They have emerged from the Hall of Birds into a central chamber. Underneath a rampant elephant Ross Drummond stands composed in his tux.

"Why, you are the picture of elegance, Miss Stephanie," Ross says in a Mississippi drawl with a courtliness that cancels the compliment. In his early forties, the lobbyist is an elongated man with thinning blond hair above a face too round for his build. To Avery he says, "I thought y'all died."

"It took forever to check our coats," Stef explains. She looks up at the silently trumpeting elephant. This is not what she had expected when Avery had told her Ross had two extra tickets to the inaugural ball. Stef had been surprised to learn that there was no single inaugural ball, but rather a series of parties held at hotels and even government buildings. Avery's two tickets admitted them to the ball at the Smithsonian Museum of Natural History.

"Do y'all know Aglaia Kazakis?" Ross asks as the woman

beside him, his official date for the evening, turns from talking to other celebrants. "Aglaia, you know Avery Brackenridge."

"This is Stef Schonfeld," Avery says.

"Aglaia Kazakis." Aglaia is at least a decade older than Ross. She is everybody's favorite elementary-school teacher, plush cheeks and warm smile beneath a halo of frosted hair.

"Stef here works for Jim Ritter on appropriations." That is the sort of detail retained in the mind of Ross, a Republican political consultant.

"Really?" Aglaia asks Stef where she is from.

"St. Louis," Stef answers. Encouraged by that schoolmarm smile, Stef starts into an epic digression about her recently completed education at Georgetown and her Capitol Hill job, then pauses, wondering if she is talking too much. The question is never resolved; like a string of firecrackers going off blocks away, applause rattles through the crowd.

"Over yonder." Ross points. Beneath a screen as big as a billboard on which the face of the president is blurring in and out of focus there is a sudden turmoil in the crowd. Cameras twinkle.

"Is it him?" Stef asks, excited despite herself.

The crowd that a few moments before applauded as one now joins in a choral laugh.

"False alarm," Ross tells them. "Some guy who looked like him. He probably won't stop by here until a little before midnight."

"What do you think, Ross?" Aglaia asks. "Are we going to stay up for the first couple?"

"Hell," Ross says, shifting from courtly Southern to redneck Southern, "I went and made reservations for a midnight breakfast. You'd better not pass out on me, woman. Jay Pierce is supposed to meet us."

"They sound like an old married couple," Stef observes as she and Avery squeeze their way through shoulders to the bar. "Except that they like each other." Stef is twenty-six and sort of Jewish. She went to school at Georgetown with Avery, who has been an even closer friend since graduation.

"She's like you, Stef. She's a fag hag." Avery is Ross's boyfriend.

"Is she a lesbian?"

"I don't think so," Avery says. He is twenty-five and black. "She's divorced. I think she just hates men. At least straight men. All of the good-looking, intelligent men are gay . . . "

"Yeah, right."

"Well, look at me."

Stef is struck again by how handsome Avery is in a tux instead of his usual black leather jacket and black leather cap. Maybe all the intelligent, good-looking men *are* gay, she thinks.

She thinks it again a little while later when Ross introduces them to Bruce Brandt. Bruce is not so much handsome as striking, with a narrow face and short, dirty blond hair. She assumes he is one of Ross's gay friends until he follows her as she follows a tray of hors d'oeuvres.

"Try these little tamale thingies," he advises her. "Your name's Stef, right?"

"You're Bruce . . . "

"Bruce. Bruce Brandt. It's getting crowded, isn't it? I almost didn't make it. My date's father had a heart attack . . . "

"I'm sorry."

"Yeah, I hope he's all right. I don't know her very well. This girl from my office. I just had an extra ticket, and I needed a date in a hurry. I don't know many people in town yet. Are you part of a team?"

"Well, I work for Congressman Jim Ritter . . . "

"No, I mean are you here by yourself?"

Stef is taken aback by his directness. "Oh, uh, yes. I mean, no. A friend of mine got me a ticket."

"What are you having?"

While Bruce jostles through the crowd toward the bar, Stef tries to figure out what is going on. Two glasses of wine have slowed her; otherwise she would have recognized what Bruce had been up to in that exchange. He had established, first, that he was not gay like Ross and Avery, and second, that he was available—not to mention that he was new in town. When he returns, Stef makes a point of asking where he is from.

"Ultimately or immediately? I just graduated from the Kennedy School last year . . . "

"Really? I have a master's from Fletcher. Did you like Boston?"

"Beats the hell out of Bartlesville, Oklahoma. That's where I grew up. My father was in the oil business. Bet you've never heard of Bartlesville."

"Sure I have. We used to drive through it on the way to see relatives in Texas and Louisiana. I grew up in St. Louis."

"Awright, the heartland! So what's with these coastal people, anyway?"

He is smooth, funny, and smart, this Bruce Brandt. Kennedy School, father in oil, working for a Cabinet secretary . . . and almost certainly a frat boy. Not her type at all. And yet . . .

"God, I need a cigarette," she says. "Is there anywhere you can smoke around here?"

"By God, there should be drinking *and* smoking at an inaugural function. But no sex or card games . . . I think there's a door onto the outside porch over there."

She follows him through the crowd into a gallery filled with skeletons and vivid plastic models of dinosaurs.

"You know who that is?" Bruce whispers to her as they pause beneath a pebble-frilled triceratops pawing the Cretaceous sod. "That's Pendleton Corliss. He used to be deputy assistant secretary of the Treasury. This place is full of wuzzenees."

A tyrannosaur swivels its head, wrinkled lips drawing back from spurlike teeth.

"What's a wuzzenee?"

The shadow of a pteranodon tents them.

"You know—'Wuzzenee somebody in the Nixon administration?' It's the mature form of the izzenee—'Izzenee some kind of government official?' Guess what the larval form is? The wannabee."

Stef giggles so loudly that several people reprove her with lingering glances.

"It's not that funny," Bruce observes.

She laughs again, in the throes of a giggle fit. This sort of thing is known to occur when Stef is on her third glass of wine.

"I need a cigarette, *bad.*"

At the end of the corridor, Bruce tests the door. It surrenders with a clang, admitting them to a gallery in the midst of reconstruction, a chaos of paint, canvas, ladders.

"I forgot who you work for," Stef confesses.

"Mrs. Gutierrez, the new drug czar. Or the 'Drug Czarina,' that's what some people call her. Actually, I don't start formally until February."

Stef yelps as she stumbles on one of the cables coiling across the floor. Her wine sloshes from the cup. "God. I am such a klutz. I'm not usually like this, I swear."

"Must be that crazy inaugural fever."

Stef follows him into a darkened corridor. "You think I can smoke in here?"

"He's smoking." Bruce is referring to a life-size diorama of a Neanderthal man holding up a torch. "Who you lookin' at, punk? Smile when you say that, you extinct old caveman-head *punk*!" Bruce presses his face to the glass, scowling at the Neanderthal. Stef cannot help admiring the muscular caveman's torso—and wondering what Bruce looks like underneath his tux.

The Neanderthal corridor is more than a metaphorical dead end. They retrace their meander and follow another hall until they encounter a squad of Secret Service agents speaking into their wrists. One of them, a blond guy who looks as though he belongs in junior high, waves them back with address.

"We're missing *the Man*," Bruce complains. Stef does not mind—she voted against this president, and hates him with the meaningless, abstract, shallow hatred that a mildly partisan citizen feels toward a public figure who is merely a name and an image on a screen. "Come on," Bruce says. "Let's see if we can get around these Secret Service pointdexters."

They clamber down marble risers beneath a banner agitated by totemic designs and enter a gallery as hollowly dark as a cathedral. In bubbles of light within the cool dimness, fish, coral, and creatures Stef cannot name hover and shine. At first she thinks they are alive.

Bruce does Jacques Cousteau: "And so ze crew of ze *Calypso* returns to ze underwater inaugural ball . . ." But levity seems almost sacrilegious in this submarine sanctuary, and his voice ends.

By now Stef is in a kind of trance, the by-product of tipsiness blended with exhaustion. She is terribly afraid that she will forget his name—she is very bad with names—so she repeats it silently, like a mantra: brucebrandt, brucebrandt. She wanders with Bruce Brandt through the dark and watches the blue light condense and then fade on his harsh features. This space is theirs alone, a separate cosmos, a limbo for two that she does not want to leave.

She wants him. She has not wanted a man so much, so soon, since she fell for Richard, the golf team captain she tutored back in high school, her first lover. She craves this new and better version of Richard with a craving that is as physical as it is emotional, a mixture of childish infatuation and frenzied adult ardor. *Bruce Brandt. Bruce Brandt.*

Far off a band can be heard clanking "Hail to the Chief."

"Come on, maybe that's him." Bruce cannot hide his excitement. Stef follows him from the idyllic gloom into a burst of color and noise. "No president-elect." Bruce sighs.

Stef wonders whether there is such a thing as a boyfriend-elect, and decides that there is now.

2

"Your wife is on report," Velma Hawkins tells Curtis. As massive as her husband, she gasps for breath as she squeezes into the car idling by a back door of the hospital. On nights that Curtis, a private security guard, has to patrol the streets of a Virginia suburb, Velma takes the bus to their home in southeast Washington. Tonight, though, Curtis is free.

"I just felt sorry for that boy." Velma explains that she broke the rules by putting a young man in a wheelchair and taking him to a TV lounge for a while. "I don't think he'd left that room in a month. None of his kinfolks come to see him. I just felt sorry for him sitting all by himself in that room in the AIDS ward."

Curtis tenses. "I thought you weren't going to be having nothing to do with those AIDS homos no more. What if you poke yourself with a needle or something? You tell 'em you ain't gonna work in that ward no more. You gotta tell 'em. You got to."

"Baby, ain't nothing I got to do except stay black and die. Don't you be telling me what I got to do."

"What if you catch something?"

"Baby, I got sick people coughing all over me all day long. If the Lord wants me to catch sick and die, I will. If he don't, I won't. It's all up to God."

"God helps them that helps themselves."

They have had this debate before. Velma is the older daughter of a lay minister in the African Methodist Episcopal Church. She took her religious upbringing to heart, unlike her sister. During the Vietnam War Curtis had met her sister Veronica, then an army nurse in Cam Ranh Bay, when he had been immobilized by an intestinal infection. The pious Velma would never have described his plight to him the way Veronica had after he had begun his recovery: "Honey, for a couple of days there you was in the jaws of Jesus."

After his discharge, Curtis had looked Veronica up in Baltimore. By that time she had been engaged to a man named Willie Wilson. She had introduced Curtis to her two sisters, Sharonda, already addicted to abusive men, and Velma. Curtis seldom regretted having married the most serious of the three sisters. As she had aged, Veronica's playfulness had curdled into spite, driving Willie Wilson to seek refuge in bars and bottles.

"Where you going?"

"Taking a shortcut," Curtis replies. "That inauguration has got 'em backed up all the way to . . . Oh, shit." The side street is mobbed by limousines and taxis.

"Don't use that kind of language." Velma sits up and peers out. "Lawd a'mercy, look at those fancy cars."

"Ain't got nothing else to look at. We sure ain't going nowhere."

Behind them a limo slides into the lane like a battleship gaining on a tugboat. "No use honking," Velma chastises the limo's unseen driver when he leans on the horn.

Curtis chortles. "They going to miss the inauguration. How much you think they paid for that limousine? I bet they're rich folks flew in from California or somewhere. And now they're sitting back there in their diamond cuff links and their pearl necklaces and they got their invitation but it ain't no damn use. Stuck in traffic."

Town house by town house, they advance down the narrow road. Soon they can see the cause of the traffic jam. A police car is splashing crimson across the herded limousines.

"Oh, lawdy," says Velma. "Somebody else got shot. Lawd a'mercy."

Gangstas, thinks Curtis. Many—sometimes it seems most—of the young men in southeast Washington belong to one of two drug-dealing gangs, the Sherman Avenue Krew and the Georgia Avenue Yungstaz. Their battles over turf and vengeance leave teenage corpses draped on street corners and splayed in alleys almost every night.

The limo ahead of them moves again, just a little. As he eases the car forward, Curtis sees a sight that he saw a hundred times when he was on the D.C. force: a cluster of police cars, cops holding back shrieking women, a knot of stunned neighbors, yellow tape: POLICE LINE DO NOT CROSS. What look like two lumps of snow glowing in the headlights of a patrol car turn out to be the high-top sneakers of a shadow in a parka on the pavement. For a moment Curtis's pulse quickens as he thinks of his teenage nephew Evander. But tonight the gunfire has ripped a hole in someone else's family; the woman screaming and swaying in the arms of a burly cop is not Curtis's sister-in-law. The pain is a stranger's, and Curtis cannot help feeling relieved.

"You ought to have a talk with Evander," Velma tells him. Clearly the same thought has appeared, unwelcome, in her mind. "Sharonda says he won't go to church choir anymore."

"Well, maybe his voice is changing."

"You've got to talk with him, baby. Lawd a'mercy, I hope that boy don't turn into . . ." Velma sighs and looks away from the red-lit tableau.

"No matter what you do, rich man or poor man, this is where you end up," Dad Johnson says as Curtis guides the car through the cemetery gate the next morning. "Tell the truth, and spite the devil."

Dad Johnson, Velma's father, spent most of his life as an undertaker. Curtis used to think that Velma had chosen to be a nurse as a way of repudiating her grim legacy. Her father buried people, and she helped restore them to life. But as Velma has grown older, Curtis has seen that dealing constantly with the sick can inspire the same kind of apathy as communion with the dead.

He belongs here more than Momma Johnson, Curtis thinks, he with his religious melancholy hanging over his thoughts like fog over a lake. From her daddy, Velma inherited her morbid temperament. Momma Johnson had been the only one on that side of the family who had known how to enjoy life. She had always been laughing and cutting up—well, not quite always, since she had been subdued whenever her pious husband was around. Curtis had not realized how important she had been until she was gone. You are not supposed to like your mother-in-law, but sometimes Curtis thought he would rather spend time with her than with the rest of her family, not excepting her daughter.

Momma Johnson had been dark, several shades darker than her husband. Her people had all been poor sharecroppers and such down in Georgia. She had gone up north to Baltimore and found herself a prosperous husband, so light-skinned he could almost pass, a God-fearing, churchgoing lay preacher who would support his family. In his youth Dad Johnson had been, if not handsome, at least dapper in the formal style of a funeral home director's assistant, and that must have appealed to her. Curtis never met any of Momma Johnson's long abandoned Georgia relatives. They must have been an improvident, disorderly bunch to make her move so far away and take a man so distant and organized for a husband. And, Curtis has often thought, to judge by Momma Johnson, those dark Georgia kinfolks must have known how to have fun.

The dirt is like granite. The wire supporting the plastic lilies bends when Curtis tries to press the arrangement into the ground. He is so fat that even this exertion leaves him puffing. He gives up and props the flowers against the tombstone. Somebody will steal them anyway.

"That's mighty nice," says the old man absently.

Black webs mesh behind Curtis's eyes when he struggles to his feet. For a few moment he sways, dizzy, then the blood fights its way up into his head. He matches the old man's small and uncertain steps as they walk back to the car across the empty plots that soon enough will cover their remains.

Good-bye for now, Momma Johnson. He knows her soul is not there in the cemetery, only her body. But he senses she is more likely to hear his thoughts in this place. As though the tiered stones were so many antennae, beaming intermittent greetings to the mute and attentive dead.

Back at the house, Velma is putting the finishing touches on the turkey. Curtis leaves Dad Johnson in front of the TV and drives down to the project.

Crossing East Capital is like traversing the border to another country. The low, modest homes of Curtis's neighborhood give way to crumbling brownstones, separated now and then by vacant lots piled with rubbbish. One brownstone, a tall, narrow building with boarded windows, sits alone, a vacant lot on each side. With its stoop in front, it looks like a giant laced boot, like the home of the old woman in the nursery rhyme who lived in a shoe. The crack house. Curtis knows he needs to slow down because there are usually children in the area—lookouts, paid by the gang that runs the crack house. Sure enough, there they are—a passel of spindly boys, not sprinting or jumping as children ought to, but lounging on the corner, hands in pockets, heads slumped forward, doing their best to look *bad*, like their teenage brothers and neighbors and friends. None of the sentries can be more than eight years old.

From the crack house, the distance to the project where Curtis's in-laws live is five blocks.

"Come on, Momma," Sharonda calls again. She kneels to adjust the ribbon in the hair of Arnetta, at four her youngest. "Evander, you got that casserole?"

Evander saunters to the car carrying a metal bowl wrapped in foil. Casserole, my ass, Curtis thinks. The only thing Velma's sister-in-law knows how to cook, it seems, is Kraft macaroni and cheese.

Curtis opens the trunk so that Evander can set the casserole inside. Curtis marks how his nephew's thin arms emerge from the sleeves on his coat. "You're outgrowing that suit jacket. You need a new suit."

"Don't never wear it," says Evander.

"Yeah, we need to get you a new suit. You'll be needing one before long, for job interviews." Curtis speaks loudly so that Sharonda will hear.

Stella comes waddling toward the car with a plastic basket full of laundry. "Curtis, I hope you got room in the car."

He almost does not. Somehow they all squeeze in—Curtis, the old lady, Sharonda and her infant Arnetta, Monique, Jamal, and Evander. The children are babbling at the top of their lungs. Curtis decides to return home by the shortest route—and almost immediately regrets the decision as the car cruises past the crack house. Some sort of deal is going down. A small crowd of young men are huddling around two brand-new sports cars. Conversation among them dies as Curtis and his kin drive past. They turn and stare.

In the rearview mirror Curtis can see Evander shrinking down in the backseat as though trying to hide behind the plastic flower he holds. Are they enemies of his? Are they friends who would disrespect him for being seen in the company of female relatives? As he often had before, Curtis wished his relatives lived in a better neighborhood. Though she would not admit it, Sharonda had moved her family here to be closer to her generous in-laws, Curtis and Velma. Maybe the children would have been better off if they had stayed in Baltimore.

When they come through the door, Velma tells Curtis that he missed a call from their daughter Marilyn and her husband in California. "Did you ask her where our grandchildren are?" Curtis huffs. Marilyn has been married for three years, without any children yet. Her sister Lorena, who just recently graduated from college, is still single. Both of their daughters have made Curtis and Velma proud—Marilyn, with her job as assistant manager of an office supply store in San Diego, and Lorena, working as a paralegal for a law firm in Atlanta.

"Y'all want to see the cat's faces?" Velma asks nine-year-old Monique and first-grader Jamal as she and Sharonda set up the ironing board in the kitchen. "Come on. Y'all can see the cat's faces in the clothes."

The little ones stream into the kitchen, leaving Curtis alone with Dad Johnson and Evander. Velma's father is sunk in one of his reveries, looking at the TV without seeing it. Evander slouches on the couch, a polygon of teenage angles that have yet to properly lock into place.

Now or never, Curtis thinks. Lowering the sound of the game with the remote in his hand, he turns to Evander. "You aren't going to choir anymore?"

"Naw." Evander looks away, toward the TV.

Curtis thinks he can see a little of Evander's dead father Luke in the boy. "How come?"

"I don't know."

"Those other dudes, they think it's sissy, going to church and all?"

"I don't know."

The old man is listening, Curtis is sure. The old man was a lay preacher for many years. Luke was his rebel son, who died of a drug overdose in his early twenties.

"That's what I used to think when I was your age," Curtis says. "Religion. I thought it was just for women. But then I went to Vietnam. I saw grown men praying. Soldiers. You get shot at, you get religion in a hurry."

"You ever shoot anybody? You got a gun, don'tcha?" Suddenly Evander is interested. Jesus Christ, Curtis thinks. He's like his father after all. We're going to lose him.

3

They look like moon men, like little astronauts crossing the lunar desert of the parking lot, the three kids bundled up in their parkas against the February gusts. Evander does not even recognize his half brother Jamal until the three walk up to him and his friend Twon.

"What time it is?" Evander asks Twon, and learns that it is one-thirty. "How come they let y'all out early?"

"They was shootin' at school," Jamal informs the two adolescents. Then Jamal's classmates join in. Evander can hardly make out the different voices in the polyphonic babble.

"It was Rasheed Bryant. He in the sixth grade. He was pissed at Otis."

"The police was there. And they took and put us in the auditorium. And people's mothers was there. And kids was crying and scared and shit."

"Otis in the hospital."

"He dead."

"No, he ain't."

"He just walked up to Otis and shot him—pakow! Right in the—you know, the inside courtyard?"

The kids retell the events with awe and a trace of pride at having been bystanders at such drama. Not that shootings are rare in southeast D.C. Every other night the wars among the gang-bangers leave somebody else dead, sometimes three or four in a night. In the year and a half since Evander moved here with his mother and grandmother and siblings from Baltimore, the family has often been awakened by the crackle and the sirens. But it has always happened a few blocks away, in some alley or on some street corner where a deal went wrong or a member of one crew spotted a soldier of another. A shooting in a school . . . The crackle has suddenly gotten closer.

"Go on home, Momma'll be worried," Evander orders Jamal. After a moment's reflection, Evander decides to go with him. At fourteen, Evander is the man in the Johnson household.

"Outta here," Evander tells Twon.

"Audi 5000," Twon replies, setting off.

Twon is one of the few kids his age in the 'hood who have been willing to welcome Evander. Most of the others are members or hangers-on of the local set, the Fourteenth Street Krew, and they are intensely suspicious of newcomers like Evander, an immigrant from Baltimore. Evander thought it would get better over time. But only two weeks ago Lookout Wilkins, a twenty-three-year-old dealer who sometimes shows up at junior high, thought he heard Evander dis him as the two passed among the lockers. Evander had not said anything at all, but he never had a chance to explain as Lookout punched and kicked him in front of his classmates. Since then Evander has been afraid to go back to school. He has spent his days loitering at Union Station, alone or with Twon, his stomach twisted, pregnant with fear.

Now some dude named Rasheed has shot a kid named Otis in the school courtyard. If Lookout had pulled the tin he had undoubtedly been packing, Evander might have been flat in the hospital, or stretched out in a casket with his jaws wired shut and skin like cold rubber. Evander pulls his parka more tightly around his spindly body in the February chill.

The Johnsons live in "the Wood," as the Brentwood Housing Project is known. The Wood consists of four five-story blocks of featureless brick planted around a cement-and-dirt courtyard. As they pass the far end of their building, Evander reflexively tenses, reacting to the possibility that a rat might at any moment skitter out. The stairwell at this end of the building is used as a kind of indoor landfill by many of the residents, who simply toss their garbage onto an ever-growing pile of offal within which the metal canisters for months have been entombed. On hot days the stench oozes through the halls into the units and drifts across the courtyard. The cold spell has brought a reprieve from the stench, but the rats must still be around. Evander has had a special horror of rats, ever since one night in their old apartment in Baltimore when he had tried to feed a squirrel on their windowsill and realized it was not a squirrel.

Bits of broken glass crackle under their wet shoes as they walk down the third-floor corridor, a zebra-striped space lit by only one remaining light. Through the door of 3B, Evander can hear the TV blaring. "Yo, who's there? Let us in!" Sometimes his mother Sharonda locks the kids out when her man Larry is in town so the two of them will have some privacy to do drugs or do the wild thing. At those times, Evander takes a malicious pleasure in interrupting. He loathes Larry, partly because he suspects his mother gives him money that rightfully belongs to Evander and his half brother and two half sisters, and partly because the idea of Larry and his mother having sex at their age when he at fourteen is still a virgin seems to reverse the proper order of the universe.

"Open up!" Evander pounds on the door. "Who's in there?"

"Monique"—his oldest half sister's voice.

"Unlock the fucking door!"

"Momma said don't let nobody in."

"She wasn't talking about me, you stupid-ass 'ho. Goddamn muhfuckin' . . . " Evander gropes in his pocket for his key, but then the door is opened from within. The soap opera blares louder: "*Jessica, I didn't want you to find out before I confronted Ken.*"

"*My God,*" a suburban voice answers. "*Does Trent know?*"

Monique stayed home from the third grade today because she woke up sniffling. "They was shootin' each other at the school," Monique tells Evander.

"I know, I know." Evander tosses his parka across the back of a chair.

"Momma took Arnetta and they went to the school, to pick up Jamal," Monique continues as Evander pulls a soda from the half-size refrigerator. The apartment is tiny, nothing but a living room that doubles as a kitchen and a small adjoining bedroom and bath. Six people live here: Evander; his mother Sharonda; her own widowed mother, known to the family as Gram; Jamal and Monique, both children of a Baltimore man named Lamont who has been in and out of prison; and Sharonda's new baby by Larry, Arnetta. Evander was two when his own father, Luke Turner, died when he smashed the car he was driving into a tree after running off the road between Washington and Baltimore. Sharonda keeps his name.

"You lied to me," one of the beautiful, rich white people on the black-and-white TV is saying.

"I lied? I suppose you and Vanessa were up at Midnight Lake on business."

"How do you know about that?"

"I know a great deal, Devereaux Preston . . . "

Jamal is digging into a box of cereal. "I'm going to Bo's," he announces between mouthfuls.

"No, your ass is staying here till Momma gets back. She'll be worried." That seems like the responsible thing to say.

Evander changes the channel. It is time for the Cybernauts, a gang of teenage superheroes. Evander tries to look uninterested as the titles flash on the TV screen, showing each teenager—the black girl, the Asian boy, the white boy, the Hispanic girl—morphing into an armored Cybernaut crowned by a helmet with a totemic animal logo. "Cobra!" Jamal shouts, miming the karate kicks of the heroes. "Panther! Falcon! . . . "

"Shut up," Evander says affectionately as Jamal dances around the room, kicking and boxing invisible adversaries.

The phone rings. "Evander!" Monique screams. "It's Twon!"

"Lookout, he been talking about you," Twon reports. "He be talking about you and calling you outta your name and shit. He say if he catch you he gonna bust a cap in your ass."

Evander clenches. Even if Lookout were not after him, some other member of the Krew would sooner or later single him out for harassment. You can never be safe in the 'hood, in this 'hood, unless you are a member of the Krew.

Suddenly Evander knows what to do.

★ ★ ★

The Funkadelic looks like a haunted house. The cylindrical turret of the brownstone Gothic town house rises the length of the building's corner, which also happens to be at the intersection of two streets, so that the upper room commands a view of several blocks in four directions. The windows on the lower level are painted black, and most of the upper-story windows are shuttered. There used to be a sign over the entrance, but it was stippled with a spray of bullets by the Georgia Avenue Yungstaz, the gang that contests the blocks to the north and east with the Krew. Now there is no sign. None is needed. Everyone in the 'hood knows where the Funkadelic is, and what it is.

Pushing his way through the narrow door, Evander finds himself confronting a balloon-armed dude with a gold chain around his neck. "I need to see Frizzell."

Inside a jukebox, a rap group is trying to thump its way out. "Nigga, what fo' you need to see Frizzell?"

Looking past the bouncer, Evander glimpses the bar, the pool tables. The inside of the Funkadelic is as dark as the bilge of a ship. "It's about . . . about the money for the parking lot. My grandmother . . . Stella Morris. Tell 'im it's about the money."

The bouncer disappears up a stairwell. Evander tries to make himself invisible as several older teenagers in blue sweatshirts enter and banter with the bartender. Evander wants to shrink until he is so small nobody will notice him.

The bouncer returns. "He's busy."

Evander panics. "I gotta see him."

"Muhfucka, you deaf?"

"Tell him it's about the police."

That works. In a few minutes, the bouncer is leading Evander up the stairs to a chamber more like a den than an office. The place is cluttered with sofas, a wide-screen TV, CD racks, stereo speakers, closets that might be wet bars. Cigarettes and reefers smolder among cans of malt liquor. On the couches slump half a dozen members of the Krew. Evander has never met Frizzell, but he recognizes the fat man in his thirties with the goatee like a charcoal O around his mouth and its echo in the O of gold looped over the black sweatshirt billowed by his flesh.

"You Stella Morris's kid?"

"Grandson."

"What's the problem? Ain't your grandma been gettin' her money?" Since the family moved in, the Krew has been paying Evander's gram for the right to use the parking lot assigned to her in the apartment complex. "What you talking about, the *po*lice?"

Evander feels the eyes of the silent jury. "There's like this dude, been breaking on me, and saying he gonna jump me and shit. But if I get beat up, or killed, the *po*lice gonna come round, and my gram and my momma, they gonna be hysterical and shit, and the *po*lice gonna ask about the parking space . . . "

"Whoa, chill . . . What's your name, l'il homie?"

"Evander."

Frizzell shifts his vast bulk on the couch. "Who say he gonna jump you?"

"Lookout. Lookout Wilson."

Gang members glance at each other. Frizzell's brows wrinkle in the double oval of his face. "Lookout Wilson? He gonna jump you? What you did to him?"

"Nothing. I didn't do nothing. He say I dissed him, but I didn't."

Inside the charcoal O, Frizzell's lips are compressed in a stifled smile. "So you telling me, if Lookout jump you, and the police come, your momma and your gram liable to be so hysterical they gonna rat me out, and the police gonna arrest me for unauthorized use of a parking lot. Izzat it? You ain't doin' this to save your own ass. You doin' this for me, huh?" Frizzell begins to chuckle. Mirth spreads in ripples from the O of his goatee, growing into waves of wobble in the fat flesh beneath his billowing black shirt.

The young men titter. Frizzell whispers an order to one, who leaves the room. Then he takes a drag on the reefer he is smoking. "Shit, nigga, you the wackest l'il homie . . . What's your name again?"

"Evander."

"Evander Morris?"

"Evander Johnson."

Feet clump up the stairs. Evander turns and sees that the soldier Frizzell sent out of the room has returned—with Lookout Wilson.

Lookout is skinny, twenty-three, with a gold cap over one tooth. Confused, he glances from Evander to Frizzell and back.

Frizzell takes a toke from his blunt. "Lookout, cuz, Evander here say you going around saying you gonna jump his ass."

"Muhfucka," Lookout hisses at Evander, who shrinks.

"Well?" says Frizzell. "You gonna jump him?"

Lookout shifts from one leg to another, cocks his head, and sneers. "I expedite his ass later."

Frizzell is out of the sofa with amazing speed for a man so fat. He rolls over to Lookout and shoves the skinny teenager back with the flat of his puffy hand. "You wanna jump him, you jump him right now. Go on."

"Aw, man . . ."

"His grandma do favors for the Krew. What fo' you fucking with him?"

"He dissed me in the hall."

"Did not," Evander manages to bleat.

"Come here," Frizzell orders Evander. He takes Evander's hand and puts it in Lookout's. "From now on, y'all are blood. You hear what I'm saying? Lookout, Evander is your crimey from now on. He is your brother. You are down for him. You hear what I'm saying?"

"I hear you," says Lookout, breaking free and backing away.

The fat man turns. "Evander, you want to be a member of the Krew? You think you got what it takes?"

Evander is so frightened he can hardly squeak out a "Yes."

"You know how much I weigh, Evander? I'm a fat-ass muh-fucka. Well, take what I weigh, and add it to how much every-body here weighs, and everybody in the Krew. And you add that weight on top of how much all our cars weigh and the buildings we use and all the kees we sell and the weight of all our guns and that weight, cuz, that is the weight that's gonna come crashing down on you if you ever rat out on the Krew. You understand?"

"Yeah."

"You know you got to be down for the Krew. I don't care what the Yungstaz do to you, or the police. I don't care if they torture your ass or kill you, you got to be down for your homies. You think you can hold up under pain and not let it break you?"

Evander's legs are weak. "Yeah," he whimpers.

"Well, let's see." With that as the only warning, Frizzell hits Evander across the face, sending him staggering. For a moment, the room blurs. He sinks, sniffling, to the carpeted floor. Nobody says anything. To the pulse in his head, the hip-hop throbs.

"Awright, pick him up."

"I can get up my own self." Evander rises unsteadily to his legs.

"Shit, man, he's bleeding."

They guide him to a sofa and tell him to lay his head back. Somebody brings ice cubes wrapped in a towel. He holds the cold compress to the side of his nose, coughing and spitting lumps of coagulated blood into a Kleenex. In a few minutes the bleeding stops.

"Give him a blunt." Evander finds himself supplied with marijuana and a beer.

"You ain't gonna throw up all over my carpet, are you?" Frizzell asks. "You already bled all over it, like a bitch in heat." He laughs, and Lookout laughs, and the other gangstas laugh, and Evander, feeling no fear for the first time in months, laughs with them.

4

Now, once again, Graciela and her babies are without a home.

Mrs. Reyes, the landlady, has thrown them out, accusing Graciela of stealing her silverware. The missing spoons and knives vanished a few days before, around the time that Miguel, one of the immigrant men in the bedroom, failed to return to the apartment. But Mrs. Reyes blamed Graciela. For a month, the Salvadoran widow has been looking for an excuse to get rid of Graciela and her two children, seizing upon the slightest incident as an occasion to shriek and storm. Mrs. Reyes had sworn like a bar girl when Graciela had lost a key. And the old lady had terrified little Rosa, Graciela's oldest, by accusing her of wetting the floor in the bathroom. Almost certainly one of the men who slept in the bedroom had done it; Graciela heard them at night, stumbling drunkenly into the bathroom they shared, fumbling with clinking belts. But Mrs. Reyes had always treated the male *mojados* better. Each one of them paid for his space in the tiny bedroom, where up to six Central American men from their teens to their forties sprawled snoring on pallets each night. Graciela and her three-year-old Rosa and her fifteen-month-old Marcelo, sleeping in the living room on the sofa and the rug, were taking up space that Mrs. Reyes could have rented to half a dozen young men.

Though they no longer have a permanent place to sleep, Graciela is relieved to be out of that cramped apartment in that old brick building in an Arlington suburb. Often Graciela had feared for herself and her children. Some of the men she liked— portly Luis, who brought candy for Rosa and who once shouted down another man complaining about Marcelo's crying. But the renters were constantly changing. Every week one of the men would not return, and a stranger, told of Mrs. Reyes's place by word of mouth in the community of Salvadoran expatriates, would appear. Several had made passes at her; each time she had been saved by the arrival of another denizen of the crowded apartment. Sometimes one of the men brought home a woman and the others would shout obscene encouragement to their pal. Graciela had been too frightened to protest.

Her cousin Yolanda and her husband Isidro agree to take them in again, at least for a few days. When Graciela first arrived in Washington eight months ago, she had stayed with Yolanda, who had been single then. On several other occasions, when Graciela had been out of money and between jobs, Yolanda and Isidro had taken her and her small brood under their roof. Isidro made little secret of his annoyance, but Yolanda could always be counted on: "Blood is thicker than water." They were the only members of their family here in the States, so far from the little town in green, grim Salvador.

Graciela and her children find only a cool welcome when they move back in with Yolanda and Isidro. Isidro has never been very friendly toward Graciela, but she is taken aback by Yolanda's curtness. Yolanda is finally pregnant, and her personality has changed.

"The least you can do is clean up in the mornings," Yolanda snaps at her one evening when Graciela, exhausted, returns after a long bus ride from the Hair Affair. "You don't have to go to work until eleven. Why should you sleep late? This isn't a hotel."

Graciela begins to sob.

"Don't give me that crybaby act," Yolanda shrieks. "We are always supposed to feel sorry for you. Life is hard for everybody."

"You should be grateful to your cousin," Isidro adds gratuitously.

Little Rosa asks, "Momma, why are you crying?"

Graciela does what she always does in trying circumstances, she resigns herself to her fate. *Así es, así será.* From that day on she rises early each morning and furiously cleans the apartment with a rigor energized by resentment. One morning, making breakfast for Yolanda and Isidro, she mixes salt and chocolate and powdered coffee creamer into the gluey eggs. Later, when breakfast is served, her hosts grimace, but say nothing.

That night she lies awake beside her sleeping children and prays for forgiveness. She prays to Our Lady to come into her life and cleanse her of sin and sorrow. How lucky those children were, to whom the Mother of God appeared at Fatima! But they were pure, not tainted by evil deeds like Graciela, who can never hope for such a vision as long as she is alive. Perhaps when she dies . . .

Graciela imagines what it must be like to be a soul floating free of the body, to be dazzled by a milky effulgence that burns through the very fabric of the universe like a flame eating through the walls and floor and ceiling of a burning house. She imagines being drawn up by an irresistible force, through cataracts of lucid light toward the figure in the center of the flow, a being whose very garments flow like water and glow like the sun. In Graciela's mind Our Lady is not a motherly figure, she is a woman not much older, in her human manifestation, than Graciela herself, a big sister who is disappointed, but never disgusted, by Graciela's misdeeds, who knows Graciela better than anyone except for the mysterious, remote, masculine Lord, and whose special concern for Graciela is not matched even by His. Graciela wants so much to see, to bathe in that light, and, though it must be a sin, she sometimes wishes she could die at once and be united with her smiling, sisterly friend.

For three months Graciela has worked at the Hair Affair, a unisex styling salon in a little shopping complex on Pennsylvania Avenue, a few blocks from the great ivory edifice of the Capitol. Every day, from eleven in the morning until eight at night, with only one half-hour break, she performs the same limited set of duties: washing the hair of cutsomers, cleaning up workstations, running a broom across the floor. She and the two other women assigned these tasks—both immigrants like her, one from Mexico and another Salvadoran—are ignored by the hairstylists. Between customers the stylists, all men and women in their twenties, banter and gossip and clown around. Graciela's English is so poor that she can follow only a fraction of their repartee. They are strange creatures, these stylists, each with a fashionably bizarre hairstyle. One of the women has shaved part of her head and dyed her remaining hair magenta. None of them, it seems, are married; although they are Graciela's age, she has babies and they do not. If Graciela's fellow immigrants are to be believed, several of the young men are *maricónes*, faggots. The Filipino boy with the earring and the big grin, strutting around in tight black jeans, is certainly homosexual. So are a lot of the customers, at least the young men; Graciela is not sure what a lesbian looks like.

Graciela worries about catching the gay disease, la SIDA, from the stylists or the customers. She is careful not to prick her finger on scissors or razors. Her cousin Yolanda tells her she should wear plastic gloves, but the store's manager, a plump thirtyish woman with short hair like a Chihuahua's, will have none of it. "We're certified by the health department," the manager assures her. Graciela is not assured. The manager, maybe she is a lesbian, maybe she is covering up for the other perverts.

One of the other hair washers claims that hot water kills the SIDA germs. When she is washing a client's hair, Graciela always makes sure that the water is just short of painfully hot. Several times she has had complaints, but most of the customers seem to enjoy a hot rinse.

She is proud of her technique. She spends little time on old ladies, and on the obvious *maricónes*. When a handsome executive walks in, though, Graciela tries to claim him before the others can. She takes her time, slowly working the foam in with her fingers. Sometimes, when she is adjusting the towel around a good-looking man's neck and shoulders, she will give him the briefest of massages. She feels a shudder of excitement when she sees one of her subjects, trying to be nonchalant, adjusting pants tented by rebellious reflex.

The devil side of her enjoys this. When she was little in Salvador, her cousin Ferno used to amuse her by sketching a diagram of a figure that was half angel, half devil. "We know which half Graciela likes," he would taunt her. The devil side is strong in Graciela, even though she prays to Our Lady and goes to mass whenever she can. She has not been with a man since she came to Washington; with the birth of Marcelo, and her constant nomadic wanderings between jobs and homes, she has not had many opportunities. But she thinks about it all the time. She thinks that maybe one of the American businessmen will fall in love with her as she washes his hair and will marry her and take her and her children to live in a big house in the suburbs where, from early spring to late fall, without ever worrying about the cost, she can run the heat or the air conditioner night and day.

The "immigration man," as Señor Martinez is known, has an office above a *botánica* in the Hispanic neighborhood east of DuPont Circle. For a fee, Martinez will provide a false green card or a Social Security card or—though this costs more—a phony driver's license. He has referred Graciela before to jobs. Now she asks him to help her find a new place to live, with some privacy, if possible.

"You're working?"

She describes her job at the Hair Affair.

"How much do you make? I've got to know what you can afford."

Señor Martinez then places a call, speaking in rapid, fluent English. He scribbles an address on a leaf of his notepad, then hangs up.

"Be there at nine-thirty tomorrow morning."

She takes the bus and arrives early. The neighborhood is desolate, a cluster of row houses and small apartment buildings near a block of boarded-up storefronts. The address the immigration man gave her is a plain building, one of three around a parking lot, each as featureless as a brick. Graciela weighs the pros and cons. The place is far from Capitol Hill and the Hair Affair, but the rent is low. On the other hand, the neighborhood does not look very safe. In the distance, she sees a black beggar staggering down a sidewalk, avoiding imaginary obstacles.

The apartment man does not arrive until 9:45. He is a big man in a black T-shirt and jeans, a bodybuilder by the look of him. His close-shaven head rests on a thick neck; only the wrinkles around his eyes show him to be in his forties.

"You Graciela Herrera?"

He takes a chiming clump of keys from his belt and unlocks the apartment. The place is tiny, a one-room efficiency with a bathroom and a shower in a space scarcely larger than the closet. The tiles in the kitchen area and bathroom are scorched and crumbly.

"There is no . . ." She waits for the English word to come. "No bed."

"*Aqui,*" he replies. "*Se llama* 'Murphy bed.'" The man tosses pillows aside, then pulls a complaining mattress from inside the sofa. A green tattoo glows on one telegraph pole of a forearm. He must have been a soldier.

His Spanish is passable, she discovers, as he drives her in his monstrous black truck to the realty office. Here, under the watchful eye of a woman in what appears to be a blond wig, Graciela signs the forms.

"Here's my card. You have any trouble, give me a call."

"*Gracias*—thank you, Señor Shelton."

"Call me Darryl."

Yolanda and Isidro help Graciela and the kids move in. The couple are friendlier now that their unwanted guests are leaving. Graciela thinks ruefully, they will be sorry they were mean to her when she is dead.

When they are finished, Isidro brings a meal of fried chicken from a nearby drive-through. They make tables of the cardboard boxes containing the small family's few belongings.

Rosa slaps the sofa again and again, hardly able to believe that a bed could be hiding inside. "Murphy bed," she sings, "Murphy bed," amazed that a piece of furniture, like a person, has a name.

In the week that follows, Rosa comes down with a cold. It does not go away. Foolishly, Graciela listens to her cousin Yolanda's advice. "If it is just sniffles, don't worry," Yolanda tells her. "She will get well on her own. Anyway, she probably just wants attention because she is jealous of all the attention you are paying to Marcelo. That's the way kids are."

A few mornings later, however, Rosa is no better, and her forehead feels like a hot stove. Trying not to panic, Graciela calls Yolanda, but no one answers. She considers calling the operator for emergency assistance, but she is afraid. They would find out she has no papers and deport her and her babies.

She calls Darryl.

In half an hour the super shows up, the big man in the big black truck. He takes the three of them to a Mexican doctor he knows who will not ask any questions.

Doctor Sorzano is an old man, a white Creole with the ocelot skin of age. Babbling, Marcelo stares from the safety of his mother's arms as the doctor places the stethoscope's tip on Rosa's bare chest. "Dog!" Marcelo shouts as the doctor looks up at him, the stethoscope drooping like a leash.

"Give her two of these, every four hours, with some food," Doctor Sorzano instructs the anxious young mother. "She'll be all right. It is just a nasal infection. The antibiotics ought to clear it up." He uses fancy words with authority. She feels relieved until he asks to be paid.

Darryl sees the alarm in her eyes. "I'll take care of it," he says, taking out his wallet.

On the way back, huddled with her children in the cab of the truck, Graciela does not dare to look at the tall American. She cannot imagine where she will get a hundred and fifty dollars to pay him back. Every cent she will earn in the next month has already been committed to the rent, food, laundry, the bus, the small fee for Mrs. Valdez, the baby-sitter.

"I know it's not easy," Darryl tells her in his accented Spanish after she has phoned the Hair Affair to explain why she will not be coming in to work today. "Maybe we can make a deal about the rent."

His hand touches her hip, so lightly that it might just be an accident.

"I can talk to the company and work out a deal, sometimes, for my friends."

His hand touches her again. Her heart quickens in alarm.

"That's just for special friends, you understand. I bet we can be friends like that. What do you think?"

Graciela looks away as his hand brushes her hair.

"What do you say?"

Her voice is almost a whisper. "I don't know."

"Well, think about it. I'll give you a call. I think we could be real good friends." He pauses on his way to the door. "Do you need any groceries? I could pick up soda, or juice . . . "

"No," she says. "Thank you."

He almost smiles. "Anything for a pretty lady."

She is so shaken that she hardly hears the truck rev up its engines and drone away. As she feels Rosa's forehead and watches her swallow the pills, one after another, she regains her composure. She wonders how much Darryl would take off the rent. They could use another hundred dollars a month. Maybe he would reduce the rent by more than a hundred. She thinks of what Darryl did for Rosa, and of how, when he touched her, she felt not only alarmed but flattered.

5

A hearing room in the Capitol is the site of the memorial service. No one from Congressman Ritter's office had been planning to attend until the organizer of the event, another representative's legislative assistant, called in an attempt to ensure a big turnout. It is a slow day, so Stef agrees to accompany the office manager, Gloria Piccoli, to the service.

"Who was this guy?" Stef asks Gloria when they discover that the hearing room is so crowded they will have to stand. Like everyone else in Washington, Stef had seen the headlines in the *Washington Post*—RHODES SCHOLAR SLAIN NEAR CAPITOL—but she had only skimmed the story. From the photograph in the paper, however, she recognizes the blond young man in the portrait photo set up in the front of the room on one of the stands used for exhibits during committee hearings.

"Those must be his parents over there," Gloria murmurs, nodding toward a solemn middle-aged couple in the front row.

A gray-haired man whom Stef recognizes as Mike Bingham, a Democrat from Iowa, rises from his seat behind the dais and walks to the lectern.

"Several years ago, I interviewed a remarkable young man for a position on my staff . . . "

"I didn't know he worked for Bingham," Stef whispers to her plump coworker.

Gloria—usually tough and cynical despite her maternal look—cuts her off with a reproachful glance. Stef falls silent. This *is* a memorial service, not an occasion for political insider analysis.

Still, she cannot feel very sad about the death of someone she had not known.

While Bingham delivers his eulogy, Stef studies the other speakers, who are seated where committee members usually sit. One is a thin, spindly elf of a man with hair the color of rust that seems to be evaporating in wisps from his head as you watch. He looks vaguely familiar; perhaps she has seen him on TV. Next to him sits a woman—Stef puts her at a youngish fifty—whose black turtleneck and cropped, symmetric, iron-gray hair reinforces the intensity of her expression. Her sphinxlike solemnity contrasts with the fidgetiness of the gnome. The trio is completed by a middle-aged man in a baggy designer suit with unnaturally black hair slicked back from a soft, gentle, Mediterranean face.

The congressman, eyes downcast, sits down. With much scuffling and maneuvering, the gnome takes his place at the lectern.

"Sir Robin Blair," Gloria explains to Stef. "The editor of *Perspective*."

Now Stef is sure she has seen him on one of those Washington chat shows. But she is surprised to learn he is a knight.

"The story has it," Blair is saying in a high, almost feminine voice interrupted by stammering and occasional sharp intakes of air, almost like giggles, "that a Stoic philosopher once chanced upon a man weeping for his dead daughter. 'Your mourning cannot bring her back,' the philosopher told him. 'I know,' said the man. 'That is why I weep.'"

By now the grim mood of the room is dissolving Stef's indifference. She studies the handsome, smiling, confident youth in the photograph, an upright young Scandinavian-American from the prairie, and thinks of him bleeding to death on the sidewalk a few blocks from the floodlit Capitol. Her face twitches as she tries to suppress unbidden, insurgent tears.

The next to speak is Naomi Segal. Stef recognizes the name as that of a famous novelist or critic. And—Stef learns now—she is also literary editor of *Perspective*. The man with the Mediterranean look, Stef learns from Gloria, is the publisher of the magazine. His last name is Kazakis. Stef does not quite catch his first name—Les, or Des, or Desi.

Stef puts the puzzle together. Steven Quist must have interned for Congressman Bingham before going off to Oxford as a Rhodes scholar. He had been returning to join the editorial staff of *Perspective*, the political monthly, when he had been murdered for a watch and forty dollars.

"My sister Aglaia and I," Kazakis is soon telling the quiet crowd, "have established a scholarship fund in the memory of Steve Quist. Our initial contribution has been matched by Jay Prentice Pierce. Those of you who would like to join us in honoring Steve's memory can find information about the fund at the table by the door as you leave."

"Who is Jay Prentice Pierce?" Stef asks as they ride the small subway train that links the Capitol with the Cannon House Office Building. Jay Prentice Pierce—she has heard the name before. The three names, united, have a certain gravity, like William Butler Yeats or Robert Penn Warren.

"Oh, he's some kind of hotshot Washington lawyer or lobbyist," says Gloria. "A fixer. A *macher*." She opens a compact to guide her as she repairs her makeup. "I always cry at funerals."

There is no warning, no warning at all. "The office is going to be reorganized," Diane, the administrative assistant, tells Stef behind the shut door, "and it looks like your position is going to be discontinued . . ." Only as Diane talks further does Stef realize that she will not be offered a new position. "The budget's gotten tight . . . "

"So how long do I have?" In spite of her attempt to sound cool, her voice breaks.

"We'll pay you until the end of the month. But we'd like to start out under the new system next week . . . "

When she walks out of Diane's office, Stef senses that she is the focus of covert attention. Everybody knows, she thinks. She has been the last to find out. Mandy, the congressman's niece, is filing letters. Stef is certain, though the subject was not discussed in her exchange with Diane, that a place for Mandy in the new "system" will (the passive voice absolves Diane of responsibility) be found.

Stef takes the key and retreats to the bathroom down the hall.

In the mirror she looks smaller, homelier, somehow. For the first few minutes after learning the news she felt a pressure swelling behind her eyes. To burst into tears—now that would have proven her unworthiness. Now, though, she is growing angry. Self-righteous umbrage displaces her terror, restores her confidence, reinforces her sapped pride. There has been nothing wrong with her work, she tells herself. She has done her job as well as anyone in the office, maybe better. She is merely the victim of office politics, of budget politics. This happens all the time in Washington. Nobody's job is secure. She will simply move on to a new position. It happens all the time . . . She is rehearsing an explanation that will minimize the alarm of her parents, who may have to support her for the weeks—she hopes it will not be a longer period—that it will take for her to find a new job.

Like an actress ready for the final act, Stef emerges from the ladies' room. That afternoon she puts on the best performance of her life, as one by one the other members of the office commiserate, or pretend to. Stef is even gracious to Mandy, who tells her, "My *God*, it's such a *shock!*" Her anger gives way to resignation as she packs the few personal items in her alcove—slowly, and in full view of Diane and Mandy and the rest. She hopes they feel sick.

Stef has no time for self-pity. She must find a new job so that her parents will not have to support her from a distance. (Returning to St. Louis, giving up her career in Washington, is not even conceivable.) After work, in a mirror-and-elbow restaurant on Pennsylvania Avenue a few blocks from the Capitol, she communes with Gloria.

"Here are some résumés." Stef hands her the folder.

"It can take a while," Gloria warns, munching on a burger. "Something will open up, and you've got an inside track, since you know people on the Hill. But you've got to pay the bills in the meantime. A lot of companies hire from their temp pool . . . "

Stef blows smoke through her pursed lips. "Stef Schonfeld, B.A., M.A., Kelly girl."

"Hey, it's money, all right? Now I know a direct-mail firm that hires people by the hour. Political stuff. It's shit work—preparing the computer to print out address labels, things like that. Okay, it's not a career. You can leave it off your CV. But it'll pay the bills for six weeks. Or six months."

"Six months?"

"Look, it can take a while. What can I say? Eat your salad, or I will."

Six months . . . Stef's stoic resolution is tested by new attacks of despair. She tries to be cheerful and serene, but there are moments when she wants to lie down and sob. One of them occurs when her former roommate Julie and her boyfriend accompany her to the Cannon House Office Building on Saturday evening to help her retrieve a few remaining items from her desk. The guard on duty cannot find her name on the list. They have already removed her name.

More regrets when, alone in her tiny apartment, she unpacks her box of personal effects from the office. She rereads her old writings from the Georgetown student paper and the long magazine article about battered women, based on research done for one of Ritter's subcommittees, that she has been working on intermittently for a year and a half. It is good, very good. She has been making excuses for not writing since going to work for the congressman, but she was meant to be a writer. Her life since college, she concludes, has been a waste of time.

A few days later, when she is alone in the apartment at midday while every other able adult is at work, she breaks down. Her period is giving her cramps and nausea, and on top of all that the can opener won't work. She melts into tears, and recovers by binging on Oreos. Afterward, contemplating the traces of her fit in the form of an empty Oreo box and tiny black-and-white cookie crumbs all over the carpet, she wonders whether she is going mad. Maybe she will end up bulimic, binging on Oreos, throwing up, thrusting more Oreos into her face. Feeling bloated as a result of water retention and a surfeit of Oreos, she repeatedly examines herself in the mirror, as though hoping to catch herself in the act of swelling like a balloon. She feels utterly useless and unattractive and alone, a horrible, bloated thing, a marshmallow oozing blood. When Bruce Brandt does not phone her, as he had promised he would when they parted the night of the inaugural ball, Stef is both depressed and yet strangely relieved. In her present condition, she must appear as unattractive to others as she seems to herself.

Allison cheers her up. Allison was her best friend in high school back in St. Louis. "You're going to find something pretty soon," Allison's phone-shrunk voice says. "You've got a great résumé. And then the senator will ask you to marry him."

"Right. Are you still sure you want to come to Washington?" Allison has been working as a paralegal in St. Louis for several years. She wants to move to the District.

"Sure. We'll share a broom closet. While you're out passing out your résumé, I'll sleep, and then when you come home I'll let you use the closet . . . "

"I thought you were trying to cheer me up."

Later Avery cheers her up with a suggestion: "Why don't you talk to Ross? He knows a lot of people."

"He's a Republican."

"He knows all kinds of people, not just Republicans. You ought to talk to him. What have you got to lose? The worst that could happen is that you'd find out he can't help you and you'll never work again . . . "

"Fuck you, too."

"And you'll end up as a bag lady. And then I can get you onto NPR as a guest commentator. The bag lady's perspective on Washington. We'll appeal to liberal guilt. We'll raise donations to buy you a park bench. The Stephanie Schonfeld Memorial Bench."

"You are evil."

The dozen blocks east of the Capitol have always reminded Stef of a European city. With their old-fashioned town houses and little yards behind iron grilles and redbrick sidewalks, these streets might be in Europe rather than in the Virginia swampland. On a winter day like this, when the fish-colored sky hangs low enough to touch, emanating a chill from its damp cells, Washington might be on the North Sea.

Trussed up against the wet wind, Stef is enjoying the brisk walk until she comes to the polygon of yellow tape that sections off part of the sidewalk. POLICE LINE DO NOT CROSS. With guilty curiosity, she looks for the chalked outline of a body on the brick, but there is nothing. Not even any blood.

Is this the site where Steven Quist was killed? No, where he was "slain." RHODES SCHOLAR SLAIN NEAR CAPITOL. Naturally, Stef thinks (a former student journalist, she is sensitive to words) a Rhodes scholar would be "slain." Slain is a noble word, almost a feudal word, at home with "dastardly" and "valiant." RHODES SCHOLAR KILLED or RHODES SCHOLAR MURDERED—no, the tragic and romantic connotations are just not there. Nor could you say that a Rhodes scholar had been "shot" near the Capitol. Gunfighters in the Old West are shot. So are black teenage gangstas in southeast D.C. But Rhodes scholars can only be slain . . .

A few blocks further Stef finds the address that Avery gave her. Ross lives in a Victorian town house molting paint from scabby bricks. Stef is puzzled to find no list of renters' names next to buzzers. Instead, there is merely a single doorbell. He owns it all.

"Come on in. Let me take your coat." Ross guides her into a parlor with a bay window that looks out onto the tree-punctuated street. "Can I get you a drink? Coffee? Tea?"

"Some tea would be nice, thank you."

The cel phone rings. Speaking into it, Ross vanishes into the kitchen. Stef takes the opportunity to explore. Ross owns the whole town house, she realizes. He must be wealthier and more important than she had suspected. All the better, perhaps, for her.

"Sorry about that. Business." Ross brings her teacup and saucer, then retrieves his drink.

Stef swirls the tea bag. "You really have nice antique furniture," she says awkwardly.

"Old family stuff. I'm keeping a lot of it for my sister and her family. They're back in Mississippi . . . "

"That's where you're from?"

"Oh, yeah. Since forever. Since Bible times . . . My nephews and nieces, they're real little Hessians. They'd just tear the stuff up, so I'm baby-sitting it until they get older." Ross stands, strolls to the mantel, and takes down a framed photo. "Here's my niece, Elin."

Stef pretends to admire the generic blond child. It must be lonely, she thinks, to be a gay man like Ross, living in a big house empty of people but full of furniture.

Ross settles back in his antique chair. "So Avery tells me you've been downsized," he drawls. "Well, that's par for the course in Washington. I used to work on the Hill, you know."

"No, I didn't."

"Many moons ago. The Senate Foreign Relations Committee." He runs pink fingers through blond hair. "Since Avery called, I've been thinking. There are a couple of possibilities that come to mind. The best bet would be Aglaia . . . Oh, did you bring your CV?"

Stef takes the satchel out of her handbag. "My CV and my portfolio."

Ross leafs through the clippings. "So you've done a fair amount of writing."

"Mostly when I was at Georgetown. I was on the student paper. But I've written reports for the committee. And of course press releases."

Ross lays the satchel on the end table and takes a sip from his drink. "I think you'd be perfect for the assistant program officer job, as I understand it. You can write, and you've got managerial experience . . . "

"I don't quite understand what the job would be."

"Well, they'd have to fill you in on the details. You know what the Kazakis Foundation is?"

"It's a charitable organization, right?"

"It's an excuse for Aglaia to throw money at whatever causes she likes. It's her share of the family fortune. She blows her money on do-gooders, and Des blows his on trying to buy up all the newspapers in the world."

"They're Australian, right?"

"Greek-Australian. Their father was a Greek immigrant. Apparently there are a lot of those. Australians aren't all Irish white trash, as I was brought up to believe. Anyway, the old man made a ton of money out of real estate and he bought a few newspapers and TV and radio stations for his son Des to play with, after he came back from Oxford. And the rest is history. Des owns a couple of tabloids in London, and the *New York Sentinel*. And he bought *Perspective*—oh, must have been about eight or ten years ago, just after Reagan was elected. It's his way of buying respectability in Washington. He contributes a lot to Aglaia's foundation. They're very close, the brother and sister. That's the way the Mediterranean people are, aren't they? Very close." Ross smiles slyly. "You know the Greek army's motto? 'Never leave your buddy's behind.'"

"Gosh." Stef laughs. Maybe by telling the joke, she thinks, he is welcoming her into the circle of his friends. "You mentioned there were other possibilities? Besides the foundation."

"We have some temp jobs at my firm, Wriston, White . . . "

"That's a public relations firm."

"So we claim, but between you and me, we're lobbyists. But the temp jobs don't pay much, and I wouldn't recommend it, unless you're facing a complete financial catastrophe."

"I'm okay for a couple of more weeks."

The surprise that shows on his face indicates that running out of money in a couple of weeks is Ross's definition of a financial catastrophe. "Look, I'll tell Aglaia you need an answer, pronto. I'm having dinner with her tonight."

"If I'm holding you up . . . "

"No, not at all. I'm not expected till eight. I'm enjoying this. You know, there's nothing one of us Southern gentlemen enjoys more than passing the time in the parlor with a lovely and erudite young lady."

They talk for a little while longer. But Stef leaves without asking Ross the question she really wanted to ask: Why won't Bruce Brandt call? If Ross could get her a boyfriend, as well as a job, he would be Washington's greatest fixer.

6

The cafetorium of Woodrow Wilson Junior High seethes with the dammed energy of half a thousand adolescents. Sitting a few chairs away from Mrs. Gutierrez on the floodlit stage, under the red, white, and blue banner reading NO MO', Bruce winces when the public address system twangs.

"Quiet . . . Quiet, everyone," the principal repeats.

It takes five minutes for the drone to subside enough that the show can begin. Bruce has been through all this before; he has visited three schools already this month in the drug czarina's entourage. While his employer speaks, he anticipates each phrase of the address he helped to write.

"Somebody who offers you drugs is not your friend," Mrs. Gutierrez is saying. "Do you know what we say to somebody who asks us if we want to try drugs?"

On cue, about a third of the students, most of them girls, chant the slogan of the campaign: "No Mo'!" Somewhere in the audience, a beeper trills, triggering an avalanche of laughter.

Her face frozen in a smile, Mrs. Gutierrez waits for the laughter to die down. Meanwhile, Bruce is scanning the audience. Most of the kids are black, but there are a few Latino and white students. Bruce focuses on a white boy, an eighth grader to judge by his size, a kid with reddish hair and freckles dressed like a homeboy in baggy pants, a hooded sweatshirt, and a gold chain. A white homie, Bruce thinks. A wigger.

"How many of you here know that alcohol is a drug?" the drug czarina asks. "Let me see your hands. How many of you know that coffee is a drug?"

The wigger sneers and whispers to a black guy next to him. The two snicker. If you're white in this neighborhood, Bruce thinks, you have to be a wigger. Adapt or die.

"How many of you have heard the word *addiction*?" Mrs. Gutierrez is asking.

Suddenly Bruce has an idea. He is only a decade older than these kids. He wonders if he could pass himself off as one of them. Learn their slang, their moves, the signals that distinguish outsiders from trusted neighbors in the 'hood. He imagines himself dressed in the homie uniform, strapped with a hidden pistol, an undercover agent for the Justice Department. Operation Wigger. He sees himself in a shadowy alley with the white kid and his black friends, taking their money, watching them reach for the crack. Suddenly Bruce cries, "Justice Department! You're under arrest!" The red-haired wigger reaches for his gun, but he is too slow; the blast from Bruce's 9 mm sends him slamming into a trash can. Bruce dodges clattering automatic fire and rolls to his feet, spraying the gangstas with the lethal metal rain from his chuckling gun . . .

"No mo'," Mrs. Gutierrez is saying. "Remember—all you have to say is two words: No mo'."

Another beeper goes off. The laughter rattles the rafters.

The backbeat starts first. Then a titter of electronic rhythm is superimposed on it. Another drum joins in, then the melody, syncopated with the flashing lights on the eye-level runway. It is as though the stereo speakers are monitoring the arousal of the men in the shadowy club on M Street, translating pulses into drumbeats and quickening breaths into synthesizer notes as the stripper takes the stage.

"Filipino," Milligan guesses. Bruce is surprised, but his colleague may be right. Beneath the cloud of white-blond hair, the features are Southeast Asian.

Milligan knows the strip clubs the way he knows the rest of Washington. After a few months of working for Mrs. Gutierrez, Bruce has come to respect the balding FBI agent more than anyone else on the staff. Milligan is a Republican operative from way back; in the past three decades, he has worked at half the agencies in town. Bruce plans to be much higher in the world when he is Milligan's age; for now, he plans to use Milligan's know-how to the fullest.

"Hey," says Bruce, watching the stripper peel her halter off conical silicon-swollen breasts, "I've got it. We'll turn the drug czar into a sex and drug czar."

"I like it," says Milligan, lighting another cigarette. "If they can't use drugs, they might turn to sex instead. Can't allow that. We've got to stamp out sex *and* drugs."

"Okay. Okay." Bruce is grinning. "I've got the motto. You ready? 'No 'ho.'"

Milligan laughs. They spent the morning with Mrs. Gutierrez watching a group of black rap singers film an antidrug commercial, using the new, street-savvy slogan of the war on drugs: No mo'.

"No sex," Bruce continues, "no drugs. No mo'. No 'ho."

"No how. . . . Yeah, another round," the veteran bureaucrat tells the hostess.

"I still think that guy was flashing a gang sign," Bruce tells Milligan. "What he did with his fingers, you know, like this? It's probably the Crip sign. Or the Bloods."

"I guess we ought to check on that before we blanket the TV screens of the nation with that piece-of-shit ad. If they're making gang signs, guess who'll catch hell for it? Remember that little sign Harry Truman had on his desk, 'The Buck Stops Here'? Well, it's a lie. 'The Buck Stops There'—that's the motto here in Powertown. Anything goes wrong, the low guy on the totem pole is responsible. The intern. The receptionist. The janitor. It's all the janitor's fault, Senator. The janitor ran amok."

The blond Filipina is naked now. Cheered on by his hooting office colleagues, a pudgy, mustached guy in his thirties gingerly approaches the dancer and puts a rolled-up wad of dollars in her garter.

"No mo', my ass." Milligan takes a drag on his cigarette. "In 1965, when I started out with the FBI, there were just a couple of agencies dealing with enforcement of the drug laws. Now there are fifty some-odd agencies. DEA, the Bureau, ATF, the IRS, the Agency—and that's just for starters. You've got the services, and the whole intelligence community, and State, Customs, the Coast Guard . . . But you know what? The enforcement budget is just about the same now as it was in the sixties. So you've got fifty agencies trying to do the work of two, for the same amount of money. Sheer chaos.

"So they thought they'd appoint a drug czar to straighten the mess out. Right. Like Customs or the Agency is going to take orders from some half-ass political appointee who'll be out in eighteen months—that's the average tenure of top federal executives these days. Yeah.

"I'll tell you a secret, Bruce. We don't want to win the drug war. Not really. It's not in the interest of U.S. foreign policy. I'm not just talking about the mujahedeen, Noriega, the Shan in the Golden Triangle, you know, the usual friends of our friends in the Agency. I'm talking about Mexico. The PRI, the government party, they're in the trade up to their butts. The DFS—that's the Mexican CIA—they are, too. The army, the police. They're all getting a cut from what comes into the States. Half the *narcotraficantes* in fucking Mexico are in uniform.

"They've got this system, the plaza, see. The town square. That's their slang for the concession in a particular part of Mexico. Whoever the local power is—the governor, or maybe a general—he hands out the plaza to the *narcos* he likes. So we traipse down to Mexico, and we say, you've got to be more cooperative, or Congress won't certify that you're making progress in helping us win the drug war. Whereupon the *Pristas* and the DEA stage a raid on some two-bit *narco*, capture a warehouse or something—but it's always the guys who don't have the plaza who get caught, see? The ones who are on the outs with the *Pristas* and the military. Oh, there's a big dog and pony show, for the benefit of the *yanquis*. The Americans and Mexicans have a big ceremony burning all the shit, and the Americans go home, and State tells Congress they ought to give our Mexican friends an A for effort. And the minute the *gringos* are on the plane, the police call up the guy holding the plaza and they say, 'We didn't burn all the shit, we saved half of it. Here it is. Just don't forget to give us our cut.' "

Milligan taps ash from his cigarette into the tray, and takes a sip from his drink. "So what are we going to do? It's not just

Colombia and Bolivia. It's every fucking government in this hemisphere south of the Rio Grande, and half of the countries in Asia and the Middle East and Europe. Are we going to send in the troops and occupy the whole world? Is the drug war worth a world war? I don't care who the fucking president is, when they clue him in to the real situation, he's going to make the same decision. Better to live with a bunch of crackheads in Southeast than throw our whole foreign policy into turmoil. Let the home-boys shoot each other every night. That's better than throwing away the lives of U.S. soldiers in Bolivia or Colombia or Honduras or, God forbid, Mexico. That's what any president is going to decide. And you know what? You know what? He'd be right."

Glumly, Bruce asks, "Well, what do we do?"

Milligan grinds out his cigarette and lights another. "You want to know what I think? Surrender. Repeal the laws. Just like Prohibition . . . "

"Legalize drugs?"

"Hell, yeah. Tax the hell out of 'em. Reduce the deficit. Or make the sale of drugs a government monopoly. Like booze in West Virginia. The ABC Stores."

"Man, the Baptists would go ape-shit." Bruce imitates a Southern accent. "'We're a Christian nation, and the government is pushin' drugs. It's the work of Satan.'"

"All right, then. Before the government sells you a rock or whatever, you have to recite a Bible verse. 'The Lord is my shep-herd. . .' Drugs for Psalms. That ought to get the Baptists onboard. And you can pay all the hicks in North Carolina to shift from tobacco production to growing marijuana. Ten years, you'd get the conservative marijuana lobby in Congress. And Coors, Pfizer Pharmaceutical, all those big-time patriotic Republican donors? They'd turn around in five minutes and start rolling Quaaludes and speed off the assembly line. Just give 'em a tax break."

Under the blue parasol of Milligan's cigarette smoke, they sit and watch another smiling blonde peel off a silver space suit.

"So we're wasting our time," says Bruce.

"As Tonto said to the Lone Ranger, 'What do you mean by

we, white man?'" Milligan gazes into the red-globed candle on the table. "Wait . . . wait . . . I feel a vision coming on." He makes passes, like a medium, over the candle, the cigarette glowing in his fingers. "I see the future, two years from now . . . I see Mrs. Gutierrez, back in Texas, making shitloads of money on some corporate board . . . I see you and me in other jobs in Washington, making a little more money . . . Yes, and . . . Wait. . . . It isn't clear . . . Yes. Yes, there are more drugs pouring into the country than ever before!"

Milligan sucks on his cigarette. "So are we wasting our time? Hell, no, because we have achieved our primary goal. *We're employed.* That's the bottom line.

"Look, I've been here in Powertown since 1963. Washington is like Broadway. You look at plays, the fashions come and go. This year it's musicals, next year it's tragedies, then comedies are the big thing. But no matter what kind of play they put on, they have to have dancers for those show-stopping numbers where the tourists hold their hands up over their heads and clap like they're retarded. They're always going to need dancers. Folks like us, we're the dancers. One show closes, another one'll open next week. We'll always find work. We're the chorus girls."

Milligan settles back in his chair and admires the blonde, now naked, thrusting her crotch in the faces of a pair of leering Marines. "Now *that's* what I call a chorus girl."

Bruce is getting aroused. It's been too long since he's gotten laid, he decides. He thinks about calling up that girl he met at the inaugural ball. In a moment her name comes to him: Stephanie Schonfeld. Stef. She's not really his type—too small, too flat, not very pretty in the face. On the other hand, in his experience ordinary girls had often been the best lovers. They were determined to compensate—and also desperate to keep a guy as good-looking as him. Stef Schonfeld . . . why not? It would be better than leering without touching, like Milligan. Bruce feels superior to the older man. After all, Bruce can have young women for free.

A few nights later, Bruce and Milligan are together again, in a police car cruising down Pennsylvania Avenue east of the Capitol.

"Down this way, it starts to get bad," the cop tells Bruce, sitting beside him in the front seat. "We get a lot of calls from that apartment complex over there. The Krew was running a crack house out of one of the apartments for a while. We shut it down—oh, must have been February."

"The crew," Bruce repeats. "That's the gang."

"That's the term they use in Washington, crews. Other cities, they got different names. This area right here, there are two crews, two gangs—the Krew and the Yungstaz. There's a kind of a no-man's-land for about six or seven blocks that they both claim."

Young black men in coats and hoods glower from the sidewalk as they pass. For the first time, Bruce feels the tickle of apprehension. He glances at the image of Milligan in the rearview mirror. Milligan is smoking and watching the streets drift by.

The radio crackles. Bruce cannot make out what the dispatcher is saying. He clutches the car door's armrest as the cop makes a U-turn.

"Got a fight on Capitol Hill," the officer says.

Bruce feels his heart quicken, feels a mixture of fear and excitement. He is heading into battle, into danger, for the first time in his life. Tonight, he will become a blooded warrior.

The Capitol Police are there before them. In front of a glass-paneled donut shop in a small strip, figures appear and fade in the rhythmic red flash. Radios crackle.

"You coming?" Milligan asks. The cop has already gotten out, but Bruce has stayed fast in his seat, hesitating, waiting in case shots ring out.

Returning from the crime scene, the cop greets them as they emerge from the car, a smile on his face. "Jesus Christ, you ain't going to believe this. The owner—see that little Filipino guy? He says these two drunken men come into his store and order donuts. And then they start throwing them at each other. And then they run out of ammunition, and they go back behind the counter, and start grabbing . . . "

"Ed . . . Ed, come on," a man's voice implores. Another voice, one that Bruce knows, says, "Call Marina O'Brien . . . Call this number . . . she'll straighten it out . . . "

Police officers part before two burly, middle-aged men in trench coats and fine suits, splotched and spattered and streaked with sugar and crumbs. The bigger one wavers drunkenly as the smaller, calling him, "Ed," leads him by the arm.

"Call Marina," the one named Ed is saying in that familiar nasal voice.

"They will, Ed. Come on."

"I want to talk to Marina . . . "

The big man brushes past. Oh my God, Bruce thinks. It's Senator Ed Shaunnessey of Massachusetts.

"I want to know who is going to pay for my store!" a small brown man in an apron is shouting. "I don't care who they are. This is America. I want to know who is going to pay!"

"Who's the other one?" Bruce whispers to Milligan as they watch the two senators stumble along the sidewalk in front of a gathering crowd.

"Brad Doyle," Milligan answers. "Senator from Connecticut."

"I can't wait to read about this in the papers tomorrow."

"Betcha money you won't read about it," Milligan says, his lighter flaring redly through the fingers of his cupped hand.

A few yards away, Senator Doyle makes a spastic motion with his arm. The donut he has hidden until now bounces off Senator Shaunnessey, who blurts out, "Goddamn you!" Giggling, Doyle dances away from his lunging friend.

The cop who drove them here returns from the shop. "Hungry?" he asks, his voice muffled by munching. "Got a French twist and a jelly donut. Go ahead. It's on the government."

7

"They gonna jump Tyrone Watkins." Teesha hears it first in the hall between second period (social studies) and third (English). Then in the girl's room, where she adds eyeliner while a couple of seventh graders surreptitiously smoke, Teesha hears it again: "They gonna jump this boy named Tyrone."

As she settles down with a couple of girlfriends in the English class, she hears more details: "Tyrone's dissed this dude, Calvin? And Calvin's down with the Krew. They gonna jump him."

"When?"

"I don't know."

The teacher, Miss McAllister, a fat white woman in her thirties, talks a little, then tells them to read the assigned story by Jack London. Though the whisper thickens into a drone, Miss McAllister pretends not to hear. She is reading a novel. Sometimes she balances her checkbook.

Teesha notices the crowd gathering around the pencil sharpener, which is affixed to the wall next to the door. She rises.

Miss McAllister calls out. "What are you guys doing?"

"My pencil broke," says Teesha.

Teesha sharpens her pencil. Outside in the hall is an eighth-grade boy she has seen before. She thinks his name is Alan. He is going from classroom to classroom with updates.

"They comin' down from high school now," the boy tells them.

"Who?"

"The Krew. I seen a couple of 'em in the hall. Remember L.B.? He graduated from here two years ago. He was standing by the lockers. They back, and they gonna jump his ass."

"I don't remember who Tyrone Watkins is."

"You know, he tall. Kinda got, like, a gap in his teeth."

"That means you're horny."

"Say what?"

"If you got a gap in your teeth. It means you like to do the wild thing."

"She Tyrone's girlfriend."

"Am not. Shut up, girl. He's just in the seventh grade."

"Your boyfriend's in the *fourth* grade!"

The laughter finally draws Miss McAllister's attention. "Come on, you guys, sit down. Quiet down." Miss McAllister goes back to reading her novel.

In the cafeteria at lunchtime there are conflicting reports. Some claim that Tyrone Watkins has been jumped already. Others say he slipped off campus. Yet another account has him hiding somewhere on the school grounds, maybe on the third floor. The third-floor boy's room is infamous. The boys go there to smoke, and sometimes, it is said, to do drugs. Once, it is rumored, a girl named Veronica, since graduated, had sex with five or six boys in the third-floor boy's room. The teachers and the principal stay away from there. They would just as soon not know.

Sitting with her friends at the lunch table, Teesha scans the crowd, hoping to catch a glimpse of high school boys who have infiltrated the junior high on their grim mission of jumping Tyrone Watkins. Some of the boys in the eighth grade are old enough to be in high school themselves, having been held back a year or, in some cases, two. Their bulk makes it easy for them to terrorize the other boys in their grades, and their maturity means they can have all the junior high girls they want.

Teesha is still a virgin at fifteen. Most of her friends, though, have had sex, for the most part with guys a few years older—sixteen, seventeen, eighteen. Her best friend, Diane, has a twenty-one-year-old boyfriend named Barry and an eleven-month-old baby girl, Janet. Janet is perfect, a tiny, dimpled candy sculpture folded up in doilied dresses like elaborate wrappers of lemon or pink. Teesha loves to play with Diane's baby, to pat her little hands together and sing to her. "You gonna be a good mother," Diane often tells her friend. If Teesha had a baby, Diane speculates, she would not have to live with her aunt and uncle anymore. Teesha and Diane and their babies could move into an apartment and be a family.

"When you gonna get a man, girl?" Diane keeps taunting Teesha. "You gonna be an old maid."

"I'll get a man, he's just got to be the right man," Teesha always replies serenely. Secretly, though, she fears that indeed she will be an old maid. No man will ever want her. Her friends tell her she is pretty, but friends lie. She doesn't like her broad face—a frog face, she thinks. She is proud of her light skin, but even that has been turned against her. Once she heard two high school girls talking about her, thinking she could not hear: "Look at that! Whole lotta yellow wasted there."

Diane thinks that Teesha just needs the right do. At the Africare Salon, Pearl, the head stylist, examines her. "Girl, we gonna fix you up." Afterward, admiring her new twin in the mirror, Teesha is impressed as much by her own boldness as by the results.

Her Aunt Shirelle, though, is not pleased by Teesha's new look. "Is that the way they wearing their hair now?" She is a bitter woman. She does not enjoy having to raise the daughter of her sister Jocelyn, who is serving time in the women's prison at Lorton.

"Girl, you *go*," her mother compliments Teesha as they embrace in the visitor's room the following Saturday. "Who did you up?"

"Woman named Pearl. At Africare Salon."

"You ain't spending too much of their money?"

"They say I'm costing too much?" From the look on her mother's face, Teesha infers that Shirelle and her husband Monroe have complained. "How come I have to live with them? How come I can't go live with Grandma like Jasmine and Joey?"

"Baby, listen to me. I want you to get a job. Then you can spend all the money you want . . . "

"I'm too young. I'm just fifteen. What if they ask how old I am?"

"Just lie about how old you are. They don't check."

Teesha looks at the floor. "I don't want no job. I want to go to design college."

"College? Oh, Lordy, who's gonna pay for design college? Baby, we ain't got no money. You know that."

"I saw this ad on TV, for this Imperial School of Design. You learn how to decorate people's houses . . . "

"Baby, those people on TV, they just want to take your money and give you some piece of paper, ain't worth nothing. Now you listen to me, Latisha Madison, you get yourself a job at a store or a restaurant or something. And you open up a bank account and you save your money. Don't think some man gonna come along and treat you like you was the queen of Sheba." Jocelyn is serving two years for having acted as a courier for her boyfriend Cy, a dealer serving twenty-five in a federal penitentiary.

Within a few weeks, as much to spite her aunt and uncle by reducing her dependence on them as to follow her mother's advice, Teesha has found a job as a clerk at Deluxe Video, a video rental store in a run-down shopping strip not far from the apartment complex where her aunt and uncle live. The owner is a Korean. Teesha dislikes him, but the job is easy. All she has to do is run the magnetic strip on the videos across a sensor and the computer will tell her the rental fee to charge.

One evening the computer shows what Teesha thinks of as a huge balance of overdue charges. She looks up at the customer, a skinny boy her age with a round face. "You've got a lot of overdues," she tells him.

"How much?" He is wearing a hooded blue sweatshirt and baggy blue pants. He looks like a gangbanger.

Teesha thinks he is fine. To spare him public embarrassment, she writes down the amount he owes the store on a piece of paper that she slips to him: $27.50.

He pulls out his wallet and hands her a note. At first she thinks it is a twenty, then she looks again. It is a hundred-dollar bill, the first she has ever seen.

Mr. Kim, the owner, sees her puzzlement and comes over.

"We can't take," he says, handing the hundred back to the teenager. "No change."

"Oh, man." The gangbanger takes the hundred back and pulls out two twenties. The people in line behind him shift impatiently. He turns and intimidates them with a glare.

"Keep the change," he tells Teesha as she puts the three martial arts movies he has rented in a plastic bag.

"Say what?"

"Keep the change." He looks at her. "What's your name?"

"Teesha."

"You go to Douglass?"

"Yeah."

"You know Diane Lake?"

"Yeah. She your girlfriend?"

"Ain't got no girlfriend. Tell her hello."

"What's your name? To tell Diane."

"Evander."

"Evander who?"

"Evander Johnson."

"I met one of your boyfriends," Teesha tells Diane. "Evander Johnson."

Diane doesn't recall him until Teesha describes him.

"Oh, he ain't no boyfriend. He hang with Tito and them."

"He a dealer?"

"They all sellin' that shit. I don't care. Long as they don't get shot." Diane looks at Teesha and smiles. "Girl, you in love."

"I am not. He's too young for me."

"You like 'em old. Like that old *Ko*rean at the store."

"Shut up!"

"He your boyfriend. Mistah Kim. With that little Asian dick."

"They got little dicks?"

"Didn't you know that, girl? That's what everybody says. Asian men is the littlest, and white men is in the middle, and African men is . . . just right to fit in your mouth."

"Ooh, girl, you nasty."

"The way to a man's heart is through his dick, Baby Sis. It's true. Ain't no man don't like a BJ."

"You do that with Barry?"

"When I was pregnant with Janet, that's all I'd do. I don't want him running around with no other womens. Baby, they ain't gonna wait for you."

Teesha thinks of Evander on Sunday afternoon as she does the clothes. This is one chore she enjoys. It gives her an excuse to be by herself, down in the basement of the apartment building, away from her aunt's family. And she finds something very relaxing in the ritual of washing the clothes and then watching them tumble in one of the three dryers. She brings the radio down with her and listens to the Top Forty.

"Our next dedication comes from a young lady in San Diego, for Paul, who is stationed in South Korea. She writes,

"'Casey, I never knew there could be a love like the one that Paul and I enjoyed after we met while he was on leave from the army. I knew our special time together could not last forever, but somehow I was not prepared when he had to return to his unit in South Korea. It was then that the doctors discovered I was suffering from Crohn's disease, a terrible affliction that strikes young women like me without warning.

"'Casey, I don't know how I would have survived the many operations without Paul's support. His duties prevented him from visiting me more than once, but he has showered me with phone calls and letters. As soon as his tour of duty is finished, he has promised to marry me and raise a family. He is more than a lover, he is my best friend.

"'Casey, please play our favorite song, "Eternal Love." And Paul, if you are listening, know that I shall always love you, my darling. Signed, Joanie.'"

Teesha is wiping tears from her eyes as she thinks of Paul and Joanie, wondering whether she will ever experience a love so tragic and beautiful. Because of the music and the droning of the dryers, she does not hear her aunt enter the basement.

"Baby, you crying?" Shirelle asks, concerned. "What's the matter?"

Teesha sniffles. "Nothing."

"You're not upset about that boy, are you?"

"What boy?"

"The one in the papers this morning. Did you know him? Name of Tyrone Watkins. They found him dead over on the corner of Sherman Avenue. Shot three times. Nobody saw nothing. I don't know what the world is coming to."

8

Once more, Jamal appears. He stands on the corner a block away, a little boy in a big parka, gazing in the direction of Lookout and Evander.

"Shit, man," Lookout complains. "There he be again. Damn. He gonna give us away."

Lookout and Evander are hovering in the front yard of a boarded-up row house. Its flight of stone steps hides them from the view of anyone in the yellow-and-brown tenement a few numbers down. Like a soldier cautiously raising his head above a trench, Evander, a Krew-blue stocking cap for a helmet, peers over the stairs. His half brother spots him and starts moving in.

"Go 'way!" Evander hisses. Jamal does not hear, or pretends he does not.

"He like a dog," says Lookout. A little while earlier, Lookout had invited Evander to accompany him as he made the rounds, checking up on his women: "Got to check my traps, man." Jamal had wanted to tag along, but he had been rebuffed: "You just a baby gangsta. OG's"—Original Gangstas—"only."

When he had seen the mint, shark-black Lexus parked in front of the building where Jocelyn and her sister live, Lookout had grown suspicious. He and Evander had hunkered down to study the doings at Jocelyn's place.

Then Jamal had shown up.

"Go home!" Evander picks up a rock. It lands a few feet from his half brother. Jamal stops and gazes at them with a mixture of sullenness and imprecation.

"He busted," Lookout agrees. It is Lookout's turn to chuck a pebble at the boy in the parka. His throw, though, is wild. The rock ricochets off the door of Jocelyn's row house with an emphatic thunk.

The door opens a minute later. A teenage girl with braids and bangs, clutching a baby, comes out into the cold bright day.

"What you doing?" she yells at Jamal. She follows his gaze to the older boys.

"Yo. Monica," Lookout greets her, emerging from hiding and moving with a gangsta limp even more exaggerated than his usual gait. "Where's Jocelyn at?"

"She upstairs. Y'all throwing rocks at the house?"

"He did."

"Did not," says Jamal.

Jocelyn emerges from the house holding a blinking baby of her own. Like her sister, she has elaborate hair—black bangs in front and, on top, a tornado spiraling up, transected by lightning metal.

"Hi, baby," says Lookout, addressing Jocelyn, or her infant, or, perhaps, the toddler who wobbles out of the house and peers at them from behind the columns of his mother's legs. "Whose car is that?" Lookout asks.

"I don't know. 'Cross the street."

His suspicions allayed, Lookout turns his attention to the toddler. "Yo, Markie. Look what I brung you." Lookout grabs Jamal and hoists him into the air. "I brung you a brother. Jocelyn, you want another baby boy? Evander says they don't want this one no more."

Watching his brother kick in Lookout's wiry arms, Evander laughs. "He a little shithead. Throwing rocks at people's houses and shit. My momma told me to get rid of him."

"Y'all gonna sell him," Jocelyn asks, "or give him away?"

"He's for sale," Lookout replies. "He's not for free."

"Baby," Jocelyn tells her sometime boyfriend, "you done give me two already. I don't need to *buy* none off you."

"Women check each other out, Deuce," Lookout says as they cut through an alley on their way to the next destination. "Deuce" is the nickname the gang bestowed on Evander after he embarrassed himself by mistaking a 9 mm for a .22—a double deuce. "Women are cold-blooded. Like they going down the street, and they look at each other's clothes and jewelry and shit, and they think like, Ooh, she ugly, or Ooh, she pretty, I wanna dress like that. And if you walking along and you checking out some other woman, man, they know. They say, 'I saw you looking at that 'ho. You think that ugly old 'ho is fly? Did you see her makeup? I like to throwed up.'" A gold-capped tooth glints as he laughs.

Women, Lookout explains, are either bamas or fly girls. The bamas are dowdy and unfashionable; the fly girls have it. *It* isn't just sexuality—both bamas and fly girls could be good in bed. Nor is *it* looks—there are bamas who were given great beauty by nature, and fly girls who overcome a natural disaster by means of art and, above all, attitude. Fly girls are hot shit and everybody else is dirt and they want the world to know it. That, according to Lookout, is why it is such a pleasure to do a fly girl. It is a humbling of the haughty.

"A-minus bama," Lookout replies when Evander asks him to evaluate Jocelyn according to his scheme. The next woman on Lookout's list is a true fly girl—a B fly, he concedes, not an A fly—named Eunique. Evander has glimpsed her at parties given by the Krew in the Funkadelic and elsewhere, a girl with an hourglass body, strikingly asymmetric hair, and a single gold earring so big it looks like a rapper's head-mike. Unlike so many of the girls in the hood, Eunique does not have any babies. Lookout says she has had three or four abortions.

Eunique is not at home. Lookout, though, is reluctant to believe it. For five minutes, the gold necklace he has brought as a present hidden behind his back, he pounds on the door. After a while he starts to unconsciously manipulate the necklace as though it were a rosary.

"She gone, man," Evander repeats. Still not satisfied, Lookout circles to the outside of the apartment complex, hops up on a low wall, and gazes in through the window as though expecting to catch Eunique with another man.

Evander wants to know what his friend would do. Lookout pats the cuff of his baggy pants where, Evander knows, the seventeen-year-old is wearing a 9 mm Glock tucked into his high-top sneakers.

The gift intended for Lookout's fly girl goes instead to his bama number two, Suzy. "Oh, baby!" Suzy smiles with delight as she lets the gold necklace run from hand to hand like a glittering snake.

"Try it on, woman."

"Who'd you steal this from?"

"I bought it." Lookout winks at Evander, who knows it was pilfered from Jocelyn's drawer.

Suzy is big, as tall as Evander, with broad shoulders like a man's. Her hips and legs are thick, her breasts drooping cones rescued by a halter. She is not pretty, but she is powerful, physical. "How come you never call me?" she asks Lookout as he plays with his eighteen-month-old daughter, a baby as dark as her mother with luminous green and pink barrettes glowing on her head.

"I call you," he says. The baby squeals as Lookout, her tiny hands globed in his, makes her clap. "I call you. You're ain't never home. You're out with other mens, ain't you."

"Shit. You know you the only one."

Lookout sputters. He has told his friends proudly that he is the father of Suzy's child, but refuses to acknowledge his paternity to her face. He brings mother and daughter cash every now and then, and sometimes jewelry and toys.

After they leave, Lookout, who had grown morose when he had found Eunique absent, is cheerful again. He punches Evander playfully as they walk. "You want to fuck her?"

"Say what?"

"You want to fuck Suzy?"

Evander does not know what to say. He is not sure whether his friend is trying to pick a fight.

"While we was in the kitchen," Lookout tells him, "she say, 'Who that boy?' She say, 'He look mighty fine.' She wants you, cuz. Word, cuz. Go for it. I don't care. If you mess with Jocelyn or Eunique, I'll bust a cap in your ass. But you can hit the skins with Suzy."

"You shittin' me."

"No shit, homes. She'll buff you. She a horny-ass 'ho. Bring her some Scotty, man. She'll do whatever you want."

"For real?"

"I ain't shitting you, man. Just go by there some time. Word, I'm telling you, she wants you. Go by there." Lookout sees Jamal in the distance. "Damn."

Lookout spends the rest of the afternoon hanging around the open-air drug mart while Evander looks out for the cops, including the plainclothes five-oh he has been trained to identify. There are only a few customers, including a carload of white college boys. Lookout never carries drugs on his person. He makes the customers wait while he goes into a nearby apartment building and emerges, nonchalantly dropping the package off in a trash can near the street. Evander is not supposed to know that Lookout keeps his wares inside a sawed-off pipe in the stairwell, where he lingers long enough to make everyone think he is in an apartment inside.

Toward evening Twon wanders up to them. "What up?"

"What the fuck you doing, man?" Lookout sneers. "Get your ass outta here."

Twon looks hurt. He has been hoping that his long-standing friendship with Evander qualifies him for special treatment by Lookout as well. Twon turns from Lookout to Evander and unzips his backpack. "I got a new Cybernauts."

Evander reaches for the comic book, but Lookout snatches it out of his hand. "What kind of pussy-ass shit is this?"

"This is phat shit, man," Twon protests. He giggles as he reads from the cover. "Listen at him, he say, 'I will avenge you, my fallen comrade . . .'"

"You making that shit up," Lookout says.

"That's what it says, read it." Twon insists. "Read it."

"Fuck this shit!" Lookout explodes. "Fucking pussy reading that comic book shit!" Swearing, he crumples the glossy booklet and tosses it aside. Evander stares, stunned. For the first time, he realizes that Lookout cannot read.

"Get the fuck away, muhfucka," Lookout shouts at Twon, "or I fuck you up." Lookout saunters away, then pauses, and calls back to Evander. "You comin' or you a pussy bitch, too?"

Tears in his eyes, Twon looks at Evander. Evander hesitates, then turns his back on his former friend and hurries after Lookout.

From that day onward, Evander is careful not to read comic books in the presence of Lookout. He hides other childish pleasures, as well. Several times, sauntering down Pennsylvania Avenue near the Capitol with his new peeps like Lookout and Willy, Evander has passed the pet store. Each time he has done a double take, fascinated by the guinea pigs snuffling in their litter-carpeted aquarium in the window. In the presence of his friends, however, he is careful not to show his interest. Gangstas are not supposed to be fond of small animals.

Alone, he visits the pet store, feeling something of the unease of a deacon in a blue-movie house. Hands in pockets, head hunched low, Evander studies the gerbils through smeared glass. Young women with children stop at the end of the aisle and take the other aisle to avoid brushing past him in the narrow space. Everyone else in this pet shop in the gentrified section of Capitol Hill is white. Evander senses the tension. It is familiar to him, this unease he inspires among middle-class white folks when he intrudes into their stores, their neighborhoods, their lives. Sometimes it makes him feel powerful to know that he can inspire such anxiety. Today, though, he does not want to be a menacing ghetto kid, he just wants to be another browser admiring the animals.

"They're neat, aren't they?"—this, from a plump, bearded young white man. His voice startles Evander, who has been watching tiny black salamanders swim and clamber onto wedges of slate.

"What kind of lizard that is?"

"Oh, they aren't lizards, they're salamanders," the young man says. He is wearing a name tag. He works for the store.

"It's a salamander lizard?"

"No. Salamanders are amphibians. Like frogs."

Evander snorts. "Ain't no frog."

The creatures seem to have neither skin nor bone. They are all surface, pliant as candy figurines come to life, little dragons made of soft licorice. One of them splits its mouth in a dopey grin that seems to crack open its very head. Evander laughs.

"I've got a book on salamanders over here." The bearded salesclerk leads him to a rack full of pamphlets on pet care, each with a photo of its subject on its cover: goldfish, turtles, a spider monkey. The man draws a pair of glasses from his pocket and puts them on. "Salamanders . . . "

Evander wonders why this white man is being nice to him. Maybe he's a homo, wants some black ass.

"Here we go. *The Salamandra*. This is from a medieval bestiary . . . "

"Say what?"

"A book of beasts. See, that's what they used to think salamanders looked like."

The clerk shows Evander an ornate initial from an illuminated manuscript. Twined within it is a serpentine creature with two legs, a human face, and pointed ears.

"That don't look like him."

"They had all sorts of misconceptions, it appears. Listen: 'The Salamandra is the only beast which prevaileth against fire; it dwelleth in the midst of the flame, neither is it hurt nor burnt in any way'. . . Listen, this is Aristotle, the Greek philosopher: the salamander 'not only walks through fire, but in doing so extinguishes it.' See, in ancient times, and the Middle Ages, people believed that salamanders could live in fire."

"You shittin' me."

"Oh, of course it's not true. Though it's possible that somebody might have seen a salamander put out a weak fire with the liquid it exudes—slime, really—to repel predators . . . "

"Like a skunk."

"Yeah. Basically . . . It says here that in ancient times people thought that asbestos was the hair of the salamander because it didn't burn. Listen, this is Caxton—the English printer?—'This Salamandre berith wulle, of which is made cloth and gyrdles that may not brenne in the fyre.' And it says that Pope Alexander II had a coat made of a thousand salamander skins . . . in other words, asbestos."

"All they had to do to check was set one on fire," Evander reasons. He likes this man, who doesn't treat him the way other white folks do.

"'In medieval allegory,'" the clerk reads, "'the salamander dancing in the flames was a symbol of moral purity. It symbolized the virtuous soul able to dwell amid the flames of sin and vice and the corruption of this world without being tainted or destroyed.'"

The clerk notices some customers waiting at the counter. Evander returns to the aquarium. Seen swimming from below, the salamanders almost look like drowning people, with tender bellies and flimsy limbs, flailing helplessly in shadows like smoke.

That night he goes to bed listening in his mind to the rap song he has made up:

My name is Evander
I am the salamander
I dance in the flame
But it's all just a game
'Cause the fire don't hurt
'Cause I can't be burnt
My name is Evander
I am the salamander

The headquarters of the DAC, the Direct Action Community, is a former elementary school built in the twenties, a drab, weather-scorched cube of yellow brick. The old trees around it create an emphatically lush smear of green on an already leafy street, a contrast to the desolate waterfront zone that begins only a few blocks away at the highway.

"They'll come to us," Lookout explains with authority.

He and Evander are loitering under a great scaly octopus of an oak, maintaining a steady surveillance of the DAC building and the metal Dumpster in the alley where they have already stashed their wares. According to Lookout, some of the homeless men and women roofed by Ryan Weinstein and his organization can always be counted on as buyers. At the moment, not much is happening. A few black men in their forties or fifties are lounging on the steps, smoking and sharing a bottle in a brown paper bag. A fat white woman now and then appears, twirling her long brown hair into knots.

"She crazy," Evander speculates.

"There yo' white pussy."

"You ever fuck one of them white ho's?"

Lookout shifts. "Yeah."

"You shittin' me, homes."

"For real. A redhead."

By now Evander can tell when Lookout is lying.

A blubbery white guy with a tangled mane fringing a face the color of brick is limping toward them. Now and then he pauses and looks over his shoulder toward the old schoolhouse.

"Yo, Captain," Lookout greets the shaggy giant. "What's up? This here's my road dog, Evander."

Evander wrinkles his nose in disgust. Captain smells.

"Man, she's gonna be pissed off." Captain gestures at the building. "Ryan's old lady. She's raising hell again. No drugs on the premises."

Lookout grabs his own crotch. "Bitch can have my premises," he snorts. Then he says, "Where you been? You ain't been here, Captain."

"I don't like this place, man. They steal your stuff when you fall asleep and you're not looking. And there are fags, man. They'll suck your dick if you give 'em some Scotty. You got some? Scotty?"

In exchange for a clump of greasy bills, Lookout watches discreetly from a distance while Evander gives Captain several plastic baggies of rock from the stash in the Dumpster. When Evander and Captain rejoin Lookout, several of the black men who have been sitting on the steps wander over. A white woman appears in the entrance portal, not the one they saw earlier, but a younger one, almost pretty. She glares in their direction.

"That's her, man," Captain growls. "Ryan's old lady. I can't go back in there with this." Captain decides to go to the crack house. He heads off in that direction with one of the black men while Lookout and Evander stroll away.

"Count it, homes. Eighty dollars."

"Where they get their money?"

"SSI. Panhandling." Lookout describes how Captain begs on Pennsylvania Avenue, near the White House, pretending to be a Vietnam veteran. "He ask me, do I know where he can get a crutch. So he can make out like he a cripple. Shit. But he a good customer. He like that Scotty. The customer is *always* right."

They pass houses where young women, sitting on the stoops, watch their children play in a vacant lot of rubble and weeds. The street ends in a cul-de-sac. Beyond is the highway overpass, a pillared cement cavern tattooed with graffiti and echoing with the rumble and rush of the traffic overhead. They scan, and seeing no one but a few beggars far off, they inspect the spray-painted walls like priests in a Mayan temple pondering glyphs. In fat rainbow letters squirming like serpents, the Yungstaz have spray-painted their logo over the sign of the Krew.

"Fuckin' Punkstas." Lookout kneels and pulls his gleaming 9 mm from his high-top sneaker. Evander's ears ring and his nostrils burn as Lookout's bullets carve off bits of the Yungstaz logo.

"Go for it, Deuce."

The gun is warm. Evander fires. Empty shells fly. A chunk of whizzing cement lands only a few feet away. Evander sees the beggars in the distance freeze in fear. He waves the gun and the beggars scramble, chased by his and Lookout's echoing laughter.

Evander hears Lookout draw his breath in sharply. He turns and tenses as he sees the beggar.

Everyone calls him Scab. Evander has seen him before, but only at night, and only from a distance. By the light of day he is hideous. His hairless head is a quilt of skin grafts of different colors and textures: brown, caramel, raw-meat pink. The hands that emerge from his layered coats are patched with skin grafts as well.

Scab gestures at them angrily, burbling in an unknown dialect. They have trespassed in his realm.

"He a retard," Lookout says, apprehension in his voice.

Scab comes closer. He smells like a sewer.

"Moke," he gurgles. "Moke." He is trying to say "Smoke."

"Sell him some, man," Evander tells Lookout.

"Shit, man, I'm outta here."

As they hurry toward the houses, they are pursued by the cries of "Moke!"

"You ever hear of Waylon Purdy?" Lookout recounts the tale of how Waylon, a member of the Krew, came across the beggar sleeping in the open one night and, just for fun, set his coat on fire with a Bic lighter. "I wasn't there, but I knew people who were. Man, he was screaming and shrieking and dancing around and shit. You know that guy in the comic book, the Fantastic Four? The human torch. That was ol' Scab, the human torch. He had third-degree burns all over his body. They had take skin from his back and put it all over his face and arms. Waylon's in Lorton now. He got twenty-five years for shooting a Punksta. Waylon, he cold-blooded."

Evander, with fascination as well as disgust, imagines Scab ablaze in the darkness of the underpass. And then he thinks of the salamander, dancing unharmed in the scorch of the flames.

In the next room, the TV is droning. The little girl is wailing. "Mommy!"

"Hush up! I'll be there in a minute." Suzy, sitting on the bed, takes another sip of smoke from the thin glass pipe. Then she hands it to Evander.

Nervously, Evander puts the pipette in his mouth and inhales. The fumes sear his nostrils, scorch his mouth. He exhales slowly, waiting for the rush.

"Mommy . . . "

"Hush. I told you to watch TV."

Standing, Evander can gaze down the cleft of Suzy's breasts. When she reaches for the pipe, he withholds it from her. "You want it? I'll give it to you on credit. You want some credit?"

"Gimme that Scotty."

"You want some credit?" Evander is now stiff with arousal, his cock straining painfully against its cloth prison. The tremolo of sexual excitement is joined by the buzz from the crack, an intense sensation that floods through his body and pools in a tingling in his left temple.

Suzy unfastens his pants. Evander's legs go weak as she swallows his stiff length. She looks up, licking her lips.

"You know what a double master blaster is?" she asks.

"Yeah." A double master blaster means getting high on rock and coming at the same time. So excited he feels faint, Evander watches as Suzy takes the pipe and lays it along Evander's brown tube. She takes both tips in her mouth. Evander's knees are so weak he has to sit down on the bed. By now his nervous system is on fire, with the blaze focused on his groin and his itchy scalp.

The little girl is scratching on the door. They pay no attention. Evander wriggles out of his pants and shirt, then watches Suzy strip. He stares at her body, and her body stares back, like a giant clown face with blind nipple eyes and a belly crease for a nose and, between her parted legs, a bearded, surprised mouth.

Her actual mouth closes on him and he feels his knees melt. He shivers with the electric jolts radiating from the moist warm pressure between his legs. As though he is watching a porno movie on the VCR in the Funkadelic's upper room, he stares at her grotesquely foreshortened head, watching her eat him and feeling it at the same time, trying to connect the sight and the sensation, like a baby staring at hands and feet that it is only half-aware are its own. He can hardly believe it. He is getting blown. He is having sex. The physical pleasure is almost lost in the rush he feels when he thinks about bragging to all his peeps in the 'hood.

She rolls onto the bed beside him and waits for him to make the next move. Evander thinks: Don't eat no cheese. Only pussy-whipped dudes eat pussy. But she wants something else. She pulls him on top of her and waits for him to position himself, some-what awkwardly, finding a place for his elbows and his knees, and then she guides him into her. He thrusts with his hips, and the shudder that sends through her suprises him and makes him even stiffer. Excited by the thought of his own power, he bucks again, and again, and soon they are rocking with a shared rhythm metronomed by her moans and the screech of the mattress and the slap of skin on skin. He tries kissing her, but she has gone into a trance, eyes closed, in an ecstasy resembling pain, clamping him in the rigid vise of her arms as he claps her, harder, faster. Soon he can do no more than pant, his hot breath swirling back at him like steam from the hollow of her neck and shoulder. "You like that?" he gasps, pausing to catch his breath. But she can only whimper and then once again he can do no more than gasp. He remembers Lookout, and when he tries to picture Lookout thrusting into her he suddenly clenches and spasms and feels the pressure ebb.

"Mommy . . . "

"Hush up!"

"Evander! Evander, it's the telephone!"

The voice belongs to Gram. Evander struggles upward through lightening layers of consciousness.

"Evander! They say it's about your friend Lookout."

Blinking, Evander follows his grandmother into the dark living room of the apartment. Outside it is black. Evander knows even before he hears Willie's choked voice. "They got him, man. They killed Lookout."

"Evander, what is it?" His mother is sitting up on the fold-out bed, holding his half sister next to her. Evander's eyes cloud with tears as he hurries into the bedroom he shares with Jamal to dress.

The wind turns to ice in his tearful eyes as he flies down first one street, then another on his bike. *They killed Lookout . . .* the Yungstaz.

Evander sees the sweeps of red light from the sirens before he turns the corner. A crowd of backs screens the scene. Evander pushes his way through, and in an instant takes it all in: the squad cars, the ambulances, the yellow tape—POLICE LINE DO NOT CROSS—and, lying on the street, Lookout. His body, in its dark hooded parka and dark pants, is hard to see in the dimness. His white high-tops, though, are glowing like teeth knocked out onto asphalt.

"Lookout!" A cop and several bystanders are holding Jocelyn back. "Lookout!" Her face wrinkles in pain, and she emits an inarticulate shriek. Evander turns away so no one can see him sob.

9

The apartment of Aglaia Kazakis is on an upper floor of the Watergate. As she makes her way through the labyrinth, Stef gets a sense of the complex—the courtyard, with its cement tiers like a crumbling sixties movie-set version of a city of tomorrow, the curving, carpeted halls beneath overbright fluorescent light. The air smells of soap and bath oil, of old people. She is disappointed. She had expected something glamorous, not a high-rent rest home.

Aglaia's apartment is no disappointment. Stef has never seen an apartment with as much floor space as a suburban house. Her boss has managed to fill it with guests even though the engraved invitations said "Stag (no spouses or companions, please)." Most of the people are unknown to Stef, though she recognizes a few from TV: news anchors, talk-show pundits, a few senators and congressmen.

Too bashful to introduce herself to the middle-aged and mighty, Stef floats like a leaf between little swirls and eddies of conversation. "You think he'll call a special session?" "How often do you get back to Wyoming?" "No, he's left. He's at Carstairs and Bryant . . . " "You've got to see it. It's absolutely the funniest movie . . . "

She notices something peculiar about the apartment. There is not the slightest trace of personality in it. The books in the shelves are first editions of classics. They appear to be unread. The pictures on the walls are faded prints of Venetian canals and English fox-hunting scenes. There are no photos of friends or family, no curios picked up on holidays, nothing that could locate Aglaia Kazakis in time and space. Aglaia is an Australian of Greek descent, but her apartment might as well belong to a rich Argentine or a Europhile heiress from Topeka.

The caterer rings a little bell, summoning the guests to tables in the mock Bourbon dining room. Stef is sitting between Des Kazakis and the senior senator from Massachusetts, Ed Shaunnessey.

Shaunnessey delivers the toast. Stef can hardly concentrate on what he is saying. She is paralyzed with anxiety at the thought of having to make small talk with one of the most famous politicians in the country. With fascination and disgust, she studies his sagging jowls, his pink-veined face beneath the helmet of silvery hair. Like most people familiar on television, he looks much worse in person. Stef wonders how somebody so old and fat could be so famous as a ladies' man.

"I, ah, I encourage you all to drink up," Shaunnessey says, swaying slightly as he lifts his glass, "because, ah, immediately after the, ah, dinner, there will be a, ah, mandatory drug test . . . "

Laughter, more polite than spontaneous. He's drunk, Stef thinks, as the senator eases his massive bulk down beside her.

"Oh, yes, I believe Aglaia mentioned you to me," Des Kazakis, sitting on her right, tells Stef when the meal is under way. "You're a writer."

"Well, sort of." Stef watches the publisher to learn which fork she should use for this course. "I worked on Capitol Hill for a couple of years. I've written an article on battered women . . . "

Kazakis listens, then invites her to submit her article to *Perspective*. Stef is amazed at her good fortune. She forgets all about the article, however, when she becomes aware that a blond young man, from across the room, is regarding her with a discreet but steady gaze. His face looks both handsome and harsh, its angles underlit by the candles on the table before him. She tenses as she recognizes Bruce Brandt.

Their eyes lock for a moment before, uncomfortable, she looks away.

"Tell me, my dear," says Senator Shaunnessey, turning from Aglaia at his right to regard Stef, "are you also an Australian?"

* * *

After the dinner, Stef looks around but cannot see Bruce any-where. "Hi," says a voice nearby. Bruce is behind her.

"Hi . . . Bruce." She tries to think of something to say, to make small talk, anything to keep him from vanishing again. "Mrs. Gutierrez. Which one is she?"

"I'll introduce you, if you want. You don't have marijuana on your breath, do you? Just kidding."

"She doesn't look Mexican to me," Stef confesses to Bruce after the drug czar has smiled and pressed her hand.

"Her maiden name was Rachel Birnbaum. Her first husband was a guy named Gutierrez, from Costa Rica. She's made a whole career out of being a fake Hispanic. I'm thinking about changing my name to Speedy Gonzalez. You ready for another drink?"

"Some coffee, maybe."

Stef watches Bruce ease through the crowd toward the caterers.

"So, ah, Julie . . ." It is Senator Shaunnessey, moving toward her like a destroyer through a scattering of lesser ships.

"Stef. Stephanie Schonfeld." She backs against a grandfather clock. Shaunnessey's face looms in front of her as gnarled as a tree stump, shocking pink.

"You know I, ah, I've been to Australia," Shaunnessey says. His breath smells like a ransacked honky-tonk. His teeth are unnaturally white. "So, ah, what part of Australia are you from?"

Beyond the vast dandruff-spangled shoulder of the senator's pinstriped suit, Stef catches sight of Bruce. He is watching, smiling, and, for some reason, waggling a donut.

"It sounds like a great job to me," Avery tells her over supper at a French restaurant in Georgetown that they had frequented when they had been in school together. "Beats the hell out of what I do." Avery is a booker for National Public Radio; his job is to line up guests for phone interviews and debates. He pretends to be speaking into a telephone. "Uh, yes, we would like you to be on our program to represent the other extreme. Would you characterize your views as extremist to the point of lunacy? You would? Oh, good. Oh, no, we don't want you to tone it down. Be provocative." He rolls his eyes and emits a gargled scream.

"How's your boss?"

"Oh, you must mean . . . The Bitch. Still driving everyone to the verge of mutiny . . . Did you hear the joke about the Polish coup? They seized the public radio station."

"At least you don't have to tag along with her to dinners." Aglaia is in the habit of bringing her staff along to public functions. "I feel like a lady in waiting."

"So you're not a Jewish American Princess. You're a Jewish American Lady-in-Waiting."

Stef looks up from her drink. "Did I tell you I've got a date with Bruce?"

"Bruce?"

"Bruce Brandt. That friend of Ross's."

"That blond guy? He's cute. Can I come along?"

Clap, clap, clap, Stef thinks. She joins the ballroom in mechanically applauding after the president of the Free Enterprise Foundation has introduced the next speaker, whom the printed program describes impressively as Dr. Kenneth Flanagan, Ph.D.

"Do you know him?" Stef whispers to Bruce. Her date for the evening gives her a reproving look before he resumes the expression of the class president listening to the principal's address, a kind of wax-museum nobility. Flanagan, Ph.D. is a small, balding man who speaks hesitantly, verbally drafting sentences and then revising them with rephrasings and equivocations: "The statistical correlation between the genetic basis of intelligence and manifest or phenotypical intelligence is nontrivial, or so our research would lead us to . . . to suggest . . . "

Stef can hardly keep her eyes open. Mildly annoyed, she turns away from Bruce and discreetly studies the other diners at the table. They are, from Bruce's left to her right, a Korean colonel affiliated in some way with the right-wing Washington tabloid, *The Washington Herald*, a lobbyist for Pfizer Pharmaceutical, whose hair is shrinking, and his wife, whose hair, if it is any consolation, appears to be expanding like a soufflé.

Just in time, the waiters arrive and fill their coffee cups. As she sips from hers, Stef stretches her legs beneath the table. Her foot bumps into Bruce's. Instinctively, she moves her own foot away.

"... The Gini coefficient—if you'll bear with me, I know this
is rather difficult for the layman ... Our work establishes a correlation between the axes of ability and hereditary potential ... "

Their feet, Stef gradually becomes aware, are touching again.
Bruce's right loafer is pressing gently against Stef's left shoe. There
is something reassuring about the contact, about this small intimacy. Stef wonders whether it is accidental.

"... The covariance is really quite telling. Naturally, the inter-
pretations that the demographic data tend to support depend to a
large degree—I wouldn't say largely, but to some degree—on the
way the parameters are defined ... "

Bruce's foot moves gently, slowly, gliding alongside hers like a
yacht ever so lightly scraping the planks of a pier. Stef feels her
heart flexing, winglike. Trying not to show her nervous excitement, she focuses on the speech.

"In cross-national campaigns, these results, at any rate, some of
these results, have been duplicated, though of course the subject is
contentious ... "

He is stroking her foot with his, subtly but unmistakably.
Energy flows from him through two layers of leather into her
body, setting her afire with anxious arousal. Coquettishly, Stef
moves her own foot ever so slightly, responding to his harnessed
ardor with a flirtatious push of her own.

"The hypothesis that there is an absence of correlation
between economic success and hereditary potential, then, appears
to have been disconfirmed ... "

His foot draws back, only to return with greater passion. It
nuzzles hers the way a wolf might nuzzle its mate, with a
poignant tenderness. Then, boldly, it rocks back on its heel and
mounts her ankle, the nose of the shoe probing the leather encas-
ing her toes.

Stef is unable to resist a peek at Bruce. But his handsome,
attentive face is fixed on Dr. Kenneth Flanagan, Ph.D.

"In layman's language, this means that rich people tend—
well, how should I put it—well, the rich tend to be genetically
superior."

Stef would be offended by Flanagan, Ph.D.'s argument if she
heard it. But the world is a haze and a buzz, centered on two shod

feet coupling like giant jungle snails. Relief is mingled with Stef's excitement, for until now she had been haunted by the fear that it was only in her imagination that Bruce wanted her as much as she wanted him. Now the signal has been sent. There can be no doubt. Liberated from that initial uncertainty, Stef's mind is free to flash ahead to what might follow: Bruce making love to her. Bruce marrying her. A town house in Georgetown or a mansion on Capitol Hill. A country place. Dogs. Children . . .

Suddenly, a clumsy foot crashes into theirs as the Korean next to her slopes back in his chair, yawning and stretching his legs. If Stef were a cobra, he would be dead. *Goddamn you, Colonel Kim.*

From that moment on, Stef's ardor begins to ebb, though not the background radiation of rapture. Passion fades further when, after dinner, they stand in line for thirty minutes to retrieve their coats only to discover they must wait in another line to catch a taxi in front of the Hilton.

"I still owe you dinner," Bruce says, shoulders hunched, hands in the pockets of his long black coat, shifting back and forth to keep warm. "Tonight doesn't count."

She wishes they could share their body heat. "Why not?"

"It was a banquet, not a dinner." His breath turns to silver in the air, like a jet from the lips of a fountain's god. She wants to curtain herself in the folds of his coat and feel the heat of his body like the radiance of a stove.

A spiky-haired black beggar, layered in dark jackets, is working his way along the line. "Quarter. Spare a quarter."

"Sorry," Bruce says. He turns back to Stef. "So."

"So," she replies.

"Dinner."

"Dinner."

"What are you doing tomorrow?"

Stef has to pause to think. "Wednesday . . . Oh, I can't. One of Aglaia's friends is giving a poetry reading. A feminist poet from Ireland. I told her I'd go . . . How about Thursday?"

"Sounds good."

A thud. A few yards away, the beggar has crumpled onto the sidewalk like a fistful of wet felt. The tuxedos and tiaras in line pretend not to notice.

Stef turns away and puts the scene out of her mind. "Oh, you know, Friday would be better." They could make passionate love all night on Friday and not have to worry about getting up to go to work in the morning. She wants to make love with him tonight, but she feels groggy. On their first night together, she has to be alert and attractive.

"Okay. Friday. Where?"

Stef toys with the dangling belt of his coat. "Surprise me."

The Hispanic doorman in his World War I field marshal's coat strides past the beggar and opens the back door of the taxi. As she bends to get in, Stef glances at the still form on the sidewalk. Maybe that poor black guy is dead.

She is disturbed by the thought, for three or four blocks.

As though swimming underwater, the two dancers move toward each other across the cafetorium stage. The man takes the woman in his arms and they begin, slowly, to revolve, his arm and her leg extended like props of a propeller. The music of the strings, glistening, expands.

So does the noise of the audience: coughing, giggles, two arguments, and one stream of muttered obscenities from an elderly black woman, clearly insane, who is crouching on the floor near Stef and rocking back and forth, oblivious to the dance being performed on the stage as she engages in a kind of dance of her own.

Stef is relieved when the music fades and the lights come up again. The dancer named Chet, looking like a Coney Island bather from the World War I era in his sleeveless body stocking, addresses the small crowd once again.

"That was the pas de deux from *Swan Lake* . . . "

"Pot o' who?" one man asks, and others titter.

Stef glances at Aglaia, whose face is a mask of imperturbable benignity. Stef wonders what her new employer is thinking.

Stef has been working for Aglaia's foundation for three weeks. This is one of her first trips to the field to check on the progress of a project the foundation is funding. They are in the cafetorium of a decayed old school building in southeast Washington that is now the home of the Direct Action Community, a homeless advocacy group run by a once-famous sixties radical, Ryan Weinstein. His followers hang around Union Station and the entrances of the Metro, thrusting printed cards at commuters and chanting, "Direct Action Community" or "DAC," as though this gives them a greater claim than freelance panhandlers on spare change. The conservatives are always denouncing the DAC as a shakedown racket; even though Stef's parents raised her to feel benevolent toward the underprivileged, she cannot help feeling disquiet at the thought of the organized, militant poor.

"When Stravinsky's *Rite of Spring* premiered," the dancer is saying in his languid voice, "there were actually riots in the theater . . . "

Stef feels a twinge of apprehension. Why does he have to mention riots? They are surrounded by thirty or forty homeless people, the vast majority of them bedraggled black men between their twenties and fifties, a few of them no doubt on drugs, some of them manifestly insane. She senses a stirring in the room, a flaring of new, nervous energy, as the dancers contort and spasm to the discordant evocation of ancient tribal Russia. Why couldn't they have programmed only gentle, calming tunes from Mozart or Vivaldi?

Stef looks at Aglaia. Ballet for the homeless must have seemed like a good idea at the time.

The monkey looks terrified. It is a squirrel monkey, a tiny creature that looks all the tinier as it crouches alone in the spotlight on the Kennedy Center theater stage. A trumpet fanfare is the cue for the entry of a bearded man in a whirring wheelchair. The two spotlights, one on the monkey, one on the chair-bound man, slowly merge to a burst of music and a wave of applause.

"He wants to know if the applause is for him or for me," the bearded man tells the audience, eliciting laughter that is too hearty. The monkey sits on the man's chest, peering out into the theater.

Behind them, the lights go up, revealing a set in the shape of a cutaway house or condo. The man, whose arms are useless, gives instructions to the monkey, which—sometimes at once, sometimes only with coaxing—carries out a series of tasks—turning lights on and off, opening and closing drawers, and, finally, feeding its crippled master from a bowl of cereal with a spoon.

"That's beautiful," Stef says to Bruce, raising her voice above a murmur in order to be heard over the applause. They are at a fund-raising benefit performance for one of Aglaia's favorite charities, a group that trains monkeys to help the handicapped: Monkeyshines.

"You didn't tell me it was monkeys *and* the handicapped," Bruce complains. "I thought it was handicapped monkeys. I want to see monkeys in wheelchairs. Monkey wheelchair races. Monkey wheelchair basketball . . . "

She nudges him playfully, and he responds by stroking her leg.

He has made reservations for them at Pied a Couchon, a restaurant in Georgetown. Over dinner they try to spot "other famous people." Bruce recognizes Skip Wriston—one of the senior partners in Ross's lobbying firm, Wriston, White—and his wife.

"Isn't Ross a partner?" Stef asks.

"No, not yet. I think he's getting antsy. If they don't make him a partner soon, he'll probably leave."

"I don't think I'd want to be a lobbyist."

"Why not? You get to do public policy work, but you get paid ten times as much as you make working for the government." Bruce plans to be an in-and-outer, spending his career hopping from government posts to lobbying and party work and back into government. "It's like leveraging your way up in the real estate market. You make a profit on your first house, and then you buy a bigger one. And then you sell that, and get a really humongous house. And then you're old, and you're sitting in this big house, and your kids have grown up and moved out, and you're crippled and you can hardly get around, so there's only one thing to do: get a monkey."

Sudden laughter makes Stef nearly choke on her potato pancake. "You're obsessed with the monkeys."

"I'm just sitting here, thinking of things they can do for crips that they couldn't show at Kennedy Center. Like helping them get off."

"You are so sick." She giggles.

"Here, monkey. Here, monkey. Bring the lubricant. Now tug on this and I'll give you a biscuit . . . "

Stef is having another giggle fit. "Stop it! You are so gross."

"Hey, I bet those monkeys could help out women, too. Okay, little monkey, bring Mumsy a banana . . . "

His talk has grown more risqué as the hour approaches. They both know it is going to be tonight. Stef has rehearsed it all in her mind for days. In the novels she used to read when she had more free time, the hero and heroine would spontaneously fall into each other's arms and make love, as though the idea had only suddenly occurred to them after a hundred pages. In Stef's experience—she has had three boyfriends and two one-night stands—everything has always been planned far in advance.

This romance is no exception. A few hours after their dinner, when she returns from freshening up in the bathroom of her apartment to the den, she deliberately sits next to him on the couch made of the folded futon. Right on schedule, his arm slides across hers, then he stops talking and gazes at her intently and his face moves toward hers till their mouths meet. When his hand creeps up her dress and delves into her panties, when another hand slips beneath her bra to compete with it for her breast, it all seems anticlimactic, since she has imagined this again and again since she met Bruce for the second time at Aglaia's party for Mrs. Gutierrez. The one thing she had not foreseen was how hairy Bruce is; beneath his shirt, his chest is a Rorschach blot of fine black fur.

If this were a novel, their foreplay on the couch would segue smoothly into lovemaking. The clothes would melt from their ardent bodies and the futon would emerge on its own initiative from the sofa like an enchanted bed in an animated fairy tale. Instead, they must pause while Bruce, shirtless, struggles to unfold the futon's wooden undercarriage until its slats lock with a click. While he is distracted, Stef strips down to her bra and panties, which she gives Bruce the privilege of removing.

His mouth moves from hers to her nipples and then traces a snail walk down her belly. She squeezes her eyes shut and stiffens as she feels his tongue delving inside her. She wants him inside of her at once, but knows that she should go down on him if she wants to win him.

Their passion is interrupted again as she unlaces his shoes and pulls them off, then peels his socks from his feet. He lifts his hips and lets her slide his underwear as well as his pants down his pale, hair-fletched legs.

She devours him. She wants to please him, wants to impress him with her erotic expertise. She does everything that had once sent her first boyfriend Richard and her college boyfriend Paul into shivers. When she tastes salt, she grows alarmed. She read somewhere that you can't get AIDS from oral sex, but you needed one for intercourse until you and your partner are tested and monogamous.

"You have a condom?" she asks, though she has no doubt that the answer will be affirmative.

Bruce looks alarmed. Shrinking, he writhes on the bed, pretending he cannot move his arms. "Damn it! Where's a monkey with a rubber when you need one?"

Twice he makes love to her. In between they talk—or rather, she talks, compulsively, excitedly, as he lies beside her drifting in and out of sleep. During the night she wakes up several times to gaze at him as he sleeps. If he considers this a one-night stand, she thinks, she will be destroyed.

As black gives way to gray in the dawn sky, she is lying awake, feeling her gloom deepen. She is afraid he will awaken and decide he made a terrible mistake. As if to reassure herself, she touches him. He awakens and pulls her to him.

"Good morning," she murmurs.

He grunts, drawing her hand with his to his lips. "I love the smell of you on my fingers," he whispered. "I'm not going to wash this hand between now and the next time I make love to you." He draws his forefinger across the top of her lip. "Can you smell yourself?" She inhales: a scent of cinnamon. She feels a rush of vertigo. "Tomorrow at the office I'll smell you on my fingers and get it up just thinking about you, just like now. See?" She feels vertigo, as though the floor has opened, and clings to him, pressing her face into the damp hollow of his confident shoulder, and he rolls on top of her again.

10

An hour before the alarm goes off, Ross finds himself lying wide awake in bed in his town house on Capitol Hill. The explanation is obvious: stress over the meeting at ten. Ross had done everything he could to relax the night before; he is angry that his subconscious, his body, is reacting in such a predictable way.

After shaving, showering, and reading the paper, he decides to go into the office early in the hope that work on other business will prevent him from brooding on the forthcoming meeting. He almost misses Graciela, who arrives half an hour early for her weekly visit to clean the town house.

"My cousin say, I ask you what to do?" The little Salvadoran woman seems frightened. She shows him a pink and blue paper from a collection agency: DO YOU INTEND TO PAY? OUR CLIENT WILL BEGIN LEGAL ACTION UNLESS YOU ENCLOSE PAYMENT IMMEDIATELY. Graciela owes $64.81 to the phone company. To judge from her stammered explanations in her broken English, she has other bills coming due. Ross infers the existence of a chain reaction leading to a potential meltdown.

When he hands her a check for two hundred dollars, her eyes melt. There is a strange disjunction between the ardor of her expression and the banality of her words: "Thank you. You are so nice . . ."

Name a baby after me, he thinks. "You need to keep up with your bills, Graciela. I know it's tough."

The meeting is a disaster. Backed by his mentor in the firm, George White, Ross had volunteered to lead a coordinated effort to defeat amendments to a forthcoming trade bill that would require quantitative proof of the success of measures by the Japanese government to open their market to American imports. This is Ross's bid to go from a bit player to a major actor among the Washington lobbyists for Japanese industry. The other founding partner of Wriston, White, Skip Wriston, who had earlier encouraged Ross, leads the attack on the proposal.

Hours later, Ross is still stunned. "That old son of a bitch bushwhacked me," he complains to Aglaia. They have met in an art gallery a few blocks off Dupont Circle. Once a week they have lunch, and sometimes they quickly take in a gallery or museum exhibit first. "The way I figure it is, it's Skip's way of getting back at George. Skip founded the firm and brought George in, and now he sees George pushing his own people, like me."

"You should have made sure Skip was on your side."

"I thought he was. Son of a bitch lied to me. Looked me in the eye and flat out lied." Ross smiled. "I can respect that."

They are moving among human-size tripods of papier-mâché and twisted metal, like monstrous roots. The artist is the youngest daughter of a prominent senator on the Commerce Committee.

"Do you know her?" Aglaia asks.

"Naw. I thought I'd send the senator a note telling him how impressed I was by his daughter's exhibit. We need his vote on this trade bill amendment, and we just can't get through to him. Maybe that's too obvious. You'd be surprised, though . . . Do you think this is art?"

"I like the forms," says Aglaia. "And the volumes."

Later that afternoon George White summons Ross to his office. "You win some, you lose some," White tells Ross. The man's ancient skin, ravaged by many noons on many golf courses, gives the lie to the artificial perfection of his hair and his teeth. "I've got a booby prize for you." White hands Ross the number of the American representative of Mitsutono, the Japanese *keiretsu*. "Mitsutono's worried about American protectionism, so they're moving more production to Malaysia and Indonesia. That way exports to the U.S. get labeled as part of the Malaysian or

Indonesian trade surpluses, instead of the Japanese trade surplus. The only problem with this brilliant scheme is the Japanese didn't count on the controversy about human rights, in Indonesia in particular. Now there's more at stake here than the Mitsutono account. Indonesia just has no presence in Washington. If we can get in there before Carstairs, Bryant, and the rest of them, we might be able to clean up. Maybe it won't pan out. Anyway, look into it, all right, buddy?"

On the way home, Ross stops by the Monocle on Capitol Hill for drinks with one of his mentors from an earlier phase of his career, when he had worked on the Hill. "I just don't know how to get through to him," Ross complains to Carl Perkins, a retired senator from Missouri. "He's not going to run again, so he doesn't need to raise any money . . . "

"I've known Bob for many years," Perkins ruminates. They are sitting in a dark, sofa-crowded upstairs lounge that looks toward Union Station. "He's not money corrupt. But that doesn't mean you can't get to him. A lot of senators are that way. They can't be bought with money. But there's some button you can push. A pet cause. Vanity. The wife or the kids. They want to meet Hollywood movie stars. Everybody's got some button."

Ross is a little drunk when he enters his big dark house on Capitol Hill. Waiting for him on his kitchen table is a child's scrawled drawing of a house and a smiling sun. THANK YO ROSA, it says.

Ross hunts for tape to put it up on the refrigerator door, reflecting all the while on how preposterously proud a parent can be of a child's primitive artwork. Then the inspiration strikes him.

In the first rush of excitement, he dials George White's number to brag about his idea, then thinks better of it and hangs up. He paces the room, like a tiger that has just made a kill, a hunter lowering his rifle from a successful shot. Tomorrow he will call the Mitsutono representatives in New York and tell them that their conglomerate is going to purchase one of the paper-and-wire constructions crafted by the senator's daughter. Better yet, commission one. That's it. A giant ugly tripod in front of some corporate office in Tokyo. They will fly the girl over for the ceremony and invite her father, too. Not a dollar, not a yen, will be given to the senator, but unless he is the world's most callous father he will be their man forever.

Ross catches a glimpse of himself in the hall mirror. You, he tells the thin blond man between the coats, are well on your way to a partnership. You're better than smart. You're cunning.

When they get to the Delta Airlines hospitality lounge at the airport, Ross immediately commandeers a corner for the three of them, folds his lanky frame onto a sofa, and dials his office on the courtesy phone. "Sue, have we heard back from Tokyo?" he asks loudly, for the benefit of his traveling companions. "Hang on a second . . ." He lowers the phone. "Scotch and water," he tells Karen. As she goes to fetch the drinks, Ross speaks into the phone again. "Awright. Now looky here, I want a fax of that press release waiting for us at the hotel . . . Here, check the number just to make sure . . . "

Out of the corner of his eye, as he scans his papers, Ross watches his audience. Jack Vincent is Ross's age, forty-something, a shoe-polish-hair, navy-blazer Republican, the legislative assistant to Congressman Lou Mayers. They are on the way to field hearings in Mayer's Florida district, orchestrated by Ross on behalf of his PR firm, Wriston, White and Associates.

"Oh, and Sue, did you check that list against the Michigan conference . . . Uh-huh . . . Uh-huh . . . Awright, now I want you to check with Bobby Conyers. I want to know what in God's green earth this United Citizens outfit is . . . "

Never miss a chance to make a case-related phone call in the presence of your clients—this is one of the tricks of the trade that are second nature to Ross now. Like displaying the signed photo of yourself with the president—off to the side of the office wall, as though it isn't really *that* important. Like taking clients to plush Capitol Hill watering holes where the waiter brings a blank receipt so that the customer can write in any amount for reimbursement that he chooses, committing the kind of petty larceny that thrills the average American businessman as much as the big score. Like wearing your watch upside down, with the face on the underside of the wrist, so that, having invited the question, you can wink and answer, "So I can keep an eye on the time when

I'm making love"—a line that never fails to impress tubby executives with dead marriages who secretly dream of rushing from sales meetings to assignations around the globe. Like confessing, of the same watch, "I got this Rolex rip-off in Hong Kong on my last trip—you know they're cheaper than the rip-offs you can get in Rome."

Karen returns with the drinks. She is in her early thirties, but affects the mature businesswoman look—a mannish jacket, short schoolmarm hair. "Thank you kindly," says Ross, replacing the phone on the receiver. He pulls a memo from his briefcase and hands it to Vincent. "See, right here, this group that calls itself United Citizens?"

"They've signed up for the hearings," Karen reminds her boss. "To testify."

"And the thing of it is," Ross drawls, "the thing of it is, we don't know who the hell they are. You know what they teach in law school—never ask a witness a question unless you already know the answer. These other groups, the committee has dealt with them before . . . "

"What are you worried about?"

Ross smiles, like a benevolent teacher instructing a slow student. "Plants. You get some of the bad guys planted in the audience, they can screw up your hearing big-time. Happened last year at this conference CARPAC sponsored in Flint. Turned out one of the groups was just a front for the Auto Workers. They had a whole speech prepared, a whole dog and pony show about how the American worker is being betrayed by management, yakkety yak. We don't want a repeat of that performance." Ross sips his Scotch and expands upon his theme. "They ship spies in, too, sometimes. You know, we had a mole from Carstairs and Bryant in our little legislative supper club last year. This woman claimed to represent this consumer group opposed to restrictions on imports. Turns out the whole thing had been set up by Carstairs and Bryant, and they were funneling everything we said back to the unions."

"Wow," says Vincent.

Karen brushes dandruff from Vincent's jacket. Ross wonders whether the two of them are getting it on.

★ ★ ★

Holding a field hearing on the pending automobile trade legislation in Mayer's suburban Daytona district had been Ross's idea. A Democrat from a mostly Republican district, Mayer had been wavering in his opposition to import quotas. On behalf of CARPAC, the Japanese-funded lobby that was the biggest client of Wriston, White, Ross had cut a deal with Mayer's staff. CARPAC would fund Mayer's reelection campaign, instead of that of his Republican challenger, if Mayer took an antiprotectionist line. The field hearing was designed to ward off an attack from the left by showing Mayer's Democratic critics the strength of sentiment against import restrictions in his own district.

Ross's staff back at Wriston, White in Washington is never able to resolve his doubts about United Citizens. Ross is not willing to take any chances: "I believe in wearing a belt *and* suspenders," he tells Vincent and Karen. At the last minute, the site of the field hearing is moved from the Chamber of Commerce building to a suburban high school auditorium. The local media and all of the groups on the list except United Citizens are notified in time to change their plans.

The hearing goes well; there are no surprises. That evening, in his hotel room, Ross falls exhausted across his bed, feeling lonely and horny. He should have brought Avery with him.

Avery is Ross's third regular boyfriend. The first was Steve, an ex-Marine to whom Ross had rented out his extra room in his condo in Alexandria. At the time Ross—out of the army and a couple of years out of Georgetown Law Center—was working on the staff of the Republican Senate Policy Committee. He was almost thirty, and had never acted on his desires. During his tour of duty in the army in the Pacific, the ROTC graduate had been too afraid of discovery and discharge to go beyond a few furtive gropings in a barracks theater in Japan and submitting one drunken night to a blow job by a PFC in an alley in Manila. For a long time, too long, he had hewed to his original plan—ROTC, army, law school, politics—the career of a Southern gentleman, a career that required a suitable marriage and suitable children. All of that ended when, two months after they had begun to share a roof, Ross and Steve had confessed to each other.

For five months they made love every morning. Ross had never been so happy, so free. He was still afraid, though, of being spotted in the area's gay bars, where Steve began spending more and more of his evenings. Steve always came home drunk. Sometimes he did not come home at all. He began to borrow money. He lost his job.

Long before he evicted him, Ross had ceased to feel anything for Steve but cold contempt. When the break came, it was complete. Ross sold the condo and paid the down payment on his present house on Capitol Hill with the earnings from his new job in the private sector as a lawyer-lobbyist working for a former Republican senator. For a few months Ross had to endure rambling, drunken phone calls from his ex-lover. He feared for his career. But Steve drifted south to New Orleans. Ross has not heard from him in years.

The experience left Ross with a dread of emotional involvement. For several years, his sex life—he did not have much of one given the demands of his job on his time—consisted of one-night stands or relationships that lasted only a few weeks before he deliberately and abruptly ended them. He developed an intense loathing for members of the gay ghetto subculture, for their mincing, their gregariousness, their unseriousness. In them he saw what his fellow soldier Steve had slowly been turning into.

His career flourished. His income doubled when he left the senator to join the Wriston, White firm. He worked as hard as anyone in his field, sparing only one night a month or so to pick someone up at a bar; his favorite was the local country-and-western establishment. His routine might have continued for years.

Then he met Paul, for whom he would have given up his career and moved to the other side of the continent, if only, instead of benevolently tolerating him, Paul had loved him in return.

Ross knows Paul's number by heart. Impulsively, though he knows it is a mistake, he dials. He gets the answering machine. He savors the voice.

After he hangs up, he stares at the phone for a few moments. There is something he has forgotten to do, someone he has forgotten to call.

Of course. He had promised to call Avery.

11

"The community has got to provide the leadership itself. We can't look to Washington for leadership."

We *are* Washington, Avery silently rebukes the speaker, the head of the D.C. chapter of the NAACP. Avery fidgets and glances around the banquet room of the National Press Club. He knows most of the faces—city council members, city bureaucrats, deans and principals, columnists and TV anchors, foundation executives, members of the Congressional Black Caucus, the Kappa Alpha Psi types from the business world. This is his mother's crowd. This is Washington. Black Washington.

He squirms. The NAACP guy is going on and on, not realizing, evidently, how badly Avery needs to pee. Avery has been squirming at events like this since he was six or seven. Now, as then, he resents having to wear a suit and tie instead of the casual clothes he is permitted to wear to his job at NPR or his preferred weekend combination of black leather jacket, visored cap, and tiny round glasses—the Bert Brecht look, though he is the only one who thinks of it as such. After two decades of appeasing his mother by attending these convocations with her, he still has not acquired the ability to sit through one of these programs without nearly doubling over with a clenched bladder.

"We cannot let them set back the clock . . . "

His mother, seated next to him at the big table, sees his fidgeting and reproves him with a glance. He is twenty-six, and yet the slightest hint of disfavor from her makes him feel guilty. He has to behave, especially in this crowd, *her* crowd, where he remains a subsidiary element of her carefully cultivated public image. He had been reminded of that fact earlier, when they had been cornered by a salt-haired member of the black establishment.

"Reverend Montgomery, you remember my son . . . "

"Leander? Little Leander? I haven't seen you since you were a baby. You must be in school now."

"He graduated from Georgetown, and he's working at National Public Radio," she had explained, instantly judging that an old black minister would not recognize the acronym NPR. If further evidence of her finesse as a politician had been needed, it had been provided by the fact that she did not correct the old man when he had called Avery "Leander."

The name on his birth certificate is Leander Avery Brackenridge. His first two names commemorate his maternal and paternal grandfathers, respectively. He had grown up known to all as Leander, the son of a schoolteacher and an assistant principal. His mother, the teacher, had won a seat on the school board, and then a place on the D.C. council, at the price of her marriage to a man who, like her children, had come to feel like a stage prop in a permanent political campaign. When Amy Brackenridge married again, this time to a utility company executive, a comfortable family became moderately rich. The former teacher pulled her children out of the public schools and parachuted them into Sidwell Friends, where they would be groomed for leadership among the children of the capital's political and media elites. The children did not protest. It was all part of the permanent campaign.

His only small rebellion in adolescence had come on his first day in that strange new school, when a teacher had asked, "Do you prefer to be called Leander or Avery?" For reasons he did not quite understand, he had answered, "Avery." Having made the decision, he ratified it, introducing himself to his new classmates as his mother had taught him to do ("Just go right up and look 'em in the eye and shake their hands"): "Hi, I'm Avery Brackenridge." He practiced signing his name as a discontinuous line, as though he were a celebrity. L. Avery Brackenridge.

He had hoped, perhaps, that she would be disappointed by his unilateral deletion of her father's name in favor of the name of her ex-husband's father. In fact, she was pleased. He had taken the initiative in redefining himself in the way that she desired. Unlike Leander Brackenridge, a name fit for some quaint, elderly Southern Negro, L. Avery Brackenridge is a patrician name, a Sidwell Friends name.

"We *shall* overcome!"

At last, Avery thinks, recognizing the signal. He usually dreads what is coming, as he once dreaded hymns at the Episcopal Church in northwest D.C. when he had still been compelled to attend. He takes some comfort, though, in knowing, as the room joins in a lugubrious chorus of "We Shall Overcome," that they soon will be emancipated. *Pee at last. Thank God Almighty, I can pee at last.*

"I met your mother the other day," Ross tells him over supper.

Avery pauses, in the midst of opening another carton of gluey rice. They have had Chinese delivered. "Yeah? Where?"

"Some downtown function. The firm sponsors a school in Southeast. Not just us, a lot of businesses. Helping out the community, you know."

"Sounds like a *Mama mia* sort of thing. Was she the speaker?"

"No. I sat next to her at the luncheon. She's a real nice lady."

"You didn't tell her you knew me?"

"You kidding?"

Avery relaxes and scrapes lumps of rice onto a paper plate. "Maybe you should have *thanked* her." The jest helps to dispel his unease a little. The thought of Ross and his mother side by side at a banquet is somehow disquieting. These universes are not supposed to overlap; one world is not supposed to drift across the zodiac into the constellation of the other.

After supper they retire to the den to watch TV. With one hand Ross sips from his scotch and water, with the other he strokes Avery's shoulder through the sweater.

"So do they still want you to apply to law school?" Ross asks as the zany neighbor shows up on the TV sitcom to a burst of canned laughter. "Your mother and them."

"They always want me to apply to law school. They've been waiting for me to graduate from Harvard Law since I was six weeks old. I was supposed to get my law degree and be the first black president. And do my duty to the race by having 2.6 African-American children, not too dark, thank you, and they'd go to Sidwell Friends and Georgetown, or Harvard . . . It's like a dynasty. I'm the black American prince."

"The king of the gypsies."

"It's the mafia. The black mafia. That's what my Aunt Lorraine calls it. I'm like—what's his name, in *The Godfather*? The one who goes to college. Al Pacino. His character. That's me. I'm supposed to carry on the dynastic tradition. *La Familia. Mama mia.*"

"You're something else, Rave." The nickname Ross has given Avery—Rave, short for Raven—is not a reference to his color. In the jargon of espionage, Ross had explained, a raven is the male equivalent of a swallow, a spy who uses sex to entrap a foreign agent or citizen. Ross has told Avery stories about a few of the ravens who had worked for Bill Casey's CIA. One of them, a gay actor on a soap opera filmed in New York, had been paid, back in the mid-eighties, to seduce a prominent Eastern European scientist. The scientist had defected, only to find himself isolated in a safe house in northern Virginia, sans boyfriend. *C'est la guerre froid.* Ross seems to know a great deal about the Agency and its workings. He claims he was never more than an ordinary army officer, but Avery is convinced he was a spook.

Ever so slightly, Ross squeezes Avery's shoulder. Avery responds by listing to starboard and drawing his folded legs and stocking-feet up onto the couch. He lays his head in Ross's lap. Ross gently removes the gold wire-rimmed glasses, and the shapes in the room suddenly grow moss on their edges. Ross's small, round face is a tan blur as it descends toward Avery. Tongues test teeth. Avery feels a quickening between his legs. Beneath him, Ross shifts.

"Hm. We've got company," Avery observes.

"Rave, it's only eight-thirty."

"C'mere." Avery reaches up and sinks his fingers into Ross's short hair and pulls their faces together again. "You taste like soy sauce."

The phone rings. "Shit and molasses," says Ross.

"Let it ring!" Avery yells in annoyance, but Ross extricates himself and walks across the den to pick up the cel phone.

"Rich? Yeah, right. I wanted to know if anybody has got ahold of Heinzelmann . . . "

Ross paces with the phone at his ear. Avery picks up the TV remote and ratchets the volume down. The sitcom characters jabber in eerie silence.

"Shit," Ross tells the phone. "I didn't think about that. Hell, we need to give him a call. Yeah, we've got to have him onboard. You want to handle that? Maybe I should."

Ross sits down on the couch next to Avery, cradling the phone with his shoulder. "Awright, now you tell that peckerwood if he goes south on us his ass is grass and I'm a lawn mower." Ross frowns in mock displeasure as Avery squeezes the pattern in his pants. "Fuck it, we have already spent enough money to burn a wet mule . . . Well, you should leave no doubt in their minds . . . I want y'all to stick to him like ugly on an ape, right up to the vote . . . "

Avery shivers a little with excitement as he carefully unbuckles Ross's belt and then unfastens his pants. He pauses for a moment, his stomach weak with anticipation. Ross winks.

"I don't want there to be any daylight between us on this . . . If he screws us over again I'm gonna personally fuck him and the horse he rode in on."

Slowly Avery pulls the zipper down, then folds the fabric back from the bulging briefs.

"The grace period is over. He's got to understand that . . ." As his tongue moves and his mouth closes, Avery hears Ross pause and draw in his breath to the depth of his lungs.

"Okay. I'll talk to you tomorrow."

Avery hears Ross turn off the phone. He twists, in order to look up at Ross.

"Hey, Mister Washington Lobbyist. If I go south on you, will you fuck me and the horse I rode in on?"

Ever since high school, Avery has been looking for the man in the Burberrys coat. In the tenth grade he cut an ad out of a glossy magazine and kept it with him all through college. Though he finally misplaced it during a move, the image is crisp in his memory.

He is in his mid-thirties, the age at which a handsome man's face outgrows a puerile prettiness and assumes its distinctive form, contoured by character but not yet ruined by age. From his sun-bronzed brow his dark blond hair is swept back to frame close-set blue eyes gazing off in the distance, as though he has just recognized someone; the supposition would explain the hint of a smile tugging at his thin, stoic lips. His face itself is framed by the upturned collar of the coat that flows, the mantle of a twentieth-century lord, from the span of his strong but not overdeveloped shoulders. The coat is parted, revealing elegance: an ornate foulard tie tucked into a vest, or maybe a buttoned jacket, it is too dark to tell. Superimposed against the darkness of his midriff is the insignia of a tiny knight charging on a horse, lance lifted, and, below that, in floating white letters, BURBERRYS OF LONDON.

The picture that Avery cut out was not an aid to self-gratification—he had more effective icons. Rather, it was a stimulus to daydreaming. The Burberrys man was a WASP, or an English aristo, or maybe a dynamic young German executive. He would know all about the best wines and how to fix a sportscar, would be a master marksman, a genius at the stock exchange. He would be up to date on the best restaurants and converse fluently in the language of the waiters, be it French or Mandarin. He would have a summer place on the Vineyard, and know the best wintering spots in the Caribbean. The mystery lover would support Avery until he discovered his destined vocation and was discovered in turn by the world. They would take long trips around the world, and make passionate love in expensive hotels in Paris and Rome and London and New York.

The man in the Burberrys coat. Avery thought he recognized him in Ross the night they met in a dim smoke-filled bar on P Street. Among the clones in their leather jackets, the forty-somethings with their mustaches, and the twenty-something twinkies with their short haircuts and attitudes, Ross had stood out. Looking professional, affluent, controlled, and confident in his trench coat and suit and tie, Ross had nursed his drink and watched the parade of regulars with a kind of sovereign reticence. He was among them but not of them, Avery sensed, someone with a life beyond a favorite bar and a circle of queeny friends, someone substantial and superior. In him Avery saw a fellow aristocrat.

He was the right age, too—early thirties, or so Avery had guessed (later, he was shocked to learn that Ross was almost forty). Stef had suggested that Avery needed to find a more mature guy, someone older, late twenties or thirties, someone who was not racking up points, someone with a real adult life with whom he could have a steady and complete relationship.

So far that has escaped him. He and Ross are physically intimate, but they are not lovers. At least Ross has never said the words, and it is impossible to imagine the reticent ex-soldier calling Avery "dear" or "honey" or "baby"; the nickname "Rave" is the closest thing to an endearment. Avery knows that Ross had two longtime lovers in the past; of one of them, Paul, now in California, Ross is reluctant to speak, leading Avery to believe Ross's love for Paul is not entirely dead.

That night, awake in the comforting captivity formed by the clamp of Ross's body and the layered sheets, Avery lies and wonders what more there could be, apart from the words. A siren somewhere on Capitol Hill wakes Ross, who stretches and shifts and begins to subside into unconsciousness once more. Feeling vulnerable, Avery takes Ross's arm and folds it across him, clutching it like a lifeline.

"Ross," he murmurs.

"Hmmm."

"I love you."

There is no reply. But there is a kind of assent in the slight flex of Ross's enveloping arm. Or maybe it is just a twitch.

Stef calls it Avery's crisis. At first Avery thinks it is funny.

"It's not his fault, I know," Avery says, lying on Stef's broken green sofa. This is his preferred form of therapy. "He just wants somebody he can get off with now and then. He's a workaholic. He's a Type A personality."

"So are you," Stef says, mixing the margaritas on the counter that divides the kitchen from the living room. "Maybe that's the problem. You guys are too much alike."

"We're not alike at all."

"Yes, you are. You're both high-strung . . . "

"I am not!"

"See? I rest my case."

He tests the margarita. "Too much tequila."

Stef dilutes the mix. "What do you want?"

"I want this blond guy who's a few years older and makes tons of money and dresses really sharp to take care of me."

"You want Ross to marry you."

"No, I don't," Avery says, but it is as though he is mooting a possibility, not emphasizing a fact.

"Well, then, what do you want?"

"I don't know," he says, this time with conviction.

That weekend Ross is out of town, and the next week he is busy every night. Avery knows Ross is genuinely busy, but he works himself into resentful rages nevertheless. He cultivates his anger as though it were a small, delicate, bristling cactus.

His resentment blooms at a dinner party at the Capitol Hill town house of one of Ross's friends. Older than Ross by a decade, David Lawrence is also a Republican lobbyist. He is known to all as "the Ambassador," from a stint in the Caribbean in the service of the Reagan administration.

"It's my little Confederate *baby*," the Ambassador says, kissing Ross on the cheek after opening the door. "You know," the Ambassador tells Avery, "Ross here says I remind him of his dear old mammy . . . "

"You do not."

"Don't listen to him. Mammy knows. She used to wrap his little white ass in the Stars and Bars."

A voice bellows from upstairs. "David!"

"His master's voice," the Ambassador murmurs. "Back in a sec. Ross, you know your way to the booze."

While Ross pours them drinks, Avery asks him about David's boyfriend.

"Wesley? He's some kind of white trash from West Virginia," Ross replies in low tones. "David took him in like a stray cat a couple of years ago. He's a fuck-up. I gave him a job in our mail room, but we had to fire him 'cause he'd show up late for work all the time, stoned out of his mind. I don't hold for that kind of shit. And he'd steal. He's bad news. I think he beats David up.

Pardner, there are some real fucked-up people in this world."

"Present company excepted?"

Wesley enters, followed by his older lover. A quiver of excitement runs through Avery. Wesley is pretty—a slender boy in his mid-twenties with blond hair down to his shoulders. He is too slender for Avery's taste, and too short—the top of his head reaches the Ambassador's shoulder. He is not a blond god, but a blond elf. A psychotic elf, Avery concludes, watching the expressions on Wesley's face during dinner.

Conversation at dinner has to be squeezed in between portions of the Ambassador's monologue. "One of my fellow underprivileged oppressed homosexuals was asking me, 'How *could* you work for Ronald Reagan?' And I said, 'Missy'—well, I didn't say Missy, but I said, 'Ronald Reagan is *God*.'" The Ambassador raises his right hand. "This is the hand that shook Ron's. I remember exactly what we said to one another. It was a beautiful moment. I said, 'I look forward to the challenge, sir.' And he said—I'll never forget—he said, 'Well, I'm sure you'll do a great job.' But it was the *way* he said it—you know, with feeling. He's a real actor. Not like that phony old Charlton Heston. You're too young to remember, but Ron was so much studlier than Charlton. Did you ever see a picture of Reagan as a male model? Of *course* he took it off. Unless it was illegal in Iowa or wherever. Well, anyway, he was a hunk. Not like that nelly son of his. Oh, and Nancy Reagan, don't get me started on Nancy. That woman is the biggest fag hag in the world."

After the meal, Avery finds himself alone with Wesley in the black-and-gold Napoleonic parlor while Ross helps David with the liqueurs in the kitchen.

"You go to school?" Wesley asks in a West Virginia hillbilly twang.

"I graduated from Georgetown two years ago," Avery replies in his crisp broadcaster-standard American English. He is torn between fascination with the blond boy's looks and contempt for his social origins.

"Is that a college or a university? I'm thinking about going to a University," he says, capitalizing the term with his voice.

Contempt wins. Silently, Avery laughs.

"David's gonna help me with my education," Wesley continues. "You think if I applied you could help me get into Georgetown? You know, pull some strings."

Help, Avery thinks. He glances out of the parlor toward the door of the kitchen. Ross is standing there with David. The two are glancing at Avery and Wesley, smiling, laughing.

Laughing about their toy boys.

All the rage that has been accumulating in Avery rushes into his mind. He is so furious he hardly hears what Wesley is saying.

He broods through the remainder of the evening. He is quiet, too, as he and Ross walk back to Ross's town house.

"What's the matter, Rave? You're quiet."

"Nothing."

They come to Ross's street. Avery pauses. "I think I'm going to take a taxi home."

"I thought you were going to stay over."

"Not tonight."

"Tired?"

For weeks, Avery has rehearsed an entire speech—about how their relationship has to either go forward or come to an end; about how afraid Ross seems to be of his own emotions; about how insensitive he is to Avery's need for commitment. Instead, Avery says, "Yeah. I'm kind of tired."

Ross walks with him until they are in sight of the Capitol, a luminous white balloon rising above the trees. A cab pulls up. "Adams-Morgan," Avery tells the driver. He does not look back at Ross as the cab pulls away from the curb. There will be inconclusive conversations over the next several weeks, excuses for postponing further meetings, and then, finally, an awkward conversation about just being friends. All of that will be an aftermath. The end has come tonight.

12

She begins to think of them as her own. She spends most of her waking hours, after all, in one or another of the big houses in northwest Washington. Not all of the places that she cleans are mansions; there are a few apartments and one condo. But it is the great homes that she loves: the ranch-style home of Mrs. Bronsky, with its blue-painted brick and black trim; the colonial house of Mrs. Schultz, with its white brick and columns, a house made of sugar; the Binghams' house—across the river in Arlington—with its facade like a grafting of a castle and its pelt of ivy and its curvy fireplace.

She has never had a better job. At first, to be sure, she did not permit herself to enjoy her new vocation. She was afraid she would do something wrong. She did, in fact, make mistakes. Mrs. Bronsky had to remind her to dust the high places, where thin pelts of gray fur had been growing on bookcases and furniture tops too high for the tiny Graciela to see. There were more serious failures, like the time Graciela had broken the vase in the foyer of the Schultzes' house. When, after hearing the stammered confession in broken English, Mrs. Schultz had smiled stiffly and said, "Oh, it wasn't worth much anyway," Graciela had burst into grateful tears. She had expected to be arrested and deported.

After a few months, she begins to relax. She is no longer afraid that if she dares to sit down for a few minutes at a kitchen table to relax with a glass of juice or a soda, a furious employer will storm in unannounced. Now she sometimes turns a TV or radio on, so that she can listen to voices as she works. She finds it easier to understand what the Americans are saying on TV because she can watch their faces and figure out what they are talking about from the circumstances. She loves to watch the *telenovelas*, including the ones on the Spanish-language channel. Her favorite is *Los Ricos Lloran Tambien*—The Rich Also Cry.

In time she works up the nerve to steal. Her thefts are minor. She begins by stealing tampons, no more than one or two at a time; this spares her the embarrassment of having the clerk and the customers at the checkout stand see what she is buying, and spares her, as well, the need to rely on Yolanda. Sometimes she smuggles out other necessities in her purse—a roll of toilet tissue, or a light bulb, or a pen or a pencil. She never touches the money she sometimes finds lying around on bedside tables or in pants or shirt pockets. The rich Americans do not count their tampons or their light bulbs, but she is certain that they count their money.

She likes to spend time in the shady backyards. She will hose down a patio as an excuse to stand and listen to the birds chatter and feel the breeze as it slowly moves from lot to lot in the neighborhood, rattling each tree in turn. At such moments she misses the Salvadoran countryside. She never paid any attention to the landscape when she was there, but now, in her memory, it acquires a special radiance, as if in a dream. One scene recurs in her memory whenever she thinks of her distant homeland. She is walking down a rutted country road through the woods at that moment when the sun has set but the blue sky has not yet forgotten the day, and the cloud-foam, piled beyond the darkening trees, appears to have the weight and texture as well as the color of clay. A stillness settles over the world. Even the dogs forget to bark. This is what she chooses to remember.

"*Dios mío*, he is so crazy," Maria says, blowing smoke as her cigarette twitches like a red-beaked bird in the cage of her wicker-colored fingers. "He called me last night at two in the morning. I don't know what I am going to do."

Graciela knows exactly what Maria is going to do. She will let her boyfriend José move back in with her, even though—Graciela suspects—he hits her around. In the three or four months that they have been friends, since they worked together at the Hair

Affair, Maria has broken up with José four or five times. After one fight, Maria found a bloody pig's foot in the grass under the window of her efficiency apartment in Arlington. José, following the instructions of a *brujo,* had been trying to put a curse on her.

"Look," says Rosa proudly, joining them. They are sitting on a cement platform projecting into the puddled slot of an alley from the Salvadoran restaurant where Maria's friend Frida works. The children have been playing around the trash cans.

"What have you got, sweetie?" Maria asks.

"What is it?" Graciela's voice has an edge of concern.

"Something plastic," Maria concludes. "Part of a bottle, maybe."

Graciela turns in time to see Marcelo raise something in his hand toward his mouth. With practiced reflexes, she lunges for him, scoops him up in her arms, slaps his hand until he drops the piece of trash. His wail wrings tears from the pink sponge of his face.

"Ay, *pobrecito,*" Maria croons. "Come here." She takes the boy from his mother and sets him on her knee. "See? You've forgotten already."

"The mouth. Anything he sees, it goes in the mouth."

"Wait till he starts talking."

"He's talking. It's just a language we don't understand."

Graciela is jealous of Maria for having a man, even a man who mistreats her. Graciela misses having a man of her own. It is not so much the sex she misses as it is the attention. And the drama. Even if she and a man were fighting all the time, the way that Maria and José do, at least Graciela would be living, like the passionate characters in the soap operas. Once her life had been full of drama—the agony of her separation from her husband, the secret joy of her assignations with Paco. Now there is nothing but a liturgy of the mundane—leaving the babies in the morning with Mrs. Valdez, the baby-sitter, lurching with every hesitation of the snorting bus, scrubbing tubs and toilets, shopping, hauling clothes to the Laundromat, sitting at Sunday dinner with Yolanda and Isidro while the TV keeps silence at bay. The cycle goes on and on, like an escalator at a shopping mall, endlessly repeating. Her life has become a sequence. She wants it to be a story.

"Dog!" Marcelo shouts abruptly, pointing at a passing car. *Dog* is the only English word he knows.

"No es perro," Graciella tells him. "Everything he sees is a dog. Wait till you have one of your own."

"I have a baby," Maria replies. "A big, fat baby. His name is José."

A lawn mower clears its throat and cackles nearby. Surprised by the sound, Graciela goes to the living room of Mrs. Thompson's house and divides the curtains.

In the street, a dusted pickup waits. A young man, a Latino, is wobbling a mower across the front yard, striping the darker with lighter green.

His name is Carlos, she learns, when she works up the nerve to bring him a cup of cool water. It is hot, so hot that his T-shirt is blotched and brindled like the hide of a dalmatian. He came from Guatemala a few years ago, she learns. He works in the yards of several of the families on this block. He is small and dark, with an Indian face, with features that almost look Chinese. He is not handsome, but he is cute.

Graciela wants to invite him inside to sit down at the kitchen table and cool off, but she is afraid that would break some unwritten rule of decorum, some *norteño* taboo. Instead, when she goes back into the house, she stands discreetly among the curtains and watches him as he toils, and she feels as she has not felt for a long time.

With each dazzle and crack, another sieve of rain scrapes down the gray-green street, outlining the cars it nets in ephemeral silver. Graciela contracts in the midst of her umbrella's cylindrical cascade as the water crawls into her shoes and speckles her dress.

She does not notice the truck until it pulls up on the corner. Then her first impression is that the driver is asking for directions. But he knows her name.

"Graciela!" It is Carlos.

She hesitates before accepting the gardener's offer. But she will be soaked to the skin if she waits any longer for the bus. She might catch pneumonia. To have a sick mother would be bad for the kids. As is her practice, she ends up excusing what she wants to do by telling herself it would be in the best interest of Rosa and Marcelo. She climbs into the truck.

"Where can I take you?" he asks as he turns the radio down, strangling a Latino balladeer.

She tells him where she lives—then, reconsidering, asks him if he minds stopping by the supermarket first. As long as she has the use of a truck, she need not be limited in her shopping by how much she can carry home.

Her first trip to Safeway had been a religious revelation. She had never imagined that there could be anything like this cathedral space, with its aisles going on forever, endless tiers of fresh food under lights like the translucencies of glaciers. The marvelous has become the mundane in the time she has lived in the States. Still, she feels something of that initial wonder as she strolls with Carlos through the produce section, with its small mountains of apples, oranges, pears, bananas, all glowing like Christmas lights on a suburban lawn.

"It's not my truck," he explains. "I rent it from a guy I know, two days a week, to cut grass. The rest of the time I work on houses." He is a *mojado*, an illegal, as well. He tells her that he and other day laborers gather in the parking lot of a church near the Latino neighborhood in Arlington where he lives in a room with three other guys. The contractors pay them on a daily basis, cash. "Sometimes there isn't much work. Sometimes there are a lot of construction projects, and you can bargain with the contractors." Carlos admires the electricians whom he watches install the wiring in new homes and office buildings. His ambition is to learn the trade himself.

"My husband is dead," she tells him, certain he must have noticed her wedding band. He seems taken aback to learn that she has children.

That evening, after Carlos drops her off, Graciela gets a phone call from Darryl Shelton. There is a problem with the lease. Her English is not good enough for her to understand him, and his Spanish is not good enough to explain. He tells her he will pick her up in the morning, before she has to go to work in the suburbs.

She has trouble sleeping that night. She does not want to move yet again. She remembers how Darryl's hand brushed against her, how he hinted to her. He wants her, she is sure of it. She would rather be with Carlos, but she fears Carlos lost interest in her on learning of the children. Maybe, she tells herself, Señor Darryl is not a bad man.

His big black truck is waiting for her in the parking lot of the apartment complex when she emerges at eight in the morning. He drives her to Yolanda's, where she drops off the children, then takes her to a run-down shopping strip near Capitol Hill, to a windowless office in the back.

"Listen, I felt sorry for you, Graciela," the big Marine tells her in a mixture of English and Spanish. "I didn't charge you for the deposit. But the owner found out, and now I'm in trouble."

"How much is the deposit?" Graciela asks. When she learns, her heart begins to pound in panic. It would take her weeks to earn that much money, and she would have nothing to live on if she gave it to Darryl.

"I want to help you, Graciela," the tall American says. "I really want to help you, because I like you. You're a very pretty woman. Did anyone ever tell you that? I bet you've got lots of boyfriends. Do you? Do you have a boyfriend?"

She looks down at the floor in embarrassment. "No," she manages to whimper.

His hands are crawling on her. "You ever had an American boyfriend, Graciela? I used to have a Salvadoran girlfriend. She used to like it when I did this . . . "

She wrestles away. "No," she says weakly.

"Come on, Graciela. We're friends. I help you out, you have to be nice to me, *comprende*? If you don't want to be friends, you can just walk out that door and come back with the check for the deposit. If you want to be friends, then be nice to me. You want to be friends with me, don't you, Graciela?"

Her voice is so faint she is not sure she said or thought it. "Yes." She will do anything not to rely on Yolanda and Isidro's charity again. It will not be so bad, she tells herself. Whatever would happen, would happen. *Así es, así será.*

Darryl unbuckles his belt.

13

The drone of a plane making a low pass over the waterfront on its way to touchdown at National Airport rattles the windows.

"You ever think about what you see when you die?" Evander says.

The colorless curtains have been pulled all the way down from their rollers. The room is suffused with an amber effulgence.

"You see God," Teesha says.

"I think when you die," Evander tells her, "it's like your soul comes out your body and it's just like floating there, like a few feet away? And you're looking down at your body, all shot up or whatever, and people come running because they heard all the shooting, and they standing round your body and screaming and carrying on and shit, and you can see them, but they can't see you. And when you, like, try to touch 'em, you know, your hand go right through 'em like they was water or something. It's like everything is water. You can go right through walls like you walking through, you know, like water from a shower. And you can see through buildings, and people's clothes, and you can read their minds and shit like that. Ain't nobody can see you, though, or hear you coming or nothing. Can't nobody touch you."

The room is empty except for a couple of dusty TVs, a broken VCR, some boxes, and a few sweaters in the half-open closet. They are lying on packing foam on the carpet.

"That ain't in the Bible," Teesha says.

She wriggles toward him and throws her arm across him, her

breasts squashed against the narrow taut drum of his chest. "Why you talking about dying?"

"Baby, I got enemies."

"Shit. Listen at you."

"It's true." Evander is gazing at the ceiling, his face a dark island in the golden haze. "It's a war. What if some Punksta bust a cap in my ass? Then I be dead. Least my body'd be dead. But my soul gonna be outside my body. I'll come visit you. I'll *haunt* you."

Teesha snuggles closer to him. "Don't talk like that."

"I'll come right through the walls—boo! It's a ghost." He cackles, and tickles her.

She shrieks, flinching. "Stop it! Boy, you crazy."

"It's the ghost of Evander!"

"I turn you into a ghost right now, if you don't quit."

His mirth subsides into melancholy as she settles down next to him again. She puts her head on his chest. She can hear—feel, more than hear—the throbbing of his life.

This is the fourth time they have had sex. The first time was hasty and confused, on a late Saturday afternoon in the uncertain privacy of a junior high power generator's shadow. Then there had been hasty fumbling and squeezing and sucking in a stairwell and the basement laundry room of the apartment where Teesha lives with her aunt's family. This afternoon Evander had ceremoniously led her to the run-down town house near the Anacostia River where the Krew keeps a room for caches of loot.

The refrigerator, they called it, the place where hot items could cool off for a while. The refrigerator had been anything but cool as the two had enjoyed languid, naked sex with one another for the first time.

"If I get shot," Evander instructs her, "I want you to put my Baltimore Orioles cap in the casket. I want to be buried with it. And my high-tops."

"You can't get buried in your high-tops."

"Make 'em close the lid halfway, so they can't see what kind of shoes I'm wearing. You got to promise."

"Shit. You crazy."

He rolls over on top of her, pressing her with an ardor that frightens. "You got to promise." His breath is stale with onions and ketchup from a hamburger. "Swear to God. Ain't nobody gonna have my shoes after I'm dead. Swear to God."

"Oh, baby." She puts her hand on the back of his neck and draws him down to her. Soon she is clenched in pleasure again as his eager bucking flares coals of burning pleasure in her core. Please, she pleads silently, so as not to alarm him, gimme a baby.

Afterward he puts on his underwear and stretches, thin as a gazelle, silhouetted against the amber curtain. With the grace of a ballet dancer, he slowly lifts one leg, draws it back, then kicks an imagined foe. "Yow! Ya!" He reenacts the moves he has seen in martial arts movies, spinning on one foot and jabbing with the other, his fingers splayed and stiff as claws. He is the most beautiful being in the whole golden world, and he is hers.

"Teesha, go and take out the rolls," her Aunt Shirelle orders. The baby has just thrown up. The phone is ringing.

"Shit!" Teesha shakes her hand, stung by the hot metal through the thin terry-cloth towel. She plunges her hand under the running tap. Wide-eyed, her cousins crowd her.

"Y'all get outta here," she says. "Y'all in the way. Go set the table. Alyssa, you hear what I'm saying? Both of you."

The telephone shrills again. Teesha hears her aunt exclaim, "I'm gonna rip that thing out of the wall." A pause. "Teesha, it's for you." Shirelle gives her a warning look as she passes the receiver on to her teenage niece. "Tell whoever it is we're eating supper."

"Hi, baby." Evander's voice sounds far away and somehow older.

"I can't talk. We're eating supper."

"I wish you was eatin' me for supper."

Teesha feels her aunt's eyes upon her. "Call me later, at the store." She hangs up, secretly thrilled.

"Lamar, call your daddy," Shirelle says. Not looking Teesha in the eye, Shirelle, setting a bowl of steaming rice on the table, asks, "Who was that, baby?"

"Somebody wants to know the answers to our homework."

Halfway through the meal, Alyssa starts to giggle. Shirelle looks at her sternly. "What's got into you, girl?"

"Teesha got a boyfriend," the nine-year-old sings.

Teesha glowers. "Hush your mouth."

"His name is 'Vander." More giggles.

"Is that the boy who called?" Shirelle asks Teesha. "Who is he?"

"Just a boy."

Shirelle and Monroe glance at one another. "What's his name? What's his name, girl?"

"Evander."

"Evander who?"

"Evander Johnson."

"He live round here?"

"I don't know." With each round of interrogation, Teesha's voice grows quieter, and her study of her plate more intense.

"Pass the butter." Shirelle sinks her knife into a roll as though it were a boy named Evander Johnson. "I hope he ain't one of them gangbanger boys. Your momma would skin me alive if I let you hang around that street trash. You hear me, baby?"

"Yeah."

Alyssa sings, "Teesha's got a boyfriend."

Shirelle whirls and slaps her hard. Stunned, Alyssa stares up at her mother, too frightened to cry.

"Hush your mouth!" With a trembling hand, Shirelle scoops up Alyssa's plate, marches into the kitchen, and scrapes its contents into the Safeway sack that is serving as a trash bag.

"Lawd a'mercy," rumbles Monroe, wiping his lips. It is the first thing he has said since sitting down at the table.

"You go to your room, Alyssa Robinson. You done had your supper."

Alyssa blinks back tears. "Why? I didn't do nothin'."

"Hush up. I'll hit you upside your head again."

Alyssa stomps off with cratering elephant steps to the bed-room she shares with Teesha and slams the door.

"Jesus Christ," says Monroe. "Do you think we can have one meal around here without all hell breaking loose?"

"What you complaining about? You get waited on hand and foot."

"Jesus Christ."

Teesha sits staring at her plate. I hate y'all, she thinks, I hate all of y'all.

On the way home from the pizza place through the steaming, puddled streets, Evander tells her about his favorite comic book, *The Cybernauts*. "There's Professor X, he's their *sensei*. Like their coach. He got, like, this super-scientific brain. He's a mutant . . ."

"What's a mutant?"

"They're, like, deformed, kinda, but not like retards. It's like they got these special powers. Like Jackal. He got these hype claws, he just rip your guts out . . ."

"That's nasty. Why you reading all that nasty old shit?"

"It's stories, girl. It's like movies. They draw the pictures like it was a movie. It's def shit. I'll show it to you."

Evander confides that he has made up his own Cybernaut: the Salamander. "Everybody think he's just this dude in the 'hood, ain't nothing special. But he can turn on his salamander powers, and he can shoot out fire outta hisself. But he don't get burnt up on account of his skin, it's like . . . you know. What do you call it? Asbestos. He got like this asbestos skin, and if there's like this three-alarm fire, he can walk right through it, no problem."

"You made all that up?"

"Yeah."

"You lying to me, nigga. Don't you be giving me no three-six-nine."

"No shit. Salamander, I'm gonna, like, I don't know, like sell him to the comic book people."

"Say what? What you talking about?"

"Shut up and listen, girl. It's my concept. The concept is mine. You understand what I'm saying? I got to sell 'em the concept of the Salamander, and then they'll pay me. Like royalties on a record. Like when one of them hip hop dudes covers somebody else's song, he got to pay 'em royalties."

"So you think they gonna buy this Sow . . . Sow . . . "

"Salamander."

"Salamander Man. Is he like Batman? Spider-Man?" Evander seems pleased at her comprehension, and his pleasure pleases her in turn. "Batman, he's the one with Robin?"

A police siren burps, once. They have been so enrapt that neither noticed the squad car following a short distance behind.

Evander's head snaps. "Shit. Fuck. It's five-oh. Come on."

"What's the matter?" Terrified, she dashes after him toward an alley. The siren barks again. Rubber squeals. Somebody shouts.

"Quick, hide this shit. Put it down your shirt," Evander pants once they are in the alley. He is thrusting Baggies of rock at her. "Hurry up!" She does as she is told.

Then a policeman is upon them. "Hey, punk!" The cop is a burly black man in his late twenties. He slams Evander against the wall. His next blow sends Evander staggering back into the street, where his partner stands by the squad car's open door, apprehensive.

"What you runnin' for, muthafucka?" Evander opens his mouth, only to be told, "Shut up. I didn't tell you to say nothing." Seeing Evander glance at Teesha, the cop snarls, "What you looking at her for? She ain't gonna help you."

"Leave him alone!" Teesha shrieks.

Grady, the cop, takes his long black flashlight from a belt sagging beneath utensils. He waves it at her in warning. "You shut up." He turns back to Evander. "Okay, muthafucka," he says, herding Evander toward the squad car with successive shoves. "Spread 'em." He pats Evander down, retrieving the shiny Glock from Evander's high-top. "Shit, Lewis, check this out. L'il homie is strapped like a muthafucka." Grady turns the gun over in his hand. "What you be doing with heat like this?"

"Don't mess with me, man."

"What you gonna do, shithead? Bust a cap? With what, your finger? Come on, muthafucka, let's par-tay. Head-up."

"He didn't do nothing," Teesha pleads.

"Tell your 'ho to hush."

The other cop is growing more anxious. "Grady, come on."

"Chill." Grady paces around Evander. "So where you hiding that rock, punk? I bet you got all kinds of shit to sell to them rock stars."

"Ain't got nothing."

"Ain't got nothing, don't know nothing . . . You an ignorant nigga, ain't you." Grady tugs at the blue chevron that Teesha has sewn on Evander's sweatshirt. "Blue for the Krew. You working for Frizzell. Where's the shit?"

Teesha says, "He told you! He ain't got nothing!"

Grady turns on her. "Your homegirl, now, she ain't holding for you, is she? Lewis, what you say we check this bitch out."

Evander lunges between Grady and Teesha. Grady's black metal torch, arcing upward, connects with Evander's face and sends him staggering. Teesha shrieks. Evander sinks to one knee on the cement, clutching his face. Teesha embraces him. Her shouted curses bring a crowd into the street.

"Shit, man, we gonna get wrote up," Lewis complains. "Come on, Grady."

Grady gets back in the squad car. "Listen to me, muthafucka," he says through the rolled-down window. "No unauthorized business on my beat. Next time you better have your contribution, or your bitch, she gonna be crying at your funeral." He holds up the 9 mm. "This'll have to be the contribution for today. Support your local *po*lice. Ninety-nine and five-one-hundreds pure." Grady cackles as the car screeches away. Teesha, sobbing in rage, clutches her man as though by squeezing tightly enough she can shield him from all his foes.

14

"I want sex," says Sir Robin Blair. "We need more sex in the magazine. There's just got to be some kind of sexual angle to this."

"The story," Daniel reminds him, "is about the infrastructure crisis."

"I find the whole essay underconceptualized," Naomi Segal announces. "There's a sort of naive positivism to the author's attitude that I find disturbing. There are distinct technocratic elements."

"It's got to be *slashing*," Sir Robin erupts. "I want us to stand out from the pack. Whatever the conventional wisdom is, we should say the opposite. We need controversy. Tell the author we want it to be a slashing polemic. Just frightfully slashing. Take no prisoners." The editor glances at his watch. "My God! I'm supposed to be at a reception at the British embassy."

The discussion breaks up. On the way out of the conference room, Stef whispers to Daniel, "What was that?"

"That," Daniel tells her, "was a *Perspective* lineup meeting."

Stef has been a deputy assistant editor at *Perspective* for two weeks. Ever since the murder of Steven Quist, the designated managing editor, near the Capitol a few months ago, the magazine has been reshuffling editors. Stef had interviewed for the position when she had been under consideration by Aglaia's foundation, and had not gotten it. The woman who had gotten the job, however, had withdrawn to accept a more lucrative position at a Condé Nast publication in New York. When the editors had asked Stef if she was still interested, Aglaia had been very encouraging. Stef was merely moving from one to another Kazakis enterprise.

Stef quickly masters her new duties at *Perspective*. Her work evokes memories of her days as a student editor working on the Georgetown University magazine. Editing the articles of others, researching her own—this is what she is meant to do. Her two years of answering mail and preparing press releases on Capitol Hill now seem to her to have been a long and fruitless diversion from her destiny.

From the magazine's veterans, Stef acquires a sense of its history. *Perspective* was founded in the 1930s by a Trotskyist splinter group in New York whose members filled the magazine's pages with abstruse discussions of democratic socialism and artistic modernism. In the fifties and sixties, it became a conventional left-liberal journal, specializing in denunciations of U.S. foreign policy and sympathetic treatments of the student counterculture. After Nixon ended the draft in 1973, the editors along with their campus readership lost much of their political fervor. For a few years in the middle of the seventies, under new owners, the editors tried to market *Perspective* as a slightly more highbrow version of *Rolling Stone*. This first attempt to transform the journal from a little magazine into a mass-market glossy failed, but the experiment intrigued Des Kazakis, who bought the failing monthly in 1981. The political passions of the early Reagan years gave the magazine a new raison d'être—combating Reaganism and the middle-American vulgarity it was thought to embody. With this combination of liberal partisanship and snobbery, *Perspective* acquired a new, older, more affluent audience more interested in political controversy than in long, learned essays on the deeper meanings of rock and roll. Kazakis completed the reinvention of *Perspective* by moving its offices from New York to Washington in 1986 and recruiting the best Washington journalists as contributing editors.

To edit the new *Perspective*, Kazakis brought over Sir Robin Blair, who had edited the flagship magazine in Kazakis's British tabloid fleet, *The Peephole*. Blair, Stef learns, is in the habit of commissioning pieces from his cronies in British journalism, with the result that the front of the book tends to be divided between earnest American investigative journalists and sarcastic Fleet Street dilettantes.

The back of the book is under the exclusive jurisdiction of Naomi Segal, who was a celebrity radical in the sixties (her 1967 *Perspective* essay, "The Ironic and the Political," has long since become required reading on many long-quiet campuses). Whereas Blair recruits from Washington and London, Segal culls heavily from the intellectual ranks of Manhattan; Cambridge, Massachusetts; and continental Europe. She seems to know every Eastern European dissident by the first name, and Prague is practically her second home.

Because the two demigod editors spend much of their time abroad—Blair in Britain and Segal in the Danubian river basin—the task of running the magazine falls on managing editor Daniel Ratner, a twenty-nine-year-old Ph.D. from Harvard. He is extremely effeminate and thoroughly heterosexual, engaging in month-long affairs with a succession of pretty young women who see something in Daniel that is imperceptible to Stef. Perhaps his accent does the trick; he has a pronounced Oxbridge accent, which he must have acquired during his brief stay in Oxford as a Rhodes scholar (he grew up in Palo Alto, the son of a Stanford professor). "Oh, how utterly, utterly *delightful!*" he will exclaim at any bit of good news, clasping his hands and rolling his eyes as though he were a high school student auditioning for a part in a bad dramatization of Dickens. Stef thinks he is irredeemably phony, but hides her opinion, since her future with the magazine depends on a good relationship with him. Fortunately, Daniel seems to like her; and even more fortunately, perhaps, she is not his type. (Stef is told that he prefers women who are not intellectually intimidating—for example, models.)

While Sir Robin reigns, Daniel rules over a staff of a dozen assistant editors and interns. Most of them, Stef discovers to her disappointment, are "heir-heads" like Mandy back in Congressman Ritter's office. Stef had assumed that the young staff members of *Perspective* would be aspiring writers and reformers, disheveled and bohemian and earnest, not a clique of rich kids whiling away the time between college and law school or a Ph.D.

program. The salaries paid young journalists in Washington, though, are only slightly better than those paid congressional interns, making it all but impossible for a middle-class twenty-something to survive. Indeed, Stef could not do it without occasional parental subventions in the form of her share of the proceeds from the rental of her deceased grandparents' house in St. Louis (hereditary income that does not, in Stef's mind at least, make *her* an heir-head).

The more Stef learns about the magazine, the odder it seems to her that Washington's leading political monthly should be owned by an Australian, edited by an Englishman, and staffed by rich kids who grew up insulated from the America of mega-malls and bowling lanes. Stef takes a certain pride in having achieved her position on the basis of merit alone, particularly after she learns that many of the other associate editors are children of friends of Des Kazakis (the magazine really *is* like a congressional office). Stef finds a kindred spirit, or so she assumes, in Ouida Covington, the only black American on the editorial staff.

In a novel by Somerset Maugham that Stef read once, the upper-class women were in the habit of telling one another, "I admire your *chic*." Stef admires Ouida's *chic*. Ouida is not so much strikingly beautiful as beautifully striking. A small woman, she has a heavyset body, tending toward a plumpness that would have been accentuated by heavy hair. But Ouida has shorn her head and dyed the skullcap of feltlike hair the color of yellow grass whitening in summer sun. Her skin is the color of caramel, the eyes framed by that blond skullcap and a single silver earring are Baltic blue.

Her exotic beauty is enhanced by the way she moves. There is always the slightest hesitation in her movements, as if she were aware of her own fragility in a world made for rougher folk. Stef has never seen any black woman like her, nor for that matter any American woman of any race. Stef is not suprised to learn that Ouida grew up abroad, the child of an air force colonel. From bits and pieces of the peoples of the world, Ouida has created herself. Next to her, Stef feels awkward and graceless. Nevertheless, she thinks of Ouida and herself as kindred outsiders, the graceful, cosmopolitan black woman and the middle-American sort-of-Jewish girl from St. Louis. They have something else in common, their friendship with Avery, a subject that Ouida, curiously, does not like to discuss.

"Guess what?" Stef says to Avery at their biweekly dinner in Georgetown. "I'm going to your mother's house." Stef explains that Ouida has invited her to join the New Columbia Movement, which seeks statehood for the District of Columbia.

"You're kidding." Avery laughs. "Oh, my God. Those people are such frauds. They're just publicity hounds."

"This is a real issue, Avery. The District has been colonized by an occupying power."

"Stef Schonfeld, freedom fighter."

"You are so cynical. I wonder what Ouida sees in you."

Avery's mother and stepfather live in an elegant baroque mansion in Chevy Chase. Stef has always thought of herself as upper middle class, but her parents, both academics, lived far more modestly than Avery's. During the coffee break in the session, Stef, munching a cookie, discovers the bookcase shelf in the living room devoted to grotesquely racist paraphernalia from the Jim Crow past: Aunt Jemima syrup bottles, Nigger Toe licorice, a nutcracker in the form of a minstrel-show black man with thick white lips.

"This is my favorite," Amy Brackenridge says, joining her. She is a buxom woman with a silver streusel swirl in her light brown hair. "We got this at an auction at Sotheby's." She cranks the nutcracker, making its fat lips clack.

Somebody is clapping. "People . . . People, can we all sit down again? Lars is going to demonstrate nonviolent resistance techniques."

Lars is a seven-foot blond Viking who works as a masseur at a health club for wealthy women when he is not demonstrating how to go limp during nonviolent protests. "I need a volunteer," he tells his audience, mostly female and about half black.

"Go on. Be brave." Stef gives Ouida a little shove. Lars sees Stef's movement and takes it for volunteering. The others applaud.

"Go for it." Ouida smiles.

"The key is to go completely limp. Don't fight back. Just let your muscles melt . . . "

As she lies on the carpet, with Lars moving her limp arms and legs in various positions, Stef tries to keep a look of solemn dignity on her face. She tries to imagine herself and the others lying down on the asphalt, jeered at by reactionary crowds, shoved around by brutal policemen, when the time for the March on the Capitol for District Sovereignty finally comes. But she finds herself thinking of joining the health club where Lars can be found most of the time, molding the backs of pliant women with his brown and powerful hands. She wonders if Bruce would object.

A few days later, she flies home to St. Louis for a friend's wedding. The smell of the house she grew up in is the same: cat litter and lemon air freshener, like a lemon orchard manured by cougars. Everything is the same. Right on schedule, Stef's Gentile mother tells her that her professor father has bought more Jewish antiques. "Show an interest," says the proverbial *shiksa* mother. "It will make your father feel good." Right on schedule, too, Stef hears, through the wall of her bedroom, her mother rummaging in the bathroom late at night, downing pills to help her sleep.

They ask her about Bruce, but Stef gets the feeling that they really do not want to know. She is an only child—the reason, perhaps, that she was so quick to find a surrogate sister in Allison and a surrogate brother in Avery. She has come to believe she was an accident. Her parents, with their division of labor between the professor, her father, and the school administrator, her mother, are old-fashioned by the standards of a contemporary academic couple, but Stef thinks they were probably pretty bohemian in the early sixties. People are most themselves at different ages—some at twenty, some at eighty. Her parents, Stef thinks, probably peaked when they were a young, trendy couple, just a few years before she was born. They were not meant to be parental authority figures, much less middle-class and middle-aged. That accounts, she thinks, for the vague depression that floats in the air of the house in the St. Louis suburb like the scent of lemon and cats.

"I'm going crazy," she confesses to Avery in a long-distance call. "It is so boring."

"It's just a few days. At least your parents live in a different city. You can get on a plane."

The fitting for the bridesmaids' dresses is an ordeal. Stef has had little contact with the bride, Linda Latham, since high school, and she was surprised when she was asked. She accepted, partly in the hope that everyone in her hometown would be impressed with her new status as a deputy assistant editor at *Perspective*. She has discovered, however, that no one in St. Louis reads the magazine. The talk is not about Stef's prestigious career, but about babies and mortgages.

"If Lacy talks about that little brat of hers one more time I'm going to throw up," Stef announces to Allison as they drive away from the mall where the bridal shop is located.

"I know," Allison says. "She is such a conceited bitch. I'm sorry, but I think that baby of hers is *ugly*."

Once again, Allison shares her scheme. "I'm thinking about moving to Washington."

You're not going to move in with me, Stef thinks. Allison is her closest friend, and she wants to keep it that way.

Allison wants to know how serious Stef's relationship with Bruce is. "I don't know. I don't have any plans. I mean, we don't have any plans."

"So when do I get to meet this mystery man? I might be coming to Washington for some interviews next month."

"I don't know why you want to move to Washington. The prices are higher, jobs are scarce . . . "

"Listen to you. You've got this great job, and met this great guy, and you're telling me I should stay in St. Louis."

"Well, I was lucky."

"You just don't want to share." Allison indicates the mall they are passing. "See the Home Depot there? That's where Richard is working."

Richard was the first man who had made love to Stef, the high school golf captain whom she, the bashful, brainy girl, had tutored in math. Stef shifts in the seat, uncomfortable. "He got married, didn't he?"

"To Dorothy Green. Did you know her? They have two kids now."

The disquiet grows at the rehearsal dinner, and then the ceremony. Apart from Allison, all of the women with whom Stef went to high school, it seems, are married now. She tells herself there is no rush. Still, she feels a flash of anger when Allison catches the bouquet.

The sentry in the booth had not been just for show. He had phoned ahead for confirmation before raising the barrier and waving Bruce and Stef on through into the private neighborhood. Though Bruce had not been invited, he had insisted on driving Stef to Kazakis's weekend place on Long Island Sound. Bruce's verdict, when he had seen the first house of several on the leafy and wholly private street, had been disappointment: "If I had money like Kazakis, I'd do a tear-down, like in L.A. I'd tear that place down and build a mansion, man."

Now Bruce, dismissed with a kiss, is on his way to visit a college buddy in Manhattan. Stef, having left her bags in the foyer, is being led through the house by a Latina maid. It might be any big suburban house—testimony, she thinks, to Des's modesty rather than to his lack of imagination.

"Mr. Kazakis will be down in a minute," the maid tells her. Stef absentmindedly touches her hair and looks down from the veranda. The view is astonishing. Steps glitter in the shape of a smile down from the house to the beach of Griswold Cove, an indentation in the shoreline in the shape of a G. The bar of the G is a spit, at the end of which an old-fashioned pillared gazebo as big as a circus tent is budding in the salt light.

She hears Des before he reaches her. "There you are. I'm so glad you could make it. Oh, you don't have a drink? What will it be?"

Glasses in hand, they descend to the boardwalk and stroll toward the spit.

"From the street, you can't tell any of this is here," she says.

"It's nice, isn't it? It's artificial—the beach, the spit. It was built in the twenties by Myron Liebowitz, the investment banker."

"Who was Griswold?"

"Oh, there was no Griswold. Liebowitz called it Griswold Cove to make it sound WASPier." He points. "That's Aglaia's place, over there. It was torn up pretty badly in the big storm two years ago. So was the gazebo." His accent is peculiarly indeterminate—sometimes British, sometimes American, sometimes residually Australian. "It looks like fine sailing weather. Unfortunately Jay Pierce won't be able to make it . . . Do you know Jay Prentice Pierce?"

"I've heard the name."

"He's a good person to know in Washington. Very well connected. Into real estate. I think he was some sort of bright young thing in the Johnson administration. I met him at Malcolm Forbes's seventieth birthday party in Morocco."

"I know people who know him," Stef says helpfully, thinking of Ross. All gay people know each other somehow.

A different Latina maid—how many does he have?—descends from the house bearing a cel phone on a litter of fingers. "Excuse me for just a moment," Des apologizes.

Stef leans on the railing of the gazebo and lets the warm sun melt on her face and the salt breeze soak into her lungs. Against her will—for she wants so desperately to impress her new employer with the acuity of her intelligence—she feels contentment oozing through her like the numbness from an anesthetic, stilling her anxiety, making her serene and complacent and a little stupid. She watches a heron struggle with a spiderlike crab a few yards away at the surf's edge, and is struck with the wonder of it all.

The young sailor's name is Yannos. He has dazzling white teeth and black chest hair bristling through the open neck of his shirt. Claudia catches Stef admiring him.

"Isn't he adorable?" Claudia says, lighting a cigarette. Claudia—a nom de plume used for her column in the *New York Sentinel*—is a woman somewhere between forty and seventy. Her teeth are much younger than she is. "He's like one of those hunks on the covers of those romance novels. You know, the guys with their shirts off, ravishing Scarlett O'Hara or Maid Marian or whatever. Have you ever read any of those things? They're pretty hot. They all have the same story. There are these two gorgeous twin brothers, one evil, one good. The evil brother rapes the heroine for three hundred pages, and then the good brother kills him and marries her."

"What happens then?"

"Nothing. End of story. The fun's over."

Stef likes Claudia better than the other guests on the overnight cruise: a Wall Street investment banker and his wife, who is half or a third his age, and the tall Englishman with bulging eyes whom Des addresses deferently as "Professor." During the meal the stewards serve in the yacht's dining room, the professor insists on explaining in detail how dogs rip apart a cornered fox.

"You go on foxhunts?"

"At every opportunity," the professor responds. "I suppose it's the sort of tradition an *Ameddiccan* wouldn't understand."

"Professor? That's a laugh," Claudia snorts as she and Stef, an hour later, watch the water on the eastern horizon turn turquoise as the sun sets. "He writes a column for a London tabloid Des owns. He's just English white trash. Don't let these guys fool you."

Stef had been quiet during the dinner, intimidated by the names being dropped around her. Everyone else at the table, it seemed, was on a first-name basis with presidents, monarchs, prime ministers, stars and starlets, models, designers, Italian industrialists, and New York intellectuals. Claudia tells her not to feel inferior. "Why do you think we're here? Why do you think Des spends all his money on buying papers and magazines? The rich are nothing unless their names are in the papers. Nothing. They're just boring people with lots of money. We have it in our power to transform them into celebrities just by talking about them in print. We have awesome power."

"But we have to use it responsibly," Stef argues.

"Of course. We have a duty to serve the public. Yannos? Yannos, darling. We both need refills."

15

It looks like a county fair, but it sounds like Halloween. The popping grows louder as Darryl steers his big black truck into the parking lot on the side of the hill amid the vans and pickups.

"Lock the door," he reminds Bruce. Darryl has some of his own guns in the cab.

A cool breeze ruffles the drab green nape of the Virginia ridge. They stroll through the throng, between rows of booths set up by gun dealers and manufacturers. Bruce joins a knot of people watching a video monitor at the Two-Tap Ammo display. "Watch the difference the Thunderbolt Mark VI makes," the man in the video is saying. The camera shows bullets blasting craters in cubes of wet clay.

"Cool," says a little kid in an orange hunting jacket to his beer-bellied father.

Most of the crowd at the Virginia Gun-A-Thon is male. There are a few women, though. A pretty blond girl, dressed like her man in a khaki combat jacket, attracts Bruce's attention.

"We just both love guns," she is telling a couple of older sportsmen in a thick Southern accent as her man looks on. "This is the first day of our honeymoon, and we couldn't think of any place we'd rather spend it."

"She loves guns," her husband confirms.

When Bruce had told Ross he was thinking about buying a gun for protection, Ross had given him Darryl's name and number. Darryl had invited him along to the Gun-A-Thon. On the way, Bruce had managed to learn a little about the tall, taciturn, cold-eyed fellow with the graying military crew cut and the black mustache. He had learned, for example, that Darryl had been in Lebanon in '82 and, a little later, in Honduras.

Bruce wonders if Darryl is gay. "How'd you get to know Ross?"

"I work for a friend of his, Jay Prentice Pierce. Do you know him?" The name sounds familiar. "He's a big lawyer in town. Big realtor, too. I work for his real estate firm, Henderson Properties."

"What do you do?"

"Oh, I guess you could call me a manager. General troubleshooter. I kind of drifted into it. I started out doing private detective work for law firms and insurance companies, after I got out of the marines. That's how I got to know Jay. I did some work for his law firm."

Darryl had taken a great interest in Bruce's own job in law enforcement. He knows the structure of the agencies supervised by the drug czar quite well, and he had asked Bruce about particular individuals in the FBI and DEA. Bruce had told him some of the names sound familiar.

"You ought to find something here you like," Darryl says as Bruce joins him at a dealer's display booth. The names are evocative—Smith & Wesson .22, Colt .45, Mac 10, Glock 19, Beretta—like the names of horses or dogs or roses or vintage wines.

"Check this out. It's a Cobray M-11/9." The gun Darryl hands him looks crude and menacing, with its stubby barrel and angular pistol grip jutting out from the middle. It is the color of dead coal and weighs as much as a severed head.

"Nine millimeters," Darryl explains. "Thirty-two rounds. You just point it and mow the motherfuckers down." He turns to the dealer. "Can he try it?"

They stroll over to the firing range. Bruce aims at one of the man-shaped targets in front of the long earthen ramp. He squeezes the trigger. As the gun rocks in his hand, the target topples, patches swirling. The earth behind ripples. Shell casings fly past Bruce's face; one bounces off his windbreakered shoulder. He stops for an instant, his ears ringing, his nostrils burning. Then he lowers the gun, pointing toward the fallen target, and pulls. The crumpled silhouette freckles into blizzarding fragments. The gun is empty, its thirty-two slugs spent, but Bruce's finger keeps squeezing, urgently.

"Cool." Bruce hands Darryl the Cobray.

They turn in time to see the bride, helped by her husband, fire a bazooka at a battered van that has been parked as a target on top of an adjacent hill. The van shatters. Orange flame drills up into the gray sky as chunks of metal streak down. An orphaned tire bounces, rolls, wobbles, and falls. There are whoops of approval and scattered clapping.

"Hey, Darryl," the salesclerk says, looking up when the two, announced by jangling chimes, stride into the display room of Guns Galore of Middleburg, Virginia. The clerk, a guy in his late twenties dressed in the redneck uniform of checkered shirt, blue jeans, and boots, is demonstrating the use of a rifle with a laser scope to a middle-aged man. "So the bad guy comes in"—the clerk aims the rifle at Darryl—"and you got him nailed. See the laser?" A faint pink spot has appeared on Darryl's marine sweatshirt. "Gotcha."

Darryl growls. "Smile when you say that, boy."

The customer decids not to buy the rifle. The clerk—his name is Warren—joins Darryl and Bruce. "Y'all been up to the gun show?"

"Yeah. It wasn't much of a crowd."

"They were saying attendance is down this year. The economy. I don't believe it. The economy goes down, burglaries go up. That's good for business."

Bruce follows Darryl through a door into the firing range, a long, dimly lit corridor lined by booths. The place stinks of cordite and sweat.

"You load it this time," Darryl says after he has emptied the magazine.

Bruce loads the Beretta and fires off nine rounds at the bull's-eye target dangling on its wire like laundry on a clothesline. He pocks only the outer circles, and as a reward for his pains gets clipped on the arm by a flying shell. Darryl presses a button and the wires begin to move, drawing the target up to the booth to be replaced.

"Damn," Bruce says, taking off his earmuffs, "I'm pathetic."

"It's not a Cobray, man. You've got to aim."

Bruce decides not to buy a pistol today, but he takes a Form 4473 to fill out. He reads it aloud to Darryl as they sit eating barbecue in a diner by the side of the highway to Washington.

"Am I a drug addict? Am I a convicted felon? Am I mentally ill? Am I an illegal alien . . . Damn! They caught me on that one. My real name is Raoul Cortina."

"You serious about getting a gun?"

"Yeah. Probably."

"Tell you what." The ex-marine shifts in the booth. "I'll talk Warren back there into giving you a discount, if you do me a favor." Darryl wants him to buy a couple of other guns, for which Bruce will be reimbursed. "I've bought a couple under my own name in the last month, and I don't want my name kicked up on some computer somewhere. Don't worry. It's all legit, man. I wouldn't lie to you."

Bruce is suspicious, but he tries to look relaxed. "Well, I'll think about it. I have to make up my mind first whether I want to even buy a gun on my own."

"Sure. Of course."

Darryl sips his coffee. His eyes follow a truck down the highway. Bruce wonders, just who the hell *is* this guy?

The place is small—an elongated efficiency in the basement of an old town house a few blocks southeast of the Capitol. Thank God, Bruce thinks as he sets another box down, she didn't get an apartment on the top floor.

"You are so sweet," Allison says as he walks past her to get another load from the U-Haul truck her father has driven from St. Louis. "You are such a saint."

"Tell Stef what a saint I am," Bruce replies as Stef walks in, her thin arms holding up a chair. "She needs to be reminded."

"Are you guys talking about me behind my back?"

Allison's father is middle America: middle-aged, middle income, middle height, middlebrow. His daughter, too, belongs somewhere in the middle between extremes: she is not beautiful—her toothy mouth is too big, her blond hair is too obviously bleached—but she is not homely, either. As he puffs and pants with his arms around her possessions, Bruce cannot help undressing her in his imagination.

That night, lying next to Stef after making love to her in her apartment, Bruce wonders how the two bodies differ. He runs his hand down Stef's side, and she rolls over onto her back. As she does so, her breasts flatten and expand. Bruce has had sex with eight women—thirteen, if oral sex counts—and he never loses his amazement at the way a woman's naked body changes shape as she moves. As a teenager, beating off over copies of *Playboy* and *Penthouse*, he had imagined that women had firm bodies like plastic rafts, with breasts that maintained their shape like balloons in all positions. Real women spread and shrink and pool like globs of mercury.

He wonders what she will look like in ten or twenty years. Probably pretty good, he concludes. She is small and slender; it is hard to imagine her ballooning up. He wonders once again whether he should marry her. Again he weighs the pros and cons. On the pro side, she is a well-connected Washington professional woman. Power couples seem to be the trend, which is just as well, since Stef is too opinionated and intellectual to be an old-fashioned Washington hostess. On the con side, she is not as good in bed as some of his other girlfriends—especially Karen, back in college. But even Karen might get boring if he were married to her. He had to look for other qualities in a wife, in the mother of his children. Stef would not be the ideal homemaker and supermom, but that didn't really matter, because they could hire some Latin American woman to take care of the kids. As for kids, it was better to have them early, so Bruce would still be young when they went off to college. With adult children, there would be no reason to keep holding a stale marriage together, so Bruce could divorce the first wife and marry a younger woman and still be young enough, in early middle age, to enjoy her . . .

Bruce stares at the ceiling. Decisions, decisions.

"So who's your source?" Milligan asks.

Bruce squirms in his chair. It is one of those corporate power chairs, a mass of red leather bumps like blisters. There are several of them in Milligan's office.

"He insisted on strict confidentiality," Bruce answers, then, thinking that sounds too official, offers an emendation: "He made me swear not to tell."

Milligan leans back in his own power chair, which gives him an advantage of six inches or so over visitors. "Look, we can pass along tips without letting on where we got them. The FBI and the DEA don't share their sources with us, so turnabout's fair play. But within this office, we have to know. I have to know. Because if I end up looking like a fool, by God you're going with me. Just a friendly warning."

Bruce tells him. He describes the cryptic call he got from Darryl, who claimed a tenant had tipped him off about the location of the headquarters of the Florida Avenue Yungstaz, one of the gangs whose territory is a maze of felt marker scribblings and pushpins on the map of southeast D.C. in the drug czar's war room.

Milligan does not need to look at the map. When Bruce hands him the address Darryl gave him, Milligan can picture it in his mind. "That's . . . not implausible. So who's this guy Darryl?"

"He's an apartment manager for Henderson Properties. Jay Prentice Pierce's firm."

"Jay Pierce?" Mention of the talismanic name has its desired effect.

"Jay"—Bruce pretends to know the great man—"owns some apartments in Southeast that Darryl manages for him. Darryl finds things out from the tenants sometimes. You know."

"So what's this Darryl guy's angle? What's he after?"

"What do you mean?"

"Come on, man, wake up and smell the coffee. There must be a couple hundred people down there, maybe a thousand, who know where the Yungstaz keep their shit. And not one of them will talk, because they're scared shitless. Now why isn't this Darryl character scared shitless, too?"

"He was a marine?" Bruce suggests helpfully.

"I don't know." Milligan reaches into his pocket for a pack of cigarettes, then remembers that Mrs. Gutierrez, the drug czarina, has ordained that the workplace be smoke-free. Nicotine, too, is a drug. "There's something rotten in the state of Denmark."

Seeing his chances of glory fading, Bruce interjects, "What difference does it make? If that's the Yungstaz's headquarters, it's our duty to shut it down."

Milligan regards Bruce with a mixture of condescension and affection. "Well, thank you, Eliot Ness."

"The real money's going to be in Asia," Ross continues, climbing into the golf cart. He and Bruce are between holes on the country club course. "You can bust the unions by switching to Asian producers. And you don't have to worry about them raising wages, either." As he steers the cart, Ross explains how it is done. "Suppose the U.S. puts the screws on Indonesia to raise its wages. That just makes Vietnam more competitive. If Vietnam gets too expensive, there's Cambodia. One of these days, Burma's gonna be the hot place to invest, because of SLORC . . . "

"SLORC?"

"Their military junta. The State Law and Order Restoration Committee. Those guys are heavy-duty. The army enslaves the men and puts the women in rape camps."

"Jeez," says Bruce, finding the idea of rape camps mildly arousing.

"Take my word for it: Burma. That's the place, a few years from now. There ain't gonna be no labor movement under SLORC."

They move on from the seventh to the eighth of the nine holes they are playing. After Bruce swings, Ross asks: "So how serious are y'all?"

The question surprises Bruce. "I don't know. I've been thinking about getting a place with her . . . "

"Wait a minute." Ross demands silence as he putts. The ball rolls toward the hole, accompanied by Ross's sound track: "Sh-h-h-h-h-h-h-h . . . it." His next putt misses. "Make it five," Ross says, pocketing the ball. They start toward the next tee.

"It's none of my business," Ross continues, "but I think you ought to think about getting married. How old are you?"

"Twenty-six. Almost twenty-seven."

"Son, you need to be married. Otherwise folks are going to start to think you're some kind of faggot like me." Ross brings his iron down with a whoosh. He watches Bruce tee off, then goes on. "I don't hold for this shacking-up bullshit. Used to be only white trash did that. And hippies. If you're going to move in with her, you ought to marry her. This is Washington. This ain't Hollywood or Greenwich Village. You can't go up to the president and say, 'I'd like you to meet my significant other, the person whom I fuck but to whom I am not married.' That's not gonna hack it."

They stroll down the green. Ross directs Bruce's attention to the older man in the red jacket following one hole behind them. "See that? That's Rich Morgan, from Akin, Gump. Senior partner."

"Yeah?"

"Yeah. He's a gold-plated asshole."

After Ross putts, Bruce asks, "What about you? You ever think about getting married?"

"To a woman?"

"No. You know, a guy."

"Spare me, please," Ross drawls. "I don't want a wife."

"So you'd be the husband, huh?"

Ross smirks. "Let me let you in on a secret, partner. The real division in the world is not between heterosexuals and homosexuals. It's between tops and bottoms. Fuckers and fuckees. If you're a top, why the hell would you be in favor of gay marriage? You're probably bringing in most of the income, right? So if you have gay marriage, even though you're pulling in eighty percent of the money, the male wife gets fifty percent of the household assets. Fuck that shit." Ross purses his lips as he concentrates on a putt, then he relaxes. "Anyway, this whole gay marriage thing is just a big deal for lesbians. They want children. And to hell with that. I don't want some man-hating lesbians raising little children. They'll rebel in adolescence and turn into promiscuous heterosexuals . . . "

Bruce laughs.

". . . and hang out at straight bars," Ross continues, "and wear disco clothes and ask members of the opposite sex what their horoscope signs are . . ." Ross notices the team behind them motioning. "Fuck you, Rich Morgan. Lawyers are such assholes."

"You have a law degree."

"Hey, watch it. I'm not a lawyer. I do something productive for society. I'm a lobbyist."

Bruce wonders sometimes whether Ross secretly finds him attractive. Stef thinks not—according to Avery, Ross's taste runs toward small, dark-skinned guys like Avery himself—and Bruce can never catch Ross eyeing him when they hit the showers after a golf game. The gay men at the gym where Bruce works out are less discreet. Every third time he attends he finds himself being chatted up by some guy with overdeveloped abs and an effeminate voice.

One afternoon, while he is straining at the Nautilus in a pool of his own sweat, he hears a soft voice calling his name. He sees Allison approaching in the mirrored wall.

"Wow, what a small world," she says. "I joined here last week."

They chat for a while, about the apartment, Allison's new job, Washington. Allison's dyed blond hair is stringy with sweat. It gives her a slutty look, like the tight black gym pants. Bruce tries not to be caught looking at the wrinkled crotch. That night, when he is slamming into Stef, Bruce imagines that he is riding Allison.

First comes the screech of braking vans and squad cars, then the snap of doors, the slap of boots on pavement, and the bellowed order: "Freeze! Everybody freeze! Don't move! Freeze!"

All of a sudden they are everywhere—agents from the ATF and FBI in windbreakers and visor caps or riot helmets, District cops in uniform or undercover mufti, hollering, brandishing double-barreled shotguns, AR-15 assault rifles, 9 mm handguns. Squad cars block off each end of the street as police vans squeal to a stop in front of the row houses, doors rolling back to disgorge dozens of troops, leaping into the 'hood like paratroopers pouring from a plane's belly.

"Freeze! I said *freeze!*"

The cops converge on the half-block of row houses next to the vacant lot on the south side of the street. Teenagers, several men and women, are lying down as ordered, guarded by cops with shotguns. Faces to the ground, they can hear but cannot see the booted officers racing past into the first of the apartment houses.

The popcorn clatter of gunfire. Officers bark orders into walkie-talkies. A policeman wielding a rifle is waving from a rooftop.

"Cut 'em off!"

Siren blurting abruptly, a squad car lunges into the vacant lot and bumps over the rubble into the alley.

"Freeze, asshole!"

Bruce, carrying his walkie-talkie upside down, dashes up to one of the vans in the lead. "Looks like we got a lot of them," he tells a cop as he kneels beside him.

The cop turns and glares at him, then barks: "Get the fucking civilians out of here!"

"Mr. Brandt, do you mind staying back here?" his guide from the DEA says wearily. Bruce is annoyed. He has every right to be in on the action, sharing the glory. He is the personal representative of Mrs. Gutierrez. What is more, he is responsible for this raid. It was he who relayed the tip from Darryl.

In a few minutes, a dozen cops escort half a dozen young men from the alley, hands cuffed behind their backs. Among them is the leader of the Yungstaz, Chuck E. His face is bloody and bruised. He spits and curses as he is forced to lie down in the street next to his soldiers.

Through the overcast sky overhead a chopper is thumping its ominous way. Standing petrified in front of a row house, a little boy stares, his pants darkened by a spreading stain.

Bruce has never felt so alive.

16

Like a castle augmented over many ages, the whitish cube is a compilation of patches and parts. The original building had been the servant's quarters in the alley behind a fancy town house. Over a century the block of row houses had grown up all around, like a coral reef, turning the alley into a court commanded by what the residents of the 'hood now call "the Bunker." The name fits. Most of the windows have been bricked in, something that layers of whitewash could not hide. The windows that remain, with their iron bars, resemble monstrous eyes peering through monstrous black lashes at anyone crossing the asphalt moat.

"Turn it off," Willie orders as Evander manipulates the radio. They are sitting in a car parked strategically next to the alley that connects the court to the street. Willie wants to be able to hear, in case anything goes down inside the Bunker.

"Who is this dude?" Evander asks. "Darryl."

"He a straw," Willie explains. "A straw man buyer, you know? He buy guns in Virginia under his name, with our money. He some kind of real estate manager. You know that place on Eighth? And that place down by the river? It's all in his name. His company's name." Willie fingers the AK-47 nested near his foot. "He some kind of marine."

Somebody is coming out of the Bunker—Daquan, who, in his twenties, is one of the senior members of the Krew. Daquan strolls over to the car.

"Man, they got some hype shit down there. It's like the

National Guard Armory. Come on, we need some help, Deuce. Willie, Frizzell say you stay here and keep an eye out."

Evander gets out of the car. Daquan signals, and a van waiting in the street enters the alley, turns around, and backs up into the cage next to the Bunker. The cage, with wire across the top as well as the sides, permits a car to serve as a shield against enemy fire while the side door is unlocked.

The massive door of the Bunker opens into a small office, with stairs leading to the second story. Most of the Bunker is occupied by a single large room, like a garage. It smells of dust. A section of floor has been lifted and pulled back. A cement stairway slants into a basement lit by bulbs like burning skulls. Those bulbs illuminate the first faces that Evander sees in the basement—Frizzell's, his number one lieutenant Tito's, and Darryl Shelton's, a pale oval bisected by a dark mustache. The three look tense.

"Come on. Boogie," Frizzell barks.

There are dozens of guns, maybe hundreds. A dozen kinds of pistols. Shotguns. Rifles. AKs. A metal-haloed Street Sweeper.

Daquan motions toward a locker. "Come on, Deuce." Evander picks it up, trying to guess how many guns it contains. As he struggles backward up the cement steps, he glimpses the leaders of the Krew again. Frizzell is talking to the unreadable Darryl. Behind Frizzell, Tito is glaring, with a look that strikes Evander as hostile. He is glaring at Frizzell.

Later Evander will reconstruct the events in a way that makes his memories more coherent than the experience. What happens is confusion, a sequence of vivid scenes. A row of old buildings, dark after hours, the brick facades splashed by a streetlight's circle. Shadowy shapes in a corner basketball court. The face of Willie, next to Evander in the car, assuming a look of rapt intensity as the Cobray swings toward the window. The shrieking tires, and then the pressure pushing Evander back into the car seat. The popping. The screams—or maybe the sound is merely the plaint of the tires. When Evander remembers it all later, the sound is definitely screaming.

"They coming? They coming?" Patrick the driver is still crying out, almost hysterical, even after he has put several blocks between them and the basketball court.

"Nobody," Evander reports, watching the block recede.

A horn blares as a truck swerves to avoid them.

"Muthafucka, watch the road."

"Fuck you."

"Hey. Y'all chill."

They sit silent for a moment in the darkened, hurtling car as the barren blocks drift past. The car smells of cordite. Evander cannot believe it all happened so fast.

"Yo, Patrick. Turn on the radio, man."

The speakers begin blasting out a pulsing rap tune. With a trembling hand, the same hand that sprayed bullets at the kids on the corner, Willie opens the beer Evander hands him.

"I got a couple," Willie avers. "I lit they asses up. I know it."

The car's tires scream as Patrick makes a high-speed turn onto Sherman Avenue.

"Lookout, man," says Pharo, sitting in the front seat with Patrick, "wherever you are, my brother, we paid 'em back. We surely did."

"Yeah," says Willie in a flat tone that makes his words all the more ominous. "And from now on they gonna be looking to pay us back."

Like a lion tamer, the scowling rapper in his jumpsuit and shades paces back and forth before the audience he has whipped into a roar. Every rhyme he barks into the wireless mike in his hand is a crack of the lash stinging the mob into a greater frenzy.

Evander is stumbling through the chanting, swaying throng. Spotlights rake the rows of hands. Every few seconds the light washes like a breaker across Evander, then he is plunged into blackness again. It is wartime, it is the blitz, the searchlights are scanning for bombers while the screaming city shudders beneath regular percussive blasts. The hammering beat coaxes his heart into sync with it; part of him wants to abandon himself to the amplified throbbing, to become one more stalk of grass in this field riffled by the thundering gale from the stage. But abandon is not part of the gangsta's code, not abandon in public, not here, in the Go-Go Palace on H Street, where at any moment the crowd might part to reveal an archenemy, a Yungsta, strapped and ready to take you out. This may be a carnival, but it is not a holiday; the club is a jungle through which Evander makes his own trail.

At the edge of the dance floor the crowd dissolves into lesser tangles. The young street soldier saunters through the zebra light, impassive, scanning every face. IFF. Identification: Friend or Foe. He spots Willy, and hands entwine in the ritual clasp.

"Check this out," Willy bellows hoarsely above the drone of the rapper and the thunder of the crowd. "Dude got a camera."

Evander takes a drag on the blunt he is handed and follows the gaze of his homeboys. Three girls are shaking furiously in front of a man with a handheld videocassette recorder. Around them, a crowd of jeering spectators is beginning to coalesce.

"Ooh, baby! What we got here?" booms a familiar voice. Evander turns, and sees Frizzell and an entourage of half a dozen lieutenants sweeping past like a Renaissance warlord and his men promenading at a ball. Evander takes another toke, breathing in the sickly-sweet marijuana fumes, and watches Frizzell swagger toward the artist and his models. Maybe the cameraman recognizes Frizzell, or maybe the sight of a thickset gangsta in a black sweatshirt, torques of glimmering gold and shades, intimidates him. Whatever the reason, the man with the video recorder does not protest as Frizzell inserts himself among the three women, bumping and thrusting with hips bigger than theirs.

Now Evander is feeling the rush. He joins Willy in cackling and pointing as the chorus line turns into a duet between Frizzell and a busty woman shaking her head as if in a trance. The cameraman circles, recording it all, as the woman peels off her tank top and shakes her bouncing breasts in front of Frizzell's belly, wobbling globes that flare and fade with each pass of the spotlight.

Evander turns away, shaking his head in disbelief, and so he misses the start of it. But he catches the rest of the fight, sees the skinny youth who has appeared from nowhere slapping the topless dancer while she claws back at him and shrieks, and stares as members of the Krew converge on the hysterical man. Now the skinny kid is writhing on the floor while Frizzell kicks him, hard.

"She that dude's bitch." Willy laughs. "*Was* his bitch. Ain't no mo'."

Several soldiers of the Krew drag the pummeled lover away into the shadows. In a series of lightning-lit tableau, as in a stop-action film, the topless dancer, more angry than hurt, puts her halter back on and then strides toward the exit at Frizzell's side, through waves of flash and darkness. Evander and Willy fall in with the set.

Firecrackers clatter. Somebody, running, slams into Evander. The force of the collision sends him staggering, bumping into others. More crackling shots, and screams, almost lost in the thud and screech of the music. At first the intermittent lightning shows Evander nothing but astonished faces making mouths like O's; then he glimpses Frizzell on the floor, propped up in somebody's arms, a look of utter surprise on his face.

Willy's gun is drawn, raised in the air. Evander reaches into his high-top and pulls out his nine. He plants his feet on the floor like a cop or a commando and stands there, washed by light and music, pulse panicking, pistol ready. With a crunch, the music dies, permitting the sirens to be heard.

Two days after he is admitted, Frizzell checks out of the hospital. The members of the Krew are told that he is undergoing private treatment at a place that has to be kept secret so that the Yungstaz do not hunt him down.

From Willy, Evander hears another explanation. "They saying that Frizzell is hiding from Tito." Tito has taken over the leadership of the Krew in Frizzell's absence.

Evander emulates Willy, and glances around to make sure they are not overheard. They are standing on a street corner at sunset.

"They saying Tito, he don't want Frizzell to come back," Willy continues quietly. "They saying he hired this dude from Philadelphia. A hit man. He'll get three thousand if he pop Frizzell."

"Shit," says Evander. "Who saying that?"

Willy's face eclipses the red sun. "People."

Blood-colored light seeps through clouds textured like gauze. The world was menacing before, but Evander felt safe in the fraternity of the Krew. Now there is no safety in the world.

17

Avery ostentatiously sits throughout the standing ovation. The show is a Kennedy Center salute to America's jazz greats. Avery has hated every minute of it, for reasons he explains to Ouida Covington over supper at his favorite French restaurant in Georgetown.

"Jazz is supposed to be raunchy and crude, it's whorehouse music, not Art with a capital A," he says, or rather declaims. "Those giant screens around the stage with the blowup photos— it was like a museum. And half those guys looked like they were dead. They were mummified."

Ouida is watching him, rapt in the candlelight.

"It's the French influence," Avery explains, warming to one of his favorite theories. "See, the problem with jazz is Paris. In Paris, in the twenties and thirties, they turned jazz into an art, they made it hoity-toity, something snobby white people in berets could brag about listening to. But in Germany, in Weimar Germany, jazz was still whorehouse music. Only it became cabaret music. Here you had this form created by the most oppressed class of people in America, and it got picked up by these marginal rebels in this bitter, defeated nation. You know Brecht and Weill, don't you? That stuff is harsh. It has an edge to it. Tinny pianos, transvestites, Nazis and Communists rioting in the streets. Not like this I-am-the-talk-of-Paris-watch-me-jack-off jazz solo bull-shit."

Her gaze, attentive to the point of adoration, encourages him, an actor before an audience demanding an encore. "They took our music, black music, and made it better in Germany, see. And sometimes when we took it back, we made it worse. Like Louis Armstrong. The version he did of 'Mack the Knife.' It sucks. It's all watered-down, happy, big-band music. It's awful. The original is chilling."

"'Mack the Knife' is a German song?"

"Yeah. From *Die Dreigroschenoper*—*The Threepenny Opera*—by Bert Brecht and Kurt Weill." Avery starts to sing, in his flawless, practiced German: *"Und der Haifisch hat die Zähne . . . "*

People at other candle-rubied tables turn to look.

"They're going to throw us out of here." Ouida laughs.

"What's the matter?" Avery mutters. "Ain't they never seen a black man singing a German *Morität* before?"

Avery had discovered Brecht and Weill during his high school years at Sidwell Friends. The irreverence of the Weimar songsters had appealed to an adolescent disgusted by the sanctimonious liberalism of his milieu. He might have become a left-wing radical, but that was too acceptable in the circles of his parents and his friends, so he rebelled by becoming a Republican and a Germanophile. At Georgetown he had been fond of shocking the radicals in the Black Students Association by telling them their contrast of Africans with unmusical, scientific Caucasians was all wrong; the Germans, the whitest of white people, the ultimate racists, were not only the world's greatest scientists but the world's greatest musicians. All the jazz and soul and blues ever written was not worth a bar of Wagner. Naturally, most of the other black students had hated him, and he had reciprocated their hatred. He had nothing but contempt for people whose idea of helping black Americans was writing letters to the Georgetown student newspaper claiming Beethoven or Cleopatra for the race.

"We lived in Germany for a while, when my father was in the army," Ouida tells Avery as he steers the car around the floodlit mall. He is enjoying their conversation, and he wants to share one of his pleasures with her, the pleasure of driving at night among the white monuments. "I didn't like the Germans," she says.

"Did you speak any German?"

"Just a few words."

"Well, then, how can you say you didn't like the Germans? You were living in this little bubble full of Americans, and the people were just part of the landscape. And the Germans a GI's family would deal with, well, let's say that they're not the cream of the crop." Avery has to defend his beloved Germans. "I spent a summer there, after my junior year in college, going around the youth hostels. Yeah, there are racists, but I'd rather be in a small town in Bavaria than in northern Florida or Howard Beach."

"Did you have German boyfriends?"

He shifts uncomfortably. The Jefferson Memorial drifts across the windshield. "Yeah." In Germany that summer, enjoying the freedom of anonymity, he had made love to other men for the first time.

"Have you ever had any girlfriends?"

"What is this, an FBI background check?"

"I had a girlfriend, once," she confides. "In college. We used to fool around."

"Really."

"A lot of people are bi. They just think they have to go one way or the other."

Jesus Christ, he thinks as the white mountain of the Kennedy Center they had left a few hours earlier rises into view, she wants to convert me.

"Do you ever think about having children?" she asks.

"Sometimes."

"You could adopt."

"Naw, I'd do it the old-fashioned way."

"Would you enjoy it?"

"Well, it's hard not to . . . I mean, unless you really hate women. I mean, I know some guys who would just die if they touched a woman, but I'm not that way. I had girlfriends in college. I liked it. What's not to like? It's just . . . Well, you don't want to hear about it."

"Yes, I do."

"Well, a man . . . I don't know. It's the broad shoulders, and the deep voice . . . It just feels right. It's not just a sexual thing, it's an emotional thing. It just feels right. It feels natural. In private. Not in public. It doesn't feel right in public."

"What do you mean?"

"Well, you can't go around as a couple. Oh, you can, but everybody will stare at you. 'Look at them, they're queer.' A man and a woman, people take it for granted. I think that's why all these gay rock stars and designers get married. Parties and openings. It's easier to introduce your wife than your significant other, Bob. Everybody knows they're gay, or bi. Sometimes both of them. They have these open marriages. He has his boyfriends, she has her girlfriends, and they sleep with each other, too, it's cool. You have to watch out for AIDS, I guess, but that's no different than for gay couples."

He realizes he is probably revealing too much as he takes them toward the white dome of the Capitol, but he can tell she is hungry for everything he can say, hungry for his body, hungry for his soul. He is not in love, but he knows he is loved, even adored, and he finds himself enjoying the experience.

"She's lying," Stef tells him. "I don't believe it."

They are having croissants downtown at Au Bon Pain. Avery has told her about his discussions with Ouida.

"She may tell you it's okay for you to sleep around with other guys," Stef continues, "she may tell you that now, but wait till you're married. And all this stuff about having children . . . "

"I want to have children," Avery protests.

"Yeah, but will you ever get to see them? What if she decides to get a divorce once you've served your biological purpose and fathered her children . . . "

"I can't believe you. I thought you were her friend."

"I am. I guess. But I was your friend before I ever knew her."

Furious, Avery looks out through the glass onto the afternoon bustle.

"Hey, I'm sorry, okay?" She reaches out and touches his hand lightly.

"You're just jealous."

"Yeah, right."

"It's true." Avery smiles. "All women find me incredibly attractive. You know the way women are always complaining about how all the good-looking, intelligent men are gay? Well, I'm the one they're talking about."

"Listen to you. Jesus Christ."

"You're just jealous. You want to bear my children, too."

"Yeah, right. And do your laundry. And cook your supper. That's what you really want."

"Only if she insists."

Their lips part. They draw apart on the couch in Avery's apartment, dissatisfied.

Avery takes Ouida's hand in his and connects her fingers like strings of an abacus. Then he puts her hand between his legs. He starts to get hard again. Then he loses it as she slides down, setting her head in his lap, the way he used to nest his head in Ross's lap.

"This is nice," she says quietly.

This is not working, he thinks. He smiles at her, but he feels his disquiet deepening. This is not right. It just does not fit.

Maybe he has changed since college. In the past few days, preparing himself to make love with Ouida, he has thought back on his two girlfriends at Georgetown. He had realized that, though he remembered sex with them as a pleasant experience, he never fantasized about their bodies, only about the bodies of his men.

"Avery?"

"Mmm."

"Let's take our time."

"Okay."

He strokes the textured cap of her hair, and leans back on the sofa and listens to the stereo. Siegfried, emerging from the cave, is singing to Brünnhilde. The Valkyries join in. The dawn sun, awakened by their aria, turns every pine on the alpine hillside into a green torch.

After he drops her off, he drives around for a while, brooding. He is angry, but he is not sure at whom, or why.

Thirsty, he parks in front of a convenience store in the row house neighborhood east of the luminous Capitol. He realizes that he and Ouida drank all his sodas; he takes his satchel, big enough for a couple of six-packs. As he enters the small store he hears a buzzing sound.

He thinks no more about it until he sets the two six-packs of soda on the counter in front of the little Korean woman. Only then does he realize that her sons have stationed themselves at the four corners of the store. He glances at the squat, burly young man watching him from the door with arms crossed.

"You open bag," the woman orders.

"Excuse me?"

"You open bag. No bag in store. We check."

Anger flares in Avery. "Excuse me, but I don't see a sign."

"No bag in store."

One of the Korean teenagers starts toward him. "Hey, I just want to get some sodas."

"No bag in store. He check."

Avery pulls his satchel away from the Korean youth. "You don't touch my bag, man. You people don't understand this country. You don't have the right of search and seizure."

"You black people," the old lady is shouting, "you come in here, you steal."

"All right, that does it," Avery says, his voice trembling. "You're not getting my business."

"I no want your business." As he starts toward the door, he hears the woman shouting something in Korean. A brother materializes and joins the burly kid in blocking the door.

"So you're not going to let me leave?"

"We check bag. Then you go."

"Well, you are not checking my bag. I don't have to put up with this shit. You can call the police if you want to."

"Fine."

"Fine. Call 'em."

Avery, shuddering with an adrenaline rush, watches the lady pick up the phone. "Man, I can't believe this. This is unreal. I'm going to sue you people for everything you've got. You aren't going to have enough money for a fucking plane ticket back to fucking Korea!"

Arms crossed, the sons scowl and stare.

18

"It's too long," Evander insists.

"No, it's not," Curtis says. "You don't want your wrists sticking out. Turn around. All right, look in the mirror."

The adolescent saunters over to the triple mirror with his best street moves, shoulders sloped, head thrust forward, body moving with an exaggerated swing from side to side. Curtis suppresses a smile. It looks peculiar, a kid in a suit doing a pimp roll.

Evander leans his head to one side, scowling like a petulant child, as his uncle feels the back of the suit.

"Can you take it in here in back?" Curtis asks the salesclerk, a young white man.

"Certainly."

As the clerk marks the sleeves and cuffs with chalk, Evander squirms. Curtis knows his nephew hates being here. Let him suffer, Curtis thinks. It's his duty. The boy has to have a suit ready to wear for his grandfather's funeral.

The end might come any day now. The old man, propped up on his hospital bed, looks better than he has for several days, but he is still a shriveled remnant of what he had been only a month ago.

"I brought you some cookies," Curtis tells Dad Johnson, his voice raised. "I hope they don't catch us."

"They threw out those green beans I made for him," Velma complains. "I put 'em in the refrigerator down the hall. But somebody'd left something in there too long, and it was stinking

up the place something awful. So they just went and threw everything out. Didn't ask nobody nothing. I'll try to bring some more
green beans tomorrow, Daddy. Cooked the way you like. Like
Momma used to make 'em. With bacon."

If the old man is listening, he shows no sign. Since it became
clear that the end was not far off, Velma has been sitting with her
father for hours when she is off duty in the other part of the hospital. Usually taciturn, Velma is showing an unusual tendency to
ramble, less to make her father feel comfortable than to stave off
the silence. With the same purpose the TV is going constantly,
adding its babble to the voices that are keeping the encroaching
nothingness beyond the perimeters of the dark and acrid room.
The screen glows all night long, a blue glow like a campfire warding off yellow eyes.

"I brought your nightgown," Curtis tells his wife.

"Thank you, baby."

For three weeks, after the first stroke, Velma and Curtis tried
to take care of Dad Johnson at home. Curtis had surrendered his
sofa bed in the living room, and he and Velma had taken turns
helping the old man relieve himself in the portable potty they had
smuggled from the hospital. Curtis understood now what the
phrase "second childhood" meant; he told Velma they were expe-
riencing their second adulthood. Having raised their children,
they were now parenting a parent.

As always, Curtis did his duty without cheerfulness but without complaint. A long time ago, he had developed the ability to
turn off natural feelings of disgust, whether at the stink of a
buddy's infected arm in Vietnam or the odor from the old man
that scrub baths and air freshener could not drive from the house.
Curtis did his duty and hoped that he would die before it was
ever necessary for Velma, if she survived him, or the kids to take
care of him as they were taking care of the old man.

One by one, most of the far-flung members of the clan gathered to see Dad Johnson for the last time. Curtis and Velma's
youngest, their daughter Lorena, came up from Atlanta. Their
married daughter Marilyn could not afford to take time off from
her job in San Diego; she agreed with her parents that it would
be best if she waited to fly in for the funeral.

By this time, Dad Johnson is too far gone to know who was visiting him, anyway. He has begun to ask where his wife is, and they stop reminding him she has died. A doctor asks him where he is, and he says matter-of-factly, "Baltimore." He thinks a sharply dressed black man he glimpsed in the hall is his employer of many years, the owner of the Baltimore funeral home. As he shrinks, his honey-colored skin tightening around his skeleton, he drifts further back, into the fifties, the forties, the thirties. The movie is being rewound.

One night Velma is awakened by a sound. Her father is answering the darkness at the foot of his bed. "I swear," Velma tells Curtis later, "they was other voices." The old man has been talking to his parents.

The house is a big two-story place on a suburban side street, lagooned in a darkness made deeper by the way the tall trees screen out the glow from a solitary streetlight. Most of these calls turn out to be false alarms; still, Curtis feels a tingling anxiety grow as he makes his way around the side of the house, the beam from his flashlight ghosting across brick and wood as he looks for a broken window or a half-open door. Somebody could be there waiting, ready to lunge or shoot at him without a second's warning. That had happened a few years ago, when Curtis had worn a shield for the D.C. force. He and a handful of other officers had been ready to call off their search of a shadowy apartment stairwell when the fugitive had fired. One bullet had whizzed past Curtis's ear; another had shattered a comrade's shoulder.

Seeing a shadowy figure at the edge of the front yard, Curtis flinches and reaches for his pistol. To his relief and embarrassment, he discovers that a neighbor has come to learn why a Neighborhood Patrol car is parked in front. Moments later, a squad car from the Arlington Police Department pulls up.

Curtis's shift is half over by the time he finishes the paperwork and sets off again on his solitary patrol. Before resuming his rounds, he stops off at an all-night convenience store, a glass and metal prism in a dome of glare by the highway. WE HAVE ICE, boasts the floodlit sign above the parking lot. That is how everybody knows the place; when its present owner bought it a few years back, We Have Ice became the official name in the phone book.

"How you doing tonight, boss?" the Lebanese immigrant manager asks Curtis as he returns from the bathroom the management lets him use. In the round mirror overlooking the cash register, Curtis sees himself reflected, a fat black man in a uniform.

"Huntin' the almighty dollar," Curtis replies. "Can't kill nothin', and won't nothin' die." The management supplies him with coffee without charge. They like to have a police car regularly parked in front of We Have Ice, if only that of a private security agency. "Gimme two of the Match Prize."

The manager hands Curtis his lottery tickets with his change. "One of these days you gonna win the jackpot, boss."

"I already won something, once."

"Oh, yeah?"

"Yeah, I won fifty dollars. And my cousin-in-law, she won two hundred in that Safeway contest." Curtis takes a sip from his coffee before pressing a plastic lid down on it. "Did I tell you I'm working on my second million?"

"Yeah?"

"Yeah." Curtis smiles slightly. "I done give up on my first."

Curtis abbreviates his usual rounds to make up for the time lost because of the false alarm. For the last eight months Neighborhood Patrol has assigned him to this Arlington suburb, a motley neighborhood squeezed in between the highway and Wilson Boulevard. Bit by bit, high-rises and malls are springing up, but the process is far from complete, so there can be striking incongruities—a new apartment block overshadowing a modest single-family home built after World War II in Tudor-cottage style; a Methodist church, all brick and white trim, squeezed between a parking lot and a prismatic office tower.

The neighborhood is a safe one, much safer than Curtis's own neighborhood in southeast Washington, so that policing it is an easy job. Curtis spends most evenings cruising up and down the leafy streets and listening to AM talk radio, following the debates over crime or taxes or illegitimacy, now growing angry, now laughing out loud. He misses having a partner in his patrol car to debate the state of the nation and the world, but that is about the only thing he misses about his lost job with the department. At fifty-two, he looks forward to a decade of ease in the private security business; his retirement has already begun.

"All right," the talk radio host is saying, "the question before us is whether we would have less crime if we just did what the Arabs do—cut off the hands of thieves. Just cut off their hands. Should we maim criminals? The lines are open."

Cut 'em off, Curtis thinks. He has grown hard after many years wearing a shield. In his youth, he had raised a lot of hell. Once, when he was in high school, he and a few other members of the football team had been drinking and zooming down a country road in what was now a subdivision near this Arlington neighborhood. They had been pulled over by white cops, two of them, an old redneck with a beer gut and a kid who hardly looked old enough to drive.

"What you been drinkin', nigger?" The fat one pushed Curtis around to impress his junior partner. Curtis remembers how frightened he was. They could torture you, even shoot you and leave you dead by the side of the road, and any white Virginia jury would have let them off. "Nigger *attacked* me! . . . " Curtis's heart had throbbed like a rabbit until he saw the look of fear and alarm and sympathy on the skinny white kid's face. The boy was more afraid of the fat man than Curtis was—afraid that his superior would see that he was feeling sorry for Curtis and his friends. Suddenly Curtis had felt sympathy for him, for this scrawny child dressed up in a man's uniform. It made no sense, but Curtis had felt pity for a white kid trying to kill the pity in himself. Later Curtis would see that look on the faces of other men, of all races and ages, in Vietnam, and later still in the mean streets of the District, the look of the conscientious fellow hanging back, afraid to break with the mob but afraid to wholly corrupt himself by joining in. There were troubled, humane, decent people like that in every mob.

Not that they would lift a finger to help you while their buddies were beating the crap out of you.

It was because of that night that Curtis wore a uniform. He went into the service so that people would look at his clothes and not at his skin, at his rank rather than his race. And so that he would never have to wait on white folks, as his forebears had done. His grandfather had been a Pullman porter. Curtis remembers him as a stately old gentleman, always dressed to the nines, with a pocket watch that he checked frequently and with great drama as though he was still clocking trains. Curtis's father had worked in the shipyards in Newport News, Virginia, until he had severely sprained his back. In his later years, after moving the family to Washington, the old man had supplemented his disability payments by mowing lawns. Curtis had despised his father for that. And now here Curtis is, protecting the homes of white folks from people who look like him.

But then, he doesn't think of them as his people. Black or white, burglars deserve to have their hands cut off.

The preacher at the African Methodist Episcopal Church that Curtis and Velma have been attending for many years is always referred to as Doctor Theodore Cameron. He is a tall man, built like a football player, and made all the more imposing by his silver hair and his slightly old-fashioned dress: a three-piece suit with a handkerchief tucked in the pocket.

"You know he was a lay preacher for many years," Curtis murmurs to Doctor Cameron as they pause in the doorway. Inside, gathered around Dad Johnson's bed, are Velma, Sharonda and her little ones, Gram, and Evander in his new suit. "He used to preach to prisoners."

"I did not know that," says Doctor Cameron.

"He's a good man," Curtis says with a tremble in his voice. "We've got to cross him over right."

"We surely do, Curtis." The tall preacher locks Dad Johnson's withered golden hand in the brown knot of his own. His reverberant voice booms. "Brother Johnson, are you right?"

The old man stammers.

"Are you right, Brother Johnson? *Are you right with God*?"

"I hope so," the old man wheezes. "I hope so."

"Brother Johnson, you've been right with the Lord for a long time. You were saved a long time ago. And you've been showing your fellowman the way to salvation for many years."

Tears are streaming down Velma's face, and her sister-in-law Sharonda is sobbing. Curtis feels his lip trembling uncontrollably.

"They tell me you used to preach in the prisons."

"Yes, sir," the old man says. "I used to tell 'em about Jesus driving the money changers from the temple. With a cat-o'-nine-tails. That's a whip, you see."

"It surely is."

"I used to tell 'em, he whipped the devil out of 'em. That used to make 'em sit up." The old man chuckles, then struggles for breath.

"Brother Johnson, will you pray with me?"

"Yes, sir."

"Let us pray."

The tears are spilling from Curtis's eyes now. Everyone is crying, the little children, because they do not understand, and the adults, because they do. Even Evander turns away, to hide a response that, with the ignorance of youth, he mistakes for weakness.

And then, as Doctor Cameron prays, the lights in the room seem to take on a softer glow. For a moment or so, it seems to Curtis, the din of the hospital grows faint, and the electric light becomes a warm haze, and the grief of the people sobbing in the room is transmuted to a kind of joy.

In his headlights, the air is scaly with rain. For long, oozing, expanding minutes Curtis sits listening to the crackle of the squad-car radio and the squeak of the wipers and staring at the evanescent streetscapes they paint on the melting windshield. The taillights of the Porsche 911 gaze back at him, the eyes of a luminescent monster from the watery night waiting for him to emerge from the bathyscaphe of his car. The wipers complain, and the radio crackles, and his pulse thunders in him with a fear he has not felt since Vietnam.

He had noticed that the car was speeding a few blocks back. Then he had seen it begin to swerve from one side of the street to the other. The odds are that the driver lives in this elegant northern Virginia neighborhood that he patrols for Sentinel Security four nights a week: a suburban executive coming back from too many hours at the bar, or maybe a rich kid who is drunk or high. The chances are low that the driver is a criminal or a psychopath from the other side of the Potomac who is waiting for Curtis with a semiautomatic. The chances are low, but they are not low enough.

He gets out of the car, leaving the door open as a shield in case he must dive back under fire. The driving rain pelts him as he shines the torch beam toward the sports car. The daub of glow snails over the fender and the trunk and lights up the inside in a snowy glitter. The reflection of the beam from the rearview mirror is like a camera's flash, imprinting in Curtis's memory the silhouetted interior, the head and shoulders of the driver. Maybe there are passengers hunched down in the front or backseat. Maybe as he approaches the shadows will swing up, and the semiautomatics begin to chatter . . .

His gun drawn, his torch the hilt of a lance of light, Curtis slowly moves closer. His own car seems so impossibly far away now, the twin bars of its headlights measuring the distance to safety. If anything happens, he will never make it back behind the door.

He lunges at the car. The beam fills the cubic space; the light is so intense the driver winces and looks away. There is nobody there but the driver, a young black man. A current of fear jolts through Curtis. A gangsta.

"Let me see your license," he barks through the half-lowered window.

"What am I accused of?"

Curtis applies the spotlight to the kid's face as though it were a brand pressed into a calf's side. "Shut up and give me your license."

"Aren't you supposed to read me my rights?" He does not sound like a homeboy. His English is clipped, educated, white.

Icy water is rippling down Curtis's face. His uniform clings like a filmy skin. "Get out of the car. Get out of the car, muthafucka."

Curtis must sound as though he means business, because the kid complies. The driver winces as a sheet of rain shatters across them.

"You ain't gonna melt."

"I'll catch pneumonia."

"Shut up. Put your hands on the car."

Curtis pats him down. He takes out his wallet and shines the torch on it.

"You see my name? You ever heard of Amy Brackenridge? On the D.C. Council? I'm Avery Brackenridge. Amy Brackenridge's son."

"Say what?"

"Just remember who you're messing with, asshole. I'm Amy Brackenridge's son."

So the kid isn't a gangsta. He's some kind of a spoiled brat. Rage dizzies Curtis. "I don't give a shit who you are, muthafucka. You under arrest." Curtis pulls the kid's hands behind his back and reaches for the cuffs. The kid wrests himself away. Curtis reaches for him and slips, or is pushed, crashing onto the wet asphalt, slamming his head against the side of the car on the way down.

For a few seconds, he is disoriented, groping in puddled ice water by the light of his own car's headlights. Then he pulls himself up, dripping. Lights are going on up and down the block. He glimpses people on porches, staring. They are actors on a stage made by headlights, he, soaked and furious, and the kid, hovering in the shimmering storm, half defiant, half afraid.

"Get your hands back on the car, muthafucka." Curtis gives him a shove.

"Man, you are gonna . . . My mother's gonna kill you, man. You're hurting me!"

Curtis snaps the cuffs on. "You have the right to remain silent . . . "

"Oh, shit! Shit! You're breaking my arm! Goddamn motherfucker."

". . . anything you say may be held against you . . . "

"Fucking Uncle Tom nigger! Shit! Goddamn motherfucking rent-a-cop. That's all you are. Motherfucking rent-a-nigger!"

Curtis slams the kid's head against the car's trunk.

"Rent-a-nigger!"

Avery gasps as Curtis grips his head and with it hammers the cold rain-rivered metal, again, again, again, again.

19

Curtis Hawkins is black.

He invites Stef into the small old house and asks if he can get her anything to drink. She declines. *Curtis Hawkins is black.* She hopes her surprise does not show. Most of the policemen in the District, after all, are black. She should not have assumed that the cop who beat up Avery was a white man. But police brutality . . . All of the images in Stef's mind come from newsreels and photos from the era of Martin Luther King. White cops in the South beating up young black men.

Curtis Hawkins is black. Stef realizes that she is not going to be able to write the story she had planned.

"I swear he hit me," Curtis is soon telling her. "One minute I'm standing there next to him, and the next minute, boom, I'm on the ground . . . Look, the company told me not to talk to reporters, but they stopped paying my salary. I don't owe them nothing. They're the ones being sued, not me. I don't own any assets. They want to collect from me, they'll go broke, that's the way I look at it."

Despite herself, Stef finds herself liking this chubby police force veteran. She wonders what he would think if he knew the reporter *Perspective* has assigned to do the definitive article on the controversy is Avery Brackenridge's best friend.

"I don't have anything against the boy," Curtis says. "He was just a little drunk. Many a time when I was his age I did the same thing. But he just went crazy. Started popping off. And then he hit me. I swear he knocked me down."

With growing disquiet, Stef realizes that she can easily imagine Avery losing his temper, shouting at the cop, maybe shoving him.

"I would have let him go with a citation," Curtis is saying. "If he'd just sobered up and promised to drive back home. Maybe I should have just let him go. If I'd known all this was going to happen, I tell you, I would have escorted him right back to his momma's house, sirens blaring, like he was a head of state or something. Yessiree. It just goes to show you, there's a double standard. The law is different for the high and mighty, and for folks like you and me . . . What's your name, Stephanie? People like us, the little guy, we get none of the credit and all of the blame."

Stef feels ill.

"I think it has to make a difference," Stef says at the line-up meeting. "This is not just a simple story about racism."

"It's a young black man being beaten up by the police," Ouida replies.

"It's a young black man being beaten up by another black man."

"In the service of white people."

"How do you know? How do you know there aren't black people in that neighborhood?"

Stef has never seen Ouida so intense. "It's structural racism. Keep the blacks in line by turning them against each other."

"That is so paranoid," Stef exclaims in exasperation. She is aware that the other editors are watching them with the hushed fascination of spectators at a prizefight. "Suppose this black cop was in an altercation with a young white guy."

"That wouldn't be structural racism," Ouida replies.

"I think," says Sir Robin Blair, ending the long moments of tension, "I think Stef is right, this isn't just white trash police brutality of the sort you had in Binghamton . . . "

"Birmingham," Daniel murmurs.

"I think we need to dwell on the larger issues here. In the old days all the cops were white. Now some of the cops are black. Does that mean we've come close to realizing the vision of Malcolm Luther King?"

Oh, my God, Stef thinks. She does not dare to look at Ouida.

She avoids Ouida for the rest of the afternoon. She considers skipping the Nonviolent Disobedience for New Columbia Sovereignty. But she has as much a right to be there as Ouida does. Sovereignty for the District is not a black issue, it is a liberal issue, and Stef considers herself first and foremost a liberal, rather than a white, American.

The nonviolent disobedience on the steps of the Capitol has barely begun when the members of the Direct Action Community arrive. One moment, the disobedience is a decorous affair of upper-middle-class professionals, mostly women, mostly *ladies*, like a meeting of the local Historical Preservation League; the next, it is an upheaval, a chaos, a melee. Ryan's soldiers, the crack troops of his army of the homeless and unemployed, are suddenly everywhere, shrilling on whistles, shouldering through the line of hand-linked protestors, pushing their faces into those of the cops like baseball coaches shouting down umpires.

"Free D.C.! DAC! Free D.C.! DAC!"

A bearded, burly white man smelling like a latrine collides with Stef and staggers on. "Watch it!" she snaps, only to wince as a bag lady with a whistle drills a prolonged piercing shriek like a splinter into Stef's aching brain.

"Free D.C.! DAC . . ."

Stef cannot see Ouida. She glimpses Mrs. Brackenridge, now baffled and alarmed. "Free D.C.!" A scuffle breaks out between a spike-bearded black man and a black cop. Clear as Gabriel's trumpet on Judgment Day comes the voice of Ryan: "Police brutality!"

After that, it is all a blur, all shoving and scraping and scuffling and searing and the nagging, insistent, insane shrill of the whistles. As policemen cuff struggling beggars, the crowd begins to chant, "The whole world is watching! The whole world is watching!" But it is not 1968, and the whole world is not watching, Stef thinks in disgust. All that these recycled sixties radicals have managed to accomplish is to ruin a nice civil disobedience.

The dogs appear. The pack looks like a tan-and-white quilt, billowing over the slopes in the gully beneath the great Virginian lawn. The red-coated riders canter after the animals. Some of the people standing near Stef in front of the country club that is sponsoring the weekend hunt start to applaud.

Stef shivers in the chill wind, sips her cider, and turns to a matronly woman nearby. "What kind of dogs are those?"

Choral barking drifts on the cold wind.

"Those aren't dogs," the woman corrects her. "They're *hounds*."

After the riders and the dogs disappear beyond a ridge, the scattered spectators climb the hill toward the restored plantation house that commands this summit near Middleburg, Virginia. Ross intercepts Bruce and Stef. "We've got better cider up the road."

In Bruce's car they follow Ross as he drives through the low hills to an unmarked lane that is little more than a large driveway. They pass several large houses, each one on its own hill, before they come to a two-story lodge screened by a ring of trees.

They set the bags inside the door. Ross gives them a tour. The living room is dominated by an immense fireplace of rough-hewn stone; a few dusty fish are mounted on the walls. "Previous owner," Ross explains. They clump up the wooden stairs to survey the bedroom on the upper level, a prismatic space warm with orange wood.

"So how many people have a share in this?" Bruce asks.

"Four. Actually, two individuals and two couples. We get exclusive use one weekend a month."

"Sounds like a good deal."

"As long as people clean up after themselves. Which is a problem, sometimes."

The leaves laugh underfoot as they follow a snaky trail down a slope, over a small cement bridge, and up a leaf-speckled slant. "She's been married twice, both times to very well-to-do older men," Ross explains. "The first one died. We're expecting the second to go any time now."

Her name is Letitia Monroe, and she has hair so black it could not be real, hair drawn up as tightly as the skin of her face. She thrusts her gaunt cheekbones forward for Ross to kiss. "Ross, darling, you look like you've lost weight."

"Clean living."

"We'll have to put a stop to that."

Ross introduces his friends. Stef watches, amused, as Bruce tries to decide which leathery cheekbone to kiss first. Smooth as he is, Bruce has a few tricks to learn if he is going to be the complete power broker.

"Kenneth won't be joining us for brunch," Letitia says. "He's in the saddle." She rolls her eyes. "Don't worry, our nephew is with him, under strict instructions not to let him go fast enough to catch a fox, unless it dies of boredom."

Cider and sweets are being served on the veranda. The prospect is much finer than Stef had imagined; the place overlooks the Shenandoah. This is prime real estate, unlike Ross's modest time-share.

"I want *this* place," Bruce tells Stef, reading her mind. With the wind mussing his blond hair as he leans on the rail, he looks beautiful, powerful. Stef is pleased to think what an admirable couple they make.

The other guests are middle-aged rich types, all Republicans, Stef assumes. The talk on the veranda turns quickly to maids.

"I've had no end of trouble with Hondurans."

"You mean Salvadorans."

"No, the Salvadorans are wonderful."

"Ross," says Letitia, "you've been using that Salvadoran girl who was working for us at our Washington place . . . "

"Graciela. I've been very pleased. She earns her five dollars an hour."

"Five dollars an hour? I've been paying mine two. Ross, you're going to spoil her."

One of Letitia's Latina maids enters with a cel phone. Letitia speaks into it, then shuts it off. "You'll never believe what's happened. Lewis Higginbotham, you know, from First Arlington Bank? He rode his horse into a stone fence. They've both got broken legs."

"My God."

"They're sending a helicopter to medevac him to Arlington General."

"That's good," says Ross, with a wicked smile. "I hope they do something for that poor banker, too."

★ ★ ★

Ross drives back to Washington after lunch, leaving Bruce and Stef alone at the time-share. The afternoon passes slowly and pleasantly. Stef works a bit on a manuscript she is editing for *Perspective*. They take a walk in the woods.

Dinner is in Middleburg, where Bruce has made reservations for them at The Chase, an upscale restaurant catering to the weekend gentry. The restaurant occupies an old house, one of many on a street lined with antique homes that have been renovated as restaurants, boutiques, curio shops. For the benefit of Stef, who has never seen one before, Bruce identifies the elaborate hitching posts planted in front of most of the buildings.

"Oh, my God." Stef giggles. "He's been whitewashed." The small metal jockey holding up a hitching post has been given Caucasian skin tones and yellow hair, but his grinning face is a caricature of a black man's.

The wine and the heavy meal make Stef sleepy. She tries to feign interest as Bruce goes on about his career plans. He thinks he could move from the drug czar's office to one of the lobbying firms on K Street, maybe Ross's firm. He wants to get a key position in the next Republican presidential campaign. Why is he going on like this? Stef wonders.

Back at the time-share, Bruce builds a fire, using old magazines and newspapers for kindling. "Hey, look, this is inflammatory," he says, holding up a sun-faded, dust-spotted issue of *Perspective*.

"You're enjoying that, aren't you?" she says as he sets fire to it with his lighter.

He is warm and strong and she feels safe as she lies in his arms and watches the fire. "Stef?"

"Mmmmm."

"Love you."

"I love you, too."

"Do you really?" He pauses. He has been acting strange all night.

Oh, no, she thinks. He's going to ask me to move in with him. She's been anticipating this moment and thinking of excuses. The truth is, she is just not ready to live with him.

"I really care about you, Stef," he is saying, his hand caressing hers. "I want us to be together."

She is trying to think of her rehearsed objections to cohabitation, but she is tired and a little tipsy and sleepy and her mind is muddled—so muddled that, when he produces a small box from nowhere and presents her with a cushioned ring, it takes a few moments for the sight to register.

"I . . . I don't understand." Her first reaction is confusion. Her second is fear.

"I want to marry you." His hand touches her hair. "I love you, Stef."

"I love you, too. I just . . . I don't know." She feels as though she is kicking in quicksand. "It's just so . . . I don't know. I just think all of this is happening so fast."

"We've been going together for almost a year. What's wrong with getting engaged?"

"I don't know . . ." Absorbed though she is in the turmoil of her own feelings, Stef senses a change in his. She senses him drawing back, preparing for a rebuff, senses that the moment is about to pass, that doors and windows in his soul are about to be closed. She is afraid again, afraid that she will lose him if she does not say yes. And so she says yes, not because she means yes without reservations, but because only yes will keep the negotiation going.

They make love in the angular orange room upstairs. Afterward, he sinks into a profound sleep. She realizes for the first time how stressed he must have been, for days or weeks, as he prepared himself to make the proposal.

Already the tenuous commitment is hardening in her mind. She stands in the upstairs bathroom of the wooden lodge and regards herself in the dramatic track lighting. Half-moons of shadow make her eyes look mysterious and accentuate her breasts. She is not a girl a few years out of college, but a woman entering the prime of life. She has finally found her profession, and now she has a husband. Her adult life, after the anxious limbo of the post-college years, has finally begun.

Back in bed, she regards the long pale canoe curve of Bruce's back and legs. She cannot sleep. Her mind is manic, fashioning scenes of the days to come, phone conversations, the expressions on the faces of her friends and colleagues when she announces, "I'm engaged," and shows them the ring. She thinks of the wedding, and the honeymoon—in Paris, maybe, or the Bahamas—and beyond. She and Bruce will be admired and envied, the way she sensed they were as they stood on Letitia's veranda earlier in the day. They will be a model Washington couple, a power couple. They will have power jobs—she in journalism, he in politics. They will buy a power house—maybe a town house in Georgetown, or a suburban mansion in Chevy Chase. They will wear power clothes and own power cars. They will have power children and send them to a power preschool. They will have a power dog and a power cat. They will be the envy of Powertown.

Bruce stirs in his sleep, and begins to snore.

20

Eunique sips her soda and gazes at him coldly. "I been sitting here for twenty-five minutes."

Evander looks at his watch. "I'm only fifteen minutes late," he tells her. "I told you *around* one o'clock."

"I been here twenty-five minutes." Her coldness makes Eunique all the more beautiful. Her style is already forbidding—from the harsh asymmetry of her hair, heavy on one side and cropped on the other, to the cruel glint of the giant golden earring. She acts the way someone who looks as she does ought to act. Imperious.

"I'm sorry, all right? I had some business going down," Evander tells her.

"Don't give me attitude."

"I ain't giving you attitude."

"Twenty-five minutes."

"What was I supposed to do? I had business going down."

Disdainfully, she gazes past him and surveys the crowded pizza parlor. Evander watches her dark-painted lips close on the straw.

"What do you want?" he says, glancing through the glossy menu. This is a pricey pizza parlor in a fancy mall in Georgetown. "It's on me." Evander hopes that by taking her out and spending money on her he can take Lookout's place in her bed.

"I'm not hungry."

"Now you giving me attitude."

"I *said* I'm not hungry."

Evander tries not to show his anger. "What do you want to do?" he says patiently.

156

"I don't know. I'm tired. I might just go home."

Evander seethes. Maybe she's not worth it. Then he remembers what Lookout said about fly girls. Half the pleasure is making them submit. They need the discipline.

"You want to go shopping?"

"I don't know," she says airily. "Maybe."

Soon they are strolling on the second level of the mall past shopwindows done up in a frilly neo-Victorian style. "Check this out," Evander says, pausing in front of a display of knives. "This shit is hype."

Eunique wants to go to Georgetown Leather. Inside, she tries on a leather jacket and models it in the mirror, her expression an aristocratic scowl.

"I'll buy it for you," Evander offers after he has checked the price tag: eighty dollars.

"Ooh, I like this one better," she says. Evander has to agree. The leather is liquid obsidian with a sort of sinister flash, like darkness made visible.

"I want it," she ordains.

Evander looks at the tag. "This is three hundred dollars."

"I thought you was doing business."

He does a quick calculation. He's sold his supply of crack and owes Tito six hundred. If he buys this jacket, he'll need to come up with three hundred from some other source. He has about two hundred stashed at home and at Teesha's . . .

He feels one of her long scarlet nails sliding along his leg. He pulls out his wallet and counts the twenties while Eunique spins, delighted, in front of the mirror.

She kisses him at the door to her apartment, then tries to shut it. He blocks the door. "Come on, baby, when you gonna give me some?"

"I'm tired," she says.

"How about tomorrow night?"

"Depends on how I'm feeling. Call me." She kisses him again. "Thanks for the jacket, baby."

Tomorrow night, he reassures himself, they will be hitting the skins. Otherwise, he has just been swindled out of three hundred dollars. He does the math again in his head, and finds that even if he uses all his rainy-day money he will still be a hundred short. Frizzell would give him time to make up the debt, but Tito is different. Tito has made no secret of his dislike for Evander, especially since the death of Lookout, Evander's only real friend in the Krew.

At home Evander takes the eighty dollars he has hidden behind a brick in the bathroom; then, while his half brothers and sisters are outside, he takes forty dollars from the broken toaster on top of the refrigerator where Gram keeps money for emergencies. His anxiety growing, he bicycles over to the apartment complex where Teesha lives.

"What's the matter, baby?" she says as he shuts the door to her room behind them.

"You got that sixty dollars I told you to keep for me?"

With a guilty expression, Teesha glances at the closet. Evander opens it. Stuffed animals topple from the top shelf.

"What the fuck is this?"

"It's for our baby," she says. "I'm pregnant."

He stares, stunned. The door opens and Teesha's aunt confronts him. "You get out of here," Shirelle tells him. "You get out of here right now. You get out of my house!"

"Fuck you!" shouts Evander. He forgets about the baby, remembers that all his money is gone. Tito will kill him for sure.

"Get out of my house 'fore I call the *po*lice!"

Teesha begins to cry. Evander slams the apartment door behind him. He can hear the female voices erupt.

The dome of the Capitol glows in the distance like the globe of Jupiter or Saturn over the icy surface of an airless moon. A dark figure makes its way through the rubble and the weeds between the railroad tracks and the highway. It disappears beneath the railroad overpass.

Evander follows. He has been trailing Scab for ten minutes since catching sight of the beggar on a street corner near the waterfront. Rumor has it that the disfigured vagrant has hidden an enormous cache of aluminum frames and fragments pilfered from construction sites. Aluminum goes for a good price at the recycling center near the waterfront. Evander, who sold his gun a few days earlier to an eleven-year-old for forty dollars, has decided that he has no alternative now but to steal if he is to make up the debt to Tito. He thought about breaking into his uncle Curtis's house to steal the revolvers he knows must be there, but his conscience would not permit that. He has concluded that it would be easier to steal aluminum from Scab than to snatch a purse or to burgle a home.

Cars and trucks whoosh beneath the railroad overpass. Evander slips as he makes his way down the slope. Pebbles slide and clatter. He can't see Scab in the cavernous cement space enclosing the highway.

Lights blaze in his eyes. A truck snorts and rattles past. Evander approaches the peculiar structure on the cement slant, a kind of nest or tipi. He tears away cardboard and planks, and discovers the shopping cart hidden inside. The cart is filled with aluminum slats and screens. Atop it rests a trash bag filled with aluminum cans. In the light from the passing cars the cans glow darkly in the translucent bag like eggs in the belly of a fish.

Glancing around, Evander grabs the handle of the shopping cart and gives it a push. Birdlike, the metal squawks. One of the rusted wheels is rigid. Tilting the cart precariously, Evander rolls and pushes it out of the shadow of the overpass.

He hears a gargled cry, then the stench hits him. He turns to confront Scab, a shadowy hulk whose scars are covered by the kindly darkness. Evander wishes he had not sold his gun. As his fist cracks across Scab's face, he imagines that he feels the rough texture of the grafted tissue. The beggar staggers, then starts at him again. Evander grabs an aluminum slat and slashes Scab's arm with it. The beggar shrieks in pain. Then Evander is flailing him with the slat, on the arms, across the back, on the face. Grunting and snuffling, the beggar dashes away into the darkness, pursued by Evander's curses.

Evander sweats through his underwear and his shirt and as he pushes and hauls the top-heavy cart to the top of the slope. He has pushed it halfway across the railroad overpass, glancing both ways for the lights of any approaching train, when his nostrils are full of the stench again.

The blow to the back of his head knocks him into the rail.

Beneath, cars whizz. He turns, only to present his face for another blow. The third is deflected by his arm.

He is next to the cart again. He reaches for an aluminum slat, but the bag of cans is in the way. Then Scab has seized the trash bag, his trash bag, and they are fighting for it like dogs contesting a stick or a bone. The bag breaks. Dozens of cans clatter over the railing onto the highway below where they are hit and scattered by swerving, squealing cars.

The lights in the distance are a train's. Evander tries to run, but Scab has him by the legs. He falls, hard, onto a track, and feels a searing pain in his back. The stink is unbearable.

The lights are closer. The train is wailing. His heart racing, Evander kicks until he frees himself from the stinking shadow. Then he scrambles off the track, tumbles off the overpass, and slides down the slope, amid a hiss of rocks in a minor avalanche. The very earth is trembling now. He looks up to see the shopping cart, a silver cage full of silvery bars, glow ever brighter on the track. Then the dark blaring mass of the train strikes, and the shopping cart explodes in a swarm of streaks like falling stars.

"Say what?"

Evander looks at the carpeted floor of the Funkadelic's upper chamber. "I said I'll get you the rest next week." When Tito says nothing more, Evander turns to walk away.

"Yo, Evander," Tito calls out after him when he has reached the top of the stairs. Evander turns, and Tito's fist connects. Then Tito has him by the throat, pinioned to the wall at the summit of the staircase like a butterfly to a collector's mat.

"Muthafucka think you can steal my money goddamn muthafucka . . ." It is all one stream of monotonous cursing. Tito's fist sinks into his gut. When Evander bends over, another fist cracks across his head.

He tumbles down the stairs, a few flights at a time. Each time he brakes his fall and starts to rise, Tito punches or kicks him again and sends him rolling a few yards more. At the bottom of the staircase he collapses.

"Get up, muthafucka!" he hears Tito's voice through the ringing in his ears. "Get up!"

Evander climbs to his feet and sways unsteadily. The room is still as death. Everyone is looking at him—the pool players, the guys on the bar stools, the girls. All staring in terror and pity. No one speaks. There is no sound except for the thump of the juke-box.

"I ought to kill your ass," Tito says. His eyes and his nostrils flare. "Muthafucka say he gonna pay me back. Shit. You fuckin' stealing from me, muthafucka. Ain't nobody don't pay in time. Goddamn muthafucka. You got till Tuesday, or you dead, shit-head."

Evander's heart is pounding. For a moment he feels faint with terror as Tito, seeming to reconsider, turns back toward him. Evander expects him to draw a gun and finish him.

Instead Tito jabs a finger at Evander. "Check in that jacket, muthafucka. Kick it in!"

Trembling, Evander takes off his Eddie Bauer jacket. Everyone is watching. It is like being forced to strip in front of a crowd. He curtains a bar stool with the parka.

"Take off your high-tops." Evander unlaces his shoes. "Hurry up!" He slides the small boats of white foam from his feet.

"Your watch. Check it in."

Evander sets his watch atop the jacket.

"Your gun."

"I sold it," Evander murmurs.

"Say what?"

"I sold it."

Several of the onlookers laugh. Tito smirks. "Louder, punk. I can't hear you."

Evander's face is burning. He blinks back tears. "I say I sold my gun." His voice breaks.

"Get outta here. Shit."

Laughter and murmurs follow Evander to the door. As he leaves, he hears Tito a final time: "Tuesday. Tuesday, or your ass is mine."

21

The entrance to the revival meeting is guarded by burly young men in crisp suits. "Six-dollar contribution recommended," one of them growls in a tone that makes it clear that the contribution is not optional.

"Tol'ja it was a hustle," Curtis murmurs to Velma as he pays.

Twenty minutes before the service is set to begin, the community center auditorium is full. Unable to find two adjacent empty seats, Curtis and Velma sit apart. Fidgeting on a metal folding chair, Curtis loosens his tie; the heat of all these bodies packed together is already turning the room into a sauna. He scans the place, trying to find people he knows. Most of the worshipers are unfamiliar, a fact that confirms him in his view that his sort of people do not come to things like this. He is determined to have a bad time.

Curtis takes out the mimeographed sheet that Velma had picked up at the hospital:

My dear Christian brother or sister:

This letter is put in your hand by God Almighty because I am on my way back to Washington for another blessing service this Sunday night and all the folk that see me will get a dead straight and one way hit on Monday, so help me God. If you got money problems or a loved one or a friend. If you need help in a hurry, come Sunday night when I upset Washington again and lots of folk will be hitting on Monday dead straight and one way and counting their cash money

after my blessing service for Washington D.C. If you need a
cash money blessing you be there Friday night when I upset
Washington and give out hits for Monday so help me God
Almighty.

Yours in the spirit of God
Elijah Drake
The Blessing Prophet

P.S. Be there for me to bless you with a hit rain or shine
Friday in Washington for one day only. Pass this letter on to a
loved one or a friend needs a cash money blessing and a sure
enough hit dead straight one way the very next day.

When women in baggy blue choir robes file in and start to
sway and swing and the crowd catches the contagious syncopa-
tion, Curtis suppresses the desire to rock with the rows around
him, thinking, Bunch of low-life trash.

The pregame show ends with the entry of Brother Elijah,
dancing his way slowly to the front of the room while the sisters
cry out ever louder. The Blessing Prophet is fat, fat in a way that
Curtis for all his humps and folds will never be; the man's head
and hands seem to be ballooning from his purple suit like smaller
parachutes around a central one. For a man so fat, the prophet can
move surprisingly fast; eyes closed, chubby hands paddling the air,
he sways from side to side, his legs working beneath his equator.
He's sweating like a stuck pig, Curtis thinks, and smirks, despite
his determination to have a bad time.

"Do y'all *believe* the Bible? Do y'all believe it's the word of
God? Look at y'all, look at you, yup, yup, yup. 'Uh-huh, I believe.'
This sister here, check it out, she saying, 'Oh, I believe!'" The
prophet braids his chubby fingers, leans his head to one side, rolls
his eyes up until the whites glow, and mews, "'Oh, Jesus, I
beleeeeeeve!'" Pacing on the stage, he waits for the thundering
laughter to fade. "Well, brothers and sisters, if you really believed,
you wouldn't have no problem to ask the Lord to help you out.
That's right. We got a lot of so-called Christians, they need cash
money, they need a job, they need a down payment on they car,
and where they go? Do they ask God for that cash money or that

job or that down payment? They afraid to pray for what they need! How many times you heard some so-called Christian preacher say, 'The love of money is the root of all evil,' and what he thinks it means is, 'Money is the root of all evil.' But you read the Bible, it don't say, 'Money is the root of all evil,' it say, 'the *love* of money.' You ever heard anybody say, 'The *need* of money is the root of all evil?' 'Course not, 'cause that ain't in the Bible nowhere." Brother Elijah wipes his brow. "Brothers and sisters, they ain't nothing wrong with the *need* of money. God wants you to eat. He wants you to have a place to live. Now how you supposed to eat and have a place to live if you ain't got no money? Jesus, he was a carpenter. You think he worked for free? You think he didn't charge union rates to build a table or raise a barn or whatever? God ain't got nothing against money, as long as it's *I need* money and not *I love* money."

"Amen."

"Tell it."

The preacher is plodding back and forth. "Now it says in the Bible, it's easier for a camel to go through the eye of a needle than for a rich man to enter the kingdom of God. Don't say nothing about no poor man. How many of y'all here think you too rich to go to heaven?" The audience erupts in laughter. The prophet jabs a finger at an old lady in a hat. "Sister! Gimme an Amen."

"Amen!" she hollers, and the crowd laughs. Curtis joins in the laughter.

The prophet sponges his face. "Can I sit? Can I sit, people?" Several of the young men dressed like bodyguards ceremoniously bring a chair to the stage and help the fat preacher settle into it, like a potentate on a throne. "Oh, thank you Jesus." He sighs. "My dogs is done give out. 'The spirit is willing, but the flesh is weak.'"

Curtis laughs. Despite himself, he is beginning to like this preacher.

"Yes, indeed, brothers and sisters, yes, indeed. The so-called Christians. They need some cash money, but they ain't gonna ask God, that would be *rude*. They think if they just pray on something else maybe God'll read their mind. Well, I tell you something, brothers and sisters, he know your mind better'n you do.

You can't hide nothing from him, he knows what you need before you need it. All he wants is for you to ask him. That's all. He just wants you to come right straight out and ask. He won't get mad. He's your Heavenly Father. He's your daddy! Your daddy get mad at you, if you hitting on him for money for fancy clothes and liquor and baubles and bangles and jewels. But he won't get mad if it's money for something you need. 'Ask, and you shall receive.' That ain't me talking now, brothers and sisters, that's what it says in the Bible. Psalms 24:5—'He will receive blessing from the Lord, and vindication from the God of his salvation.' Amen. Hallelujah. That's the word of God. Psalm 34:6—'The poor man cried, and the Lord heard him, and saved him outta all his troubles.' Amen. The poor man cried, and the Lord, he heard that poor man, 'cause if you poor, the Lord wants to help you. He is your daddy, and God Almighty loves his children. Hallelujah! Thank you, Jesus! 'They feast on the abundance of thy house, and thou givest them drink from the river of thy delights'—Psalm 36:8. Amen. Amen. A-hey-men!"

Then the music starts again, and the women in their robes of billowing blue are swaying and clapping and the preacher is up out of his chair and spinning, a purple planet wobbling on its axis, and Curtis, though he refuses to clap, finds himself rocking and tapping his foot.

"Boy, that preacher hollered, didn't he?" Curtis laughs, shaking his head, as he drives home.

"Daddy wouldn't have liked him. He didn't hold for those hollering preachers."

"That's what they used to call a chicken-eating, jack-leg preacher. For sure. I hope he can give us a direct cash-money hit."

"Baby, we gonna need one, since you ain't drawing no salary."

Curtis falls silent. He has not told Velma that the security company has suspended him without pay.

"Baby, I don't know why you didn't tell me they stopped paying your salary. It ain't your fault, baby. Ain't nothing you can do about it. It's out of your hands."

His embarrassment gives way to relief, and gratitude, at her understanding.

"I'm gonna look for another job," he says quietly.

"You ought to think about SSI."

"I ain't going on welfare."

"It ain't welfare. SSI is on account of you're disabled. With that heart condition of yours . . . I bet some doctor can say you shouldn't be straining yourself."

"Shit."

"They do it all the time. All the time. Lawd a'mercy. I bet that heart condition of yours goes back to Vietnam. You served your country. You deserve it."

He feels more tenderness toward her that night than he has for years. It is not a desire for physical intimacy—as always, she repairs to the bedroom, and he to the fold-out sofa in the living room, where he will doze off listening to the police radio. Rather, it is like a friendship undervalued and then reaffirmed.

A collision at Fifth and East Capital. A fight near the Marine barracks . . . Sitting in the backyard, listening to the police radio, Curtis follows the events. He wonders how many of his friends are still on the force. And how many of his enemies.

The crisis had come in the late eighties, a few years into the crack epidemic that turned the District into a version of Capone's Chicago. Responding to a call, he and his partner had watched as a young cop named Grady and Grady's partner beat a minor drug dealer bloody.

"Where the fuck is it?" Grady had demanded, his uniform darkened by spattering blood.

The whimpering dealer, a kid in his teens, had limped over to the drawers they had already searched and knocked out a false bottom. Grady had whistled at what must have been ten thousand dollars of pure powdered cocaine.

"Here's yours," Grady had told Curtis and his partner, handing them a slab.

Curtis had felt a spasm of vertigo, as though the floorboards beneath him were on the verge of giving way. "What the fuck you talking about?"

"You got a problem, muthafucka?" Suddenly Grady had been in his face, pressed up close against him, glaring through red-veined eyes. "You want to dance, muthafucka? Head-up. Let's go."

Curtis had backed away. "You can do whatever you want," he stammered. "I don't want to mess with none of that shit." He turned to see his partner taking his share.

For a few weeks, Curtis had thought about alerting Internal Affairs. He had decided it would be too dangerous. For all he knew, IA had been in on the secret that cops were dealing. Curtis was well aware he could be taken out by one of his colleagues at any time, and the department would say he had been shot by a common criminal.

He had noticed a new coolness toward him in the locker room, down at the District courthouse where he hung out with other cops waiting to testify. The word had spread. He wasn't participating. He wasn't willing to share their guilt. That made him potentially dangerous.

Curtis had done what he had always done. He had avoided making any trouble. He had offered his resignation and had gone to work for a downtown building security service. Eighteen months later he had won his present job as a private security guard.

Why should he be a hero? He was the low guy on the totem pole, he always had been. He had enough trouble trying to help pay his and Velma's bills. The system was corrupt through and through. His slow and painful crucifixion by the lawyers confirmed it. He makes the mistake of stopping the drunken son of a city council member, and now the whole black establishment is trying to destroy him. His own company, reversing its initial promise, has refused to pay him during its legal negotiations. It was always like this and it always will be, Curtis tells himself. The game is rigged, and there's nothing one person like him can do about it, nothing at all.

Curtis sleeps late. Awakening, he finds that Velma has taken the bus to the hospital. When he checks to see whether the mail has come, he discovers an envelope she has addressed to Reverend Drake.

Goddamn it, he thinks, tearing it open and finding the check for twenty dollars, with only one of them working, why is the woman sending money to that preacher? Then he reads the note:

Dear Rev Drake

I know its OK to pray for myself but me and my husband we are OK. Im a nurse at DC General and they are so many sick people and a lot of them is shot up children too. Like the girl lost her eye she is just a baby. Can you give them a blessing please. I put in a contribution.

Velma Hawkins RN

PS My father was a preacher too

He sets the note down and finds himself weeping for his wife, who is a saint, and for himself, because, as he only vaguely understands, he wants a wife and not a saint.

22

He has seen this before. Avery realizes, after he sits down, that he must have glimpsed the bookcase dozens of times behind different talking heads on TV. He can see, as the viewing audience cannot, that the books are fake—mere titled bindings, glued together in bunches of three and four.

"Hi, I'm Craig Conway." The handsome, beefy, rusty-haired TV reporter clasps Avery's hand, then waits patiently as a crewman fastens the mike to his tie. Like the backdrop, Craig Conway is familiar to Avery from TV, not just the name ("And now, back to Craig Conway in Washington"), but the face. The face, of course, looks different on the man than on the homunculus who appears upon the screen. Having grown up in Washington among celebrities, Avery is used to meeting people who in the flesh are shorter or taller or have wider heads or narrower faces than their TV personas would lead you to believe.

"Can you make sure I'm identified as L. Avery Brackenridge? Not Avery Brackenridge. The papers have gotten it wrong."

"Sure." Conway explains the format. "I've just got a few questions. We'll talk for ten, fifteen minutes. We'll get maybe two minutes on—" The reporter freezes in mid-sentence, like a medium in a trance, as he listens to a voice only he can hear on his earpiece.

"—light a little more?" Suddenly, startled, Avery is hearing the same producer's voice. It seems to be echoing inside his head. "Okay. Five seconds from the cue . . . "

★ ★ ★

Ouida wants to watch *Nightline* with him at his apartment, but Avery tells her over the phone that he is feeling ill. The truth is that taping the segment has only deepened the listless depression into which he has sunk since the incident. He sleeps through the afternoon—he has ended his leave of absence by formally quitting his job at NPR—and feels his dread deepening as the hour approaches.

To his relief, he seems articulate and even good-looking in the two-minute segment that begins the program. Craig Conway and the news crew have done a good job in culling a few convincing sound bites from Avery's rambling remarks. "As a black man, I shouldn't be considered guilty until proven innocent," the TV Avery is declaiming. "As a citizen, I should be able to go into any neighborhood in this country without fear of being brutalized by mercenaries . . . "

After the commercial break, the program resumes. "Neighborhood patrols—are they out of control?" Ted Koppel looks into the camera. "In the opening segment of tonight's broadcast, we heard from Avery Brackenridge, the young man who was beaten by a private police officer in a tony Washington suburb. The NAACP's Legal Defense Fund says Avery was beaten because he is a young black man. On behalf of Avery, they are suing Sentinel, the private security company whose employee was involved in the incident. We asked Sentinel if they would send a spokesman to appear on *Nightline*, but the company declined, citing the pending litigation. We will keep you updated in future broadcasts as to the status of that litigation."

Koppel, camera angle two. "To discuss the broader issues of race and private neighborhood police forces, we have with us a noted criminologist, Dr. Irving Weisberg of Harvard University, and the Reverend Ike Jefferson of the New Zion Baptist Church in Los Angeles. Gentlemen, thank you for joining us. If I may start with you, Professor Weisberg . . . "

The phone begins to ring.

"You were terrific, honey," his mother tells him. "Ron thought so, too." Well, if the utility-executive stepfather approves . . .

Avery hears a beep. "Somebody's trying to call. I'll talk to you later."

"All right. We're proud of you."

Ouida is on the other line. "You were very impressive. Are you feeling better?"

"Yes." The answer is no.

He always sensed he would become famous. Amy Brackenridge's son was raised in the expectation that one day he would be at least a local celebrity like his mother, and quite possibly a national figure. He would be a famous politician, or a celebrated journalist, or a great novelist, or so he had always assumed.

Now he is famous as a victim, as a black man beaten up by a policeman. He has been famous for more than a month, though by now the stories have dropped to the back pages after a few days on page one: D.C. COUNCIL MEMBER'S SON BEATEN BY COP. The physical pain had been minor to begin with, though X rays and photos attested that the bruises and contusions had been real enough. Though the pain has faded, the misery endures.

Even before he had been stopped by that cop, the fragile structure of his life had been about to fall apart. It had been provisional, anyway, a lean-to, a windbreak, a makeshift shelter for him as he deferred any decisions about returning to school, or deciding on a career, or coming out to his parents and the world, or risking a deeper emotional commitment than his now-dead relationship with Ross. The lean-to has crackled and split, and Avery is kicking away its last splintered fragments by quitting his job and severing his friendships.

The hardest tie to cut has been the one that bound him to Stef. In the past several years she has been a surrogate sister, a confidante. But if what Ouida reports is true—and Stef will not deny it—Stef did not take his side in the battle at *Perspective* over the story of his beating. At least Stef did not side with him one hundred percent, and that is what L. Avery Brackenridge has a right to demand of his friends. One hundred percent loyalty. Two hundred. Five hundred percent.

Having broken with Stef, he is now thinking of breaking with Ouida. She has been devoted to him. But he finds her devotion as disgusting as everything else in a world that seems to have been fouled by a sticky film like the smear of a cosmic snail, sliding like an eraser through the universe and leaving colors minus warmth and foods minus taste and people like puppets minus souls. He wants no friends, no family, no lover, no job, no life. He just wants to lie in his bathrobe in his apartment all day with the curtains drawn, listening to Wagner.

Maybe, he thinks, this is what is meant by the phrase "a nervous breakdown."

The law office looks out onto Pennsylvania Avenue. Across the street rises the pale Gothic tower of the Old Post Office.

"Why didn't you tell us about that, Avery?" his mother asks.

Avery is cornered. There are four of them—the two litigators for the NAACP Legal Defense Fund, John Conyers and Sheila Rubinstein, the family attorney, Dan Adams, and his mother.

"I don't know," says Avery. "I didn't think it was important."

"Can you keep it from being introduced?" Adams asks Conyers.

"Well, we'd have to try."

The defense team for the private security company has somehow discovered the incident at the Korean-owned grocery.

"They didn't press charges," Avery repeats. "I should have pressed charges, I guess."

"Avery, anything you can remember," his mother says.

"They weren't going to let me leave without checking my satchel. Because I'm a young black man. That's the only reason. If I'd been white, I would have been in and out of there. But they barred the door. These damn Asians are racists. This woman, she says, 'You black people, you are always stealing from my store.' That's what she said. So I said, fine, call the police. Then I waited, and the police showed up, and I explained what was going on, and who I was, and that was the end of it."

"Dan," says his mother, turning to the family lawyer, "do you think there's a case here?"

"I don't think," Conyers, the NAACP litigator, interrupts, "it would look good if Avery sued two different people for racist harassment."

"Even if it's true?" Avery snaps.

Dan Adams sighs. He is a tall, stately gray-haired man, an

experienced litigator who marched with King and Evers in the South. "What are they offering?"

Sheila Rubinstein answers, "Eighty thousand."

When Amy asks what he thinks, Adams says, "Take their offer."

"Why?" says Avery. The tremor in his voice gives his anger away. They have asked for half a million.

"You've got a black jury. You've got a black cop who lives in the community. You've got a kid from a well-to-do family with a history of making scenes in public—at least if they get that Korean incident introduced."

Avery sits up. "Making scenes?"

His mother cautions him. "I asked for his opinion, Avery."

"I know these juries," Adams says. "They're law and order. They'll side with the cop, especially a black cop. Settle," he repeats. "And next time you decide to get beaten up by a cop, make sure he's a white man with a KKK card in his wallet and a Confederate flag on his bumper."

In a Weimar theater of the imagination, as well as Avery's ear, Jenny the bar maid is singing to Kurt Weill's jagged melody of the vengeance that will be wreaked on her enemies when her ship comes in. Over Lotte Lenya's voice Avery does not hear the knock.

His mother's mouth is moving soundlessly. He takes off his Walkman. "We need to go, dear, if we're going to make it to the studio on time." She smiles and returns downstairs.

Avery sets the Walkman with its cassette of *The Threepenny Opera* on his desk. The desk is exactly the way he left it when he moved into the dormitory at Georgetown six years before. The room has been preserved by his mother as a monument to the first Brackenridge to attend high school at Sidwell Friends. Avery's gaze moves over the graduation photo, the plaques from the academic competitions he won—journalism, art, track. This was the old Avery, the bright black kid whom all the white liberals wanted to know so they could invoke their friendship with him as evidence in philosophical arguments about race. His mother has now found a new Avery, the Avery who has been asked to appear on the Don Morgan show on Black Entertainment Television, the Avery of *Nightline* and the newspapers: BLACK COUNCIL MEMBER'S SON BEATEN BY COP . . . Avery the passive victim of a cruel racist society. Like the old Avery, this new Avery is as much his work as his mother's.

"Avery, please!"

"Come on, Avery!" The voice is Ouida's.

The walls of the Chevy Chase mansion are closing in. Suddenly he wants to flee. He wants to get on a plane for anywhere and never return to Washington again.

He washes his hands. As he towels them, he stops and gazes at the towel.

"Avery . . . "

He savors the expression of puzzlement and annoyance on their faces as he completes his descent of the stairs. "This is what they want, isn't it?" He models himself in the mirror of the coat-rack in the front hall. He has tied a towel like a bandage around one eye, and made, of another towel, a sling for his right arm.

"Avery, if you're through clowning around . . . "

"I'm through, period." He pulls the towels off and tosses them onto the coatrack. He searches in his pocket and finds his keys.

"Call the show and tell them I'm not coming. Tell them I'm sick. No, wait. Tell them I'm well."

"Avery, please!" The pain in Ouida's voice does not move him, it merely disgusts him.

His mother comes out onto the porch as he climbs into his sports car. "Avery, I will be humiliated."

For a moment he pauses, arrested by reflexive guilt. Then he purses his lips, shuts the car door, turns on the engine, and pulls out onto the street.

He finds himself cruising among the monuments in the great marble city of the dead. He parks near the Capitol and strolls the grounds. From a marble wall he gazes out across the mall toward the obelisk of the Washington Monument and watches the sun go down. For the first time in a long while he feels at ease.

He tries several pay phones at quarter-hour intervals before he reaches her. "Stef? It's Avery. You mind if I drop by?"

23

Graciela feels Darryl's eyes upon her as she dresses.

"A cold front is supposed to be coming in," he says, pulling on his T-shirt. He straps on his holstered pistol. "Looks like we might get some rain."

Graciela takes her clothes into the bathroom and finishes dressing there. Somehow she always feels more naked afterward than before.

They are in a building that Darryl's company owns, a free-standing garage or converted warehouse that looms in a parking lot between rows of shabby town houses. Downstairs, opening into the giant two-story main room in the building, is a small office with a desk and a calendar on the wall. This tiny bedroom, with its bathroom and shower stall, is directly above. This is the third time that Darryl has brought her here—twice in quick succession, and then after the space of almost a month. Graciela has been relieved that he wants to get together with her only infrequently, though she assumes he has other women, too. She is less worried than she might be, because he always uses a condom.

"Ready?" he asks. She follows him downstairs and outside. She watches him press a code into the computer alarm, then snap padlocks and loop a chain over the door as added precautions. They are standing in the locked cage where he parks his giant black truck. The neighborhood does not look dangerous, but to judge from the building's fortifications it must be.

"I've got to make another trip to Middleburg tomorrow," he says, guiding the truck through the alley and out onto the boulevard. "It's nice getting out of town into the country, though. You like the *país*?"

"*Sí*," she says. She feels nothing for him. On the other hand, she does not dislike him. He does not hurt her when he is with her; indeed, he is tender, in a way that seems incongruous for such a giant of a man. He tries to make friendly conversation. And he has reduced her rent from two-fifty a month to sixty dollars.

"Rosa! Rosa, get away from there!"

The little girl looks at her from a vantage point half way up the jungle gym. Graciela knows that look, that hesitation before obeying, that pause, in order to give Mama a chance to reconsider and revise her instructions—or to confirm them.

"Rosa, I'm not going to tell you again."

Rosa climbs down. Half hopping, half skipping, she rejoins her. "Mama, I want to go on the swing."

"Not now," Graciela says, irritated. "We don't have time. Tía Yolanda is coming to pick us up." She lifts Marcelo before he can toddle off further in the direction of the tree-roofed suburban street.

"Please? I want to go on the swing!"

"I'm not going to repeat myself."

Mrs. Valdez has been in and out of the hospital since she fell and broke her hip in her kitchen. Graciela has been forced to bring the children with her to work more often. She does not like doing that. She falls behind in her cleaning when she has to keep an eye on them, making sure they do not break anything in one of the big houses. At least when she finishes at Mrs. Thompson's house she can bring them three blocks to this playground on the premises of the Epiphany Episcopal Church.

"Please? Please, can I go on the swing? Please?" As though demonstrating what she would like to do, Rosa swings at the end of Graciela's purse. Where is Yolanda? Graciela wonders, growing ever more annoyed.

Then she notices the two American ladies approaching her. They look like people from this neighborhood, the sort of upperclass Americans who populate the English-language soap operas.

"Hello," a lady with frosted hair says pleasantly as the other one smiles. They introduce themselves, but Graciela does not get their names.

"If you don't mind our asking ... We belong to the church ... "

Graciela glances at the brick building with its ivory steeple and feels alarmed. They must have trespassed. "We don't come here anymore," she promises hastily.

"Oh, no, please," says the other lady, whose hair is unnaturally blond. "You and your children are welcome to use the playground any time you like. What are their names?"

"Rosa. And Marcelo. He is two."

"You're sweet, aren't you?" the lady with frosted hair tells Marcelo. "Yes, you are. Yes, you are."

The other lady is writing a phone number on the back of a brochure. "We have a day-care program. Preschool and kinder-garten. Here's the number if you're interested. Janey Carrington is the coordinator. I hope you can join us in church sometime."

"Bye-bye," the ladies tell the kids.

"Wave good-bye," Graciela whispers to Marcelo, moving his tiny hand.

"Bye-bye," Rosa sings.

Yolanda pulls up in the old car Isidro recently bought. "Who was that?" she wants to know, then, on learning, asks, "Did you tell them you are Catholic?"

She plans it long before it happens. Graciela knows it is going to happen the second or third time Carlos drives her home, when his hand floats across the truck's cab to rest lightly upon hers.

Over the next few weeks they spend several evenings together. Paying for the use of the truck, Carlos takes them to a movie, though they have to leave when Marcelo will not stop shrieking and bawling. A few nights later Carlos barbecues ham-burgers for them on the pit in the courtyard of the run-down brick apartments where he shares a room with three other day laborers. One of them, Julio, bemuses Rosa by showing her his silver-capped tooth with the pattern of a star.

They enjoy a few fugitive kisses in the cab of his truck and in the darkness of the parking lot after the kids have been put to bed. Carlos suggests a motel. She has a better idea. The day after the Thompsons leave for their two-week vacation in Ireland, she meets Carlos at their house in northwest Washington.

"Did you park down the block?" she asks him after the door closes. She does not want the neighbors to report to the Thompsons that his truck has been parked in front.

"Come here," he says, pulling her to him. Their mouths meet.

She shows him the upstairs. "There are three bedrooms," she boasts, as though the giant house were her own.

He emerges from the closet in the master bedroom with one of Mrs. Thompson's dresses.

"What are you doing?"

"Put it on."

"No, I can't."

He holds the dress up in front of her. She looks into the mirror, seeing his reflected smile. "You are too small," he teases. "You're a shrimp."

He tries to pull her down on the bed right there, but Graciela feels uneasy. She leads him out of the master bedroom and into the den, a warm orange room with dark bookcases and a tall TV stand. The sofa is long and plush.

He has wrestled her shirt off her by the time she remembers the window. She draws the curtain, even though the room looks out into the backyard. When she turns, he is standing in his socks and underwear.

He walks over and kisses her again. She is reminded, not for the first time, of slender, ever-boyish Paco back in Salvador. Then she is writhing on the sofa and his tongue is probing inside her. Then she is swallowing him. He seems so small and slender after Darryl. His body is so golden and smooth. At first, when he starts to ride her, she clenches in panic at the sound of every passing car outside. But as the waves of pleasure wash through her with each impact she forgets everything except for the beloved man flattening her with his warm weight and gasping urgently next to her ear.

The Saturday before Thanksgiving, Carlos drives them to the Fall Folk Festival in the Adams-Morgan neighborhood of northwest

D.C. The schoolyard site simmers with humanity. Graciela cannot enjoy the festival, so possessed is she by the fear that Rosa will disappear into the throng. There is so much to attract a four-year-old: the stalls of craftsmen selling votary candles or faux-African metalwork or felt paintings of unicorns and matadors; the vendors cooking barbecue or shish kebabs or egg rolls on open grills, the aromas blending in a spicy fog that immerses the fair-goers.

And then there is the dinosaur: a plastic apparition, half balloon and half tent, with a gullet full of squirming, screaming youngsters. Graciela holds Marcelo and watches anxiously as Carlos waits with Rosa in line, then helps her up the steps to the monster's tail, a slide. Rosa vanishes inside the trampoline belly of the behemoth. A few minutes later, weeping, the victim of a small elbow's collision with her temple, she is retrieved from the rubbery maw by Carlos. Graciela notes how Carlos kisses and holds her daughter, and thinks he would make a good father for her children, and for new children of her own.

On their way back to the rented truck, they see a photographer taking pictures of a blond child on the steps of a renovated brownstone while the young parents adjust a giant silver mirror as big as a satellite dish. Only rich people can afford private photographers for their children. But the incident gives Graciela an idea. On Sunday afternoon she invites Yolanda to go with her to the Sears in northwest D.C. Here, Graciela has a photo made of herself with Rosa and Marcelo while Yolanda watches. On their way out, they see a black family in fine clothes waiting to have a picture taken. Yolanda says that black people are lucky, they can wear any color.

Yolanda invites them over for Thanksgiving. "Tell Carlos he can come, too," she says, even though Isidro does not care much for Carlos.

Graciela sets the alarm to wake her early Thanksgiving morning. She puts a few dishes into the oven; Yolanda has been baking the turkey all night. While the dishes cook, she wakes and bathes and dresses first Rosa, then Marcelo.

The knock on the door at nine-thirty surprises her; she is not expecting Carlos until eleven. At first, when she sees the two ladies from the Episcopal church there, she thinks that she must have done something wrong when she enrolled Rosa in the preschool program.

"Happy Thanksgiving, Graciela," one of the ladies says, handing her a pie covered in plastic wrap.

"I hope you don't mind," says the other lady. She is carrying a bag of apples, oranges, cantaloupes.

Graciela's English fails her. She furrows her brow and shakes her head. "No, no, no . . . "

"It was the least we could do," the lady with frosted hair says, setting the pie on the drain board. To her amazement, Graciela sees that teenage children, a girl and a boy, are carrying yet more food into her efficiency apartment. They make trip after trip, the ladies and the children. Soon food is stacked in piles on the counters, the end table, in the refrigerator—pies, cakes, platters of baked ham and sliced turkey, dishes of rice and corn and potatoes, croissants and rolls and cornbread, platters of cookies. Rosa and Marcelo are silently astonished.

Graciela is in tears. "Thank you, thank you," she repeats, wiping her eyes. "Tell them thank you," she instructs Rosa.

"Y'all have a happy Thanksgiving." The blond lady flashes a toothy smile, and they are gone.

When Carlos arrives, he does not at first understand her explanation. "You go to their church?"

"No, Rosa goes to their church school."

"And they brought you all this, even though you don't go to their church?" Carlos smiles. "Don't tell Yolanda."

"Why?"

"Tell her you made it all herself. Tell her you were up all night cooking. See what she says."

A knock on the door. Graciela half expects to see the church ladies with another load. She does not expect to see Darryl.

"Graciela, brought you some . . ." His voice fades as he sees Carlos standing behind the counter that divides the kitchen from the rest of the little room. The building manager's eyes take in the pyramids of food. "Don't let me interrupt your party," he says in his accented Spanish.

Graciela glances anxiously from Darryl to Carlos. She hesitates for a moment, a fatal moment. Then Rosa runs to Darryl and wraps her arm around his leg. "Uncle Darryl, Uncle Darryl!"

Darryl gently pushes her back. With a cold glance at Graciela, he turns silently and strides out the door.

"Who is that?" Carlos hisses.

"Just the apartment man."

"Why did you look at him like that?" Carlos nods at Rosa. "Uncle Darryl, she calls him. Uncle Darryl."

Darryl's truck can be heard driving away.

"Who is he?"

"He's . . . nobody," Graciela says, turning and picking up a pie.

"Who the fuck is he?" Carlos shouts. He grabs Graciela's hand so violently she drops the pie. It cracks and oozes across the floor. Graciela slaps him, and he hits her. She shrieks.

The children are staring at them. Rosa begins to cry.

Carlos walks out of the apartment. Graciela bursts into sobs as she hears the door of the truck slam shut. Then she rushes out into the parking lot. "Carlos!" The tires screech as the truck lurches away.

She turns and sees Rosa standing in the door, and beyond her, tier after tier of festival food.

24

Telephones clatter across the 'hood early one morning as members of the Krewn awaken each other with the news that their leader is dead. Tito has been found in a vacant lot near the waterfront, his hands tied behind his back, two bullets in his head.

"It wasn't no drive-by," Willy observes to Evander. They sit subdued, conversing in low tones as they munch on their french fries, glancing over their shoulders whenever anyone enters the McDonald's restaurant. "It was a *essecution*."

Everyone knew that Tito must have been ambushed by someone he knew. Willy purveys a theory that Evander has already heard. On the night of the slaying, someone had seen Tito talking to Grady the cop. There are even reports that Tito had been seen getting into a squad car.

Why would the five-oh kill Tito? One theory holds that the cops were upset by the upsurge in violence by the Krew under Tito's leadership. They were afraid that the attention of the federal government, and the newspapers, might lead to exposure of their own profitable dealings with the gang. Another version of the theory suggests that the police executed Tito in order to restore Frizzell to power. Frizzell, it is said, has been hiding from the Baltimore hit man whom his former protégé Tito had hired to track him down. The master was not to be outdone by his student; if Tito had hired a contract killer, Frizzell had hired an even more formidable assassin or assassins from the ranks of the D.C. blues. Blue for the Krew.

Evander does not know what to believe. But the theories

seem more plausible when Frizzell appears at Tito's funeral and, in the following few days, reassumes his position as first among equals. From the Funkadelic, the word goes forth that all offenses against Tito are now to be amnestied. The infighting must cease. The Krew must be a brotherhood once again.

Evander does not return to the Funkadelic until he is summoned by the man himself.

"I hear tell you and Tito had words," Frizzell says when Evander nervously enters his upstairs office.

Evander looks at the floor and shrugs.

"Man, we can't afford to fight among ourselves." Frizzell has lost weight; the fat hangs loosely from his cheekbones and his jaw. "That's how the Punkstas could take advantage of our weakness and take out Tito. You hear what I'm saying? All of y'all? Now we're gonna fuck those muthafuckas for killing Tito. But it's got to be by strategy. Meantime, we got to rebuild our customer base."

Frizzell has $400 of rock in Baggies issued to Evander. "Don't fuck up on me, Deuce. You my ace kool."

"I need a gun," Evander says. When he feels the cold weight in his hand, he feels as though he, like Frizzell, has completed a long convalescence.

When, as he departs, Frizzell flashes him the sign, it is less like a salute than a benediction. Evander does not know whether Frizzell was behind Tito's execution. He is glad, though, that somebody had the muthafucka killed.

"Yo, Evander!"

Twon is standing on the corner talking to a couple of junior high girls. Evander stops, then waves at him dismissively. He used to be Twon's friend, but now Twon is on the margin of the set. Evander doesn't have time for punks.

"Yo, Evander! I hear Scab kicked yo' butt!"

Evander halted. "Wha'd you say?"

"Ol' Scab, that old homeless with the burned-up face? He whupped yo' ass." Twon cackles, then turns back to the girls.

Stunned with shame, Evander starts off down the street. He can hear Twon's laughter, feel the girls looking at him. *I hear Scab kicked yo' butt.* Evander feels the pressure of tears in his face. *He whupped yo' ass.* From Twon it will spread to the Funkadelic, throughout southeast D.C. Everyone will know he lost a fight with a beggar. Everyone will know . . .

Evander stops and slowly turns around.

"Twon!" Faint with rage, Evander charges toward his former friend. "Twon!" Evander snarls.

Twon turns. Evander's pace drops from a run to a brisk stride. He pulls the gun from his pants and holds it straight in front of him. His rival's mouth opens. The fear on Twon's face is Evander's reward.

Nothing else is supposed to happen. Suddenly, though, the gun is going off, the pistol, spitting shell casings, is kicking in Evander's hand, twice—three times? The smell of cordite splits the air, and then the screaming of the girls. Twon's face wrinkles in pain as he capsizes, a blotch shaped like a butterfly darkening the right side of his blue sweatshirt.

"He's killing him!" a girl is shrieking.

Evander stands slack for a moment, bewildered. Twon is looking at him from the grass, more in surprise than in pain. Evander stares back. He has shot Twon.

Then Evander is running, passing astonished children on the sidewalk, veering into a sunlit alley, clambering over a fence and crashing through somebody's garden, scattering flowerpots with a clatter and clink, scraping his hands on fence wire. When he is a few blocks away, he slows to gulp a few cool drafts of air.

He is clutching the 9 mm. The metal is still warm. He thinks of the police as he jogs, and looks for a place to hide the gun. There—he spots a metal Dumpster in an alley. Glancing around, he wraps the Glock in a bit of greasy brown paper and tosses it into the giant canister among the plastic trash bags, cardboard boxes, and rotting melons.

He walks on, emerging on H Street. He tries to look cool, to look bad, to give no hint that he has just gunned down and maybe killed a man. He saunters along the sidewalk, his expression an imperious scowl, past the dusty barbershop window, beneath the broken H Tel sign, past the hardware store with its graffiti-laced metal gate rolled up for the duration of the business day. Evander scans the street ahead: a few boys, ten or eleven, a bearded pipehead stumbling along and mumbling to himself, a fat lady lugging a bag of groceries.

Then the squad car turns the corner.

They are looking for him. They have to be. Evander plunges through the nearest door, into the Africare Beauty Salon. Chimes clatter, and air thick with lotions and perfumes hits him. The hair-stylists and the old ladies look up.

"Evander!" exclaims Pearl, one of the stylists. She used to cut Evander's hair before he decided he was too grown-up to accompany his mother and grandmother to the Africare salon. "You come to get your hair done?"

"Yeah."

"Baby, it's going to be a while, if you don't got an appointment. You don't mind waiting, baby?"

"Naw." Evander sinks down in a chair and picks up a copy of *People* magazine. He flinches as a beam of light sweeps across him—but it is only the reflection of a passing car.

Where are the cops? Evander experiences another flashback: the crack-crack-crack, the scream of the girls, Twon's face warping in surprise and pain . . .

"So he say, 'Ooh, girl, come down and listen to this preacher.' He say, 'God want to make you *rich*,'" Pearl is telling an old lady as she washes her hair. "He say, 'That preacher, he swear up and down, if you make him a contribution, you know, if he pray for you, you're guaranteed to get a lucky hit.' Win the lotto, get a raise—you know, something like that."

"Mm-hmmm."

"So I say, 'Don't you listen at no lying-ass preacher like that. He just want yo' money . . . '"

"He sure do."

"And you know what he say? He say, 'I got a friend in Baltimore, and he gives this preacher a contribution, and the next day, one of them Safeway things, you know? He won twenty-five dollars.' And you know what I say? I say, 'He ain't worshiping Jesus, he worshiping Safeway!'"

"A-hay-men."

Evander is staring at a black-and-white magazine photo of a

happy white Hollywood couple strolling the beach hand in hand, but he does not see it. He is going over the inevitable sequence in his mind: the squad cars in front of his house, splashing the neighborhood with melting crimson; the policemen cuffing him and leading him away as his mother and grandmother and siblings watch; the humiliation of being forced to strip naked under a cold fluorescent light in the police station. He does not think about the trial, since it does not occur to him that he might not be convicted. Instead, he begins to prepare himself mentally for prison. He has heard all about it from other members of the Krew. If you don't make them afraid of you on the inside, some dude will try to make you his bitch, make you suck his dick and take it up the ass. Evander resolves to pick a fight on his first day inside, his first hour, just to show what a crazy, mean muthafucka he is. It does not matter if they beat him until he passes out; after he returns from the infirmary, the word will be out: Don't mess with that Evander. He may be skinny, but he bad. He a stone-cold killer. He shot his own friend down like he was a dog just for making fun of him.

Evander flinches, shocked out of his reverie by the touch of Pearl's hand on his head. "Baby, I think we ought to give you some Jheri curls. Like Michael Jackson."

"Don't want no Jheri curls."

"It'll just be ten more minutes, baby."

The door chimes tingle. A middle-aged man in an orange delivery suit comes in.

"Hi, Otis," says Pearl.

"Did y'all hear about that shooting? They is police all over, down near Eighth and Georgia. Some kid got shot."

"Oh, Lordy," says one of the old ladies.

Evander's muscles shrink into knots.

Pearl joins Otis at the door and looks down the street. "There goes a police car. Who was it got shot?"

"I don't know. Some teenage boy. He in the hospital. Nobody seen who done it. Ain't nobody seen nothin'."

Ain't nobody seen nothin' . . . For the first time, it occurs to Evander that he might escape arrest.

He goes to the bathroom in the back of the store. When he is finished washing his hands, he looks at his twin in the mirror. The round baby face on its thin stalk of a neck ages before his eyes, hardening into a contemptuous mask. The face of a stone-cold killer.

Ain't nobody seen nothin' . . . The code of the street is already working to protect Evander. He thinks of all those teenage girls, all those children, who had watched him pull his 9 mm and pump two or three slugs into Twon. Every one of them, questioned by the police, will say the same thing: "I don't know." They have all grown up learning what happens to snitches.

Suddenly Evander is no longer steeling himself for battles in prison. He is thinking of ways to beat the rap.

"Hold still, baby," Pearl tells him as she rinses his hair.

Warm water rills over his temples, his ears. He wonders whether it was a mistake to toss the gun into the Dumpster. Maybe the cops have found it already.

"How much of a fade you want, baby?"

Evander shows her with his hands. "Kind of like up to here . . ." Pearl will be his alibi.

"I gotta use your phone," Evander tells Pearl after he pays her. Closing the door of the salon office, he leans back in the desk chair and dials. He listens to the other phone ringing and gazes at the picture on the calendar, a giant red barn in an arcadian Midwestern landscape.

"She ain't here," Alicia's little sister tells him.

He hangs up and dials the number of the Funkadelic. But Frizzell is out, too.

Walking home, Evander flinches every time a car turns the corner, thinking it might be a squad car. Back at the Wood, he tenses when his mother says, "You look different."

Can she tell her son just shot a man?

"Oh, it's your hair! Where'd you get your haircut?"

"Pearl's," he mutters. He goes into his room, shuts the door, turns the stereo on, claps the earphones to his head, and lies down on the bed.

. . . Cuz I told the bitch
Babe I got an itch . . .

Evander is unable to think of anything but the shooting. He relives it, again and again, replaying it in his mind so that familiarity will rob the scenes of their frightening vividness. Again and again, the look of agony that replaced the look of surprise on Twon's face, the popping . . .

His little brother Jamal opens the door. "Evander! Telephone!"

The voice belongs to Willy, one of Frizzell's retinue. "Frizzell say get yo' ass down here." Click.

Frizzell, Pharo, and several lesser members of the Krew are waiting for him at the Funkadelic in an upstairs room. When Evander walks in, Frizzell turns from the video game he has been playing and glowers.

"You shoot Twon?"

A quiver of fear goes through Evander, but he cannot let them see his doubt. He puts his hands in his pockets, lolls his head to one side, and growls, "Yeah."

"He in the hospital," says Willy.

Evander says, "I hope he die."

"You better hope he die," Frizzell replies. "You shoulda killed him, you stupid-ass nigga. You don't never shoot nobody unless you kill him. Or he come back at you."

"Then I shoot him again."

Pharo snickers and takes a sip from his beer.

"You think you hot shit, don't you?" says Frizzell. "What the fuck you go and shoot Twon for?"

"He fucked with me."

"Shit. So you go and shoot him. You stupid-ass little nappy-head nigga . . . "

"Hey, chill, man," Pharo rebukes Frizzell. "Twon dissed him, so Deuce paid him back. We woulda done the same thing."

A chorus of assent from the others in the room.

"But Frizzell's right, man," Pharo continues. "You shoulda made sure his ass was dead."

Frizzell rubs his face. The video game makes blurping and beeping noises.

"All right," says Frizzell. "Let the word go forth. Nobody better not say nothing to the police."

"What about Twon?"

"That nigger better not say nothing if he don't want nothing to happen to his family." Frizzell turns to Evander. "Where your gun at?"

"I hid it." Evander tells them about the Dumpster.

"Man, you the stupidest nigger I ever seen. That's the first place the cops are going to look. Shit." Frizzell dispatches two of his soldiers to retrieve the pistol from the Dumpster, if it is still there. "Go on, get out of here," he tells Evander.

At the door to the clubhouse room, Evander turns back. "I need another gun."

"Oh, shit." Frizzell shakes his head in disbelief.

"Willy." Pharo nods. Willy takes a pistol from his sneaker and hands it to Evander. Then Pharo, with a solemnly approving look, flashes Evander the sign.

Feeling proud, Evander swaggers down the stairs, now and then touching the new pistol in his pants.

That night Evander keeps waking in the dark to flashbacks more vivid than dreams, harsher than life. Again and again, the gun pops in his hand, again the girls scream and Twon falls . . . Muhfucka dissed me, Evander repeats to himself, the words incantation to drive away the fear and guilt and remorse crowding just outside of his mind.

He dreams of his old neighborhood in Baltimore, and the friends of his childhood. Incongruously, Lookout is there. Then the scene changes to junior high. Frizzell is the teacher, and he doesn't recognize Evander, who has cut class for months. Evander, sent to the principal, goes down a locker-paneled hall that turns into a subterranean Metro station. A train pulls up, the doors slide open, and there is the president of the United States, just like on TV. Suddenly there are Secret Service agents and policemen everywhere. . . .

His stepbrother is shaking his shoulder. "It's the police," says Jamal.

Evander is wearing only his briefs. He jumps into a pair of jeans and emerges, blinking, into the den.

Two cops are at the door, where they are physically blocked

by his mother. "We just want to talk to your son, ma'am. We just want to ask him some questions."

"Evander!" Sharonda motions for him to come forward. "Tell 'em you don't know nothin' about that Antoine."

"Are you Evander Johnson?"

"Yeah."

"Put on your clothes. We'd like you to come down to the station and answer a few questions."

"He don't know nothin'," Sharonda insists.

Evander returns to his room. He pulls on a Baltimore Orioles sweatshirt and laces his high-tops. It is over. He is resigned to trial, conviction, imprisonment.

As he emerges from his room, he hears a walkie-talkie crackle. One of the officers asks for permission to search the apartment.

"Why you want to search?" Sharonda shrills. "What you lookin' for?"

"Ma'am, we just want to look around. If you deny us permission, we'll wait until somebody brings us a search warrant."

"Baby, let 'em in," Evander's gram persuades her daughter. Much more upset than Evander, Sharonda follows the cops around as they lift up pillows on the couch and open drawers.

"See? Shit. You ain't find nothin' here! My baby ain't did nothing. Y'all ought to be out there looking for the real whoever did it. He out there right now, laughin'. Shit. Wastin' yo' time."

As the officers search his room, Evander's cool gives way to nervousness. His mother's taunts fade away as one of the cops pulls the shoebox from under his bed and removes the pistol Willy had handed him the night before.

"Is this yours?" the cop asks Evander.

"Lawd a'mercy," says his grandmother.

"Is this yours?"

"Naw. I'm keeping it for a friend."

"All right. Let's go."

"My baby!" Sharonda shrieks.

A policeman restrains her. "We're not arresting him, ma'am, even though we have cause for illegal possession of a firearm.

We just want him to come with us downtown. If we have to, we can come back with a warrant for his arrest."

"Go with 'em, baby," says his tearful grandmother.

Evander bites his lip as he is led out to the squad car. A small crowd has gathered. "Go for it, Deuce!" somebody shouts.

At the police station they do not fingerprint or photograph or strip Evander. They ain't got enough on me, he thinks, as he sits in a room with two burly cops, one black, one white.

"Do you know Antoine Drake?"

"Yeah. I know who he is. I didn't shoot him. You wastin' your time."

"When was the last time you saw Antoine Drake?"

"I don't know. Week or two ago."

"Where?"

"The Funkadelic. He hang there sometimes."

"Where were you yesterday afternoon around three o'clock?"

"Getting a haircut."

"Where?"

"The Africare Salon."

"How long were you there?"

"About an hour, hour and a half."

"Why'd it take so long?"

"I didn't have an appointment. You call 'em."

"We will."

"Ask for Pearl."

The white cop leaves. The black cop produces the pistol.

"Where'd you get this?"

"I told you, I'm keepin' it for my road dog." Instantly Evander regrets using gangsta slang for friend.

"Your road dog, huh? Your road dog got a name?"

Evander looks at the floor.

"Do you know it's illegal in the District of Columbia to possess a handgun?"

"Uh-uh," Evander replies, in all honesty. Since practically everyone he knows has one or more guns, the idea that they are illegal seems absurd.

The white cop returns and motions to the other. The two

leave Evander alone in the room. Evander tries not to let his growing apprehension show. Maybe they are watching him through a
spy camera. With his best, baddest scowl, he slowly scans the room,
looking for a place where a camera might be hidden.

The minutes seem like hours. Evander fidgets in the hard
chair. Maybe they found the gun in the Dumpster. Maybe they
traced Willy's gun to some other crime, so that Evander will be
convicted for a crime he did not commit. Maybe they have found
a witness who was willing to talk, who wasn't afraid of the Krew.
Unbid, the scene crashes into his mind once more: Twon falling,
the girls screaming, the sequence of pops . . .

The cops return. "All right, you can go, but we may want to
talk to you again."

"That's it?"

"That's it."

The cops escort Evander to a reunion with his tearful mother
and grandmother. Puzzled, he watches as the black officer lectures
Gram. "Mrs. Hawkins, we're not going to file any charges against
you, but we're going to keep your gun."

"I don't never want to ever see it again," Evander's grandmother says, shaking her head and blinking back tears. "Lawd
a'mercy, I should never have gotten that thing and asked Evander
to keep it for me in the first place. Lawd a'mercy. Ain't nothin' but
trouble comes of them things."

"Evander," his grandmother says sternly when they get home,
"I don't know who gave you that gun, but I don't want no more
of them things in the house."

"Yes, ma'am," Evander murmurs.

"You listen to your gram," Sharonda says.

Evander mutters.

"What you say? What you say to me? Don't you go talkin' no
trash to me, Evander Johnson. You ain't too big, I can't slap your
ass like when you was a baby. You hear me? You say 'Yes, ma'am.'"

"Yes, ma'am."

The next night Evander has a third gun.

He wears it as he wore the others, tucked into his high-top,
the metal chafing his ankle through his sock. They all had guns

hidden on them, all of the members of the delegation—Frizzell, Pharo, Willy, Hasan, and Evander.

They swagger down the halls of the hospital like samurai through the corridors of a Japanese castle, affecting unawareness of the alarm they inspire in nurses and orderlies, patients and doctors. They are in full regalia, these knights of the street, in their hooded coats and baggy pants pulled down on their waists, their shades masking eyes that would otherwise have been the only windows in demonic masks.

"Yo," Frizzell gestures. Like marines on the parade ground, they turn with precision.

Twon is not alone. His sister rises from the chair by his bed as they move in.

"Yo, Twon, my man. What's up?" Pharo's sunglasses hide his thoughts.

Twon stares in terror at his unexpected visitors. When he sees Evander, he scrunches up in the bed as if expecting to be drilled a second time. Anxiously, Twon glances at his sister, who hovers by the window in dread.

For a moment, seeing his friend crumpled and terrified in bed, Evander feels pity and remorse. Nigga dissed me, he reminds himself. Ain't nobody dis the Salamander.

"So who's the muthafucka done this to you?" Frizzell asks.

Twon shifts. Underneath an open pajama shirt, his right side is plastered with bandages. "I don't know. Didn't see him."

"It was the Punkstas, wasn't it?" Pharo suggests. His hand slightly touches his crotch, where he, too, wears a gun.

"Yeah. I guess."

"You told the police it was a drive-by?"

Twon looks down. "Yeah."

Frizzell is helping himself to the cupcake on the tray next to Twon's bed. "This what they feeding you?" he asks, squinting at the empty soup bowl. "Word, they ought to be feeding you some red meat."

"C'mon, man," Pharo complains, "you eating all his food."

"If they be anything we can do for you, my brother," Frizzell says, clasping Twon's hand, "you let me know. Cuz you my ace kool. Don't never forget it."

"Yo," Pharo commands. "It is time to go."

"Outta here."

"Audi 5000."

Evander is the last. At the door, he turns to give Twon the red eye. Twon stares back—but then he looks away.

Later, Evander wonders what he would have done if Twon had tried to stare him down. "I woulda shot him, prob'ly," Evander tells Eunique, hoping the tremble in his voice does not give the lie away.

They are in a dark stairwell of her apartment complex. Evander looks up as a door opens several stories above. The sound track of the building—TV noise, voices, barking—momentarily blares a little louder, then the stairwell echoes with a metallic clang as the door shuts again.

Evander resumes. "I woulda lit his ass up like Christmas right there in the hospital, just like the first time." He points his finger, feels a thrill of guilty pleasure as he makes popping sounds. "I demo'd him something serious. That nigger be *chastised*."

"You crazy!" she protests. But he can see, as he pulls her to him, that his ferocity excites her.

25

"They need crossing guards at that school," Curtis tells Velma one evening over supper. "I used to see Mr. Carnahan there. I think he's been sick."

"Why don't you do something about it?" Velma says.

Curtis mulls it over for a few days. The SSI disability payments he has been receiving since his heart condition was diagnosed have ended the financial crisis and relieved him of the need to hunt for another job. He still wants to do something useful in the world, though. He knows that sleeping late and staying in the house all day is bad for his spirit.

In a few weeks, he is out on the corner every morning and every afternoon in his nylon serape with the orange reflector stripes, escorting individual children or little groups across the intersection while he holds back cars with the extended flag. The job is not as easy as he imagined it would be. Discovering he cannot stand for hours, he brings a lawn chair. He feels guilty, moreover, when he has to take a bathroom break at the convenience store down the street, leaving a sign for the children: BACK SOON. DO NOT CROSS. The rainy days are the worst, but he checks his self-pity by thinking how much more difficult slogging through the rain is for the tiny students who depend on him.

He gets to know their names, and something about their lives. He feels young again—not like a student, but like a young parent. When he and Velma had moved into the neighborhood and sent their son and daughter to the school, they had known the other children in the neighborhood by name and had met many of their parents. Curtis had not realized how easy it is to lose contact with the neighbors after the children graduate.

The neighborhood has changed, more than he had realized. Half, perhaps more, of the kids he speaks to have no fathers at home. They seem to be poorer than the classmates of his own children, though at the time Curtis and Velma were hard-pressed to pay the bills themselves. The neighborhood seems to have lost a lot of married people with jobs. It is filling up with the people Curtis thinks of contemptuously as street trash. He despises them, but he cannot bring himself to despise their children. They are like children of any class, at least the younger ones. The older ones are already on their way to ruin, he thinks. The boys, especially, even eight- and nine-year-olds. They are embarrassed to be seen waiting to cross under his protection. Sometimes they saunter past him with a sneer, then jaywalk across the middle of the street, dodging cars. "You gonna get yourself killed!" Curtis will shout. They make him furious, even though he knows that spasms of anger can only weaken his inadequate heart.

The scorn of the bigger boys is the exception, though. The little ones adore him, thinking of him as a benevolent supernatural figure like Santa Claus or the Easter Bunny.

"Mistah, cross me over."

The words of the little girl are not a request so much as a command. Curtis is surprised. As he waited on the corner for the light to change he had not even seen the girl approach.

"All right," he says. "Take my hand."

She is embedded in a coat whose purple and pink and green matches the colors on her Barney the Dinosaur lunch box. When the light changes, she takes Curtis's hand. He reminds himself to take small steps. To her, he thinks, the four-lane street must seem like a huge expanse.

"Thank you," she says mechanically, without the slightest trace of real feeling, and hurries on. Her mother, or maybe her sister or grandmother, has trained her well, Curtis thinks. Still, something disturbs him. He realizes it is her choice of words: *Can you cross me over?* Crossing over is something that Curtis and Velma had lately helped Dad Johnson to do.

★ ★ ★

The streetlight gives each of the kids a spidery giant as a double. Two worlds meet in this corner lot with its basketball hoop, this world and a shadow world. Here they are joined and yet distinct. As Curtis drives alone through the 'hood, the boundaries blur.

The streetlights drift by. Outside the small castle that houses the Funkadelic, the members of the Krew are lounging. As Curtis drives past, the young men slowly turn and fix him with basilisk glares. Curtis almost expects to see Evander among them. Since the police questioned Evander about the gun he had hidden in the apartment, Velma has pressed Curtis to do something to help save their nephew from the street. Curtis does not know what to do.

He has been driving for an hour through the part of the 'hood he used to patrol when he was on the force. He knows the secret architecture of the Krew's little empire: the command post at the Funkadelic, the crack houses, the safe houses used for prostitution and storing loot, the parking lots for whose use the Krew pays residents of the old brownstones and apartment buildings. He catches a glimpse, down an alley, of the Bunker, rumored to be an arsenal for the Krew, a whitewashed brick building owned by a white guy named Darren or Darryl whom everyone on the police force knew or at least knew of. The raid on the headquarters of the rival gang, the Yungstaz, a few weeks ago that made the television news had left the Bunker untouched. Indeed, shutting down the Yungstaz would drive up the street value of the drugs the Krew deals in. Less competition. The Krew, Curtis concludes, must have protectors in the federal government, or on the force.

Curtis drifts through the dark labyrinth of southeast D.C. listening to the police dispatcher, and broods and thinks about the war. He has not thought of his platoon for a long time. A few of its members are vague shadows in his memory—that black guy from Detroit, whose name he cannot even recall, Turner? Others he remembers vividly. Tim Wilson, their lieutenant, a ROTC graduate, a white boy from Iowa—almost literally a boy. He looked as though he was fourteen years old. At first he thought he had to prove his authority by being strict, but his harshness had not survived the first few patrols. Soon he accepted his position as first among equals, even waiting, one night, to take his turn with a dink prostitute the platoon shared at the side of a road.

Curtis had a grudging respect for Wilson, but he did not like him. Nor did he like one of the other white guys in their unit, an Italian from Philadelphia named Tony. Tony thought he was John Wayne in *The Green Berets*. He overloaded himself with weapons: an M-16, an M-1 carbine, a 9 mm on one hip, a .38 on the other, grenades strapped across his chest, knives. Most "cherries" who took too much firepower with them into the woods ended up abandoning one weapon after another as the days went on and their strength ebbed. But Tony did not change.

The white guy Curtis liked the best was a hick from West Virginia named Earl, a big guy with black hair and crooked teeth whom the guys in the platoon sometimes called L'il Abner. Evidently Earl had never seen any black people before he joined the army; that accounted, perhaps, for his curious lack of the usual prejudices, even though he called Curtis and the other black guys "niggers," thinking this was the accepted term. Earl was superstitious, and he asked Curtis once if it was true that black skin warded off bullets. It had long been rumored that VC snipers refused to shoot black soldiers as part of a strategy to weaken the American forces by inflaming racial divisions; enough white soldiers believed the story to think that they would be safer in platoons with a lot of black GIs. Some garbled version of this, no doubt, had inspired Earl's confidence that his black buddies would act as talismans, shielding him from fire.

Mookie laughed the hardest when Curtis shared the tale with him. Mookie was the jester of the outfit, a kid from Harlem. He was high much of the time, but so were most of them in the unit. There was never any shortage of drugs—not just marijuana and speed, but every kind of pill you could ask for. The officers— including Tim Wilson, so strict at first—looked the other way. Wilson, after a while, began taking downers himself to counteract his panics.

It happened one night when they were out on patrol in the woods north of the air base at Tuy Hoa. There were reports of NVA infiltration and everyone was even more nervous than usual. Still, when Curtis woke Mookie to replace him on sentry duty at two or three in the morning, the kid from Harlem seemed to be all right.

Curtis will never forget the terror he felt when he was ripped from his dreams by the clatter of a machine gun. "What the fuck . . . ?" A shadow lunged at him. But it was only Tony, as scared as he was. Hearts pumping, they crawled through the darkness toward the clearing where Mookie stood in a delirium, spraying the trees with fire from his chuckling M-60.

When he saw them, Mookie screamed, "Vee Cee!"

He stopped firing. They pulled him down. His eyes were bulging and his forehead was damp. He was feverish; no, he was high. "Vee Cee," he began to sob.

They lay there in the wet grass for a time, listening. After a while, when they heard no sounds other than their own troubled breathing, they ventured forth.

"Jesus Christ," Curtis heard Tony say. The flashlight showed Tim Wilson's dead face, blood trickling from his mouth. The black guy from Detroit was dead, too, his face pulped by Mookie's bullets.

Earl, though, was hanging on to life. He looked up at them, uncomprehending, wheezing as blood bubbled through his chest. It took him a few minutes to die. Curtis threw up.

"They'll think we fragged Wilson," Tony whispered as the survivors huddled in the dawn light, all except Mookie, who had shrunk into a knot on the ground, moaning and whispering to himself in the throes of withdrawal.

"Ought to kill that muthafucka Mookie," snarled Jake Turner.

"Shut up, man, listen," hissed Tony. "You want to go through a whole investigation? If they court-martial Mookie, they might go after us, too. We got to bury them here. It was NVA. We were attacked in the middle of the night. It's what we got to do, you know?"

They buried their buddies and returned to camp and the story of the midnight NVA raid was soon official. No one said anything to Mookie, whose tour was soon over. Not long after Mookie left, Curtis came down with a severe gastrointestinal infection and was put in a hospital at Cam Ranh Bay and then the States. His Vietnam war was over.

Curtis has not thought about those days in a long time. Now he cannot stop thinking about them.

The monthly meeting of the Jefferson Elementary PTA is on a Thursday night. Curtis and Velma are there. Curtis pitches in, helping the menfolk in the cafeteria kitchen cook a supper of griddle cakes and sausage, and enjoys the horseplay. "He wears that apron every night!" Joe Russell says, ribbing an ex-marine named Leroy Stephens. "Yeah," says Leroy, "I may wear the apron, but I got the sausage!"

At the beginning of the meeting, the principal asks Curtis to stand. "Most of you know Curtis Hawkins, and you know that he has committed his life to serving his community. He served the country in uniform in Vietnam, and when he came back he put on a different uniform and helped to keep our neighborhood safe when he served for many years as a member of the District police force. His wife Velma, as many of you know, works at D.C. General. Their own children graduated from Jefferson many years ago and moved away, and their grandchildren are going to school out of state. Even so, Curtis came to us and said, 'What can I do to help?' If you know Curtis Hawkins, you wouldn't be surprised, that's the way he is. That's the way he always has been. If something needs to be done, he'll volunteer to do it, no questions asked, no complaints, no need for glory. I know Curtis, and I know he is a modest man and he doesn't expect any praise for pitching in and helping others out. But we shouldn't take him for granted. We see him out there every morning, rain or shine, always ready with a smile, keeping our children and our students safe from harm. Curtis, you have given this school more than we can ever repay. As a token of our appreciation, though, we've designed a plaque. It says, 'Curtis Hawkins, In Gratitude for Service, the Students and Parents of Jefferson Elementary.'"

Curtis tries to remain stoic, but as the cafeteria rattles with applause his lip begins to tremble. "I just want you to know," he manages to stammer as he accepts the award, "I just want you to know that I will do anything for these kids. I've been in the army, and I've been on the police force. Anybody who messes with the children of this community, they are going to have to answer to me."

★ ★ ★

A faultline in the wet green earth, the Vietnam Memorial glows darkly. Beneath the long sweep of the wall, a tour guide is lecturing to a knot of Japanese tourists. A burly, bearded white man, in a flight jacket and a military cap, is standing alone before a cascade of names. Here and there, tributes have been left—a plastic Baggie of photos, a wreath sagging in a puddle.

As he had approached the wall, Curtis had felt himself being smothered by the dread that had kept him from ever visiting this place before. If he had been alone, he would have turned back. But he is not alone.

"Over here," Evander calls.

Evander has found the name, a ghostly shimmer in the liquid black. Timothy Wilson. "Is that him?" Evander asks.

Curtis works his mouth, in a slow-motion wince. "Yeah."

"He got killed by the Vietnamese?" There is awe in the boy's voice.

"Yeah," Curtis lies.

A Latino man watches as a woman—his sister? his wife?—holds up their little girl to make a tracing of a name on the wall. Evander watches the procedure with interest, then follows his uncle.

"How do you join the army?" Evander asks.

"You thinking about joining the army?"

"Yeah."

Curtis realizes that Evander isn't joking. "Why do you want to join the army?"

"I don't know."

"You want to play with guns? Like that gun you had you said was your gram's?" Evander looks away. Curtis realizes he has made a mistake. He tries again. "Let me tell you something, Evander, they don't play in the army. They're serious."

Curtis watches his nephew's thin finger glide and bump over names.

"I'll tell you what," Curtis resumes. "If you're serious about the army, I'll look into it. But you got to have a high school diploma. You hear what I'm saying? They ain't going to take no dropouts in the army. You got to have a high school diploma, or a

GED, that's the same thing. And they'll pay your way through college." Curtis tries to read the expression on his nephew's face, but cannot. "Might not be bad, the army. Tell you what. Let's make a deal. You stay in school, you go on to high school and get your diploma, I'll help you out. I'll help you out with an allowance. You get your diploma, and you can join the army. Or maybe by that time you'll want to do something else. Like go straight on to college."

Evander's back is turned to him, so Curtis cannot tell whether he is getting through to the boy or not. "Well?" Curtis asks. "We got a deal?"

"I don't know."

"Yes or no? You want to join the army?"

"I don't know. I guess so."

"Well, then, you're going to graduate from high school. Deal?"

"I guess so," Evander mumbles.

Evander moves on. Curtis, frustrated, cannot tell whether he has reached Evander or not. Curtis pauses and scans the wall. In a few minutes he finds it: Warren Earl Stanton. Earl. The big, dumb hillbilly. Despite himself, Curtis finds his face twisting and his eyes wet.

He reaches up to touch the name on the smooth, cool plane. Then he sees Evander, a few yards away, solemnly extending his fingers to touch the wall that, for a moment, connects them.

26

This is not air, but something between air and water. The Indonesian air is a kind of steam—but no, the steam of saunas and vaporizers is healthy and purgative, soaking up poisons and germs and dirt. This substance conveys them. Miasma.

Ross knows miasma. He knows the glutinous haze that rises from Mississippi swamps on humid summer noons and leaves a trail of sweat on people and animals like the slime of a snail. And he knows the sticky whiteness that thickens in downtown Washington on simmering August days until the buildings only a few blocks in front of you are reduced to hazy polygons in a blizzard that does not chill. Nothing could be more noxious than Washington's midsummer compound of Potomac steam and traffic-jam gases, or so Ross had thought until he came here to Indonesia in the rainy season. He had seen the stuff first from on high when he had descended in the Singapore Airlines jumbo jet through a Wagnerian cloudscape: blue cotton mesas, canyons of black foam, rows of knobby cumuli like weird formations in a sandstorm desert, the whole splashed with films of lightning. Then they had passed through the lowest floor of the blue-black clouds and hovered for a few minutes in a zone of quartz translucency above a brown lake from which islands rose. But the islands were mountaintops and the brown lake was the gelid blend of car exhalations, the fumes of smokestacks, and the charring twisters of a million chimneys. In this miasma Ross has been submerged for two days.

"The land over there—it will be industrial park," the assistant minister of industry says, leaning forward from the backseat of the Toyota.

"Is that right." Gazing out the window, Ross tries to imagine a high-tech complex in the countryside drifting past. The land is venomously green and much of it is not even land; like the air, it is alloyed with water. Men and boys stand waist-deep or neck-deep in emerald ooze like statues of forgotten gods emerging from lacustrine muck.

The assistant minister says something to the driver, and they turn off onto a side road. Ross feels a flash of disappointment on leaving the highway. Out in the open, clean, new, with its signs in Phoenician script and its Japanese cars and trucks, the highway is the least alien place in Indonesia. Jakarta is partly familiar; it is industrialized without being modern. It is what a dark, squalid, muddy town in the Dark Ages might have been if goatherds had worn Walkmans and if merchants in between sales at their stalls had stared at flickering blue television sets.

The country, though, is old Asia, older than Samsung trucks or American-style four-lane highways, older even than the small black cannon mounted in front of the governor's palace in the old Dutch section of the metropolis. The country is another planet, with a gravity greater than the world where Ross belongs, so that everything is heavier, everything sags and bends and flows. The tile roofs on the farmhouses are warped and buckled by that mysterious force. The clumped trees droop, the peasants slump, even when they are not bowed beneath poles balanced on their shoulders with bottled water or bundles of food swinging from the ends.

"All of this, industrial park," the assistant minister explains.

The paved road beneath them gives way to a gritty gumbo of gravel and muck. They bump through a fence of trees and a more formidable fence of barbed wire to a cluster of old stone farm buildings. Reluctantly Ross gets out, leaving the pure encapsulated air of the Toyota for the miasma.

The assistant minister is talking to a middle-aged man in a suit. They all look alike to Ross's unfamiliar eye, these small Malays, and to him they all look peculiar. Unfamiliar with this part of the world, Ross had expected the Indonesians to resemble

East Asians. He has never seen any people like these, with their dwarf-like proportions and dark brown skins and round faces. To Ross the men all look like boys, but for their thin black mustaches. Maybe that is why they wear them.

Ross forgets the supervisor's alien name the moment he hears it. "This is factory," the supervisor explains, leading them into what Ross guesses had originally been a barn. It takes a while for his eyes to adjust; the place is as dark as a galley or a mine. Ross's idea of a factory is a clean space with high ceilings and antiseptic lights. Here there is only a crazy clutter of women, some of them girls, sitting at tiny workstations with trays of implements before them gleaming under tiny lamps. Ross remembers seeing a photograph of a sweatshop in New York's Garment District.

"We have contract with many American companies. And Japanese." A plastic computer keyboard is offered to Ross for his inspection.

Outside, his guides unroll a map. Where the main complex will be now stands a little shantytown. The workers live there, Ross guesses. The homes are little more than lean-tos wedged into the mud. From the quilt of roofs and walls a brown slope slides down to a greenish pond. A naked child and a dog are playing on the chocolate slant.

"Your plans are very ambitious," Ross says, noncommittal. The air moves. It is not quite a breeze, but a shift, a resettling. The smell of the pond is the smell of a latrine. Ross glances back at the brown beach, turns, staggers toward some shrubbery, and begins to spew.

He is no longer vomiting a few hours later, alone in his room at the Hotel Indonesia, and the worst of the diarrhea has stopped thanks to the little blue pills. But anything he eats turns to tobacco juice and passes through him.

He is miserable. But he is not very afraid. He was sick several times when he had been stationed in Asia, and he acquired a respect for the recuperative powers of his own body. At any rate, he has no time to be immobilized, either by sickness or fear. He has work to do.

His mind whirs and flashes as he rolls in the sweaty sheets. He keeps seeing the pitiful faces of the women trapped in that sweatshop. They remind him of the faces of the poor in magazine advertisements for Save the Children or other charities. He knows all the conservative arguments by heart: every country must go through a sweatshop stage if it is to industrialize; the sweatshop may be appalling by First World standards, but it is an improvement over the Third World farm; the best way to help the poor of the Third World is to buy the products they make. The conservatives have the arguments, but the soft-hearted, soft-headed liberals have the faces, the pathetic faces.

Then he has it. The inspiration comes in a stroke. He feels his mind afire with creativity, the images and phrases tumble through his consciousness more rapidly than he can comprehend. He is Michelangelo and William Blake, he is Shakespeare and Dante. He writhes on the bed possessed by the vision that his office, following his instructions, will turn into pixels and print and fax back to Jakarta to impress the admiring officials of the ministry of trade. He sees the face of a forlorn, beautiful young Malay woman, and above it, or below, the text:

YOU CAN HELP THIS YOUNG WOMAN
WITH AN INVESTMENT OF FIVE DOLLARS.

An investment of five hundred thousand would help even more. This young woman and others like her are struggling today to build a better life for themselves by making products for American consumers. They do not ask for charity. They ask only for a chance to earn the rewards of their hard work and dedication.

Some in America want this young woman to remain poor. They do not want countries like Indonesia to develop. And they want American consumers to be forced to subsidize bloated, unionized workers in the United States.

You can help your company by investing in Indonesia, where the business climate is as healthy as the fresh, transparent air. You can help working Americans by reducing the costs of the goods they buy. And, most of all, you can help this young woman build the better life she dreams of.

Do good by doing well.

While Paul slices onions on the cutting board in Ross's kitchen, Ross studies him. Paul has never looked better. Before, he was always a little too soft. Now, he is slender, almost gaunt. It is a week later, and Ross, back home, is astonished and grateful that Paul asked for a place to stay on his way to a vacation in New York.

"You're not cooking," Paul concludes when he is told that the strainer is packed away on a high shelf. "Lots of dates?"

"Naw. Well, I told you about Avery."

Since Paul surprised him with his call, Ross has been rehearsing their reunion in his mind. He was disappointed by the perfunctory hug when Paul arrived at his doorstep. He had been hoping, unrealistically, for a passionate embrace. Ross had hoped when he had helped carry Paul's bags to the guest room that they would end up in the same bed, as in the old days. That is why, during the meal, Ross talks, perhaps too much, about his good fortune: his promotion, the money pouring in. Though he is losing his looks, Ross is more prosperous than ever. Surely that must count in his favor . . .

After the meal, while the coffee is brewing, Paul tells him. "Ross, I'm sick."

At first Ross does not understand. He is still muddled by jet lag from the Asian trip. "I've got some stuff upstairs . . . "

"I tested positive."

Ross feels the walls rushing away from him, feels as though he is falling through space in his chair. As though across a great distance he hears Paul saying, "Have you been tested?"

"I'm fine!" Ross snaps, immediately regretting the sharpness of his response. "I haven't done anything . . . You know."

Paul smiles slightly, looks at his plate.

Hours later, Ross lies clothed on his bed. Paul, a few minutes earlier, disappeared into the guest room for the night. No kiss, no hug, just a smile. The door shut behind him with the slightest of clicks.

Ross stares at the ceiling. He hears the hiss of the guest room's shower.

Paul is trying various medications and treatments, he had said. He was sure he was going to beat it, he had said too smoothly, as though it were a line he had learned in a counseling session. Then they had talked of other subjects, listened to some of Ross's new country-and-western CDs, caught part of a movie on HBO, as though everything were normal, as though the world had not suddenly become an alien planet in a forbidding universe.

The shower hisses. Ross pictures the water streaming over Paul's naked body, a body whose terminal wasting he had mistaken for athletic perfection. He should be grieving, Ross tells himself, he ought to be in tears. Instead, he is emotionally numb and physically aroused. Paul is dying. He, Ross, may be dying as well, and yet stupid, suicidal instinct is undeterred.

In the other room, the shower is turned off. The abrupt metallic clunk is echoed by smaller concussions throughout the plumbing that veins the old house like reverberations from a terrible crash.

"We've redefined our categories," the woman is saying. "We took another look at the polling data and the returns, and we decided that six clusters make more sense than four."

Her name is Linda and she works for a list-broker firm. She is spreading her wares on the table of the conference room at Wriston, White. Six brochures in red, white, and blue, each describing one of the categories of voters on her firm's direct-mail list: New Dealers. New Age Progressives. Christian Conservatives. Market Libertarians. Middle-Class Disaffecteds. Urban Americans.

"The New Dealers—this is the older group?" Ross asks.

"That's right. Mostly over sixty. Their main concern is the funding of Social Security . . . "

Ross tries to pay attention, but three o'clock is approaching. In a few minutes, his test results will be ready. He will soon learn whether he, like Paul, has AIDS.

His thoughts are far from voting clusters. He can't get an image out of his mind. He is sitting in the doctor's shabby office, watching the nurse, a black woman, twist the little sample bottle onto the syringe in his arm. Dark blood spurts into the glass tube, a purple orgasm.

For two nights he has lain awake, pondering. He is reconciled to dying. He is almost forty; no one will remark on the tragedy of a young man cut short before he can begin to live. He has lived a full life. He has reached the peak of his profession. He has had nothing to look forward to but twenty or thirty years of ebbing energy and slow physical decline, the slow transformation of the mammal into the scaly and splotched reptile. Better to die in his early forties than to live as long as his mother has, to outlive sanity and continence and much of consciousness itself, to become a ward of his sister and her husband or their adult children. How horrible, he has been thinking, to be childless in advanced age with the result that to your closest relatives you are merely a senile and hideous great-uncle or great-aunt, a relic of somebody else's past who must be maintained out of duty rather than love.

He is prepared to die. He will not permit himself to dwindle. He will prevent that by using one of the guns in his big house on Capitol Hill—the .22, maybe. Or the Colt. He will go out like a soldier and a Southern gentleman, having left his papers in perfect order to deny his colleagues and his sister the opportunity to complain. The Drummond family line will be carried on by his sister's family. And if it dies out, what does it matter? In five hundred years America will be repopulated by Mexicans and Chinese anyway. The United States will go the way of the Confederacy. At least the Drummonds of Mississippi outlived the CSA.

The wall of the foyer is paneled with photos: presidents, senators, congressmen, movie stars, musicians. It is a bit much, Ross thinks, as the maître d' hurries toward him. Dino's Restaurant likes to advertise itself as a Washington institution, along with the Capitol, the White House, the Supreme Court, and the Lincoln Memorial. Its character has changed, though. The original Dino's had been a smoky hangout on the Hill for congressional staffers and lobbyists; Ross had gone there a few times when he had been on the minority staff of the Senate Foreign Relations Committee. When the management moved the restaurant to this bright space in the basement of a K Street office tower, a certain intimacy as well as a certain picturesque sleaziness was lost.

"Mr. Drummond, yes. They are expecting you."

The maître d' leads Ross past tree-size potted jungle plants and tables into a private room where George White and another senior partner, Skip Wriston, are waiting. The waiter takes Ross's drink order—scotch and water—then Ross waits for the older men to start. He assumes this will be a discussion of the Indonesian project.

"Ross," George says slowly, "we've come to an impasse, and we want your advice about something. We really need your expertise."

"Shoot."

"Well . . . Skip, why don't you explain."

"It's the letterhead," Wriston tells Ross. "We just can't decide the format, and we wanted an outside opinion. Here, take a look." He hands a folder to Ross.

Inside are several sheets of letterhead. Baffled, and more than a little irritated, Ross glances at them and sets the folder down. "Looks fine to me."

White glances at Wriston, then turns to his protégé. "If it was a snake, it would have bit you." A wrinkled pink finger jabs at the names on the letterhead. Wriston, White, Greenstein, Mills, and Drummond.

The two older men burst into laughter as they see the surprise on Ross's face. Then they are pumping his hand and congratulating him, and he is downing his scotch.

"When you landed the Indonesia account, you were in," George White explains. Ross looks at Wriston. The old buzzard is cordial enough tonight. He still does not like Ross, no doubt, but money is money.

The other partners will arrive in a few minutes, George tells Ross. "Dino!" A small man smoking a large cigar enters the room. "Dino, I'd like you to meet the newest partner at Wriston, White."

"How ya doing," says Dino. Make partner and you get to meet Dino, Ross thinks, shaking the fellow's hand. Will wonders never cease.

The party drags on until close to ten before the partners disperse to their homes in Chevy Chase or Vauxhall or Arlington. Ross catches a taxi back to Capitol Hill.

Only slightly drunk, he is savoring his victory. He has done it. He is a made man. In the next few weeks, his name and photo will be displayed in the *National Journal* and the trade magazines.

His income will climb. He will have a new office, and a secretary all to himself. Clubs will offer him memberships. He will be able to golf with a better class of businessmen and lobbyists. He will be one of the powers that be in Powertown.

He goes through a mental checklist of what he can now afford: a new house, his own country house instead of a time-share. A new car. Some tailor-made suits . . . It seems to him that he had forgotten something. Oh, yes. A lover.

The AIDS test had been negative. He feels no relief, only a sort of emptiness. He has been granted not a pardon but merely a reprieve. He will die, but not before he has mutated into a reptile, dry and harsh and cold.

He finds his only comfort in the thought that at least he is not the murderer of Paul. Or of Avery.

He thinks of how strange it will be to be alive after Paul is dead. How unnecessary. For he had never given up the hope that if he racked up enough honors, made enough money, acquired enough power, Paul would be impressed. Being impressed would somehow take the place of being in love, and Paul would move in with him and they would spend the rest of their lives together. In the back of his mind, he had always thought of Paul as the audience for his triumph—Paul, who would melt with admiration and repent, or at least suffer from regret for all the years he had wasted without Ross at his side. No doubt he could impress someone else, but it just would not be the same. He had done it for Paul. Or maybe he had done it for himself and used Paul as the excuse.

Through the cab window Ross watches the bone-pale dome of the Capitol revolve, the monstrous moon of the alien world in which he suddenly finds himself.

27

On his way home from the airport after his Christmas visit to his parents in Bartlesville, Bruce is stranded in traffic near the Capitol. He hunches forward in the backseat of the cab. "What's the problem?"

"That man Weinstein." The cabbie, a Nigerian, explains that Ryan Weinstein, the leader of the Direct Action Community, was gunned down on Christmas Day while trying to buy some drugs. "He was a criminal," the cabbie observes with satisfaction.

Bruce watches the weird procession pass. Weinstein's casket has been mounted on a cart and covered with the star-spangled banner. Several of his homeless charges are pulling the cart. A crowd of forty or fifty beggars, most of them black men in filthy coats, are marching alongside. Some of them are blowing whistles. Others are shaking their fists in the air and chanting, "DAC! DAC!"

"The blacks," the Nigerian cabbie says with contempt. His skin is the color of obsidian. "I do not pick up the blacks. They will rob you. They robbed a friend of mine. They will shoot you. In my country, we do not have crime like this. If you rob somebody, you are killed."

"That's the way it ought to be here," Bruce says as the taxi pulls ahead, leaving the procession to wend its way through the coldly transparent December air toward the Capitol, a light gray arc against darker gray.

His apartment is as cold as an ice cave. He turns on the heat, but leaves the lights off. There is a certain austere beauty in the way the gray natural light of the windows illuminates the kitchen and the living room.

While the coffee is brewing, he checks his messages. A few calls from the office. Christmas messages from acquaintances. Two messages from Stef.

He dials her number at her parents' house in St. Louis. He is still a little annoyed at her for not having joined him with his parents in Bartlesville. "Bruce, is that you?" Her mother has answered the phone. "How was your trip?" They chat for a few minutes. "Just a minute, I'll get Stef."

"Listen," Stef tells him a few minutes into their conversation, "Avery has gotten invited to this really terrific party in Greenwich Village on New Year's . . . "

"We can't go," Bruce says. "Remember, I've already got the tickets for the deal at the Hilton."

A pause. "I told him I'd go."

"You'd go? By yourself?"

"Bruce, there will be lots of people there. The sort of people I need to meet for my career. We're staying at Jay Prentice Pierce's apartment. I mean, *Jay Prentice Pierce*! Des thinks I should meet him. He could open all kinds of doors for me."

For a moment, Bruce is impressed that Stef is going to meet the Washington fixer that everyone talks about. Then he remembers to be affronted. "Okay, wait a minute. Let me see if I've got this straight. You've agreed to go with your friend Avery to New York on New Year's without even consulting me. I guess I'm supposed to go to the thing at the Hilton by myself."

"I'm sorry, Bruce, but it just came up . . . "

"Cancel it."

"Excuse me?"

"Tell him you're not going. You're coming back to Washington and you're going to the Hilton with me."

"Is that an order?"

"No, it's not an order. It's an ultimatum."

"Bruce, I really think you're overreacting . . . "

"I just can't believe you'd pull something like this on me at the last minute. I would look like a fool if I showed up all by myself. 'Where's your fiancée, Bruce?' 'Oh, she decided she'd rather spend New Year's in New York with her faggot friend than with me.'"

"Oh, my God. We're having a fight, aren't we?"

"I don't think this is funny, Stef. I'm serious. You're going to be at the Hilton with me on New Year's Eve."

"Bruce, look, this is just getting too intense. I thought we had a relationship where we could work things out. I thought . . . ."

Bruce hangs up.

A few moments later the enormity of what he has done strikes him. His hand trembles as he pours himself a cup of coffee. Maybe it is over, he thinks.

The phone is ringing. He starts toward it, then changes his mind. He sits down on his favorite chair and waits for the answering machine to come on.

"Bruce, I can't believe you hung up on me. I think you're being really immature. I thought we were able to talk about things. Oh, I know you're upset. I'm sorry. I shouldn't have just sprung this on you. Look, Bruce, I don't want to fight with you. I love you, okay? When you cool down, give me a call. We need to talk. Okay? I love you. Call me."

Bruce sips his coffee, sits, and ponders the stereo rack and the end table next to it. The apartment grows warmer, but the light from outside dims. The shadows expand and pool in the cozy little den.

He has to look up the number—he does not yet know it by heart—before he can call Allison.

At midnight the balloons come bouncing down. The sound of their popping echoes the popping of the corks.

"Happy New Year, Mr. President," Uncle Sam says to Bruce, who has dressed like George Washington for the Patriots Ball. Uncle Sam—in reality, a portly lobbyist for Met Life—chuckles and fills two glasses from the champagne bottle he has commandeered. Bruce takes a sip from one and offers the other to Martha Washington, a.k.a. Allison.

"Happy New Year!" she cries, embracing him. Champagne sloshes from the glasses he is holding. He winces as somebody blows a kazoo in his ear.

More balloons are descending. A sky-blue sphere bounces off Allison's eighteenth-century version of big hair. The sight is like something out of an old hippie's acid trip: Abe Lincoln, Uncle Sam, the Statue of Liberty, Davy Crockett, and Calamity Jane, all drifting past one another in a void filled by blue and red and white globes while a ghostly band plays "Auld Lang Syne."

Soon George and Martha are drifting with the other phantoms in that void. Bruce hasn't waltzed since his high school prom; it is just as well, then, that they are not so much dancing as swaying in a mob like the crowd on the Metro Orange Line going west to Virginia on a Friday evening at six. Perhaps it is the spirit of the occasion, perhaps it is merely the effect of the wine and champagne—they had taken a cab to the Hilton, so they could indulge themselves—but Bruce feels a new tenderness toward Allison as he rocks with her in his buff-jacketed arms. He leans close to her, close enough to breathe in a redolence of roses, and murmers, with all the husky passion he can muster, "You look like my great-grandmother."

"Well, I'm in the right place," she giggles as they bump into a septuagenarian couple wearing little party hats on their white heads.

The music changes from "Auld Lang Syne" to big band tunes of the forties, in keeping with the spirit of nineties conservatism. Bruce squeezes Allison a little more tightly, and is pleased to find that she does not resist. This is nice, he thinks, having a woman who wants to be with you, who doesn't have to be cajoled and negotiated with. Once again, the bitterness churns up like bile as he thinks of Stef. She should be here, at this very moment, waltzing with him in the eyes of Washington as his fiancée instead of partying in New York with her faggot friend. Not for the first time since he slammed down the phone does he think he may have made a mistake.

Fireworks are popping an hour later outside Allison's apartment. As he helps her unbutton her dress, Bruce trips and presses against Allison. "George, we're not newlyweds!" she says.

Impulsively, he kisses her on the cheek. She purrs. He kisses her again, this time on the lips. Their mouths lock. His hand slides into the open back of her dress, down the cool smoothness of her back.

"Bruce," she says at last when they draw apart, "I don't know . . . Do you think . . . ?"

Bruce pauses, but he does not hesitate. Some hours earlier, his choice was made.

28

The apartment occupies the whole length of the third floor of a town house on New York's Upper West Side. The present tenant, a middle-aged man with a mustache named Kenneth, addresses Stef and Avery in the clipped tones of someone who is not pleased with their presence.

"Here is the inside key, and this is for the outside. There's a futon under the bed that you can pull out. You're just here tonight, right?"

After Kenneth retreats to his bedroom, the two guests snicker. When he had learned they planned to spend New Year's Eve in New York, Des had phoned his friend Jay Prentice Pierce, who has been staying in Europe but keeping a pied-à-terre in Manhattan.

"It seems like everybody knows Jay Prentice Pierce," Stef says, admiring the furniture. The apartment is decorated in the elite style of the late fifties and early sixties: abstract paintings, a glass table, Barcelona chairs. "Did I tell you Des met him at Malcolm Forbes's birthday party?"

"Oh, he's just a fixer," Avery explains. "He sets up deals. My mother knows him. She's got some kind of investment with one of his real estate companies. He used to come to parties at our house when I was growing up. He's a major homo. Maybe that's why mama mia and the wicked stepfather stopped inviting him about the time I reached that awkward age."

"Isn't it kind of weird?" Stef says. "I mean, a gay man being a Wasington power broker?"

"It makes perfect sense," Avery responds. "You can't be an elected politician unless you have 2.8 children and 1.8 wives, so if you're gay you figure you'll have to make it behind the scenes. You work that much harder to get to the top, to be so rich and famous and awe-inspiring that noboby will dare make fun of you. And finally, if you don't have a family, you can spend your evenings and weekends conniving. That's why gay men make the best diplomats—and criminals." Avery smiles. "I'll introduce you to him tonight. Though I don't know why you need Jay Prentice Pierce as a mentor when you've got me."

The Soho loft is more striking than Pierce's apartment. It is a geometric exercise in intersecting planes—tall white walls, a blond wooden floor—softened only by chairs and couches freckled with postmodern designs. But it is the guests who amaze Stef. She has never seen so many beautiful men.

"Are they all models?" she asks Avery.

"I think it's a safe bet there are a few ballet dancers, too."

The crowd is not entirely male and gay. There are a few women, beautiful in the forbidding way of New York—tall, pale, poised, expensive. Like herons eyeing a duck, they assess her.

"Everybody here is, like, a god or goddess," Stef complains.

"That's New York. This is the crème de la crème. They come here from all over. They wake up one day in Dubuque or wherever, and they look in the mirror and they think, I'm fucking beautiful, what the hell am I doing here? So they catch the next bus to New York or L.A." Avery sips his wine. "You've heard of the brain drain? This is the beauty drain. The Midwest, man, with all the pretty types leaving, it must be state after state of butt-ugly people."

"Oh my God," says Stef.

At first she thinks he is naked. Then the reflexive progress of her eyes downward confirms the presence of a black loincloth, scarcely more substantial than the bow tie of the same shade binding the tan muscles of his neck.

"Wine or champagne?" the waiter asks. His hair is so blond it is almost white, like his glowing teeth. His body is the color of polished wood and looks as hard.

Stef takes a glass of champagne, feeling naked herself in the glare of his nipples. Suddenly quiet, Avery has forgotten everything in the world except the waiter, who presents an equally pleasing far side as he strolls on.

"So where is he?" Stef asks, trying not to seem too anxious. "Jay Pierce?"

Avery looks around. "He's not here. I'll let you know if he shows up."

Stef does her best not to show her disappointment. She has not admitted to Avery that the real reason she decided to come here for New Year's, at the price of a fight with Bruce, was in the hope of meeting Jay Prentice Pierce. In an almost superstitious way, she was convinced that Jay Pierce held the key to her career. The notion could be defended with perfectly rational arguments; after all, if her acquaintance with a B-team Washington insider like Ross could land her jobs first with Aglaia Kazakis and then with *Perspective*, it was reasonable to stake a lot on acquaintance with the king of Washington power brokers. But the feeling remained just that, a feeling, a sense, a premonition.

The loft rings with cries of "Happy New Year!" and the cicada clatter of kazoos.

"Is it midnight?" Stef embraces Avery and kisses him on the cheek.

"Please, woman! You'll ruin my reputation!"

They join the crowd looking out of the loft's window at the Manhattan skyline, splotched with rainbow blasts. One of the pretty boys at the windowsill says, "I *always* see fireworks when I come."

"Really?" another responds. "*I* always see the back of his head."

It is somewhere on the far side of two in the morning when the cab drops them off at the town house. There are a few minutes of gut-clenching alarm before Stef discovers, yes, she does have the spare keys after all.

Inside, they blink in the blazing light of the foyer. "Shh." Stef giggles as she helps Avery climb the switchback stairs, but every riser screeches warning of their arrival. Inside 4B, a few strategic lamps have been left burning to guide them to the second bedroom. The door of Kenneth's master bedroom is shut.

"I'll sleep on the futon," Stef volunteers in a spirit of tenderness. Avery had tried to flag a cab for half an hour without success; not until Stef took over were they able to hail one. "Young black man," he had muttered, gazing suspiciously through the parted plastic window at the Afghan driver. "They won't stop for a young black man."

Stef unrolls the futon as Avery finishes up in the bathroom. When she in turn emerges, she sees him curled up in bed with the covers around him, apparently asleep.

She turns off the light, slips out of her robe, and slides between the sheets on the futon. Filtering through the windows, along with the wintry cold, are the noises of New Year: bangs, pops, rocket whistles, and ominously close explosions, over and above the usual sirens, honking horns, and the rumble and snort of trucks.

Unable to sleep, Stef listens to the detonations. The evening has been a true experience, a bohemian experience of the sort that she should enjoy more while she is yet young. She still feels a little guilty about having deserted Bruce for the night, and rehearses the arguments with her own conscience. She was not asking for some extraordinary indulgence. How can their marriage possibly work, except as a partnership, with the partners continuing to have lives of their own as well as a shared life? As a journalist, Stef has to see the world, do the unconventional, go to parties in Soho, at the expense, if necessary, of attending dull functions at the Washington Hilton. That's what Stephanie Schonfeld does. That's what she is . . . So she tries to persuade herself, absently touching her ring.

Gradually she becomes aware of a faint scratching sound. It stops for a while, then it starts again. She tenses. A rat between the walls? In the room? Then she realizes the sound is coming from the bed.

Oh, my God, she thinks, he's jacking off.

She lies as still as she can so that Avery will not realize she is awake. The soft sound of his hand moving under the sheet is joined now by a faint creaking of the springs.

At first Stef feels embarrassed. It is almost like incest, like a sister listening to a brother masturbate. Then she decides that this, too, is a bohemian experience to be enjoyed in a spirit of worldly-wise amusement. Feeling very daring, she tries to picture him clutching himself as she listens. She wonders if it is big, if what they say about black men is true.

For the first time, she tries to picture Avery's body. She has never done so before. She feels uncomfortable thinking about her friends and acquaintances naked, having sex. The very thought seems like a violation. Everyone except for her boyfriends tend to consist of a face and hands emerging from a set of clothes, as though through slots at one of those carnival exhibits where you are photographed with the painted body of a cowboy or a pinup girl. To Stef, Avery has always been a neuter spirit whose body, below the waist, might as well taper into a cloud after the fashion of a cartoon genie. She hasn't thought of him as being a man, an adult sexual animal, in the way that sisters find it hard to think of their brothers as members of the same category as the men they sleep with and wed. Much less has she ever been able to think about Avery in bed with Ross or another man for more than a moment without shrinking and thrusting the images from her mind.

The faint scraping of knuckles on linen stops. Stef wonders what he is fantasizing about. Then she wonders if Bruce is lying in bed that very moment, fantasizing about her, stroking himself. She lies and listens to the rockets as they whistle and crack, to the braying of the horns.

Stef tells Sir Robin Blair he is looking better. In fact, she is shocked by how much her employer has declined in a week. His cheeks have capsized, the flesh under his eyes has become a pair of dark half-moons. The intravenous pipe going into his pale arm seems to be the trunk of a metallic mosquito, draining life and energy from the editor.

"I brought you the *Post* and the *Washington Herald*," she tells him, pulling the papers from her purse.

"Oh, yes, the *Herald*. I need my dose of right-wing hysteria. It does more for me than all these medicines they have me on."

They talk about the magazine, about some of the articles under consideration, gossip a bit about authors. He seems very tired and not very interested in business. He had entered the hospital for pneumonia, and the doctors had discovered advanced cancer.

When a nurse enters, a plump, middle-aged black woman, Stef rises to leave.

"You don't got to go," the woman says. "I'm just here to take his temperature."

"Stef, this is Velma . . . What is your last name, my dear?"

"Velma Hawkins."

"She is my best friend in this place. She brings me extra servings of ice cream, violating all the rules, of course."

"You gonna stop talking so I can take your temperature?"

Stef leaves the hospital deeply depressed. The reason is not Robin's unexpected illness, though watching him dwindle and wondering what her future will be at *Perspective* would be trying enough in the best of times.

Her engagement is about to come to an end. She was not sure at first when she returned from her trip to New York with Avery. For a week and a half, though, Bruce has been making excuses for not seeing her. He has been distant and curt on the phone. She has called Allison, but her oldest friend seems to be busy; she has not returned any of Stef's calls. Avery has, and his diagnosis has been as depressing as the one that Robin heard.

"If you want my honest opinion," Avery said to her a few evenings ago, "I think it's over. That's the only way to explain the way he's acting. He just hasn't figured out how to formally break it off." Stef had grown angry with Avery, unjustly, she knew. He had only been telling her what she already knew. Don't shoot the messenger . . .

A little after seven Bruce arrives at the apartment. From the perfunctory way he hugs her after several weeks of separation, she knows for certain. After that, there is only painful awkwardness and diplomacy. The maneuvering is literal. When she sits on the sofa where they had first embraced, Bruce approaches, reconsiders, and sinks down in a chair. He crosses his legs. She crosses hers.

"Look, I know you've been wondering what's been going on," he says with a hesitancy that she has never heard before. "I've been going through a lot, what with the job and all, and I've been thinking, I just haven't been fair to you."

She shifts and says with an edge of irritation, "What do you mean?"

"I just feel like I've been neglecting your career for mine. I mean, I know how important it is for you to have your own career, and, well, your own life. I guess I just assumed that I wouldn't be imposing on you, with my career . . . "

"If you're talking about New Year's, I think you're blowing one incident out of proportion." She finds herself growing angry. She knows she has lost, but she feels like fighting anyway. She doesn't want to concede.

"It's not just that. That just illustrates the problem. Look, I'm not blaming you."

"I didn't say you were."

"Well, I'm not. It's my fault, partly. Maybe it's mostly my fault. I was so busy concentrating on my career, I just didn't take your feelings into account. I'm willing to take the blame. It was unfair of me, to expect you to . . . I don't know, be like a political wife. It was my fault."

"I don't see why one person has to subordinate himself or herself to the other person," Stef says, warding off panic with abstraction. "There are plenty of couples in Washington who manage to work things out." She has rehearsed a speech along these lines for the past several days, not in order to persuade him, but simply for the record.

"You know, you're right."

She is growing annoyed and frustrated at the way he is constantly retreating, tactically. She's right; it's all his fault.

"I just don't see things working out in this case," he says. "Because I'd have to constantly be asking you to do things you don't feel like doing, and that isn't fair to you. And I really care about you, Stef . . . "

"Oh, thank you."

"I do. You're very important to me, and I don't want to be unfair to you." His voice is soothing, almost a croon, and at the sound of it, suddenly, she is once again hopelessly in love with him. The Bruce of the past several weeks, a heartless, ruthless, cold careerist, is suddenly another Bruce, the man who would hold her all night long and make her laugh at his jokes and frustrate her with his frat-boy assurance. Suddenly she is no longer resigned to losing him. She is terrified of losing him, in fact.

She struggles, but her voice breaks anyway. "Why don't we just see if we can work things out?"

He rises and comes over and leans on the side of the sofa, his hand resting gently on hers. "I just don't think that would be fair to you, Stef."

"Stop being so fair!" she exclaims with a single sob of rage.

He withdraws, suddenly cold. She feels her momentary weakness giving way to fresh anger, an arctic anger that cools and hardens her. He is the new Bruce, a polite, distant stranger once again.

"I want us to stay friends," he is saying as she leads him to the door. "Can we be friends?"

"We'll see," she says. She looks at the floor while he hugs her, a bit more heartily this time. "I'll give you a call," he says, and then he is gone.

She goes into the bedroom and sinks down on the bed under the harsh ceiling light. She reaches for the phone and dials Avery's number. Well, she prepares herself to tell him with a sort of giddy gallows humor, I've been dumped by my fiancé.

The phone rings several times, and the answering machine clicks on. "Hi," says Avery's voice. "I'm not at home right now, but if you'll leave a message and state the time you called . . . "

Stef glances at her watch: 7:25. Her engagement ended at, say, 7:20. For the record.

Her eyes move up to her hand, to the band on her second to last finger. He forgot to ask her to give the engagement ring back. As she studies it, she feels a numbness seeping through her like an anesthetic. She feels whole cells and arteries of her soul shutting down.

Lying on the bed, she stares at the ceiling. She knows too much to cry. She knows that tomorrow she will go to the office as though nothing has happened. Her work will not be affected in the slightest. She will laugh with her friends. And in time, she knows, she will have other lovers. When the time comes, she will not only be engaged again but will be married. She has told herself this many times in the past few days to prepare herself for this moment, and she repeats it in her mind.

Her very tranquility makes her uneasy as she lies still on the covered bed beneath the bright ceiling light like a patient in an operating room. She wonders whether she has grown too old, too mature, too realistic, too soon; whether her serenity is merely a kind of numbness, and that numbness a kind of partial death.

29

Like greasy slabs of bacon, the salamanders are piled in a stack.

"That's a salamander?" Teesha asks. "They ugly. Ooh, look, he grinning."

A salamander yawns and scrambles into the water. There it hangs, its head in one element and its limp body in another.

"They can't catch on fire," Evander explains to her. "They can live in fire."

"How do you know?"

"It was in a book I read."

Teesha can tell the salamanders are special to Evander. "Which one is Salamander Man?"

"Salamander Man is a superhero, not a real salamander." He boxes her head playfully. "Hello? Anybody home?"

"Look." Another aquarium has caught Teesha's eye. She presses her face close to the glass.

"They're just minnows."

"Look at the diver." Next to the bubbling pump, above a ripple of coral, a little plastic model of a diver is suspended. "That's what our baby looks like."

"Say what?"

"That's what a baby looks like, inside you. I saw it in a book."

The book was a photo book Teesha had leafed through during one of the prenatal classes at the hospital. She likes looking at the pictures of the stages of development: cell into fish into baby. She is in her fourth month of pregnancy now, and it has begun to show. Inside of her, if the books are right, their child is beginning to look like a human being.

Teesha also likes the doctor who teaches the prenatal class, a young black woman named Mary Callahan who speaks very proper English. But Teesha does not like the other girls in the class. Some of them are even younger than she is. One is thirteen. The class has turned into a fashion show. Each week the girls show up with new jewelry or new dresses, trying to show each other up. They brag about their boyfriends, too, how much money they make, or how old they are. Why should they think they are better than everyone else, Teesha thinks, just because their boyfriends are twenty-two and have their own cars?

Sometimes at the hospital, as she is going to or from the prenatal sessions, Teesha runs into Evander's Aunt Velma. At first Teesha was afraid of the plump, powerful nurse. Evander said she was very religious, and Teesha feared that Velma would consider her a 'ho. But Velma has treated her just as though she were Evander's wife. Teesha has discovered that Velma disapproves of abortion. "I'd rather see a young girl going to that prenatal class," she told Teesha once, "than killing her baby. God didn't mean for women to go and have no abortions. It ain't right."

Teesha sees Velma not only at the hospital, but sometimes at Evander's home at the Brentwood apartments. She finds herself spending more time there, because she feels more comfortable with Evander's family than with her Aunt Shirelle and Uncle Monroe. Evander's grandmother, the lady they call Gram, regards Teesha with some suspicion. But Evander's mother, to Teesha's surprise no less than Evander's, has become Teesha's friend. She looks forward to having a grandson. She goes shopping with Teesha for baby things, and rummages through drawers for hand-me-downs from her own babies. She is only a little over thirty herself. It is strange to think that she will be a grandmother and that Evander's half brother and half sisters will be the uncle and aunts of their child.

As she comes to spend more time in Sharonda's household, Teesha notices something disturbing. Evander seems to be losing interest in her. Her suspicions are confirmed one day at school, when one of the girls in the bathroom between third and fourth period taunts her. "Yo, Teesha! I hear Evander's been hanging with Eunique!" The teacher notices her weeping, and sends her to the school nurse, who gives her a Tylenol. Teesha pretends to swallow it, then throws it away. She is terrified that if she takes the wrong medicine her baby will be born retarded or deformed.

"You got to keep him coming back for more," Janet advises her. As part of her campaign to regain his interest, Teesha agrees to accompany Evander to the room the Krew uses. This time of year, the icebox deserves its name. They make a cavern out of the blankets and foam rubber that they pull from around the stolen TVs and radios and VCRs. Teesha refuses intercourse, but she goes down on him. Afterward, he lays his head on her slowly expanding belly and listens.

"I can't hear nothing," he says. "You sure you pregnant? Maybe you just fat." He cackles as she slaps him.

"Evander," she says, her voice becoming solemn. "You been seeing that Eunique?"

"What you talking about?"

"That's what people say."

"Why for you listening to people? That's just he-say she-say bullshit. That's just a bunch of girls talking."

"You swear to God?"

He clasps her hand. "I swear to God."

Teesha talks him into accompanying her to see her mother in prison. He is as interested in seeing the prison, she thinks, as in meeting her mother. Some of his friends in the 'hood have been in and out of prison, and she knows he thinks he might spend time behind bars in the future. "You go to prison, don't expect me to wait for you," she says as a warning, though of course she does not mean it.

They make a special trip, apart from the weekly visit with Aunt Shirelle, who makes no secret of her dislike of Evander and her distress at Teesha's pregnancy. The family room at the prison is decorated with cutouts of Santa Claus and reindeer and Christmas trees. Teesha's mother embraces her. "You getting big, baby." Then she turns to Evander.

"You Evander Johnson? You gonna take responsibility for this child?"

Evander shrugs, looking at the floor. The gates they had passed, the guards, the stamp on the wrist—all of these reminders of confinement have left him feeling trapped.

"You a gangbanger, ain't you?"

"No, he's not."

"Child, I run with the gang for many years. You with the Yungstaz or the Krew? You wearing blue. You with the Krew, ain't you? Well, I hope you planning to spend some of that cold cash money of yours on my grandbaby. That ain't just Teesha's child. That's your child, Evander. Are you a man, Evander?"

"What you mean, am I a man?"

"It don't take a man to make a baby. It takes a man to raise one. You gonna help my Teesha raise your baby?"

Evander shifts from one foot to another. "Yeah."

Teesha's mother extends her hand. "I want your word of honor. As a man. Shake."

"Aw, man," Evander complains. Then he relents and shakes her hand.

That afternoon, on the bus back into town, they see the first fat flakes drifting down. A greater wonder waits at the Brentwood apartments. A cloud of seagulls, moving inland in search of food, has descended on the Wood.

"Go on," Sharonda encourages Teesha. "We was going to throw it out anyway."

Teesha takes the bread into the courtyard and shows the little children how to break it into pieces and toss it to the gulls.

"Snow gulls," Evander's little half sister exclaims.

"That's right, baby," Teesha laughs. "They're snow gulls."

One by one, the residents of the apartments gather in the yard to watch the white birds arc and wheel amid the flickering flakes. Teesha will always remember the way that Evander, hooded in his blue sweatshirt, his half brother Jamal on his shoulders grasping at the birds, slowly pivots, the soft center of the feathery storm.

30

"Do some of that Cybernaut shit," Frizzell commands.

The two nine-year-olds pretend to kick-box in the space between the pool table and the bar of the Funkadelic, where Frizzell has perched his bulk. The gang leader chuckles and sips his beer.

"You ever seen Cobra?" one of the nine-year-olds asks in a piping voice. "He do like this"—he demonstrates—"and this."

"We gonna call you Cobra," Frizzell ordains. At nine, the boys are already working for the Krew, acting as lookouts, spying on the Yungstaz, even serving, sometimes, as couriers.

"I'm outta here," Evander announces, finishing his beer. He has been hanging at the Funkadelic for a couple of hours and has grown sleepy. Frizzell, watching the young kick-boxers, does not see Evander leave. Frizzell has been in a good mood for days, ever since the Feds and the District cops did the Krew a gratuitous favor by decimating the Yungstaz in a raid.

As he walks home, Evander invokes his favorite daydream. The row houses in a neighborhood not unlike this have been reduced to pyramids of rubble by a battle between comic-book villains and their superhuman nemesis. Evil mutants stand in front of a tenement and watch it burn. "No one can survive those flames," one of the froglike humanoids croaks.

Suddenly the flames part. Out strides a muscle-bubbled figure in a green and orange body stocking and a cowl that covers all but the lower part of his face, revealing he is black.

"Pathetic fools!" the Cybernaut thunders. "Know you not I am the one men call . . . the Salamander?"

Evander rounds the corner as, in his imagination, the Salamander directs a bolt of coruscating energy from his out-stretched fingers. Mutants tumble.

A motor hums. Rapt in his vision, Evander has not heard the car until now.

He turns just as the black Fiat accelerates. He does not see the gun, only the flashes.

Something thuds in his gut, his chest. He is aware of the punches first, then hears the cracks. Only instants later, as the car squeals past, does he feel the razor pain.

Like a piece of paper in a flame, he crumbles. The cement sidewalk is cold and rough against his cheek. He is gazing across the darkened street at a row of parked cars. Oh, shit, he says, or thinks, in disbelief. Oh, fuck.

Somewhere a car's tortured tires are shrieking. Another wave of pain. He wants to vomit.

He blurs.

31

POLICE LINE DO NOT CROSS. The yellow tape flutters.

Two police officers have to grab him, to hold him back from the twisted body on the sidewalk. "He's my nephew!" Curtis shrieks, over and over again.

32

For a few minutes, Teesha manages to suppress her sobbing. She stands before the casket and gazes at the thin body in its new suit. Then she looks up and speaks into the empty air, as though in a trance. "I kept my promise, baby," Teesha says as she reaches into her purse.

They are upon her when they see her attempting to put something into the casket—Curtis, Velma, and Shirelle. Intercepted, Teesha lets loose a shriek like the cry of a bobcat caught in a metal trap in the loneliest of woods.

"What has she got?"

"It's a Bal'more Orioles cap."

"I promised," she shrieks, sagging in her Aunt Shirelle's restraining arms. "I promised, I promised! He told me!"

"Lawd a'mercy," says Velma.

"Let go of that child." The command is from Evander's mother. Sharonda has risen from the seat where she has been sobbing for an hour. She speaks calmly, drawing on some hidden store of dignity. "Let me see, baby."

Teesha's sniffling subsides. She hands Sharonda the cap.

"He told me he wanted us to bury this with him."

"When he told you that?"

"Once upon a time."

"If my baby told you that," says Sharonda, "then that was his wish."

"We went through all this with the tennis shoes," Teesha hears Evander's uncle Curtis complaining. Curtis had won the battle over whether Evander would be buried in his high-tops. But now his wife Velma silences him: "Hush."

Teesha forgets all the eyes upon her as she tucks the cap next to Evander's left arm. Her fingers lightly stroke his dry hard brow. "Good-bye, baby," she says, and then her eyes melt and her knees melt in turn. They have to help her away.

Her greatest trial comes after the funeral service at the home of Curtis and Velma, where the wake is held. Teesha is noticeably pregnant now; others can see the swelling that she feels. She finds she has to visit the bathroom more often. Returning from a trip, she is intercepted in the hall by Sharonda's boyfriend Larry.

"Baby, I want to help you out," Larry says. "Now I know you were holding all kinds of stuff for Evander . . . "

"What are you talking about?"

"I know he hid money and rock and things at your place, so it'd be safe. Now you got to get rid of it, without letting people know how much you got. I want to help you out."

"Leave me alone!" She tries to pass him in the narrow hall of the Hawkins house, but he blocks her.

"You've got to get rid of it, and I can help you. Plus make you some money on the side."

Her heart pumps in fear and fury. Her eyes are wet once again. "Leave me alone!"

She backtracks, veers into a bedroom, and slams the door. Sobbing, she sinks onto a neatly made bed. Outside in the hall, voices join Larry's.

"What did you say to that girl?"

"I didn't say nothing."

A knock on the door. It's Aunt Shirelle. "Teesha? Baby, you all right?"

An hour later, Teesha is alone in the room she shares with her cousin. The members of her aunt's household have deferred to her wish to be isolated. They can be heard through the door and the walls, bickering unseriously. In the living room, the TV drones.

Teesha lies on her back on the bed. She can almost feel the

baby ripening in her gut. She moves her hand across her belly as she had once guided Evander's.

She remembers what he said about ghosts leaving their bodies and walking through walls as though they were water. "Evander?" she whispers. "Are you here?" She thinks she senses a slight change in the quality of the table lamp's light.

"I love you, baby," she whispers, her eyes overflowing. She spreads her arms and waits to feel a transparent body sinking down atop the heaviness of the body she now shares.

33

It is the sound of power itself.

It can be heard in Virginia, as far away as the commuter suburbs of Arlington, Fairfax, and Vienna, and it makes the dogs in the bricked-in courtyards of Georgetown stiffen and whine and yowl. But it reverberates at its most intense in the region to the south and east of the floodlit iceberg of the Capitol, in the area where the candy-clean town houses of the professional gentry give way to scabrous storefronts and black-eyed buildings in a progression of decay that culminates in the rubble-toothed lots on the loop of the Anacostia River. Here, the streets and alleys that ring most nights with the pop of semiautomatic pistols and the whine of sirens and the rumble of jets banking toward National Airport are vibrating beneath wave after wave of a praetorian noise.

The choppers wake Graciela from a dream of Salvador. She has been, in her dream, back in the icehouse of her native town. Her *abuelita*, her long-dead grandmother, had been there among Graciela's own children, whom she had never known. Something had happened, there was some kind of trouble, but before Graciela could learn what, she is awake in her little room in the Bunker, feeling, more than hearing, the helicopters hovering overhead.

A dog nearby is barking frantically. Her little Marcelo, though, still sleeps on his mat. Rising from the cot, Graciela peers through the window and the grate of black bars that protects them from the anarchy of southeast D.C., but sees nothing unusual between the alley's tiger stripes of shadow. It is only a little after nine, but the midwinter blackness makes it feel like midnight.

Again she regrets having stayed. For weeks Isidro had been raging. He did not want Yolanda's cousin and her children living forever under her roof. At night Graciela had lain awake listening to her cousin and her husband argue until she grew sick with anger and grief. Anything would be better than living where she was not wanted. That was why, after several months, she had called Darryl again.

She should have left with Yolanda when she had driven up earlier tonight. "I don't care, I will divorce him if I have to," Yolanda had said. Graciela had refused. She could not face Isidro, at least not tonight. She had allowed Rosa to go with her Aunt Yolanda, though. Now she regretted staying here alone with her son. Tomorrow, she tells herself, they will return to the apartment of Isidro and Yolanda. Tomorrow they will work something out. Maybe she can pay more toward the rent.

She squats beside Marcelo. In twisting and turning, he has freed himself from the blanket. Gently, she adjusts it. The midwinter cold, seeping through the single window, makes the tiny room feel like an icebox. If it gets too cold, she will bring Marcelo into bed with her. She is trying to train him to sleep on his own, though. And on those occasions when she has relented, because he was sick or frightened by a bad dream, his twisting has prevented her from getting any sleep.

She pulls the covers up around herself and tries to go back to sleep. Tomorrow night they will all sleep in her cousin's house, where her four-year-old daughter is staying now. Graciela knows it was a mistake to come here. She did so only because of her obstinate pride, only because she did not want to be dependent, once again, on her cousin and her cousin's husband. But she has the babies to think about, and the Bunker is too cold.

The dog down the road stops barking. As she sinks back into sleep, Graciela hears the sound of the choppers moving away in the direction of the river. This is the language of the State, the authentic voice of power in the waning years of the twentieth century—not the grumble and creak of tanks lurching across a field or a flag-quilted square, not the rush of jet engines nor the roar of rockets, but syncopated thunder, the thudding of a dozen dragon hearts, a hammering in the starless violet air.

Bruce's heart pounds in answer to the hammering of the rotors. He stands with his arm around Allison, gazing from the small group of administration officials at the floodlit pyramid of confiscated drugs: packets of cocaine, bags of marijuana, thousands of bottles of pills. The producer of the "No mo'" commercials had come up with the idea. The cameras would show the choppers rising in the sunset, then streaking toward their target through the night. The rails on the gunships would fire their meteors into the contraband mountains as the voice-over was heard: "America is at war. A war in our cities. A war in our own backyard. Under this president, the United States is winning that war . . ." At least some of the footage, it was hoped, would make its way into reelection campaign commercials.

Allison squeezes Bruce. "This is neat," she says, her head on her shoulder.

"Yeah."

The floodlit bellies of the choppers shine like moons slowly sinking in a hail from space as they hover over the pyramid of flame, the thunder from their halos brooming the smoky glow out across the Anacostia River. The sound of traffic echoes down the brick alleyway. In the distance a siren wails. Curtis sets the gas can down carefully, so no drips run back to the car. From a safe distance, he clicks his lighter. He tosses it and watches the blue flame spread into orange. Then, his hypnotic calm giving way to panic, he scrambles into the idling car and backs down through the alley into the street.

Then he is home free. He is turning at the corner, gliding into the traffic. He wonders whether the whole place has gone up. He hopes so. After many nights of agonizing, he has finally worked up the courage to punish the Krew. They had killed Evander by inducting him into their ranks, just as surely as the drive-by shooter from the Yungstaz who had pulled the trigger. He had hit the Krew. Hit 'em hard. Hit their supply lines. He had taken out their arsenal. He had made them pay.

★ ★ ★

The luminous fog fills the room where Graciela sucks air and wheezes and coughs. She pounds on the pane. Curtis purses his lips as a sports car pulls up beside him at the intersection, stereo pumping a thumping beat like the hammering of the rotors.

As the choppers rise one by one into a purple sky marbled by smoke and crisscrossed by beams, the sports car screeches into the lane ahead of Curtis and hums away into the night. Graciela sobs, "Please, God, please. *Dios mío!*" Curtis parks, and walks into the steel-and-glass cube of the all-night store. Hysterical, Graciela slaps at the sparkles winking like fireflies all over her nightdress. Curtis opens the glass door and takes out a carton of milk from a swirl of arctic air and the smoke sears and turns to acid in Graciela's eyes. The paper bag crackles like fire beside him as he sets it on the front seat, and she, blinking in the fog, gulping the acrid air, realizes that her baby isn't crying anymore. As he cruises down the dark lanes between the one-story homes brooding like low hills, she is shaking Marcelo, and the boy's head is flopping like a puppet's in the weird orange light. She sinks down, the pressure crushing her lungs, her throat, her temples. Her mind is splintering but she cannot scream because, as he pulls into the driveway, she can no longer breathe.

Home again, Curtis takes a leak. He washes his hands and studies the stoic brown bulldog face in the mirror. An officer's face. A soldier's face. It all seems like a dream, but he did it. Mission accomplished. Target acquired and eliminated.

He rolls the gloves up in the emptied paper sack and puts the sack in the trash bag. By the time the trash truck arrives in the morning, Curtis will have turned in the rental car and picked up his own. No witness will ever be able to identify him by the car he was driving. No vengeful gangbangers will come after him or Velma. The Krew will never know what hit them. Just as Evander never knew.

The lawn chair squeaks beneath his weight. Curtis twists the cap off his beer and turns on the police radio, low so as not to awaken Velma or the neighbors. In the distance, the thunder of the choppers is receding, while nearby new sirens—first two, then three—howl ever louder.

All the dogs in Washington begin to bark.

34

Every few minutes one of the cameramen crawls across the space separating the table from the high, wooden U-shaped platform where the committee members sit. The TV audience cannot see the guy, but everyone in the Senate hearing room can. Bruce tries not to let it distract him.

"I find it hard to believe," the junior senator from Nevada is saying, "that an operation of this magnitude could have gone on for years, right under the nose of this administration, without anyone noticing it. And yet, Mr. Brandt, it seems to me that is what you are asking this committee to believe."

Bruce has been testifying for two and a half hours about his role in the scandal that has come to be known as "Piercegate." He is growing increasingly combative. They have gone over the same few facts a dozen times—how he met Darryl Shelton; how he received the tip from Darryl that led to the raid on the Georgia Avenue Yungstaz' headquarters; how he knew nothing about Darryl other than that he was a real estate manager with a background as a private investigator and seemed to know something about the underworld of the District of Columbia. Now the senators—especially the liberals, who want to belabor the Bush administration, but also conservatives taking an opportunity to express their shock and outrage—are simply using Bruce for target practice.

"Didn't it occur to you, Mr. Brandt, to look into the background of this individual? You are on the staff of the drug czar. Surely you had the resources of the FBI at your disposal . . . Mr. Brandt?"

Bruce looks up from the pad where he has been doodling—little cubes connected by dotted lines and curlicues. "Excuse me, Senator, was that a question?" He is tired, he has sweated through his clothes, and he is growing defiant. "Was that a question? I'm sorry. I thought it was a speech."

From the packed hearing room behind comes scattered laughter and applause. Flustered, the junior senator from Nevada cedes the floor to the chairman, who gives it, in turn, to the senior senator from Idaho. Bruce has never heard of Senator Ted Chappell, but he can tell at once that the man is an ally.

"Thank you, Mr. Chairman. I've been sitting here listening to this proceeding all morning, and frankly I'm beginning to wonder, and I'm sure the American people are beginning to wonder, whether we don't have anything better to do with our time than to go back and forth with Mr. Brandt here. He has told us everything he knows. It is clear, or it seems pretty clear, that he did nothing illegal; indeed, that he was simply carrying out the duties of his job to the best of his ability. I think it should be pointed out that if Mr. Brandt had not passed on the tip from this Darryl Shelton, there never would have been a raid in the first place, and presumably there would have been no retaliatory strike against this warehouse, and the government never would have looked into Jay Prentice Pierce's enterprises . . . So I suppose you could say that we owe it to young Mr. Brandt here that this entire network of corruption has been exposed to the light of day."

"Do you have any questions for the witness, Senator?" the chairman interrupts testily.

"I just have one question, Mr. Chairman." Senator Chappell theatrically puts on his glasses and shuffles through his notes. "Mr. Brandt, I understand from your previous testimony that you were introduced to this individual, this Darryl Shelton, by a mutual acquaintance, a . . . a Mr. Ross Drummond, when you expressed an interest in purchasing a handgun."

"Yes, sir, that's correct."

"Now, correct me if I'm wrong, Mr. Brandt, but are we to conclude, from your desire to purchase a handgun, that you considered your physical person to be in some danger? And would we be correct in concluding that your concern was related to the hazards of your job? After all, as an assistant to Mrs. Gutierrez, you must have been a target for a lot of angry drug kingpins."

Bruce sees where the senator is leading. Thanks for the softball question. "Well, Senator, I don't want to exaggerate, but this was a concern."

"You mean, the possibility that some of these ruthless drug lords would try to gun you down? You saw a need to defend yourself?"

"Yes, sir, that's right. You have to remember," says Bruce, warming to his theme, "that this is possibly the most ruthless criminal element in our society. They will stop at nothing to evade capture by the law. So far this year, in the District of Columbia alone, in drug-related violence there have been one hundred and six homicides . . . "

"Excuse me for interrupting, Mr. Brandt, but did you say that one hundred and six people have been murdered by the Washington drug lords so far this year?"

"Yes, sir, according to the latest information."

"That is a remarkable number. And it is only April. Tell me, are there any estimates as to the total number of people who will be murdered by the drug kingpins in Washington this year?"

"Well, as you know, I have resigned from Mrs. Gutierrez's office as of last week, so I can't speak for the government in an official capacity. But I believe that the estimate is somewhere in the range of four hundred."

"Four hundred people will be shot this year in drug-related violence in the nation's capital."

"Yes, sir, if the estimates are correct."

"So these drug lords are dumping a mountain of bodies right outside this Capitol building every year. They have proven they will murder and murder and murder in order to make their illicit profits and keep from being imprisoned. Mr. Brandt, I for one can understand why you saw the need to obtain a handgun for self-defense. I think the American people will agree that it was a perfectly reasonable thing to do."

"May I add something, Senator?"

"Please."

Bruce gazes at Senator Chappell's face, a soloist reassured by the conductor. "Senator, I knew when I took this job that there were risks involved. I don't mean just the risk of being dragged through the press and, with all due respect, through hearings like this one." He feels a wave of interest and enthusiasm washing over him from the unseen audience in the hearing room behind him. "I mean physical risks, Senator. I mean the risk of being gunned down in cold blood and never knowing what hit me. But that was a risk I was willing to take, Senator, and I'll tell you, if you've been to the street corners of the District of Columbia the way I have, and if you've seen the bodies lying there of teenage kids, sometimes of elementary school kids. . . . Senator, if you could see some of the crack babies I've seen in the hospitals of this city, of our nation's capital, then you would see why these drug kingpins have to be stopped." Bruce is riding the wave, he is surfing on one leg. Look Ma, no hands. "Senator, I don't think it's an exaggeration to say there is a war on. It is a war for the survival of our society, I guess you could say of our very civilization. For the past year and a half I've been a soldier in that war. We've taken some casualties, and I've been knocked out of the combat for a while. We've got ruthless enemies, and we've got a lot of people sniping at us from the side." He can feel the wave growing into a tsunami beneath him, he is rising up, up into the sky on the curling crest. "But I'll tell you something, Senator, we are going to win that war. The American people are going to win the war with the drug lords. And when it's all said and done, all that matters, to me, is that I got to play my own little part in fighting in this war for the soul of my country, of our country, the United States of America."

The chairman's banging of the gavel can hardly be heard through the roar of the ovation. At last the chairman gives up and brings the hearing to a close. Bruce is gathering his papers when the babbling crowd surges around him.

"That was wonderful!" A woman is sobbing. "God bless you, son," says an old man. "Mr. Brandt! Mr. Brandt!" Hands are snatching at his, faces tight with excitement are bobbing in front of him as he shoulders his way through the crowd to the door.

"I'm Jack Dougherty, Senator Chappell's LA," a young man

shouts at Bruce. "Great job." Milligan is there, too; he emerges from the mob, he flashes Bruce a thumbs-up: "Remember. Chorus girls." Bruce mouths the phrase "No mo'."

"Way to go, Bruce," Milligan tells him when they meet in the coolness of the marble hall. Cameras flare. "The bit about the kids and the crack babies . . . "

Bruce whispers to Milligan, "I wouldn't know a crack baby if it bit me on the ass."

The light is as intense as the one in the hearing room. Bruce thinks about asking Allison's cousin to turn it off, but decides not to. Allison has insisted that every stage of their wedding in St. Louis be captured on film, even the opening of their wedding gifts.

"Look, darling," his bride tells Bruce. "This is from Ross. Aren't they neat?"

The burnished brass pots and utensils flare in the light of the camera as Allison holds them up for posterity to admire.

"Can you cook with them?" Allison's mother asks as they are passed to her.

"I think you're supposed to put them on the wall," Bruce's father suggests, somewhere in the background beyond the blazing light.

"Okay. Ross." Bruce adds Ross's name to the list of people who are to receive thank-you notes. In two weeks, after the honeymoon in the Bahamas, Bruce will return to Washington as the newest employee of Wriston, White. Already the press is losing interest in the complicated story of real estate deals, drugs, and suicide. Soon Piercegate will join the list of forgotten successors to Watergate: Irangate, Briefing-gate, Koreagate. Those who remember Bruce's role at all remember his dramatic performance at the hearings. For weeks C-Span played it again and again. I'm not even thirty, he has been telling people, and I'm already in syndication.

35

The prisoner is wearing a suit and tie, not the orange jail jump-suit in which he had stood before the judge when Curtis had watched him being arraigned. He is twenty-two. He is a member of the Florida Avenue Yungstaz, and he is accused of killing Graciela Herrera and her infant son and burning their bodies in the now infamous warehouse owned by the rivals of the Yungstaz, the Krew.

"What about TV reports?" the defense attorney asks the elderly woman on the witness stand. "Have you followed the story on TV?" The trial has not yet begun. This is the voir dire hearing.

Curtis shifts in his seat in the back of the courtroom. He attends the proceedings when he is free from his duties as a school crossing guard.

"Have you discussed it with anybody?" the defense attorney asks.

In the first few days after the fire, Curtis had grown almost physically ill with anguish. He had been certain he had killed the Salvadoran woman and her child. He had not meant to hurt any-body. He had sought only to destroy the arsenal of the gang in whose wars his nephew had lost his life. He had tried to avoid injuring the innocent. But he had, just like Mookie back in the woods north of Tuy Hoa, blasting away blindly into the darkness.

Then there had been another story in the paper. Not what they were calling "Piercegate"—Curtis hardly followed the unwrapping of that scandal—but the news that a member of the

Yungstaz had been arrested for murder and arson on the testimony of a former gang member turned government informant.

"It looks like they was breaking into that warehouse to steal the other gang's guns," Veronica, the clerk of the court, had explained when Curtis had called. They had known each other since the days when Curtis, as a member of the D.C. force, had been frequently called upon to testify. "And they didn't know this Spanish woman was staying there. And they surprised her, and they figured they ought to kill her so she couldn't identify them. And then they burned the place down."

Curtis's relief gave way to awe as he pondered the significance of all this. He had not killed those poor Salvadorans after all. They had been dead when he had arrived. By torching the place, he had inadvertently done the community a service by turning a terrible light upon the murders. Clearly a higher power had been guiding him that night. Curtis had meant to carry out God's will, and so he had, though in an astonishing manner. So be it. As Velma might say, *The good Lord works in mysterious ways.*

Curtis gets up to leave. The young gangsta at the table in front sees Curtis and gives him the red eye, that glare as cold as the scrutiny of a 9 mm or a .45. The boy's scowling face looks somehow familiar. Then Curtis realizes the kid reminds him of Evander.

It is hot.

It is hot, and he does not know where he is. He is walking down a dingy street checkered by storefronts. Above a dusty door, a sign reading H TEL dangles. A delivery truck snorts out of an alley. A rhythmic clatter draws his attention to a homeless woman shouldering a cart full of blankets and cans.

He pauses and wipes the wet from his forehead. The padded orange vest he is wearing puzzles him. He stares at the flag in his hand with its shiny strips. He is supposed to be somewhere. He has a feeling he is late.

Maybe somebody can tell him. He pushes his way through a door. Bells tinkle. Air moist with shampoo and perfume oozes over him. From beneath their dryers, women peer out like startled turtles.

"Hi," says a woman who is standing beside another woman in an elevated chair. "Can we help you?"

He opens his mouth to ask where he is, but the words won't come, only garbled noise. Frustrated, he slaps his knee with the flag.

Another woman approaches him. "You're Mr. Hawkins, aren't you? Curtis Hawkins?"

"He don't look well, Pearl."

"Mr. Hawkins, do you remember me? I'm Pearl, remember? Do you want us to call Velma?"

Velma. The name is assuring. His mind presents him with the image of a plump woman whom he thinks must be his wife. Or his sister. He can't recall her name. He turns to the women, but his mouth won't make the words right. Only a snort of frustration emerges.

"Mr. Hawkins, you sit down right here." The woman helps him onto an elevated chair. His left arm is trembling. "You just sit right there. You want a glass of water?" Then, in a low tone, to someone else: "Call the school. Ask them where Velma is. And do they want us to call 911."

36

From the moment the Lufthansa jet touches down on the Tempelhof runway, Avery's spirits begin to rise. He is jaunty as he shoulders his bags through customs, and positively ecstatic as he peers from the window of the taxi taking him to his hotel near the Kurfurstendamm. The sights are not remarkable in themselves, the blocks of square turn-of-the-century edifices, the dreary post-war stores, all cement and glass. It does not matter. He is delighted. He is far from home. He is in Berlin. He is free.

Back in Washington, it is assumed that a young black man is a gangsta. In Berlin, Avery learns on the first day of the tour the Korean grocer's settlement has purchased, a young black American is universally taken to be a GI. "You are in the army, yes?" a German cabbie asks. "Hey, man, where you stationed?"—this, from a baby-faced U.S. Army private who walks up to him on the street. Avery assumes that soldiers, of any race or nationality, are not in favor in the better Berlin establishments, and concludes that his Bert Brecht look, the leather jacket and leather cap, will not help. He spends a morning, therefore, at a men's store on the Ku-Damm, running up several hundred dollars on his parents' credit card. Soon he has remade himself in elegant European style: turtleneck, thin, stylish leather jacket, Armani pants, and black shoes with white socks. Thereafter no one mistakes him for a GI or even for an American of another sort. He hopes they take him for a French African.

He spends a day and a half seeing the sights: the park, the Reichstag, the remnant of the Wall. On his second evening in

Berlin he visits several gay bars, only to find them dingy and dim, their patrons effecting a grim macho look—jeans, leather, mustaches, earrings, stubble. These are not the blond boys of his daydreams.

He is about to give up and leave the final bar on his list when he becomes aware that he is being transfixed by a blue gaze. The fellow, somewhere between twenty and thirty, has a broad, almost Asian face and hair the color that Avery likes.

"Guten Abend," Avery says.

His accent must give him away. "You are American," the guy says in passable English. His name is Helmut. "I live near here."

The street where Helmut lives is spooky, and the building, an art nouveau apartment house, is eerier still. Inside, there are no lights in the stairwell. Blue light from some neighboring source streams through a tall ornate window, giving them spectral shadows. The stairs, as they ascend, anticipate the creaking to come, and the groans.

"I do not like Washington," Helmut tells Avery the next afternoon.

They are sitting in a cafe near the Ku-Damm having coffee and cake. At a table nearby, a group of well-dressed Italian teenagers are striking poses.

"You'll visit me, though, in Washington," Avery says, trying not to plead. Once again, he finds himself falling irresponsibly in love.

The German takes a drag on his cigarette. He has spent the day driving Avery around the city. "It is like Bonn. It is not a real city. Like Berlin. Or New York. I love New York. Why don't you move to New York?"

"Do you go to New York often?"

"Sometimes. On business."

The Italians burst into laughter.

"Italians," Helmut murmurs.

"Do you speak any Italian?"

"A little. You know the joke about the Italian tanks? They have five gears. One forward, five backward." The joke sounded like one handed down from a relative in the Wehrmacht. "I will visit you when you move to New York," Helmut promises solemnly. In a few days Avery's latest infatuation will fade, but he will not forget the suggestion. New York.

"New York. Or L.A.," Avery tells Stef in a pub near Bond Street in London. Two days have passed, and Avery is on his way home to the States. Stef has been flown by Des Kazakis to attend a function at the American ambassador's residence. "New York or L.A. What do you think?"

Stef's verdict: "New York. I can visit you there more often. L.A.'s too far away."

They talk briefly of the Piercegate scandal, to which Avery's mother has been connected in a minor way. "It looks like Jay Pierce was using this minority-owned company she owned stock in as a front for tax evasion." Avery does a cruelly accurate rendition of an underclass accent: "They gone put my momma away! I might have to visit my momma in *Lorton!*"

The waiter brings them another round. "Is smoking allowed here?" Stef asks.

Avery consoles her on her breakup with Bruce. "He's just like Ross. He's like a young, straight version of Ross. They're just operators. Why do we fall for these guys?"

"They're not healthy for us," Stef agrees.

"We need sensitive men," Avery suggests.

"Men who aren't afraid of showing their feelings," Stef adds.

"Men," Avery continues, "who don't sacrifice their lives to their careers."

"Men," says Stef, "with lots of money."

"Old men," Avery says, "old, old men, who die and leave all their money to us. Like Jay Pierce. I bet when all is said and done he'll have a huge estate. I wonder who'll end up getting it."

"You should have been nicer to him when you were a kid," Stef suggests.

The energy is the same as that he had sensed on the Ku-Damm. But Broadway is grittier, meaner.

Avery likes it just the same. Swift, confident strides carry him away from his interview for a job at NBC News toward home.

Faces lunge at him and swerve, cars blare, sirens burp and wail. Ahead of him, an endless line of red brake lights glow like coals in the dark masonry canyons with their walls checkered by lit windows.

He is utterly alone in the honking, yelling, blinking, stinking metropolis, and utterly free. He feels as he had never felt in Washington, free and anonymous. Here in his new home he is no longer the black American prince, the dynast, the son of Amy Brackenridge. He is nobody's son. He is an orphan, surrounded by millions of strangers, and utterly, blissfully alone.

He catches glimpses of himself in the shop windows he passes, wearing the armor he had brought back from a shop on Bond Street after his visit with Stef, self-assured, sufficient unto himself, dependent on no one, a striking young man in a Burberrys coat.

37

The U.S. ambassador to the Court of St. James is a narrow silvery Texan who reminds Stef of daguerreotypes of Andrew Jackson. After the meal at the ambassadorial residence in London's Regents Park, as the little party is moving through the marble entrance hall, Stef finds herself next to her host.

She tries to think of something clever to say. "Do you miss your ranch, Mr. Ambassador?"

"Oh, I brought my cattle along." The ambassador winks and guides her to a door near the entrance that opens into a small storage room where pop-art cutouts of cows are stacked together. "These here are my low-rent cows."

"He puts them on the lawn to 'graze' in good weather," Des Kazakis explains as the limo takes them away from Winfield House under the floodlit flags of the United States and the Republic of Texas. "The State Department is not pleased."

Des summoned Stef here abruptly less than thirty-six hours ago. A plane ticket had been waiting for her at Dulles, a driver at Heathrow, a hotel on the edge of Hyde Park. She had not seen the publisher before the ambassador's dinner party, and they did not get a chance to converse. Now she waits for him to speak. Her working hypothesis is that he wants to help her get a diplomatic appointment, perhaps at the U.S. embassy in London. She has been mentally reviewing her banking history; bad checks and overdue student loans are the only problem that the FBI might uncover as it does a background check. And once in college she took a toke on a reefer . . .

"Look into that satchel," Des instructs her. Stef discovers a tape recorder. She looks at her employer, puzzled. "I've got an assignment for you," the publisher says. "Sorry to be so cloak-and-dagger, but you'll understand. I want you to interview Jay Pierce."

Stef feels a twinge of disappointment. So she will *not* be the American cultural attaché in London.

"Jay's an old friend of mine. Not a close friend, a . . . Washington friend. I've been in touch with him, through an intermediary, since this whole thing blew up. He wants his story told, and he's willing to give us the scoop."

"Where is he?"

"Frankly, Stef, I'm not at liberty to say. I'm waiting for a call from him tonight. If all goes well, we can get you together with him tomorrow or the next day."

"Great." This might be even more exciting than being a cultural attaché. Then, alarmed, Stef says, "I hope I'll be able to come up with enough detailed questions . . . "

"Oh, that's right. I nearly forgot." Des rummages in his briefcase and produces several manila folders choking on faxes and clippings. "I had the office FedEx this stuff about Piercegate."

The limo emerges from Regents Park into dark blocks buttoned by streetlights.

"Don't spend too much time on the scandal," Des instructs her. "I want this story to be about Jay Prentice Pierce, the man. The Washington power broker. Who is he? Where did he come from? How did he climb so high, before his fall? What makes him tick? What does his career tell us about America, and democracy? This is big-picture stuff. But we need detail. Jay's promised to give you a couple of hours. You'll have more material than we can use in one issue. You might be able to turn it into a book."

The car arrrives at Stef's hotel. "We'll talk in the morning," Des says as she climbs out, clutching the satchel containing the tape recorder, cassettes, and clippings. "By the way, I've been very pleased with the job you've been doing as managing editor. But that talk will have to wait until later. Good night."

Stef watches the limousine pull away. A bellboy asks her if she needs help with the satchel. She is exhilarated. Not for the first time this evening she thinks, if only Bruce could see me.

"So you're from Scotland?" Stef shouts.

Her gut tightens as the helicopter rocks again. She is trying to make conversation, in an effort—unsuccessful, so far—to divert herself from terror.

"I fly back and forth to the rigs, most of the time," the Scots pilot says while Stef tries not to look at the crisping slate waves of the North Atlantic, all too near them below. They have been flying for forty-five minutes, from the small port town in the north of England where she waited for a day and a half in a small refrigerator of a hotel until the interview finally was set.

The chopper shudders and shakes. Stef clenches and unclenches her leg muscles in an asymmetric rhythm. This, she has discovered, helps to break the transmission of the shocks from the frame of the flimsy aircraft to her body.

"There she is," the Scotsman says. Stef sees the white V of the wake before she sees the yacht. It is bigger than she realizes at first—an ocean liner's calf. More terror as the chopper hovers over the boat's deck. Stef imagines the aircraft tumbling sideways into the water, dragging her and the Scotsman down, icy water roiling through splintering glass, screams . . .

"Welcome aboard. I'm Captain Jan van Meusen," says a balding man in a white uniform as they hurry, heads ducked low, beneath the slowing rotors. "I hope the flight was good, yes?" The steady vibration of the big boat is reassuring. "Mr. Pierce will join you momentarily."

Stef returns from the ladies' room to the stateroom, where she accepts a steward's offer of coffee. Once more she tests the tape recorder. As an exra precaution, she has brought another tape recorder, a small Japanese model that she bought on Bond Street in London. As Ross might say in his folksy style: I wear a belt *and* suspenders.

The door to the stateroom opens, admitting a slender, grayhaired man in a turtleneck and plaid jacket. At once she recognizes a face familiar for decades to the power brokers of Washington and New York, but unknown to most of the public until a fire in a warehouse in southeast Washington triggered the latest capital scandal. The face is more emaciated than in the photos that have paneled the papers and magazine covers. Stef wonders if the rumors about AIDS are true.

"Hi. You must be Stephanie Schonfeld." A thin smile. "Jay Prentice Pierce."

So, Stef thinks, this is the man I wrecked my engagement to meet—a fugitive from federal charges. Some mentor he would have made.

Half an hour into the interview Pierce can sell her anything. He is at his best, this virtuoso of insider politics, mixing self-deprecating humor with anecdotes about the White House, Hollywood, and K Street that allow Stef, and through her the readers of *Perspective*, to imagine that they are insiders, too. She can understand why so many liberals and conservatives, Republicans and Democrats, could consider him not only an advisor and an ornament of dinner parties but a trustworthy friend.

But Jay Prentice Pierce talks too long. His meandering monologue acquires the aggressive desperation of the talk of the old, whose fear of letting go of the listener is a fear of letting go of life.

"We'll get to the bottom of this," Pierce is telling her, leafing through one of the two enormous Rolodexes he has brought as though they were evidence and this were a trial. "Here. Sammy Blumrosen. He used to be with the SEC. You have to call him. Here's his number and address . . ." Pierce finds another name in the file. "And Marty Vandenbrock. Give him a call. Marty's an old friend of mine. I met him through Peter Lawford, believe it or not. Did I tell you that story . . . ?"

The helicopter will be returning in an hour, and Stef is more confused than ever about Piercegate. Maybe when she listens to the tapes she will be able to find some pattern in Pierce's ever more agitated rambling.

"Did I tell you I knew Rock Hudson? I had a party for him in Washington once. I think our friend Ross Drummond was there . . ."

Why, Stef wonders, do so many famous people insist on informing you that they know other famous people? Des Kazakis drops names the same way, as though they were tickets admitting him to esteem. It is as though personal fame is not enough, it must be reinforced by connections with the fame of a multitude.

Connections. Jay Prentice Pierce has told her little about his boyhood as the child of a New York Irish political dynasty, his military service and his Ivy League education, his years on Wall Street and the Ford Foundation project on urban poverty that won him his job as a general in the War on Poverty. He has said just as little about the way he had parlayed his mastery of the arcana of urban redevelopment policy into a career of making fortunes for his black and white friends through minority-owned companies qualifying for federal subsidies. What he has talked about, instead, has been his connections.

"Here you go," Pierce says triumphantly, extending a card from the Rolodex. "Margaret Holtzmann. You should talk to her. She's a good person to know. Could help you out. Tell her I gave you her name . . ."

At the beginning of the interview, Jay had been bitter about the legion of friends and acquaintances and business partners who had ostracized him after the fire in southeast D.C. had uncovered links between his employee Darryl Shelton and a ghetto gang. "When they're finished using you," Pierce had said, "they just toss you overboard." As the interview had continued, though, Pierce had become ever less critical of the constellation of names orbiting around him; indeed, he built them up in importance, even the ones who had betrayed him. He had to. His friendly business relationships and businesslike friendships were all he had, all he was.

"It's all timing," Pierce is saying. "Timing is everything. It's all strategy, just like the military. Have you ever read Sun-tzu? Ancient Chinese military classic. You should read Sun-tzu. And the *Tao Te Ching,* too. Amazing stuff. Here, I'll write it down for you . . ."

Reaching for a pen, Pierce knocks over one of the bulging Rolodexes. Bits of paper with names and phone numbers and addresses flutter through the air, the way that the screaming gulls will spin tomorrow morning when the Dutch Coast Guard fishes the body of Jay Prentice Pierce from the cold gray waters of the North Sea.

* * *

The black waters of Griswold Cove twin the paper lanterns of the gazebo. The symmetrical structure of light looks like two tangent galaxies, a new constellation in the firmament.

The gazebo glows tonight for Stef. No doting patriarch could be more proud of a debutante than Des Kazakis is of his protégé as he introduces her to his guests. Half of them she recognizes from TV or National Public Radio or book jackets and magazine photos. These are the intelligentsia of the East Coast, the thinkers and writers and reviewers and editors, and they are all here to see her.

The interview with Jay Prentice Pierce, published in two installments in *Perspective* in the month after Pierce's suicide, has made her the most famous young journalist in America. Just as she had begun to savor that first taste of celebrity, Des had chosen her to succeed the late Sir Robin Blair. She knows what people are saying—that Des, not she, will be the real editor—but she does not let malicious gossip bother her. She is suddenly and deliciously famous as the first woman chosen to edit *Perspective* in its long history. She has been on *Nightline* and *Crossfire* and C-Span. She has received a six-figure sum to expand the celebrated interview into a quick and dirty biography of Jay Prentice Pierce. Her phone has been ringing with offers to write from *Vanity Fair, The New Yorker, The New Republic, The Atlantic Monthly, Harper's Magazine, The New York Times Book Review.* Profiles of her have appeared in the *New York Times* and *The Washington Post.* On college campuses, she has learned, she is the latest feminist heroine, though she knows next to nothing about feminist theory or politics. She is a quick study.

To think that she had ever considered being Mrs. Bruce Brandt. Bruce would have been lucky to have been Mr. Stephanie Schonfeld.

"People," Kazakis booms, "people, please . . ." He motions and the chamber musicians amputate the piece in mid-chord. At his cue, one of the caterers taps loudly with a stick on a wooden tablet, a British custom Stef remembers from a dinner in London.

"Thank you," says Des. "On behalf of the editors and staff of *Perspective*, I would like to welcome you all here this evening." The measure of his stress is the way a native Australian twang creeps at odd moments into his denatured mid-Atlantic English. "As you know, the magazine is going through some changes, which we think are improvements. We're building on the success of our last few years, under the editorship of Sir Robin Blair. Many of you knew Robin, and all of you know of him through his legacy, *Perspective* as it is today. I wish Robin could be with us here tonight . . . "

The crowd grows hushed.

"Robin can never be replaced," Des continues. "At most, he can be succeeded. In searching for an editor, we wanted someone who can bring a fresh approach to the magazine and a new out-look on the issues that we address. *Perspective* has always prided itself on pushing the envelope, on being at the cutting edge of social and intellectual change, and the magazine will be living up to that tradition, I have no doubt, under the editorship of Stephanie Schonfeld."

Stef smiles, trying to look neither dopey nor arch, as cameras bloom and applause rattles.

"I could go on, but I'm just the publisher . . ." Des pauses for the laughter. "In the months ahead, readers of *Perspective* will be coming to know Stef's distinctive voice. I thought it only fitting that you, the friends of the magazine, should hear it tonight. Stef."

"Thank you, Des," she replies. "Louder," he whispers, then smiles and joins the ovation. When the applause dies down, Stef looks over the heads of the expectant crowd at the blazing lights that ring the gazebo.

And completely forgets what she has planned to say.

Nervous shifting, the shuffle of feet. Stef stammers, "I'd like to . . . thank Des for the . . . confidence he has shown in me . . . and everybody at *Perspective*. It's the most wonderful honor . . ." She is losing her audience, and she knows it. Then she thinks of a way out. "But most of all, I'd like to take this opportunity to thank the person who made all of this possible: Sir Robin Blair. If we could take just a moment, to remember him, in silence."

She bows her head.

"Oh, my God!" Stef shrieks three hours later when Claudia shares her observation. "Oh, my God!"

They are alone on the beach, half an hour after the last guests have departed. Stef stops strolling and doubles over, laughing.

"Oh, my *God*! I hope nobody else took it that way."

"I'm just evil, I know." Claudia giggles. "But I couldn't help thinking, Robin made all this possible . . . by *dying*."

"Oh, God." At another hour, in another place, Stef might have been offended, but after an evening of tension and drink she joins the gossip columnist in a fit of giggles. "Pour me some more, you evil bitch."

The women have taken their shoes and stockings off to stroll in the surf. They have some difficulty balancing shoes and wine-glasses and a bottle between them.

"God, it's true," Stef reflects as they weave on, the surf hissing coldly around their ankles. "I wouldn't be editor if Robin hadn't died. Or if that kid, Steve Quist, hadn't been shot on Capitol Hill. They were going to make him deputy managing editor."

"And then there's Jay Pierce," Claudia reminds her. "You're a regular black widow."

"Stop it," Stef laughs, wiping tears from her eyes.

"Oh, dear me." Claudia pauses to light a cigarette. "Wait up. We're not all as full of . . . what was Des saying? Distinctive voice? God, he sounded like an advertising agency."

"Did I tell you," Stef says as they trudge on through the cold surf, "about the part of the interview with Jay Pierce I left out? I'm going to put it in the book. He told me to read the *Tao Te Ching*. It's this ancient Chinese book of wisdom. And he quoted this passage—I don't remember it exactly. It's something like, 'To the powerful, people are like straw dogs. On the day of the festival, they are paraded with honor. But after the festival, they are thrown aside in the dust, trampled on by all who pass.'"

"You can see why this man was considered the life of the party in Washington," Claudia replies. Then, stung by a cold wave, she yelps.

Stef studies her friend. In the dim light from the floodlit boardwalk a hundred yards away, the signs of age are not visible— the skin stretched to drumhead tightness by face-lifts, the dentures, the dyed hair—or is it a wig? Looking at Claudia, Stef sees herself as she might be a couple of decades into the twenty-first century, a creature of sags and artifice, a divorcée several times over, living from party to party.

So be it, she thinks. Better to be Claudia in middle age than an aging Allison, waking up each morning next to a plump, balding, dull Bruce. She still resents Bruce, but not for turning to Allison after she rejected him. She resents him for growing up, for not remaining her twenty-seven-year-old lover, for wanting a wife and children and a house with a garage that has a dusty lawn mower in it. Stef's new career lets her rise in the world without growing up, and she does not want to grow up, not for now. Maybe, like Claudia, she never will.

"Where are you going?" Stef cries in amusement and alarm as Claudia wades into the booming surf. The gossip columnist pulls her dress up to her waist with one hand, holding the empty wine bottle aloft with the other, a caricature of a Degas ballerina. "Sleep with the fishes!" she bellows as she flings the bottle into the darkness.

Stef smiles. Then she breathes in sadness with the soft salt wind, sadness and the disquiet she felt in that awkward moment earlier when all eyes were upon her and speech and confidence briefly failed. She stands on the barren beach like an actress on a stage when the applause has faded and the waiting, focused audience slowly shares her realization that she has nothing, absolutely nothing, to say.

38

"Am I presentable?"

Ross remains still as a mannequin while Jim examines him one more time, tugging the new suit, thumbing the tie securely beneath the collar. This is how they met, in the men's store near K Street downtown where Jim works.

Brushing a few bits of fuzz from the shoulder of his new lover's coat, Jim says, in his sweet voice, "Okay, Mr. Drummond. You're ready to go."

"Awright, partner. Let's rock and roll."

On their way out of the town house, they move through piled boxes. The movers are scheduled for Tuesday. Ross has bought a new house in Chevy Chase, Maryland, a freestanding mansion suitable for someone of the station to which he has been elevated.

Jim drives. Though he has said nothing yet, Ross is thinking of buying a new car that Jim can use as his own. They have been living together for only a month and a half, but Ross is determined to make this relationship last. He needs stability in his private life now that his business and social responsibilities will be increasing. Jim is not the most accomplished lover Ross has known, nor the best-looking, though at thirty-one this third-generation Italian-American is fit as well as stylish. Jim is, however, the perfect wife, of the sort that Ross decided he needed to permanently settle down with after learning that Paul was positive. Jim likes to cook, he does not resent keeping the house tidy, and, best of all, he prefers staying at home in the evenings reading or watching TV to patrolling the bars with a mob of acquaintances. A few months before Jim met Ross, the younger man's six-year relationship ended when the older dentist he had been living with insisted on the right to start seeing other guys again. Jim is monogamous, it seems, by instinct, and Ross is not averse to reinforcing nature with material incentives, like the use, though not the ownership, of a car.

When they arrive at the church in the Central American section of Arlington, Jim accompanies Ross like a bodyguard. Most of the celebrants look like Salvadorans. Ross and Jim are spotted by Yolanda, who leads a little black-haired girl in a daisy dress. Her husband Isidro follows, bearing their own infant in his thick arms.

"Say hi, Rosa."

Ross kneels and looks into the child's frightened eyes. "You're getting bigger all the time, darling." He hoists the kid up in his arms. She squirms and reaches for Yolanda, but Yolanda is holding her own baby now. "She's adorable," Jim says, admiring the tiny squirming creature, and Ross agrees, "*Muy bonita.*" Jealous, Rosa begins to kick. Ross sets her down and she flees to her uncle's arms as the priest, who looks Latin American but has an American accent, joins them. "Are you familiar with the ceremony?" the priest, Father Vallejo, asks after introducing himself. Ross is surprised to learn that the rite is not much different from the Episcopalian version.

"From this great tragedy," Father Vallejo is soon saying above the noise of creaking pews and coughing and the babble of infants, "God is showing us the way to new life, and a new affirmation of what binds us together in faith . . . "

Beside him in the front pew, Yolanda is dabbing her eyes with a Kleenex. In spite of himself, Ross feels the tears welling up, tears not so much for the lost mother as for the motherless child. His own mother is now in a rest home, her mind dead in a body that lingers on. The Drummond manse has been rented out to a Japanese-American ophthalmologist and his family. Ross is putting a substantial part of his share of the rent into the trust fund he established for the education of Rosa. He had not intended, at first, to spend so much on the orphaned daughter of a maid he hardly knew. But he had been shocked by the miserliness of Graciela's other employers in contributing to the fund. None had wanted to part with more than a few hundred dollars. Most of them have more money than Ross, but he knows he has one thing they lack: class. Yolanda and Isidro sense this. That is why they have naturally turned to him for aid, as their *padrone*, in the first weeks after the horror, and why they have asked him to stand godfather to the orphaned niece they have decided to raise.

"In the name of the Father, and the Son, and the Holy Spirit . . ."

In six months or two years, Ross thinks, he will be sitting in a church like this for a memorial service for Paul. His feelings toward Paul have already died; it is as though, as an emergency measure in the interest of his own survival and sanity, the power has been turned off in that entire department of his being. With clinical aloofness Ross imagines the inevitable service, and wonders if it will be attended by more people than the little service held in a Catholic church in Washington for Jay Pierce. Jay's apparent suicide, and the Piercegate scandal that had preceded his death, had made the lawyer as unpopular in death as he had been well connected in life. Ross had hesitated about attending—but what did he have to fear? He had made it. He could do provocative things. Though he would not be too provocative. That was Jay's downfall. He did not know when to get out of the game and cash in his chips. Ross might inherit the role of Jay Prentice Pierce as the man you had to talk to in order to get things done. But unlike Jay, Ross tells himself with satisfaction, he will not let success make him go hog-wild.

After the ceremony, the small crowd closes around them. Unable to follow the rapid-fire Spanish, Ross, rejoined by Jim, stands in silence and beams at the little girl with the benevolent aspect that his great-great-grandfather George Washington Drummond in Mississippi was in the habit of assuming when his colored people would gather below his pillared stoop and listen as he suggested names from the classics for a squirming newborn: Iris. Philander. Phyllis. Otis. Portia. Leander. Curtis. Evander.

39

When the baptism is over, the pews unload their burdens into the vortex swirling around Teesha and her child.

"He's such a sweet baby," a blue-haired lady in a bonnet says, inspecting little Evander. "He's so quiet."

"I know," says another blue-haired member of the amen corner. "He didn't cry during the service or nothing."

Teesha is blissful, rocking the baby in her arms. Curtis peers over her shoulder. The boy's eyes are clamped shut. His mouth works. Teesha daubs the drool.

"He's tired," Velma observes. "This has been a big day." Curtis grunts in assent. He has regained much of his ability to talk since the stroke, but out of a residual fear of embarrassment he prefers not to.

"Yo. Lemme see." Frizzell, accompanied by several teenage men wearing Baltimore Orioles caps backward, shoulders through the cluster toward Teesha. When he sees him Curtis tenses. Then he uncoils with the apathy of resignation. His illness has taken the fight out of him.

"What up, my man? What up?" Frizzell peers at the baby. The infant squirms and stretches, extending a small hand. Before Frizzell can take it, Velma, frowning, extends her own hand. Around her forefinger, the tiny fingers of the second Evander lock in uncomprehending and justified trust.